Praise for William Hazelgrove's Novels

"American Fiction is not dead...Hazelgrove has skillfully revived it. Highly recommended."

—Library Journal

"Hazelgrove writes with warmth and feeling, his characters richly drawn, moving and evocative of it's time."

—Booklist

"Its a steam roller of a story, starting small and getting bigger and bigger..."

—Starred Review American Library Association

"Hazelgrove has a natural grace as a storyteller that is matched by his compassion for his characters."

—Chicago Sun Times

"Hazelgroves writing has the natural arc of a baseball game."

—Junior Library Guild

"Proof that despite the fleeting nature of trends, good writing survives."

—Time Out Chicago

"Hazelgrove is skilled at creating fully fleshed out characters and the dialogue carries the story along beautifully."

—School Library Journal

Jack Pine
by William Hazelgrove

ISBN 978-1-94019-268-0

Published by
köehlerbooks™

210 60th Street
Virginia Beach, VA 23451
212-574-7939
www.koehlerbooks.com

Cover design by Dalitopia Media

JACK PINE

A Novel of the Northwoods

William Hazelgrove

Author of *The Pitcher* & *Real Santa*

VIRGINIA BEACH
CAPE CHARLES

For Kitty, Clay, Callie and Careen
Who all lived the dream of the Northwoods

It was a beautiful dream...
the nation's hoop is broken and scattered.
There is no center any longer,
and the sacred tree is dead.

—Black Elk

Jack pine, n.

A pine tree of northern North America that has a narrow trunk, short needles arranged in pairs, and curving cones. It has soft wood that is used especially for paper pulp.

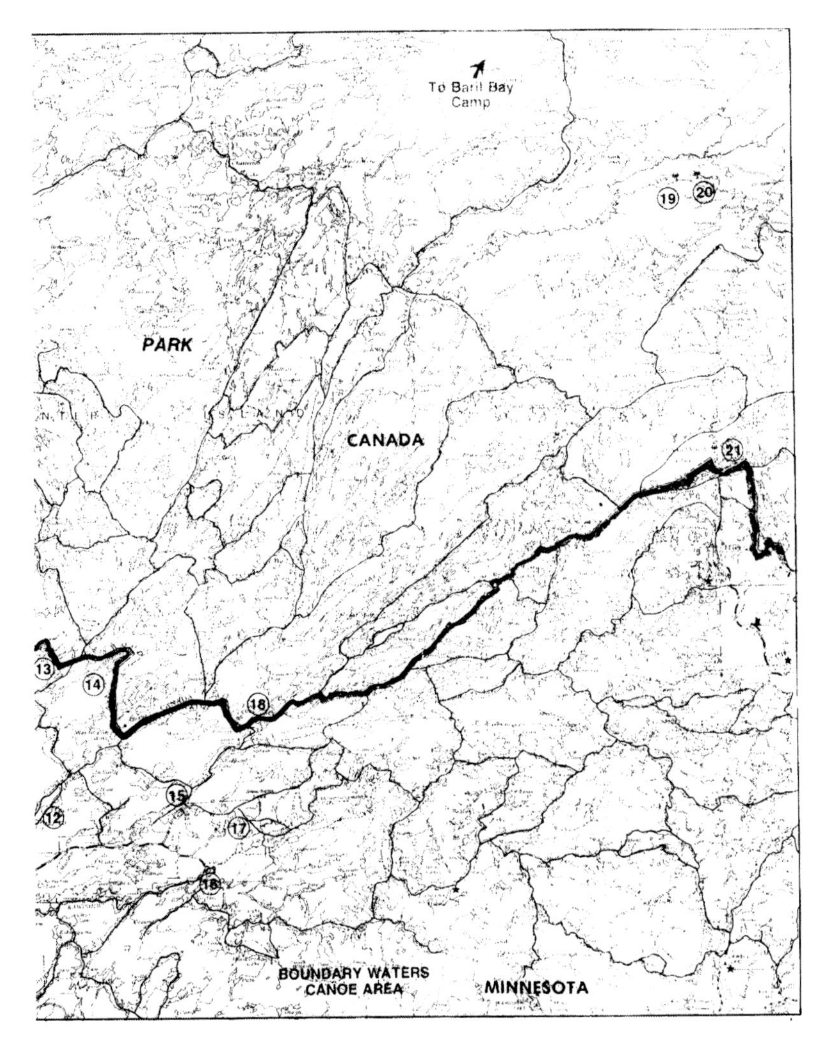

Northern Minnesota just below the Canadian-American Border
Boundary Waters Canoe Area Wilderness

1

DEPUTY SHERIFF REUGER London squinted at the smoke over the trees. He twisted the motorcycle throttle with wind tugging a Colt .44 and sun flashing the badge pinned to his vest. The sand road zigzagged among smaller red and white pines then disappeared into a scraggly wall of trees. He rode through the speckled pines into a valley of spruce and balsam firs, stumps, and cut logs. The fresh sawdust smelled like turpentine on a warm day.

He downshifted on the sharpest S-turns and flew through grass past white and gray boulders of granite and greenstone then up a hill to wide blue sky and saw the smoke roiling over the far pines like a swollen thunderhead. Reuger passed back into the trees and smelled charcoal then rubber melting then burned wood. He winged another curve and locked the back wheel. He pulled the rifle from the scabbard and the radio from his cowboy belt.

"10-6 here."

"Ya, Reuger, copy that."

"I have a burned-out slasher in the Boundary Waters."

"10-4 on that."

He levered the .30-30 Winchester, pulling out brass cartridges from his vest pocket like cigarettes and walked slowly into the clearing of logged trees, keeping the short-barreled rifle toward the sky. Charred wood crackled under his boots as fire smoldered from logs like an abandoned village of Indian fires. A hulk of blackened metal smoldered indiscriminately. Smoke steamed from the hood of the Ford truck with the blackened hydraulic claw crushed down on the cab. It was a cherry picker used for grappling logs and stacking or feeding them into a six-foot hydraulic saw on wheels. It was the standard setup for the independent logger, and the saw and the cherry picker were known as a "slasher."

He brushed back his blond hair and glanced into the truck cab and saw vinyl icicles hanging from the dashboard. The side mirror showed a man just over thirty-five with sunburnt skin, a bleached mustache, and red-rimmed blue eyes. He saw the stick shift had become a melted candle. Scorched springs poked through the bench seat. He walked past steel bands on tandem hubs past blackened melted cables leading to the control cab and the birds flying off the roof.

Reuger hunched down and peered under the truck, but it had sunk to the ground. He crossed to the hydraulic saw on a trailer resting in sawdust turned to red oatmeal from an earlier rain. The saw and the hydraulic cables were untouched by the fire.

He turned and stared into the limp trees. *Jack pine.* Foster Jones had been logging jack pine before the fire. The scraggly trees had taken over the land of the Northwoods after the big Norwegian red and white pines were logged out in 1890. Foster would sell his logs to the paper mills and the processing plants that churned out particleboard. It was like the sharecroppers who farmed the worn out soil in the South and tried to produce cotton. The modern logger was left with jack pine as the only legacy of the big trees.

"Foster!"

His voice was small in the breathless forest. Reuger didn't like the feel of the scene. The fire was too neat and too intense, and Foster Jones had been logging too long to let an accident like this occur. Usually the new loggers had the mishaps that put them out of business in the first year. The old loggers, the shaders, knew the fine margin between disaster and limping through to another year. Foster most of all.

Foster!

He shouldered the Winchester then stumbled over a red extinguisher and checked the gauge. The needle was in the red area of the gauge. That meant he had used it to try to extinguish the fire before it hit the gas tank. Foster would have fought the fire with everything he had because his equipment was his livelihood. Reuger set the extinguisher down and walked through weeds to a metal gas can with the sliding cap open. He smelled the jerrican then set it on the ground. He turned slowly as a crow arched the sky and landed. The crow cawed loudly, and two others landed on an old cedar spared by loggers.

Reuger watched another crow descend farther off in the fireweed. The crow hopped from log to log then pecked down, and a flash of blue cloth jumped. He swung the Winchester down and walked slowly through the fireweed and felt his heart in his chest. Something was mashing down the weeds. He saw a white beard ruffling in the wind.

Reuger kneeled beside Foster Jones. His mouth was open in the approximation of death where it seemed the life force had rushed out violently with the body contorted to the sky like so many Civil War photos. Blood had stained Foster's matted white hair and flecked his beard. His eyes had rolled back and were the color of a pale blue sky.

Reuger noted the suspenders stretched over his flannel shirt and the blue jeans worn at the knees and cuffed over double- tied construction boots. His gnarled hands were stained with black oil from a chainsaw. Reuger breathed deeply. He had seen death many times, but he never got used to it. Foster Jones was simply no longer. This hunk of meat was left in the woods like any other animal that had died.

Reuger leaned close to the clotted hole drilled jaggedly just behind the right ear with the blood trailing down. He examined the pockmark blowing out the other side of the skull. The blood had spattered on the weeds for fifteen feet and the explosive force of the bullet sprayed brain matter like compressed air and had dried into a sticky paste on Foster's neck.

He unclipped his radio.

"Hector!"

"Ya, go ahead."

"I have a 10-72 here."

Roger that. Need any assistance?"

"I'll let you know, it's Foster Jones."

"Foster, huh? Jeez…10-4."

He hooked the radio and walked with his head down through the fireweed. He paced off from the body twenty feet one way then twenty feet the next. He looked at the position of the head and went off to the right twenty more feet. He walked back to the corpse and stopped, then picked up a black-handled .45 Colt automatic hidden in a bed of wildflowers. It was less than five feet from the body. He swung the radio up.

"Hector, need a registration check."

The radio hissed.

"Go ahead."

He gave him the serial number then got down on his hands and knees and brushed the weeds, watching spiders and ants and jack pine beetles escape. Reuger dogged around with his Colt, grabbing briars for twenty minutes. He dropped his hat then wore it far back on his head like a rodeo cowboy. He watched the ground closely then got up on his knees. He saw something glinting sun. Reuger stood and walked to the brass cartridge lying on some weeds. He wrung out a plastic baggy then scooped the shell.

"Reuger, have that registration."

"Go ahead."

"Registration belongs to a Foster Jones, repeat, Foster Jones."

"10-4. Thanks Hector."

Reuger clipped the radio and dropped in the warm weeds and dogged around again for twenty minutes. He covered the ground going thirty feet out from Foster on all sides, but found nothing. Reuger stood and swiped his hands together. He smoothed his mustache and stared at the old man he had been out to see the day before.

"How she go, Foster?" He called, swinging off his motorcycle.

Foster lowered the saw and shook his head. He was a wiry man with the build of a wrestler and just as strong. Reuger guessed he was well into his sixties, and his fierce blue eyes burned out from beneath bushy white brows. He slept in the cab of his truck sometimes, and other times he slept out in the open. Foster was the last of the old lumberjacks.

"If the bank don't take my slasher here, then she'll go all right," he said spatting a glob of tobacco juice into the cut of the tree.

"Tough times," Reuger nodded.

Foster spat into the sawdust again with one eye shut.

"Them tree huggers are winning the war, and I say it's every man for himself now." They stood in the quiet forest, then Foster shook his head slowly. "Man has to do what he has to do, and I'm too fucking old to do anything else."

Reuger hunched down to the body again and saw a flick in the left side of his eye. He raised his head and saw the branches waving up and down. He stood slowly then pulled the Winchester to his cheek.

2

THE SILHOUETTE DISAPPEARED into speckled leaves, and he heard footsteps crashing through the second growth. Reuger ran with his Winchester to his chest to the tree line then into the diaphanous forest light. He heaved past sap-oozing trunks and slabs of granite knifing the pine floor. Reuger dropped and centered the aiming pin on the elfin figure.

"Freeze!"

The man tripped and fell face first to the ground. Reuger stood with the rifle pinned on the center of the man's back. Blood pulsed in his temples, and he kept his index finger tight on the trigger.

"Hands on your head! Turn over slowly!"

The man reached his hands to his head then rolled to his back. Reuger stared over the aiming pin with his finger curled in the trigger guard. He felt heat in his face, and sweat draped his body. Emotions he hadn't felt for years nauseated him. Fifteen years later, and there he was. The eyes had the same almond shape and something else. He dropped the rifle and got hold of himself.

"What in the hell are you doing up here?"

The boy stared up with saucer eyes.

"I've...I've been camping," he stammered.

Reuger clicked the safety on the rifle and held the barrel to the ground. He wiped perspiration from his forehead and the back of his legs felt weak. The boy looked about eleven, maybe twelve, with long shorts and new tennis shoes and the white skin of a city dweller.

"Where are you staying?"

"In a tent," the boy shrugged, closing one eye against the sun. "I've been living off the land."

Reuger reached down and pulled him up by his hand. The boy brushed back his shiny black hair then crossed his arms.

"Staying at Pine Lodge?"

"No sir." The boy shook his head. "I'm a woodsman," he declared, hands on his head with a defiant gleam in his brown eyes.

Reuger pulled his hands down and checked the safety on the Winchester. He had seen himself shooting the boy. It was his training. The use of deadly force required a trained procedure where normal emotions are circumvented and the training takes over. Once he went into those procedures, pulling back was hard. He had been close to shooting the boy, and he only now realized how close he had come. If he had spun around on the ground he didn't know what might have happened. He had a man with a bullet hole in his head and then someone running away through the woods.

"How old are you?"

The boy shrugged again.

"Eleven, but I'll be twelve in another month."

"How'd you get up here?"

He puffed out his chest.

"I've been out here in the Northwoods, hiking and canoeing! I've been camping out in the wilderness on my own."

Reuger saw the shiny bucket with the Pine Lodge tag lying a few feet away. He wondered why he hadn't seen it before.

"That your blueberry bucket there?"

The boy's eyes rolled to the shiny bucket.

"Oh, yeah, I guess it is," he mumbled.

"Have you been picking along the road?"

"I told you, I've been *camping*."

"You're staying at the lodge then?"

He broke his stare, and the boy shrugged again.

"Yeah, with my mother." He hooked a finger behind him. "Our car's back on the road," he muttered.

"Do you know how to get back there?"

"Oh, yeah," he nodded quickly. "Sure I do." The boy kicked the ground with new tennis shoes. "I never had a gun pointed at me before....Are you a bounty hunter or something?"

"No, I'm a deputy sheriff, but you shouldn't run like that when someone tells you to stop."

He shrugged and brushed his muddy legs.

"I thought you were some kind of mass murderer or something."

"Can you get back to your car then?"

The boy tucked in his T-shirt, glancing around expansively.

"Oh yeah, no problem."

"They're no blueberries this far in. Along the road back there you ought to find some good brambles."

"Sure, thanks a lot," he shrugged, starting off through the woods.

"Road's the other way there."

He stopped and glanced around. "Yeah, I know, I was just looking around," he said, glancing to the sky as if to take a bearing. "Maybe, I'll see you around somewhere."

"Kurt?"

The boy stared at him, his face turning red.

"Kurt, where are you?"

"I think that's your mother."

The boy blushed and shrugged. "Oh yeah, maybe it is."

"Kurt!"

The boy turned nonchalantly and began walking.

"I'm over here, Mom," he shouted.

Reuger turned and walked back through the woods. He emerged and saw the smoldering logs still wicking smoke into the morning sunlight. He smelled the corky scent of burned wood and turned his mind back to the bearded man in the grass. He kneeled and brushed the surrounding weeds.

"Foster Jones is dead as a doornail there, as I see it."

Reuger jumped and wheeled with the rifle to a man in a Confederate cap and low-cut moccasins. The man reached for the sky with his mouth pinched beneath a scraggly mustache. John Mcfee yelled out something neither man heard.

"Take it easy there!"

"Don't sneak up on me like that, John," he muttered.

"Well, I didn't expect yer to be so gosh darn *jumpy!*"

Reuger rubbed his eyes and pushed his hat up from his curly blond hair.

"You always listening to the scanner?"

Mcfee held his arms wide as if for rain.

"Readers of the *Ely Standard* and the listeners of WELU deserve to know what's happening and I have to be responsive to their needs here!"

Reuger stared at the local historian, then bartender, then part-time radio personality for the ten thousand-watt station WELU. That nobody wanted to fill the noontime slot and spin the polka records was his opportunity. By the time Charles Kroning descended on Ely, Minnesota, John had fashioned a program of homespun logic with local color and local history intermingled with nostalgia for the old days. Kroning ate it up and bought the radio station with one condition: John Mcfee would continue his *End of the Road* Program as WELU's only paid employee.

"The press can't be denied, Reuger." He drew a pencil from his ear and licked the tip, pulling out a white note pad from his top pocket. So what do we have here, environmental wars? Tom Jorde finally gone too far?"

"Suicide."

Reuger kneeled again by the spattered weeds and followed the trajectory of the blood back to the head wound. The blood matched up with the force of the bullet blowing out of the other side of the skull.Mcfee squeezed his right eye shut.

"Are you still doing yer security work there for Johnson Timber?"

"None of your business."

"Now, Reuger, you have a slasher burned, you have illegal logging in the Boundary Waters, and you have a man shot with a handgun there." He chewed on his lower lip. "And you got Tom Jorde declaring just the other day to WELU that he'd do whatever it takes to stop logging."

"Suicide," he said standing up.

"Quote you on that?" Mcfee cocked his head back. "Imagine Ben Johnson have a different view on this here crime. Of course you being a *former logger* for Ben Johnson, I guess I know where your sympathies lie here."

Reuger turned and tapped him on the shoulder.

"You owe me one for the Basswood hanging."

"And how would you figure that?"

"Gave you an exclusive."

"Exclusive be damned! The *Ely Standard* is the *only* paper in town!"

"That's why it was exclusive."

Mcfee scribbled onto the pad.

So then, the deputy sheriff is tight-lipped here on this murder?"

"Suicide, John."

He rolled his tongue.

"Ya, well then, let's say it's not the environmentalists here." Mcfee looked up from his pad, gray eyes plain like sheet iron. "Then you have a serial murderer here, as I see it."

"Need at least two bodies."

Reuger brushed the weeds again with his palms flat.

"Ya?" One eyebrow danced high. "And with Knudsen there, I see Foster as the second victim."

"Knudsen disappeared in one of these lakes," Reuger stood up, "and one of these days he's going to wash up."

He reached down and lifted the automatic from the weeds with a handkerchief.

"Gave you an exclusive on that story too, John."

"Well now Reuger, that is your opinion, but my public believes differently here. He was a logger who disappeared amongst the turmoil of environmental wars."

Went the way Rusty Green went, John," he murmured, smelling the barrel of the .45.

"Don't know about that now."

Mcfee looked up.

"Tell me what you think here of this lead....When Jim Carpenter called from Pine Lodge and said one of his guests reported smoke around the area Foster Jones logged, the sheriff assumed the logger was burning scrub trees. But what the sheriff found on this day was Foster Jones shot in the head and his slasher burned—"

"Where you going with that, John?"

"I've been looking the other way for a long time here, Reuger, and I know you been keeping a lot to yourself here." He stabbed the pencil back. "I can't keep quiet about slashers in lakes and tree huggers getting beat up and Earth First activists chaining themselves to trees."

"That's a bunch of shit, John."

Mcfee rolled his shoulders.

"Just give me the facts here."

Reuger pointed to the body.

"Foster Jones with a bullet in the right side of his head with his own gun ten feet away and a spent cartridge that matches that gun." He turned to the smoldering carcass. "A gas fire on a slasher started from the engine cage. Suicide by a man out of options."

"Well, that was all I wanted then, was yer version of events," Mcfee nodded, writing on his pad.

"And since I just gave you another exclusive, John." Reuger barreled the .45 in his gun belt. "You can help me get Foster up to your jeep."

"Well, now, Reuger," Mcfee held up his hands and backed away, "I'm the press here and in the legacy of Charles Kroning..."

"You'll help me pick up this dead logger," he said, clamping his shoulder.

3

THE RESERVATION SIGN was pockmarked by .22 rounds and speckled with buckshot. Reuger passed through a gate dull with noon light, past trailers with chairs, a bony dog veering through yards, and children playing beyond sagging porches. He bumped down the street toward a man in calf-high mukluks and feathered black hair hawking a store porch. Wheeling in, he snuffed the motor of the jeep.

"How she go?"

"Oh, you know, not bad." Gary Chatoee pulled the cigar away and shrugged back his hair. "Too hot, though. You know, I really think the weather is changing up here. We used to never get days like this; now it's like Florida during the summers. But you look at the forest now, and the trees are all dried out and the lakes are low. I think global warming is ruining the land up here." He braided his arms and jabbed the cigar. "Out for a drive to see our part of the country?"

"Oh, ya." Reuger stepped out of the jeep. A saw screeched like a mechanized locust in the distance. "Going to log out these hundred thousand acres and become rich?"

Gary Chatoee puffed the cigar then crushed it underfoot and scratched his belly resting on an oversized belt buckle. He paddled the sun with brown hands.

"Ya, sure, after Johnson Timber stole all the good timber, but I'm working on getting it back. That's just some Indian loggers off the south end of the lake logging some jack pine. Only about 30,000 acres is still tribally owned, you know. "

Reuger climbed the porch and saw water glimmering down the road like a promise. When he went to the Ojibwa reservation, he often thought of pictures he had seen in a book of Indians before they entered the reservation. The first photograph showed a proud people staring defiantly at the camera with long hair and braids and earrings. The later photographs showed middle-aged men with short hair sitting stiffly in suits utterly expressionless.

"How's the Outfitters?"

"Not bad. Lot of swampys who never been in a canoe before, so they buy everything in the store." He grinned yellow teeth. "They like having an Indian wait on them. I tell them I still live in a teepee, and they buy even more."

"Between the store and the Outfitters, you must stay busy."

"Ya, and then I have to go to those village meetings, but I figure that's what I went to college for, you know, to come back and help the people."

Reuger tapped his radio, shifting the Colt on his leg.

"Looking for Tommy Tobin. Seen him hereabouts'?"

"Tommy Tobin." Gary shook his head. "Nope, not seen him in a while. He still has a cabin up in the Boundary Waters. The last one, you know." He crossed his arms. "He getting in trouble in Winton again?"

"Trouble up toward Pine Lodge this morning. I found Foster Jones with a bullet in his head and his slasher burned. Looks like a suicide, but I heard Tommy's been working with him so I wanted to ask him some questions."

Gary frowned down the dusty road where two dark children played. Small jets of sunlight creased his eyes. Ever since Reuger could remember, Gary had been the model Indian. He had grown up on the reservation. His hair was always combed and he looked like an ad for collegiate wear in his teenage years. He had gone off to college and then returned to start two businesses and represent his people in the ongoing struggle over timber rights.

The local people could point to Gary and say here was proof the reservation system worked. But Tommy Tobin proved the system of reservations didn't work at all. He was the Geronimo to Gary's Sitting Bull. They had grown up side by side, but Tommy had been the bad boy all along. He had dropped out of high school and began stealing cars before he was sixteen. He became a lumberjack and fell into the drinking and drugs that went along with the life of hard labor in Ely, Minnesota. When he pulled a knife on a couple of canoeists, the judge who had heard his misdemeanors over the years had enough. He went down to Stateville for a year and came back an ex-con. He had settled down for a while, but Reuger had found him lying drunk in the middle of logging roads several times. If Gary was the poster child for the new Indian, then Tommy was the wanted poster for the old.

"Foster, huh? That's too bad, you know." He shook his head slowly. "Tommy Tobin, he's a good lumberjack and can do the work of three men, but he grew up on this reservation and took a lot of the bad habits with him; mostly he drank too much, you know."

Reuger watched the children in the street.

"Might been last to see Foster alive."

"Foster the old shader." He shook his head. "Just doesn't seem right, you know."

Reuger saw mist on the pines where the land dropped to the lake basin. He touched his mustache, smelling the rubberized body bag. Foster wasn't a heavy man. He had lifted him like a baby into the zippered container Mcfee held open. John had been fine until the eyes slapped back.

"But maybe Tommy will know what happened then," Gary shrugged. "That tree hugger from town was out looking for him last week, you know."

"Jorde?"

"Ya, says it's important he talk to Tommy Tobin. I told him I haven't seen him, but he told me to let him know he come by. He always wants to talk to Indians. They think we're too stupid to know what they're doing? He thinks Indian rights are hot again, so they want to jump on the bandwagon." Gary nodded slowly. "But you watch, once it swings back the other way, them granola eaters will all pack their sandals and Patagonias and leave just like everybody else."

Reuger watched the children with silky black hair playing in the dust with two sticks. He looked at the tin shacks with corrugated roofs.

"Hear from Tommy, let me know."

"Sure thing," Gary nodded, opening the screen door. He paused with his hand out for rain. "You know, sometimes he pulls boats at the portage."

"Reuger."

He unclipped the radio from his belt.

"Go ahead."

"Reuger. This is Sheriff Riechardt. Bad trouble here at the lodge. Apparently a girl has been attacked and says it was some big Indian...I make it out to be that Tobin from her description...didn't he just get out from Stateville?"

"Affirmative."

"You better get up in the Boundary Waters before he heads for Canada."

Reuger pushed his hat up, watching the children kick up dust.

"Who's the girl?"

"...girl named Dana Reynolds. She says she was attacked in the woodshed there."

"Attacked?"

"Maybe raped there, Reuger."

He stared at the Indian children and heard the whine of the chainsaw.

"She a guest at the lodge?"

"Ya...lower forty-eight....Jim Carpenter and I are here with the parents at the lodge...get a seaplane...I would think he's headed for his cabin up there first."

"10-4."

Reuger clipped the radio and felt Gary Chatoee's eyes. They stood under the hot sun and Gary shook his head.

"Ya, I know what Tommy did for you...pulling you out of the snow and all you know before."

"He didn't just pull me out of the snow."

"I know what he did, and you've been good to Tommy here." He breathed heavily, leaning in the doorway. "But you can't change the way some people are. You may think you still owe him something, but you're way paid up. I grew up with the guy, you know. You can't change what it's going to be with some people."

Reuger watched the boy in the road swing a stick over his head.

"You'd have done the same thing for him."

He looked at Gary Chatoee then unclipped the radio and pressed the receiver.

"Hector!"

"Ya, go ahead Reuger."

"Put an APB on a Tommy Tobin ...T-O-B-I-N."

"T-O-B -I -N...Ya, 10-4."

He clipped the radio and felt tired. Gary held his hand out palm flat.

"What will be, will be."

4

THE SEVENTEEN-FOOT MOTOR boat winged smoothly up Moose Lake toward Newfound, then toward Sucker Lake, then the Prairie Portage where International Falls spilled water down to Basswood and Canada. Reuger squinted into the northern wind snapping the lake into sparkling peaks and steered past a troop of Boy Scouts in canoes following a scoutmaster. He saw old logs sticking up like lost buoys.

The wild cloud scudding sky lifted his spirit. He loved this land carved from glaciers making their way down from the North Pole thousands of years before. The glaciers scraped the soil away and left graywacke, greenstone, and granite. The ice melted and filled the thousand lakes of Minnesota and then the trees grew on top of the rock. Many times after storms the trees fell and pulled up their root structure and a foot of earth. Beneath the tree was rock, and it was amazing that a sixty-foot tree could find purchase on a slab of granite.

But it was a beautiful country. The lakes were so clear you could drink from them. The sky was a brilliant mosaic of stars at night and a cerulean blue during the day. The cedars and jack pine and dogwoods and few remaining white pines filled the land like so many cheery Christmas trees. The weather always had the feel of a fall day. It was hard to believe he had been up here fifteen years already.

When he thought about his life in the lower forty-eight it, was like thinking back on a bad party. That life before was crowded and confused and smoky to him now. Confusion floated up on the television shows and the newspapers blaring the catastrophe of a system gone amok. The drive-by shootings and drugs and school shootings now seemed the chaos by which that society lived. Reuger didn't have a television and caught up on news when he went to Pine Lodge, but for the most part he lived his life like the mountain men or the pioneers trudging westward.

Reuger looked at the man sitting in the front of the boat with his white hair blowing wild and his beard smoothed back. He saw the channel where the lake narrowed into a sharp S before breaking open for the next lake. Gus always hated the way he went through the channel. Most people cut their motors, but Reuger had done it so many times he knew exactly where the boulders were underwater. Then again, there weren't many men over sixty-five who enjoyed riding in the front of a boat to go look for an armed Indian.

Gus Vanzant kept his feet on the nineteen-inch sawed-off shotgun and the Winchester and watched as the lake squeezed down to a boulder-rimmed passage. He braced himself as the boat roared into the channel past scraggly trees and roots and carpet moss and waving canebrake before swiveling back into sun on Newfound Lake. He saw a boat come around the bend, barreling like a wedge on a wave with *Conservation Officer* skimming the water.

A man waved in a blue hat and a green coat behind a low center console. Reuger cut the motor as the other boat rolled up. The men felt heat in their faces, their ears ringing from motors. The boats bumped along side. Dollops of water spouted.

"How she go there, Pete?"

"Oh, pretty good," Pete Hauser nodded. "Bit sleepy with the cold here. Need some more coffee, you know." He wiped a bushy mustache with a balled tissue. "So you're up here looking for a little rest and relaxation, I take it?"

"Gus and I needed a boat trip. Haven't been to the Boundary Waters for a while."

Pete Hauser laughed. He had a five o'clock shadow chaffed red from longboat rides between lakes looking for poachers or violators of fish limits. DNR men were known as fish police to the Sheriff Department, but Pete took his job very seriously. Reuger had seen him coming back more than once with men in handcuffs who had violated the ever-changing limit on walleye, bass, and northern pikes. He was a big man who vacationed in the West where he hunted waterfowl and referred to the Boundary Waters as a biological desert compared to the fecundary wetlands of Montana. He pushed back his cap with the gold star and yawned.

"You're early here."

"Get a jump on it."

His chin beckoned.

"So then, you be coming up fishing here?"

"Might say that."

Pete grinned and leaned back in his seat, swishing his green parka.

"Ya, had a busy week here getting ready for the burn, you know."

"They going to do her then?"

"Ya, well, after the blowdown, you can't even get back to a lot of the portages you know," he said, rolling his shoulders. "The environmentalists been protesting and such, but they'll do it when she dries out enough. They're just going to burn a couple hundred acres." He shook his head. "What they should do is let the loggers get back in there, you know, and take all the downed timber they can carry. That would solve everybody's problem here."

The storm of the century had descended on the Boundary Waters the year before and knocked the trees down like so many matchsticks. Now they had a tinderbox waiting for the right lightning storm to ignite the rotting trees. The forest service abandoned its long-standing policy of letting nature take her course and started planning limited burns to do away with the timber, but the environmentalists saw this as an encroachment. This annoyed Reuger. It only made sense to burn out the old wood.

He shook his head slowly.

"Don't think that's going to happen anytime soon?"

"Ya, probably not. So then, yer on official business up here?" Pete nodded. "Brought your reinforcements, I see."

Gus leaned over and spat into the water. His white beard was smoothed back from wind still and his watery red eyes glared out from a cliff of a forehead.

"Survived the channel crossing so I'm ready for anything."

Pete grinned. "Oh, ya, now you're supposed to go through there quarter-speed, but if yer on *police business* then that's different here."

"I'm looking for a big Indian, Pete."

"Ya, who's that?"

"Tommy Tobin."

He leaned back.

"Oh ya, picked that up off the wire." He smoothed his mustache and chinned his shoulder. "Heard he was up pushing boats there for Jeep for a while. I see you're expecting some trouble from the look of that hardware there. You aren't after him for not paying his taxes, then?"

Reuger thumbed his hat up.

"Trouble down by Pine Lodge. A logger shot and his slasher burned. Maybe a rape."

Pete's face darkened. He turned around, pointing over his shoulder.

"You be headed for his cabin, then?"

"Don't find him at the portage."

"Ya, that Tobin could be a hard one to find there if he wants to disappear."

"Think so?"

"No one can disappear like an Indian, you know. "

Reuger tugged the brim of his hat.

"Keep an eye for me, will you, Pete?"

"Oh ya, you bet."

* * * *

An hour later, they puttered toward a man in green waders with a camouflaged cap. Blue buoys strung the bay marking the convex bend of the falls roaring like a far train. International Falls separated the United States and Canada, and on the far side, a steel peg drilled into a slab of granite marked the official line. Reuger watched the clear green glass sheer the rocky cliff before exploding into white snow where four or five deadheads lay on the break. The man pulled his oily cap lower.

"Ah, the sheriff, it is," he called wading toward them.

Reuger raised his hand.

"How she go, Jeep?"

"Oh, not bad here."

The falls dumped water from Moose Lake down to Basswood but to get a boat down to the lower lake required the boat be manually towed down a road. Reuger watched another boat on a trailer of spoke wheels plunge into the lake and float off. Six young men in cut-off shirts and crew cuts manned the modified boat trailer. Reuger cut the engine and guided his boat into the slide of the empty trailer.

"Fishing, sheriff?" Jeep asked, guiding the boat.

Reuger jumped down into the water.

"What say, Jeep?"

"Fishing, I say?"

"Might say that."

Jeep Pardu stood in the water, facing a high school boy in a cut-off shirt and bathing suit. Jeep was a wiry man with a mottled nose, pockmarked cheeks, and small, squinty eyes. He wore his hat low and wiped a bulbous nose. He'd been working the portage as long as Reuger could remember and took his name from the broken down jeep he used to pull the boats across.

"So, now, where are the others?" he asked the boy.

He shrugged and pointed down the road.

"Bringing up some fisherman's boats there."

"Well, tell them to hurry here, damn it. Sheriff's boat here going to need taking across."

Jeep turned back to the bay hearing the motor of another approaching boat.

"Now what in hell? They get a good workout here, and I get a lot of trouble taking these here boats down from Sucker to Basswood Lake and back up again, that I do!"

Four boys jogged up the road like a squad of soldiers, and Jeep barked two up front and two in back. The trailer streamed water as it rolled ashore onto the sand road.

Jeep hollered down the road.

"All clear!"

Reuger leaned against the transom of the boat while the boys pulled the trailer toward the steep hill. The tires rutted canals smelling of dead fish and algae. Jeep kept one hand on the trailer.

"Not yet! *Pull back!* Don't want to lose this to the forest here!"

Reuger dug his heels into the packed road against the strain of five hundred pounds of metal and gear starting to roll. The boys trenched the road with legs locked.

"NOW! *Let her go!"*

They ran the clay-packed road with the giant tricycle boring down the incline of International Falls with the wheels spinning water. They reached the bottom then rolled up a brake hill before slow-rolling back down to the landing ramp. The boat floated free and the boys pulled out and started up the hill with the empty trailer. Reuger splashed water on his neck and cupped the cold water to his mouth. Across the bay, the red maple leaf of Canada flapped in the strong breeze. Men in wide-brimmed hats and boots walked between tidy cabins with new boats lining the shore.

So now, what be yer business, Sheriff?" Jeep called walking down the hill with Gus. "By yer hardware I guess you not be fishing today!"

"Nope," he said, wringing his hands then climbing onto the briny dock.

The men stared at the Canadian side of Basswood Lake with the pines clipped around cabins like homes in suburbia. The bay was so small they could have thrown a rock across and hit one of the cabins. A man with binoculars peered across the bay.

"Assholes always looking across there." Jeep grumbled, picking a scab on his scarred cheek. "Give them the finger when they use them binoculars."

"How come yer don't have new cabins like them Canadians there?"

Jeep turned to Gus with hot eyes.

"The government is too cheap here! So there's that, but they aren't too cheap to let them tree huggers take away me jeep! Been pulling my boats for twenty years here with me own jeep, and they come up and say people have to pull their own boats now?" He stared accusingly. *"People!* People! They give me this goddamn tricycle here to haul a five-hundred-pound boat loaded with gear up a steep hill? By God, and who am I going to get to pull these boats here?" Jeep shook his head. "Them tree huggers shrug and say people wantin' to go to Basswood Lake here have to pull they own boats. Weren't for high school footballers here with the coach a givin' me his linemen every summer to pull these here boats, I be out of business and that I would!"

He glared at the Canadians once more then turned.

"Now, would yer like some coffee, Sheriff, here, afore yer head on?"

"What say, Gus?"

"Could use a warm-up here."

"Well, come on then," Jeep grumbled, hobbling to a bark cabin of screens stuffed with tissue paper.

The cabin smelled of burnt wood and wet rugs. A chipped enamel sink was against one wall, next to a dirty white refrigerator. *Property of the United States Forest Service* was enameled to a wood-burning stove squatting in the far corner with ash snowing beneath. The warped planks groaned and moved as the men crossed the floor. Jeep filled the mugs by the sink and gestured to a pine scarred table with four folding chairs.

"This cabin here isn't fit for a dog while them damn Canadians look like they just a come out of a store!" Jeep pulled off his greasy cap and squinted across the mirror-perfect bay. His head was smooth and brown with gray at the temples. "Country here with our size and wealth, and we should look so bad to them Canuckians!" He jabbed the window. "Make sure I get me flag up before that damn maple leaf of theirs starts a flapping, I tell you that!"

He shut one eye with the craters and crevices of his skin deeper in the window light. Jeep rested forward on his elbows like a man about to spit.

"So what brings yer up this way here, Sheriff?"

Reuger put his hat on the table and hooked a boot over his knee.

"Looking for an Indian. Tommy Tobin."

"Oh, ya! Now *he* could pull a boat, *that one*. Give me four of them Indians, and I could get rid of these sniveling kids here," he shouted, hitting the initial carved top. "*God, ya*, that Tobin pulls a boat up by himself! Strong as an ox that one, yes sir!"

"When did he work for you last, Jeep?"

He tugged his cap and rubbed his jaw with blackened fingers.

"So, now, let me think here, Sheriff, you know I employ a lot of people and don't ask a lot of questions, just give me an honest day's work and I'll give you cash is my motto." He lowered his voice. "So now of course that don't hold for the high school boys here, but they get a good work out, way I see it." He looked at the ceiling. "So there, then, let's see, weren't in the last two weeks, so must have been week before he was up here....Course I never knew if he were coming back that one, but he would appear at the landing and pull boats until nightfall most times."

Reuger set the mug down.

"Last time he worked for you?"

"Ya, course, I almost asked him yesterday if he wanted to work, but he slipped by that one, by God he did!"

"Yesterday?" Gus stared. "Yer just said you ain't seen him for three weeks!"

"No." Jeep shook his head. "Now, that's not what I said here. Sheriff asked me here when he worked for me *last*. But no one asked me when I *seen him* last. Now, that's a horse of a different color then."

"Saw him yesterday then, Jeep?"

"Oh, ya, by God," he nodded. "Come through here like a bat out of hell, that one, carrying his canoe across, walking through them boys here and putting his canoe in the other side, and by the time I come out, he was paddling for Canada. By God, he was!"

"Thanks for the coffee," Reuger nodded standing.

"Ya, sure, always my pleasure here, Sheriff."

They walked the dock with sun glaring hotly off the water. Reuger started the motor while Jeep untied the boat. A seaplane banked the far trees.

"Ya, them Canadians still get their goods flown in by God," Jeep grumbled as the plane skied down on the far side. "Used to get steaks and beer flown up here until them tree huggers badgered that Nixon into banning the flyovers, but them Canucks have a plane come in every damn day!"

"We'll see you, Jeep," Reuger called turning the boat into the lake.

"So then, almost forgot, Sheriff." He put his hand up. "What do you want with this Indian here?"

"Ask a few questions," he shouted back.

"With that hardware there," he yelled. "He's likely to answer them!"

5

REUGER ZAGGED UP the muddy path disappearing into the forest with the pump-action shotgun in his right hand. He saw a flicker flying through the trees as sun seared his shirt back. He turned to his boat far below nudging a fallen tree. He turned back around and stared up toward the hidden cabin cresting the island. The government had made a deal with the Ojibwa, and part of the deal was Tommy Tobin's grandfather was allowed to keep his cabin in the Boundary Waters. Tommy was the last of the line.

"Something!" Gus whispered.

They moved up the trail slowly until they saw a roof peaking the trees. The cabin burrowed into the hill but the roof had caved in over the door and some of the logs had rotted to dust. The door hung partially open by two straps of leather. Moss and sod eaved the roof and hung low like an awning. Reuger held the shotgun tight with the steel slippery in his palms.

"Cover me. Going to take a look inside here," he whispered.

They were crouched down ten yards from the cabin. Gus gripped the Winchester like a man holding on for life. His face was red.

"Reuger, I ain't that good a shot."

"Just watch my back then," he whispered, standing from the scraggly jack pines with the shotgun waist high, creeping over crackling fireweed and dead life.

Reuger hunched and tried to peer through the plastic wrap stretched across the windows. He flattened himself against the log wall then nudged the door with the barrel of the shotgun. An orange refrigerator with a gallon of Jack Daniel's inside and a box of Spic and Span. Green painted cabinets stood empty, and a wood-burning stove had rusted orange. He lowered the shotgun and motioned Gus forward.

"No Indian, huh," Gus called, appearing from the woods like some old trapper.

"Doesn't look like he's been here for a long time."

"Not very good at housekeeping, is he?" Gus walked into the cabin. "Finished his whiskey, I see." He dropped the bottle. "So, what yer think?"

Reuger went to the door and stared into the forest. The trees didn't move. There was something, an extra vibration. Something that shouldn't be there. He turned as a thrash of cold air whipped his ear with the sonic whine trailing the arrow into the back wall. Reuger dove to the floor and kicked the door closed with tree dust winding the planks. He stared at the arrow buried halfway up the shank in the back wall.

"Think we found him here," Gus muttered with dust in his beard and mouth, flecking his cheeks, lying on the floor like a cripple.

A second arrow creaked the door with the head thrusting the other side.

"Gettin' better with them arrows." Gus spat floor dust. "By God, just when you think yer seen everything, you get shot at by an Indian with an arrow!"

"History's a cycle." Reuger crawled the floor. "Going out the roof there, Gus, and see if I can circle behind him."

Gus levered up a shell and lowered his eye to the aiming pin of the Winchester.

"I'm goin' to lay here, and anything come through that door I'm goin' to shoot."

Reuger jumped on the table and peered over the roof sloping back to the hill. He laid the shotgun on the thatch and lifted himself onto the moss-covered grass and sticks then crawled back to the trees. He picked up the shotgun and crouched low through the forest delving through light and shadow with needles cushioning his footfalls. Plunging down toward the lake, he then ran along the water with the shotgun heavy in his hand.

Reuger started back up the hill bent over like a man stalking an animal. The barrel of the shotgun snagged fireweed and reeds slapped his face. Birds flitted the branches and a yellow butterfly on a mossy stump was strangely vivid when the arrow shot out like a black dot growing larger. He rutted the hard ground and lay flat, breathing hard. Reuger heard a crush of second growth with the footsteps prowling closer. He brought the shotgun slowly to his face and wiggled his finger into the trigger. He counted to himself then jumped up with another arrow whisking overhead. Reuger pulled the trigger and the shotgun blasted branches and scarred bark. He dropped and pumped out the smoking red plastic cartridge and fired again with the gun butt in his shoulder and the barrel compressed up. He shucked the shell and stared at the tree branches moving from the buckshot. There was silence after the explosions. Reuger heard someone crashing down the hill.

He bounded toward the lake through trees and bushes with branches slapping his face and tripping over hidden vines like a drunken man. He heard a splash and ran faster, crashing down to the boat roped to a fallen tree. He stopped with his breath loud in his ears. The bow bumped the log as the swells flapped and souped the break. He saw a space by the seat with the gas line lying on the bottom and swore. Reuger grabbed the gas tank from the shallows then turned to a man far out on the lake paddling toward Canada.

* * * *

Oars jumped the oarlocks as he rowed with his hat and vest beside him and a canvas coat the color of yellow deerskin. Reuger scooped his hat in the water and drank before flushing his neck. He smoothed back his hair and tore skin off blisters and picked up the oars again.

"Gettin' to be purty good there. Sure yer don't want me to give yer a hand?"

"Nope. We're there now."

Gus turned to the landing with the Canadian flag flying over the pines. He smoked with the arrows beside him and the guns in the bow. The arrowheads were slate and jaggedly sharp, greasy tallow coating the stems with the feathers dark and long. He watched Reuger pull the oars then turned and saw the Canadians watching their slow progress.

"Figures they come out and watch us and not offer a damn hand here," he grumbled.

Reuger glanced over his shoulder, pulling harder with his left oar and guiding the boat toward the American side. Jeep walked the dock with his boys pulling the trailer behind. The oars ricocheted the oarlocks again and he gave one more heave toward the dock.

Jeep grabbed the bowline and scuffed the boat along.

"Where's yer gas tank, Sheriff?"

"Reuger here wanted to get some exercise," Gus nodded.

"Now is that right? Didn't see you for one of them fitness types, Sheriff."

He stepped onto the dock and smoothed back his hair. Jeep picked up the red tank of gas and shook it.

"Now, I can't believe yer would run yourself dry here!" Jeep stared at the four greasy arrows. "Well, I'll be damned. Did you find them arrows or did they find you?" His eyes glimmered under his hat. "Don't be tellin' me that Tobin been slinging arrows at you now!"

"Found Tobin's cabin, and them arrows come a looking fer us," Gus nodded, banging his pipe on the boat.

Jeep stared down at the crudely shorn arrows and rubbed his jaw.

"Now isn't that something. Bet them arrowheads are from Knife Lake there. You can stub your toe on them along the shore. Now sheriff, you think this was the man who you was looking for then?"

"Might be," he murmured, watching the boys milling around the arrows.

"That Tobin, then?"

"Dropped a barrel on him," Gus nodded again. "But them Indians have strong medicine, and he disappeared when Reuger had him and headed for the Canadians in his canoe."

"After he left yer gas tank at the bottom of the lake I wager."

"Ya Reuger, this is Hector, can you hear me?"

He hefted the radio still hot from sun.

"Go ahead, Hector."

"Ah, just got a call from the sheriff....The girl at the lodge recanted her story there....Says she's not sure what happened now."

He stood with the radio for a moment.

"She still at the lodge?"

"Ya, sheriff has gone home."

"I'll be there in an hour."

Reuger clipped the radio and turned to Jeep still holding the empty gas tank.

"Have a boat I could borrow there, Jeep?"

"Oh, ya, you bet, Sheriff, whatever you need here." He gestured to the high school boys. "You boys here get this one here up to the top and bring the sheriff's gear and put it in my boat up there."

"We'll meet you at the top, Jeep," he called starting up the hill with Gus.

"What in hell is going on down there, Reuger," Gus grumbled, limping next to him.

"Hurt yourself there?"

"Jest a little arthritis in my hip there." He shut one eye. "Don't yer worry I can keep up with yer. But what's Riechardt up to with this girl?"

He squinted up the hill where sun lay like a fleece of gold.

"Find out."

6

HE WALKED THOUGH the charred timbers. Dusk had already shadowed the land, and burned wood smelled like a damp fireplace. He walked toward the blackened slasher and glanced around again. *What the fuck had happened? How did it go so bad?* He glanced around the quiet land and reached up to the gas tank for the motor that ran the hydraulics of the cherry picker and the saw.

The cap screwed off roughly from the heat. He saw the brittle wire just inside the tank and carefully pulled out the bare light bulb. The filament was still there and, amazingly, so was the gas. The truck had burned and somehow the gas had not ignited in the smaller tank. *So the fire didn't start from there! Somebody really fucked up.* He walked over the crackling wood, holding the bare wires going to the filament. The rest of the wire had burned away.

He stood back. When the slasher started up, the bulb should have ignited. That would have blown the tank, and there would have been a neat fire. *But…this. No.* He walked away from the truck and stared over the landscape. The fireweed was crushed down, and he walked like a man approaching a dangerous animal. This was where he was. He could see the blood spread out in the weeds. It looked like someone had dressed out a deer. A man had a lot of blood.

He turned and shook his head. *Not so easy this business.* He stood in the shadow of the forest and wondered if things were spinning out of control.

7

A BOAT GLIDED on the shell-colored bay with undulations rippling from its sides. Reuger watched the boat for a moment then turned from the window to the girl in a chair among the five adults. Dana Reynolds wore sunglasses and had bleach-matted hair and pink-painted lips and fingernails. She scuffed her sandals on the plank wood and chewed gum every few minutes. A halter-top barely covered her breasts, her shorts were so tight her vulva bulged.

Reuger's eyes drifted to the bearskin rug next to mining lanterns and snowshoes and an old chain saw from 1955. The faded green tiles of the floor, pine walls, and comfortably saggy couches were familiar to him. Pine Lodge was like a VFW hall with an A-frame ceiling and long windows facing the lake. Reuger looked at the owner, Jim Carpenter, standing with his arms crossed, wearing a checkered shirt and sagging blue jeans and a BWCA belt buckle. He was pale and looked like he might get sick any minute.

The lodge had survived the Wilderness Act when many others didn't. When the law was passed in 1968, there was a bloodletting of lodges. The Forest Service bought the lodges at market value and then lit the timbers. They burned twenty-seven lodges on Basswood Lake. The line was arbitrary and sweeping. Anything above the line that was not a canoe or of nature was forbidden. The line swept down through Snowbank and bisected the lake. Lodges were put on sleds and pushed to the Southern End to escape destruction. Pine Lodge had just made it and ended up being the only lodge close to the Boundary Waters.

Jim's father had bought the abandoned logging camp after World War II and built a lodge on the horseshoe bay off Snowbank Lake.

The lodge resembled an old ranch house with a sagging roof of red cedar washed to gray from melting snow. Originally, the site was a logging camp, and the roads left behind became the lodge road and the network of cabins. Down the road from the lodge was the woodshed where Dana Reynolds said she was attacked.

Reuger stared at the girl. He had yet to hear the word *raped.* He had brought his rape kit along just in case, but Jim Carpenter was careful to use the word *attacked.* Raped, and he could kiss the lodge goodbye. Attacked, and he might have a chance. Reuger rested his right hand on the Colt. It had been a while since he had a crime of this nature. Not since Annabel Günter.

A year ago, he found her walking on the old lodge road, stumbling with cuts and bruises and one sandal missing. She wouldn't talk about it. Annabel now worked at the lodge, and every time he came there she avoided him.

"*Well!*" Joel Reynolds barked. "What the hell are you going to do?"

Reuger turned to the man standing before him. Joel Reynolds was bald and brown and heavy lipped. He stood in the middle of the room with a cell phone blinking under a raft of weight on his belt. A laptop sat open and glowing behind on the round kitchen table in front of the coffee pots.

"I want everyone's names here," he declared, swinging around.

The girl rolled her eyes.

"Chill, Dad."

"Shut up! I'll handle this."

He sat back down at the computer. A phone shrilled, and he was up again.

"What...yes. I want the *best* investigator you have...yes my daughter has been molested in some lodge up here in the middle of bumfuck I don't know where." He passed Jim Carpenter.

"You better find another lodge, my friend, because I'm going to sue you into oblivion and then back....What? Yes, call me back when you get hold of him and see when you can get him a flight up here."

He clapped away the phone and faced his daughter. When he had come to the lodge, the father had said the daughter changed her mind and that she had been attacked. A phone clipped to her pink shorts rang. Dana Reynolds brought it up to her ear.

"Oh hey...I can't hear you..."

Her father wheeled around like a general.

"Get off the phone, Dana!"

She glared at her father.

"I have to get off, my dad is being an asshole."

She folded the phone and scowled.

"There, I'm fucking off, *all right?*"

Joel Reynolds paced the room. He was sweating and his forehead and upper lip glistened in the window light.

"Were you molested, Dana?" Joel Reynolds whipped around and stared at Reuger. "We already went through this!" he shouted. "Of course she was molested!"

Reuger squeezed one eye closed and tipped his hat to the girl.

"Asking your daughter here, sir. I understand there's some confusion."

Joel Reynolds crossed the room and stepped close. He was wearing a cheap aftershave Reuger hadn't smelled for years. It reminded him of a drugstore in the lower forty-eight from when he was a boy. This man oozed sweat from almost every pore on his face and his brown eyes darted from side to side like caged bees.

"Listen to me, no backwoods sonofabitch is going to interrogate my daughter. You think you can fuck with me because I'm not from around here, well you have another thing..."

Reuger clamped his shoulder and pulled him close. He hated to do it this way, but this man was so used to giving orders he was no longer listening, and now some boundaries had to be established.

"Don't stand so close to me," he said in a low voice. "And don't threaten people with closing their business. I'm the deputy sheriff of the Northern Territory, and I'll ask your daughter what I need to here." He leaned closer with his hat brim touching his forehead. "You call me a sonofabitch again, and I'll have you out in that road."

The eyes pushed against the glass lenses and the man breathed heavily.

"Are you...are you *threatening* me?"

"Oh shut up, Joel, and let the man do his goddamn job!"

He turned to the woman behind him. Her curly hair sprouted from a hat waging war with humidity and wind, and gold sagged on low cleavage. She looked wearily at her husband.

"You didn't ask her one question, Joel, before dragging us all down here, so let the man do his job!"

Joel swept the room with his hand.

"I'll handle this, Myra!"

"Yeah, sure you will," she nodded slowly, her eyes hard as bullets.

"Will you for once quit being the lawyer?"

Joel wheeled around to his daughter, speaking in a low voice.

"This man is going to ask you some questions."

She rolled her eyes and shook her head.

"Yeah... I know that, dad."

The man glared at Reuger, then went by his wife and crossed his arms.

Ben Johnson had been quietly sitting in the corner and crossed an embroidered three hundred dollar boot over his knee and lifted his tan Stetson. He looked like he might bust out laughing any minute. Jim looked like he might puke.

Reuger pursed his lips and concentrated on the girl again. She tilted her head and fingered a pink nail. "So...where were you when this man came up on you, Dana?"

She shrugged, whisking her blond hair back behind her shoulders.

"Inside that old shed with boards and stuff."

"The woodshed?"

"Yeah."

Reuger nodded and rubbed his eyes.

"Where were you before that?"

"At the campfire." Her eyebrows lowered. "Like I said before."

"About what time?"

"Close to midnight," she muttered, smacking her gum loudly.

"Midnight!" Her father marched across the room. You said nine o'clock before! What the hell were you doing out at midnight!"

"Yeah, so what," Dana shrugged, pulling back her blond hair. "I snuck out of my window."

Myra Reynolds grabbed her husband's arm.

"Joel, let her talk!"

He went by his wife and crossed his arms again wearily. Reuger walked the planks with his boots creaking the boards. The girl's body language suggested nothing had happened. She was sitting with her legs apart and her shoulders slumped. Her whole body suggested boredom, not someone who was just raped.

"What did you do after the campfire, Dana?"

"I started walking home and went past that shed and heard a noise," she said nonchalantly.

"In the woodshed then?"

She nodded, pulling back her hair again.

"Yeah."

"What did you do then?"

She crossed her legs, bobbing one knee over the other.

"I went in to see what it was."

That's when you saw the man there?"

"Yeah, right." She nodded quickly. "That's when he snuck up on me."

Reuger looked at her directly.

"What'd this man look like?"

"He was...I don't know...he was dark." She opened her mouth and hesitated. "Big. He had this long black hair...you know... like an Indian."

Reuger smoothed his mustache.

"Did he grab you, Dana?"

"I think...I think he tried to," she said slowly. Her eyes flicked up to him, and Reuger saw something like the flash of a cooling match. The nonchalance was stripped for a second, and it made his stomach sink. She was squirming in the chair again. "But I ran before he could get to me."

"You think he did!"

Her father was moving again and Reuger turned away. The girl was already sullying up against the parental intrusion.

"Well...it was fucking dark."

Joel Reynolds lorded down on her with a fat forefinger.

"Watch your language, young lady!"

"Oh, big fucking deal," she muttered.

"*Dana...*" Her father shook his finger at her again. "I'm warning you."

"Joel!" Her mother crossed between them. "Let her talk!"

"Myra...*please!*"

Reuger turned back to the window. The sun had touched the lake with gold and he watched a boat heading out for the evening fish. He felt like he was watching one of those shows from the lower forty-eight. It was controlled chaos, and he had a room full of it. He had no way to tell what happened to the girl because the air was filled with static from the father. He turned back to Dana Reynolds in the kitchen chair.

"This Indian who came into the shed...he didn't actually touch you?"

"Well..." She opened her mouth and hesitated, a pink blush rising on her cheeks. "I guess not...I mean, *maybe*, I mean... I don't know if he did or he didn't!"

Joel Reynolds clapped his forehead.

"What!"

She glared at her father.

"He didn't touch me—but he wanted to." She said it with the shorts riding high like a bathing suit. "Most men want to touch me! You were the one who said I was attacked!"

"Because you said you were!"

The gum started a quick rotation and she examined her pink nails.

"I said I was sort of attacked," she muttered.

"Sort of!"

Dana shrugged and crossed her leg again, bobbing one foot over her knee. Reuger tapped his gun belt, biting the inside of his mouth, choking off the annoyance he felt. He looked at the lawyer struggling with some creature contorting his mouth. Reuger turned to the girl.

"Is there anything else you want to tell me, Dana?"

"No," she said in a small voice.

Reuger tapped his gun belt and looked up at Joel Reynolds.

"You can file a report if you like, sir."

"That won't be necessary," Mrs. Reynolds snapped. "Come on, Dana. We're going home for a little talk. Get your computer, Joel, and let's go!"

The lawyer stared at his daughter, his wife, then Jim. Myra Reynolds held the screen door open in a slash of twilight. The lawyer opened his right hand.

"I think gentlemen. I owe you an..."

"Oh, come on, Joel," Myra shouted. "Before you make a bigger ass out of all of us!"

He shut his mouth and slinked out behind his family. Ben Johnson stood up from the chair and walked to the picture window. He shook his head slowly, pushing up his hat to a line of sunburn.

"Well if that isn't the damnedest thing," he growled, shaking his head. "Damn swampys from the lower forty-eight they come up here like a disease." He turned to Reuger. "You knew she was lying all along, didn't you?"

"I don't know about that," he murmured, watching the family.

A door behind them swung open, and they turned to Diane Carpenter with a shotgun in her right hand. Jim's wife walked to the window and blossomed smoke rings on the glass, her Annie Oakley curl of brown hair flowing down over a flannel shirt cuffed at the sleeves with Marlboros.

"Ya," she nodded. "Telling stories like that about people here, you know she keeps her parents busy, that one," she nodded flaring the cigarette again and turning in the dusk light. "Thought I'd show you my birthday present, Reuger."

He took the shotgun and fingered the mahogany stock then sited the barrel. Gun oil slicked his palms and he could smell the new wood of the slide. He lowered the gun.

"Mossberg 20 gauge?"

"Oh, ya," Diane nodded, flipping her hair back with her shoulders. "Go ahead and check out the action there."

Reuger worked the slide and pumped the gun once. It was smooth and clean. Diane crinkled her lips, popping the cigarette in a torrent.

"Can't wait for the fall, you know. Shoot me some partridges from the jeep," she said, taking the shotgun from him.

"So did you hear all that?" Jim motioned with his coffee cup. "We almost just lost the lodge."

Diane tipped ash in her palm with the shotgun over her forearm.

"Ya, I heard it."

Reuger watched her smoke, the heavy mascara sooty in the retreating light. Diane Carpenter was the daughter of a taconite miner. A waitress when Jim Carpenter went to the Ely Diner and sat all night drinking coffee, trying to get up the nerve to ask her for a date. After they turned off the lights of the restaurant she walked up to his table and said, "Ya, Jim, we're closing, would you like to go get a drink?" Jim had nodded and said, "Just about to ask you the same thing."

She shook her head slowly.

"I was just baking my rolls and cookies here and such and hear all this yelling and see Reuger there, and I knew something was going on."

He turned to her. Where Jim was slow and methodical and didn't speak much, Diane had the frankness that comes from watching a father die of black lung disease and going to work full time when she was just sixteen.

"What do you think about the girl, Diane?"

"Oh, ya, the little bitch was lying." She christened the glass again with a wreath of smoke and looked at Reuger. "Anyone could see that, you know."

8

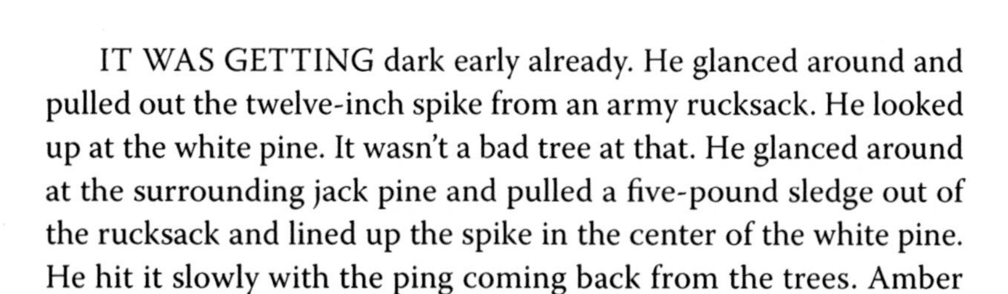

IT WAS GETTING dark early already. He glanced around and pulled out the twelve-inch spike from an army rucksack. He looked up at the white pine. It wasn't a bad tree at that. He glanced around at the surrounding jack pine and pulled a five-pound sledge out of the rucksack and lined up the spike in the center of the white pine. He hit it slowly with the ping coming back from the trees. Amber sap squished out around the spike.

He finished pounding the spike into the tree. He hit it three more times until only a small circle of steel was visible. He scraped off some of the sap and added some bark then smoothed it over the spike. There. Not bad. He stepped back. Nope. No one could see the twelve-inch rod inside the tree. He glanced around at the other trees. You never knew what tree the motherfucker was going to cut, but it looked like he was headed this way.

He envisioned the man with the chainsaw. The whirring chain would fly through the wood and then there would be a shower of sparks as the teeth of the cutting chain lost the battle to the steel spike. The chain would snap then and fly from the guides of the saw.

He pulled out another spike and raised the sledge. He pounded the spike into the tree and smoothed over the hole again. Nope. No one would ever find it. Only a man with a chainsaw would find the steel rods now. He finished with the four other trees then put his tools in the rucksack. Tomorrow was Sunday. He would come back on Monday and see what happened. It was for a good cause. That's what he had to keep in mind. The end justified the means.

They had done a lot worse. This was nothing. You had to strike when you had your chance, or you would never get anywhere. That's the way it was in this country.

9

REUGER SHOT OUT of the bay in the seventeen-foot lodge boat, sending curls of green gelatin toward the shore and clearing the last buoy. Tim Carpenter, Jim's son, was in the bow staring straight ahead at a large slab of granite rising out of the lake less than a mile across in the shape of a wineskin with the mouth close to the lodge. The dark trees of Center Island grew larger as they passed fishing boats with the red and green navigation lights. Granite slabs and jagged graywacke cliffed the shore with scraggly jack pine and overhanging swamp tamarack.

Tim pointed to a slab-slopping water, and Reuger maneuvered between the boulders. The bottom rutted shore as they lifted the trashcan to the flat rock. Reuger looked at Tim across the opening of fish offal smelling sour and horrible. Reuger was in the lodge bar with Ben Johnson and Jim Carpenter when the boy came in and said he saw a canoe over on the island. Tim also said he had seen a man back in the woods with long black hair. Ben Johnson had been ranting about the environmentalists before that.

"So when you going to pick up that sonofabitch, Reuger?"

Reuger turned slowly and stared at him. Men like Ben Johnson had always owned logging companies or ranches or plantations. Johnson Timber was Ely's sole employer since the mines played out in the sixties, and all the power came to reside in one company. He employed most of the town and had become the rallying point against the environmentalists who wanted to stop the logging.

Reuger turned away and sipped his coffee.

"What sonofabitch is that?"

"Don't give me that crap." His white eyebrows knitted together.

"You know who—*Jorde*! He's the one that's done it. He's the one that has the motivation to kill Foster." He dropped the whiskey like Kool-Aid and looked up, eyes red and small. "Bet your last dollar Jorde had a hand in this, Reuger."

He put his coffee down. Tom Jorde was the leader of the militant environmental group, Earth First. He had come to live in Ely five years before and made life hell for the loggers and for Reuger. The Earth First used a commando-style assault on industry. Logging equipment was ending up in the lakes and cars were left without tires on logging roads and salt was poured into the gas tanks of skidders and slashers and trucks. But there had been no violence yet and Reuger intended to keep it that way.

"Not their style, Ben."

"Like *hell!* They chain themselves to trees and move boulders into the logging roads, and I hear Jorde carries a gun. Forgetting, aren't you, that sonofabitch tried to put Jim here out of business?"

Reuger shook his head.

"That was the Wilderness Act, Ben."

"Tell that to all the lodges the government came in and burned down," Ben Johnson thundered, holding the bar like a man about to tear it away. "Shit, only reason they didn't get this lodge was Jim happened to be just south of the line."

"Yep, just a sixteenth of a mile short," Jim nodded, leaning against the bar holding a bottle opener. "Been any shorter an' we'd be sitting in the woods having a beer."

"And how you can rent to goddamn tree huggers—"

"Don't ask what people do for a living," Jim said, looking down to the bar. "Long as they pay up."

"I'd have thrown that environmental lawyer right out in the road," he grumbled.

"He's talking about the lady and the boy in cabin eight," Jim nodded, filling Reuger's cup again. "So...was Tommy still working with Foster?"

Reuger nodded, as the Colt clunked the bar again.

"Indians go bad sooner or later," Ben muttered.

Reuger set the enamel cup down on the bar.

"We took everything they had."

"Shit, they have the courts." He gestured to the ceiling. "Hell, they have more lawyers than I do!"

Reuger looked at him from the brim of his hat. "And all it takes is a court order to abrogate an Indian treaty made a hundred years before in blood."

"You've seen the Indians on that damn reservation. They're just like the *blacks*—living off the government and drinking all they can get their hands on!" He laughed shortly. "You have more sympathy for the Indians and tree huggers than the people around here who work the land?"

"You've stolen enough logs from them." Reuger looked down at the grounds in his cup. "I would think you liked the Indians. Never had to pay a dime for timber rights on their land."

"Stolen!" His eyes narrowed. "Whose fucking side are you on? You know where I just came from, Reuger?" He scooped the dice up. "Just come back from an auction in Washington state to pick up some equipment because the tree huggers decided a fucking owl was more important than people's jobs!" He held the cup up to the light. "I saw the owner too, sitting in a damn folding chair in the middle of his lumberyard while they auctioned off his life's work."

Ben's eyes pushed out from under the brim of his Stetson.

"I'm supposed to give the Indians a pile of money, because my grandfather didn't give some tribal chief an extra blanket for logging out the territory?"

Then Tim had come in with his breathless story of the man in the woods. Reuger now looked at the boy who had grown into a teenager over night.

"Did you see that Reynolds girl at the campfire last night?"

"Oh, ya," Tim nodded, veins swelling in his neck as they dragged the trashcan.

They sloshed the fish offal onto the rock then dunked the trashcan and poured out the water that congealed in the cold water. Reuger carried the trashcan back to the boat and saw a moon over the trees.

"Was Cliff there at the campfire?"

"You bet."

Reuger lifted the can into the boat.

"The girl leave with anybody?"

"Nope."

Reuger walked back up the shore and they watched the first vulture land then fast walk to the fish guts. The turkey vultures were long-legged birds with matted fur the color of charcoal.

"I sure hate turkey vultures," Tim muttered, watching more black-winged creatures waddle to the rock.

Reuger gestured to the trees.

"Why don't you show me where you saw that canoe."

* * * *

Tim walked across the granite and second growth to the tree line then pulled a canoe out of the brush. Pine Lodge was stenciled on the back and one paddle lay inside. He turned and frowned at the dark pines.

"Fire was a ways in there."

"Lead on then, cowboy," Reuger nodded, standing up from the canoe.

They ducked into the interior of the island through witch's branches curled and knurled. Storms had submerged the island and left driftwood and thatches of sticks and even some trash in the trees. The second growth had died. Their shoes sunk into the mud under the canopy of trees. They passed through dim light into a small clearing. Tim glanced around nervously.

"Right about here."

Reuger hunched down and touched the charred wood. He felt the mud and smelled charcoal from the fire and remnants of urine somewhere. Maybe feces. The grass was tramped down and mashed. It was a man's lair back in the swamp. He picked up a wrapper from a candy bar and turned slowly around to the flattened grass, bordered by pale green tamarack and scraggly aspens.

"Here's where his sleeping bag was," he nodded, glancing at Tim. "Grass is already rising up, he probably left after you come out with that fire smoldering."

Reuger touched the wood again and looked around the clearing. The half light gleamed dully on the cylinder wheel of the Colt and was bright on his badge. He paused then looked up at the boy.

"Better get your dad back his canoe, Tim."

10

THE WOODSHED WAS off the left side of the lodge road. Reuger turned on the low fluorescent tube. Tools were strewn on the planking with sledgehammers, shims and axes in the corner. Cutting chains gleamed from the rafters. He saw an ashtray with a pack of Marlboros on a shelf. Jim had said Tim often went to the shed to smoke and thought he didn't know. Reuger picked up several fresh cigarettes and smelled them. The woodworking table was swept clear of sawdust and two-by-four remnants.

He shook his head slowly. If a man wanted to attack her, he would have no trouble trapping her in the shed. With the door pulled shut, it would be dark as a coal mine. If the girl was attacked, why didn't she say so, and if she wasn't, then why make up something? He stared at the chainsaws and axes and drifts of sawdust on the floor then turned out the light.

Reuger stepped out of the shed. Lights flared the trees, and he heard the roar of an engine behind him. He turned in the road and saw a jacked-up Ram four-by-four pickup. Reuger stood in the middle of the road and heard the heavy-metal music as the truck leaped toward him. The truck didn't slow and splashed through a puddle, roaring ahead with the spotlights on the cab turning the trees white. At the last minute, the wheels locked and the pickup slid to a halt a foot away.

Reuger shook his head and saw the bumper sticker, *Save a Job, Kill A Tree Hugger*. He walked to the side of the pickup with a gun rack in the rear window and a CD hanging from the mirror. Chromed wheels gleamed like polished silver. He saw three Yamaha chainsaws in the bed of the truck with several axes and a coiled heavy chain.

In the corners were drifts of yellow sawdust and firewood. Metallica blared from the open window.

Cliff Johnson swigged a beer then threw the can to the floor. The sweat and dirt made his eyes stand out like a minstrel. He was the owner's son complete. Reuger had watched Cliff Johnson grow up and marveled at the swagger of youth and power in the potent cocktail of an athletic body and a razor sharp aim. Cliff could drill a dime at one hundred yards with a rifle and had been the star fullback on the high school team.

"Little late-night logging?"

"Ya, you betcha," he nodded, spitting tobacco juice from his swollen lip. "Fucking tree huggers put up a bunch of shit on the road, but we just bulldozed it out of the way."

He cracked open another can of beer and nodded to the shed.

"You hanging around woodsheds now?"

"Only when sixteen-year-old girls complain about getting attacked."

Cliff swigged the beer then burped and jumped his hat back from his forehead.

"Oh, ya? Little trouble then."

Reuger leaned against the pickup and nodded.

"This is new, isn't it Cliff?"

"Ya," he grinned, beating time on the steering wheel. "I rolled the last one.…So what happened in the shed?"

Reuger pushed his hat up and turned to the cant hooks mounted outside the shed.

"A girl here at the lodge said an Indian came up on her."

Cliff rested the beer on the steering wheel and stared straight ahead.

"Do anything?"

"Scared her mostly. I think."

He burped and spat out the window again.

"Sounds like that fucking Tobin."

Reuger eyed Cliff closely.

"What makes you say that?"

He shrugged and scratched a lightning bolt on his arm.

"He's a convict.…Isn't he up there helping that old man?"

"He was, but Foster's dead now. Shot in the head."

"Oh man," he said shaking his head. "Them tree huggers are getting out of hand!"

"Looks like a suicide."

Cliff shrugged and spat again. "Maybe Tobin did that too. Got all liquored up and shot the old man....That's who I'd look for, you know."

Reuger nodded to the beer.

"Against the law to drink and drive."

Cliff finished the beer then crushed it and threw it on the floor.

"Seen my dad around?"

"He was here earlier. I don't know where he is now."

Cliff yawned and lifted his oil stained cap with *Johnson Timber* in dirty green script.

Reuger nodded to the gun rack.

"How's the shooting?"

"Don't have time to shoot in competition anymore." Cliff yawned again with the dash lights on his face. "Well, it's been great talking with you, Reuger, but I think I'm going to go take a shower."

"Staying above the boathouse with Tim this summer?"

"Oh, ya. I work here for the ladies." Cliff jammed the truck in gear. "Keep your eye out for the injuns," he called back, roaring down the road.

* * * *

Patricia Helpner dipped her hand into the water and watched the dusk retreat toward Canada. The shadow of northern light fell over the land, and she wondered whether she would ever feel the peace she was seeing unfold in front of her. Her son was hanging over the edge of the dock making small rings in the ink-colored surface. She watched him and realized how big he had become.

He was growing up without her. She was working and he was growing. She wanted to stop him before he grew up and left. Something had passed out of her life, and she had to be careful with what was left. After her divorce, she assumed dating would come as a natural event, but being a working mother took everything and sometimes, late at night, she saw the rest of her life. It was a lonely vision, and she sat up feeling her thirty-five years. Life was fast. It sounded trite to say so, but once life took a course, you suddenly became one of the lonely joining empowerment courses, buying self-help books, embracing new-age religion.

"I'm hungry, Mom!"

Patricia wiped her eyes and looked at her son with his new tennis shoes and shorts. At least they had this moment together. No one would take this vacation. It was a stretch, but she had wiggled her way into a situation and now she was here.

"All right, I'll go up and get our groceries," she announced, standing up. "Why don't you put away your clothes I laid on your bed."

"Sure," Kurt called out, running ahead of her down the warm dock planks then letting the screen door slam behind him.

Patricia walked down the dock and navigated the trail through the woods to the lodge road. She pulled open the trunk of the station wagon and picked up a bag of groceries. The trees lit around her. Patricia squinted into the headlights as the bag tore and groceries spilled out in the white glare. There was movement behind the lights, then a voice.

"Lend a hand?"

"No, no." She smiled quickly. "I can handle it."

The engine stopped then boots sanded the gravel. A tall hat of some sort cut the afterglow of sky. She wiped her eyes quickly as Reuger saw her in the light. She was a small woman with the tight build of a gymnast. She bent over from the waist with her legs rock straight.

"Anything the matter?"

"What?" Her eyes were red rimmed. "Oh, just a cold." She sniffed again, brushing back her hair. "You really don't have to help."

He had glimpsed her eyes and even in the darkness saw they were green. Her breasts rode high and a shiny belt looped her waist.

"Don't mind," he said picking up the apples, tomatoes, lettuce, deodorant, pasta, pasta sauce and ten yogurts.

He saw this as another strange event in a day of strange events. He had seen the car with the Illinois plates and watched her bending over the trunk and had braked long before he saw the bag tear. Reuger scooped a box of vegetable burgers then a package of vegetable hotdogs and soy ground beef and two boxes of herbal teas. The Tampax fell from the torn bag again and Patricia threw the box into the station wagon. She saw the gun on his thigh and badge on his chest, but his face was lost under that hat.

"Really," she felt her face growing warm. "I can manage my own groceries."

He picked up the other bags and stood. He liked the perfume waving from her. It smelled like sweet lemons to him.

"Lead the way."

Patricia glanced down the path and felt annoyed. It was as if someone was already intruding on her vacation. At home, the neighborhood kids were in her house and her own work continually stole time from being with her son. She had looked forward to coming up to a place where it would just be she and Kurt. She decided to dispense with the situation as quickly as she could without being rude.

"All right, I'll take the suitcases and you carry the groceries."

Reuger looked at the trunk brimming with groceries and suitcases. He noticed the cell phone blinking on her belt and the new jeans showing the curve of her legs. She pulled back her short hair cut like a chow and auburn as a sunset.

"Why don't you unpack and I'll bring the rest of your things in?"

Patricia stiffened.

"I'm perfectly capable of carrying my own luggage," she said tugging a suitcase from the trunk.

"Not too heavy, I hope there."

"Don't worry, I can handle it," she gasped, dragging the suitcase across the ground. "Go ahead."

Reuger walked down the path and waited several times for her to catch up. He heard the suitcase fall twice and heard her curse twice. He saw the franticness in her. When people came up from the lower forty-eight, they seemed to be ready to jump out of their own skin. It was as if they were still running in some race that had already ended. Her movements were short and fast, and her eyes flicked and never focused in.

He reached the cabin with a stovepipe and a fire pit with logs neatly stacked. The cabin had an old green sofa, two armchairs, a white refrigerator, and gas stove with box matches. Knotty pine bronzed the overhead light. He set the groceries on the counter and went back to the door. The woman stood at the bottom of the stairs breathing heavy.

"Help you get that up the stairs?"

She shook her head, smoothing back her damp hair.

"Not a problem," she gasped. "It's not... *heavy*."

Reuger nodded and walked back into the cabin. He opened one of the bags.

"Hey!" A boy bounded out of the bedroom like Huckleberry Finn. "Did you catch the bad guys you were looking for today?"

Reuger stared at the boy from the forest with the bowl haircut and big brown eyes. He remembered the feeling again in the forest and saw this was the answer to a day of questions. Of course this boy was her son. Now the day was complete. At least he didn't look like his son anymore but just another boy up on vacation.

"Not yet," he said, shaking his head. "Did you find a lot of blueberries?"

They heard the suitcase clunk the stairs of the porch. Reuger opened the door as his mother reached the top stair.

"Can I take that for you?"

"No," she gasped again. "I have… it!"

The boy and Reuger watched her wrestle the suitcase into the cabin.

"My mom likes to do everything herself," the boy muttered behind him.

She was struggling up the last stair when Reuger grabbed the suitcase and brought it into the room. Patricia breathed heavily and wiped perspiration from her brow. He watched her towel the back of her neck under her short hair. He noticed how small and slender her hands were.

"That wasn't so bad," she said, turning around flushed.

The boy jumped and down and pointed.

"Hey Mom, this is the *bounty hunter* I told you about today!"

Patricia dabbed her face and stared at him. Reuger thought her eyes were the color of an emerald in sun now. She stared at him suspiciously.

"This is my son Kurt….You two met before?"

"I *told you,* Mom," the boy nodded wildly, jumping up and down on a bedspread of bears and loons, "he's the bounty hunter I met in the woods when we were blueberry picking! I told you and you didn't believe me!"

"Kurt! Calm down! I believe you."

She breathed deeply and looked at the sunburned man in the green hat.

"I saw the boy in the forest," Reuger explained, clearing his throat. "Deputy Sheriff Reuger London."

"Patricia Helpner," she said, shaking his hand firmly. "Thank you for your help, Deputy. I think I can handle it from here."

He paused.

"You arrived earlier today, then?"

She smiled tightly. "Mr. Carpenter had told us of an area to look for blueberries."

"Jim knows where all the berries are for sure," he nodded, standing at the door. "I could help you with the rest of your things."

"Kurt will help me bring in my luggage." She smiled tightly. "So I really don't need your help."

"Yeah, sure," Kurt shouted, pouncing from the bed. "We'll both bring in the groceries, right?"

Patricia glared at her son.

"Every boy in the Northwoods helps his mother," he said, winking at the eager boy and avoiding her eyes.

Kurt ran out of the cabin singing.

"Every boy in the Northwood's helps his mother!"

Patricia snapped up her purse.

"I'll pay you for your time."

"That's not necessary."

"I can take care of myself and my son," she said crisply, handing him a ten-dollar bill.

Reuger handed the ten back and shook his head.

"No thanks."

"Look," she continued, stepping toward him. "I don't like owing people."

He filled the door with his hands.

"You don't owe me for anything."

This is my vacation," Patricia snapped, touching her neck. "I don't need anyone feeling sorry for me!"

There it was again. Life must be like combat down there, because the people coming up were battle-hardened soldiers.

"Slow down. I was just trying to help you out." Reuger nodded to the door. "I'm going to help your son carry your luggage in and then go home."

Patricia breathed heavily and felt some of the stress lifting. She wanted to go for a run or have a beer or just sit in the darkness on the dock. She wanted to put down this load of stress in the middle of her chest, and here was this calm man.

"Look..." She looked at the floor then met his eyes. "Most people have an agenda, and I just don't need the shit, all right?"

Reuger nodded slowly and tilted his head back.

"What type of law do you practice?"

Her eyes narrowed in.

"I saw your briefcase," he explained, heading her off. "Jim told me you were a lawyer."

"Environmental law." Patricia crossed her arms and caught his eyes. “Don’t patronize me, Deputy, I know what’s going on up here.”

Reuger smiled and tugged the brim of his hat down.

“Good. Maybe you can tell me sometime.”

Patricia stared at him then turned away.

“I’m going to unpack…at least take half of this.”

“No thanks.” He stared at the bill. “Besides I don’t have change.”

She tore the ten in half and put it in his hand.

“Now you do.”

11

DANA SAW HIM on the porch, and then she didn't see him anymore. She thought she saw him outside the game room window when she leaned over the video games but she wasn't sure. She was wearing a bustier and a low-cut blouse. She saw her breasts in the reflected light of the window. They were huge.

But now the night had ended, and she had to walk back to her cabin. He was an asshole. What he did in the shed was hard to even think about, but also it was wild and dangerous. She didn't know what she thought of it all. One minute she hated his guts...then the next she wondered what it would have been like. It would have hurt. It hurt before.

Dana looked out at the bay. A breeze blew in from the lake. She heard a few people in the bar, but other kids had already gone home. No one was her age. No one at all. There was one girl but she had nobody to speak of and wasn't interested in talking about boys or drinking or sex. She was up here alone in these fucking woods with her fucking parents. *Vacations suck!*

Dana started down the lodge road. She walked quickly and felt her sandals wobble on the loose gravel. She would go home and masturbate. Then she would listen to her iPod in bed until she fell asleep. After that she would have the last piece of chocolate cake.

* * * *

He watched her walk down the logging road and spat tobacco juice. He watched her from the doorway of the shed and swigged the Budweiser already warm. He leaned against the doorframe with the smell of sawdust heavy in the air. She was just about to walk past the umbrella light. He looked down toward the lodge then walked into the darkness.

He swung wide from the light and trailed the darkness, then his eyes adjusted and he saw he had closed the gap. She was walking to the far cabins down the road. He looked at the woods and knew no one was still awake. He had waited for her outside the game room and watched her from the darkness playing the video games. Those tits hung down well over the glass. He stood beyond the light, feeling the breeze in his wet hair. He drank six beers waiting for her to leave the lodge, then he began to follow her.

He quickened his pace. Women were so fucking stupid. You treat them like dirt and they come back for more. He glanced around then began to run lightly. He felt the thrill inside. He lived for the thrill. *Fuck it. It's my forest.* People want to come up from the lower forty-eight, then they were in his backyard.

He could see her clearly now. She was striding with those long legs and that ass was sashaying back and forth. He grinned and saw himself slipping one hand around her mouth and one hand going right for the mother lode. He would tear those fucking shorts to shreds this time. He heard the soft crunch of gravel. He was hard already. *Goddamn. This is going to be fun. Tight sixteen-year-old ass.* He was moving like a missile now, running low. His eyes were locked in on the target.

"Dana!"

A light flicked on in the woods, and she veered down the path to her cabin. He went down to his hands and knees and didn't move. He clawed the dirt.

"I'm coming," he heard her shout, crashing through brush.

"I told you to come home an hour before!"

He breathed heavily then backed up slowly and crept down the road. By the time he reached the umbrella light, he had calmed down and was bored again.

12

BIRCH SNAPPED AS flames wrapped the logs like lovers. Firelight spilled over the two men in the armchairs pulled up to the hearth. Reuger held the book in his lap and peered at Gus with his white hair and beard yellowed by the firelight.

"Seen men cut trees since I was a boy. Seen 'em with crosscut saws flexing in the cold and pulling them logs to the lakes with horses so black you thought they were greased, and through snow so high a man could disappear and you see just his ax a stickin' up. Might git yer head cut off by a steam donkey or back broke by a tree, and I seen 'em in good times and I seen 'em in bad where it was so cold them trees chipped like blocks of ice and axes broke like flint."

Gus shook his head slowly. "But I ain't never heard of a logger shooting himself because his equipment burnt up. Nope, can't believe Foster done that."

Reuger reached for the glass of beer on the table by his chair. When he came back to the cabin the phone rang. Sheriff Riechardt was officious, efficient, and re-elected every four years with Ben Johnson's support. He'd been a sergeant in the Marines before law enforcement and ran the department much the same way. He didn't have much contact with his deputies. They were more like salesmen with territories who checked in every now and then. Reuger expected a call from the boss about Foster Jones. He expected a lot of calls after this day.

"Floyd said powder burns on his left arm here consistent with a self-inflicted wound. Time of death probably early Sunday morning resulting from a gunshot wound to the left side of the skull behind the ear. I'd say by that fire he was shot around seven a.m. or so."

"Any prints on the gun?" Riechardt interrupted.

"Hector's gone home." Reuger yawned. "Have him give you a call tomorrow."

Reuger heard the sheriff breathe heavy.

"Now who told that crazy Mcfee about this?"

"He put it on his radio program?"

"Yes, and the crazy bastard said the deputy sheriff is being tight-lipped, and this is leading him to speculate the murder is the result of either environmental warfare or serial murderer. Where the hell?"

"He's listening to the scanner, Sheriff," Reuger said dully, massaging his forehead.

Riechardt breathed heavily in the phone again.

"If I had my way, I'd have that fucking station burned to the ground and that one-horse printing press thrown into the lake."

"I gave him the facts on the suicide, he just chose to ignore it."

The sheriff paused, and Reuger felt a prickling on his forehead. He knew what was coming. It was the thing that irritated him most about Riechardt, and one reason he avoided the man every chance he got.

"Ben Johnson called me, Reuger. He's convinced Tom Jorde had a hand in this."

"He thinks Jorde does everything in the Superior National Forest, Sheriff."

"Ya, maybe, but why don't you go shake him upside down and see."

Reuger breathed out impatiently. He hated the way Riechardt came in like an armchair quarterback. He had been through this before. Leave him alone, and he would do what it takes to solve the crime.

"That's Ben's agenda, Sheriff," he said tiredly.

"Makes sense here, Reuger. Why the hell would..."

"Because that's where the evidence is leading me."

The sheriff was silent. Reuger could hear a faint clicking on the line. They all wanted him to hang Jorde from a tree and that was why he would look everywhere else first. Right now it was a suicide. It wasn't glamorous and it wasn't pretty, but there it was.

"I want you to talk to Jorde."

"You mean Ben wants me to talk to him," Reuger replied, knowing he shouldn't have.

The silence was there and he thought Riechardt had hung up.

"Just do it. Now, I heard you talked to that girl there."

"Girl said she was attacked then recanted her story and said nothing happened."

The sheriff paused again and Reuger could almost hear the small squeak of the cigars he cherished.

"Anything happen up there at Tobin's cabin?"

Reuger looked at Gus and shook his head.

"Not much, found some old arrows lying around, but that was all."

"The father believed she was attacked... possibly raped."

"She said she wasn't, Sheriff."

"Ya...well, let me know when you talk to Jorde," he said, hanging up.

Reuger stared at the fire, hearing the click of the phone in the popping wood. Gus shook his head again, watching the flames with one hand on his pipe.

"So that girl, she give up the ghost yet?"

Reuger picked up his beer again.

"She said nothing happened in the shed."

"Then we went up there and got arrows slung at us for nothing?"

"About the size of it."

Gus squeezed one eye shut.

"Then who was slinging them arrows, Reuger? I notice you didn't say nothin' to Riechardt about that."

"Nope, not until I know more. They're all hot to find something to hang on Jorde, and I'm just going to keep all things separate right now." Reuger paused, watching the tumblers of sparks flying up the chimney. "Might have been Tommy, and if he shot Foster then I would bet he's in Canada by now. But I'm not saying anything until I'm convinced."

"Well that makes more sense, unless that Jorde done it."

Reuger raised his eyebrow.

"Been listening to John Mcfee?"

"Now yer don't have to go comparing me to *crackpots*. I'm sayin' here that I known loggers my whole life, and they are used to hard times is all. Hell," he said gesturing with his pipe. "Yer logged long enough to know that sort of business ain't in a logger's temperament."

Reuger looked at Gus. He still wore the clothes of the lumberjack, high-cut pants so briars wouldn't grab on, laced-up work boots, a heavy flannel shirt and suspenders that kept the pants up while lifting logs or bending down to buck a tree. Gus was dressed the same way fifteen years before when Reuger logged his first day.

When he became a deputy sheriff, Reuger could think of no man better to help him. Gus had long since quit logging and their friendship over the years had become something akin to a father and a son. Gus knew the loggers and had a knack for discovering clues in the wilderness where crime scenes lasted precious few hours before rain, wind, snow, or critters obliterated any evidence.

Gus shrugged and held his pipe out in the darkened room.

"Yer know we ain't had a murder up here for the last twenty years, since old man Winston hacked his squaw up there on Knife Lake, but it don't mean we ain't goin' to end up with another. I know yer like to keep a tight rein on things around here, but Jorde might be in on this one."

Reuger stared at the hat and Colt hanging on a four by four above the hearth. A man who couldn't decide whether he wanted to live in the suburbs or the wilderness had built his cabin. Outside it had blue painted siding with large rectangular windows. Inside, the stone fireplace and knotty pine were concessions to the wilderness.

"Accident was the last straw for old Foster. Probably meant bankruptcy." Reuger looked down at his book again. "I'll know more when I talk to Johnson Timber."

Well, yer may be right there." Gus tapped his pipe on the hearth. "But seems to me Foster jest started over, is all."

Reuger stared at the leaping flames. "You remember Knudsen, Gus?"

"Yep, disappeared last winter. Found his saw in the Boundary Waters." He brushed back the hair touching his collar. "Thought you figured he fell through the ice."

He nodded. "Foster was up in the Boundary Waters also."

"Lot of lines in the forest now, Reuger. Hard put to know where I'm 'sposed to be and where I ain't." He gestured with the pipe. "Think you stumbled over the line every now and then, if I recall correctly."

Gus piped the corner of his mouth and examined the books lining the shelves. *Custer and Geronimo, Poetry of Emily Dickinson, Leaves of Grass, Poetry of World War I, Scott and Amundsen, Call of the Wild, Shackleton.*

"Now then what's the book?"

"*Writings of John Muir.*"

"Never heard of him."

"Naturalist from the turn of the century." Reuger put the book down. "I'm still willing to believe Foster shot himself. But someone was shooting those arrows for a reason. I'm going back up to where

Foster was logging tomorrow—"

"What time?"

"Get an early start."

"Around six then," Gus said standing up and tapping ashes on the firebrick. "Think I'm goin' to sleep well tonight. See yer in the morning."

"Good night, Gus."

Reuger listened to the door close then watched the devouring flames again. The crackling filled the silence. He pulled the torn ten-dollar bill from his pocket and thought about the woman with the boy. Reuger shut his eyes and listened to the expiring wood. He saw the arrows coming toward him again. They were sharp phantoms of his past, and they filled the small cabin. It was the reason he didn't tell the sheriff about the arrows. Tommy Tobin was slinging those arrows from a day fifteen years before when snow fell like tufts of cotton.

13

THE RECOIL OF the Winchester kicked down through his shoulder and the men stopped the way he knew they would. It was a picture of logging in the twenty-first century; flatbed trucks in a wagon train with chippers to mulch the wood, a feller buncher with a twenty-four-inch titanium cutting head. The feller buncher, or cutter, resembled a steam shovel and could cut a seventy-five-foot tree in minutes then lay the tree down. The skidder looked like a giant backhoe and picked up trees with a single clamp and brought them to be sawed. Men stood around in green hard hats.

Reuger lowered the rifle and levered up another shell, then walked through the weeds. The men backed away from the pale-haired man with galvanized link crisscrossing his chest like a drummer boy. Tom Jorde sat in the dirt with a bloody nose, dirt creasing his cheeks, and a chain linking him to a tree. When Reuger kneeled he smelled urine.

"Hey, Tom."

"What!"

He watched the blood flow bright red and thought nosebleeds always looked so much worse than they were. Reuger rattled the heavy chain on his shoulders. Tom Jorde was a slight man who never seemed to tan. His eyes were blue and washed out.

"How'd you end up chaining yourself to trees, Tom?"

"Sierra Club knocked on my fucking door ten years ago, and I answered, all right?"

The diesel engines breathed hotly around them. Men laughed and spat. Reuger pushed his hat back and looked at the trucks from Johnson Timber. Exhaust bloomed into the trees.

"How'd you join Earth First?"

Tom wiped blood with his wrist then smeared it on his pants. Reuger liked Tom Jorde. He even shared his view of the natural resources, but he didn't approve of his methods. The logging would stop because the resource of trees had long been depleted, not because environmentalists spiked trees or sabotaged logging equipment. All the carrying on and raising blood pressures with antics just complicated what would be a natural process.

"I was in Oregon protesting the logging in the Olympic National Forest."

"The spotted-owl deal?"

"Yeah," he said tilting his head back again, blood finding new paths like some errant river. "I was tracking the owls and met some guys there from Earth First chained to the trees."

"No shit."

Reuger glanced around at the college kids chained to the other trees. Goatees and beards and beads, sandals and moccasins, and defiance painted over fear. The chains were new from the local hardware store and could be snipped in thirty seconds with bolt cutters. He shook his head slowly. It was all just a statement. A nuisance. Like all protesting in the modern age, it was just free drama.

He took out some jerky from his vest and split the wrapper.

"How'd you end up here?"

He looked at Jorde again. Someone had kicked him in the face and broke his nose open like a plum. Tom's eyes rolled down, and Reuger saw the anger snap through his gaze.

"They needed somebody up here to stop the clear-cutting."

"Ya, too fucking bad, I'd say."

The voice was behind them. Reuger turned to a bearded man with a neck like a bulldog and small, cruel eyes. His cheeks were burned red from the cold, and his forearms were so thick his flannel shirt couldn't be rolled. He smirked like a man playing a practical joke. Al Hanes fit the role of the foreman perfectly.

"Don't you have something better to do here, Reuger?"

"Nope." He shook his head. "I don't, Al."

He took off his hard hat and palmed his crew cut. Al Hanes spat a glob of tobacco behind him and put his hard hat on.

"Ya, just more waste of taxpayers money here keeping men from working."

Reuger met his eyes. He knew all right. He must have known when his wife started coming home late from the timber office. She wanted to escape those small eyes and rough hands, and Reuger came late one night to get his check from Ben Johnson's office. It wasn't his fault Al Hanes's wife hated her husband's guts and went looking. He was young and hungry and alone then, but that was a long time ago.

He stood and faced Al with the Winchester in his right hand.

"That what you call it, Al? He has an injunction, then it's illegal logging here."

"Ya...fucking tree hugger," he muttered, crossing his arms. "So you know we're going to log this section here today starting with that tree there."

Reuger looked away and did a slow count. Al Hanes was the worst that an industry under fire could produce. He headed up the familiar local attitude of *us versus them* and justified any action under the banner of protecting a way of life.

Tom Jorde unzipped his blue vest and slipped out the injunction with the scent of a leather briefcase clinging to the paper.

"I tried to serve this injunction at your office yesterday, asshole, but you know what, suddenly the office was closed!"

Al Hanes spat just short of Jorde's foot. The glob of juice and spittle rolled in the dust.

"Ya? I don't see anything, except a tree-hugging sonofabitch here!"

Reuger kneeled down and put the jerky in his vest and thumbed his hat. He paused and realized how close Jorde had come to getting the shit kicked out of him.

"Let me see that injunction, Tom."

He crooked the rifle and read legal verbiage describing the forest quadrant. He felt a prickling along the back of his neck.

"Ya, Reuger, what's your twenty?"

He pulled up the radio.

"Headed for Foster's slasher."

"10-4."

He clipped the radio and read the injunction again.

"You're right, Tom." He looked up. "They can't log these trees."

His face turned red. "Yeah, tell the *fascists* that!"

Reuger stood and faced Al Hanes leaning against the fender of the truck now. He was surrounded by his men and had the swagger of a schoolyard bully.

"Has an injunction here, Al. Can't log today."

"Ya?" He shrugged, sleepy-eyed. "I don't know that paper is real there."

The men laughed, and Reuger smiled down at the ground. He walked the four steps to the truck and put his boot on the fender with his hat touching Al Hane's forehead. He could smell his last cigarette and saw how small his eyes were.

"You know the paper's real, and I know it's real," he said in a low voice. "So, you take these men here and your trucks and get out of here before I cuff you and throw you in the back of the jeep like an old hog."

Reuger watched Al's cheeks redden and his eyes grow even smaller.

"Ya, I know what you're about Reuger."

He didn't blink from those dull eyes and stepped closer.

"What's the matter, Al? You can only beat up women and environmentalists chained to trees?"

He saw the pulse in his temple, the set of his jaw. Al was itching for this moment, and he was going to give it to him. Reuger lifted his head slightly.

"Go ahead, Al."

He glanced at the Winchester.

"You gonna shoot me?"

"You betcha."

Al swallowed then smiled uneasily.

"Ya, you were never any fucking good as a logger either," he muttered, swinging up into the truck. "Come on, let's get the fuck out of here!"

The trucks grinded gears and rumbled back down the road. The road dust tornadoed into the trees as the diesel engines thundered off through the forest. Reuger watched the last one clear the trees before he turned back to Jorde.

"Have keys for these chains, Tom?"

He cocked his head.

"Over there, under that rock."

"I got it, Reuger," Gus called, bending down to a slab of granite.

He returned with the keys and began unlocking the padlock that the chains were looped through. Reuger counted the college kids chained to other trees.

"Getting them awful young now aren't you, Tom?"

"They volunteer," he muttered, wiping a smear of blood and dirt from his nose.

Reuger helped unravel the chains and saw the chrome of a small handgun. He tapped the gun under the vest.

"What's that, a .22? Standard equipment for an environmentalist now?"

Tom brushed dirt from his pants and shirt. He glared up.

"They carry them. I've been threatened and beat up enough times."

Reuger shook his head slowly. "Could get you killed there, Tom. Next time I might not make it in time."

"Yeah?" He nodded. "Then I guess it's good I have it."

Reuger saw the dark stain spreading from Tom's crotch. Jorde nodded down to his pants.

"Yeah, you missed the Hitler youth in-training."

"Cliff?"

"Yeah that… " Tom's face reddened, his eyes tearing suddenly. "I don't appreciate a deer rifle against my fucking forehead!"

Reuger breathed deeply

"You want to press charges, Tom?"

"Oh yeah," he scoffed. "Get real far in this town where everyone is sucking off Ben Johnson."

"I'll talk to him."

"Yeah, whatever," he muttered, spitting more dirt from his mouth.

Reuger watched him for a moment.

"Tom, you do any chaining further up, closer to the Boundary Waters there?"

His eyes hardened.

"No, should I be?"

"I don't know."

"Uh huh," he nodded. "Just let me know what crime I've committed will you? I know I'll get real far with a logger turned cop."

Reuger watched him walk toward the college students still chained to trees. The college students slapped palms high.

"Feel sorry for that fellah there, Reuger. They shouldn't a done that to him even if he is getting in everybody's way," Gus said shaking his head. "And that Cliff Johnson, he—"

"Yep," he nodded.

Gus patted the tree Tom Jorde had chained himself around.

"A Norwegian red," he murmured. "Should have been logged along with the rest of the forest." Gus squinted up. "Don't see many old ones like this around anymore."

Reuger looked at the tree.

"Nope," he said, turning toward his jeep. "Not for the last hundred years."

14

REUGER SMELLED THE charred timber as they got out of the jeep. The wood no longer smoked but crusted off like stale bread under their boots. Even the beetles snapping away were black. Gus and Reuger walked slowly toward the blackened slasher and saw a man with a Civil War cap walk out from the trees.

"Looks like she burned up pretty good!" John Mcfee called then shook his head. "Jest too bad for old Foster."

The three men met in the suffocating scent of burnt cork. Jack pine beetles snapped around them in the high grass.

"As if yer cared," Gus muttered. "Yer jest cryin' now that yer have something to write about, aren't yer?"

Reuger breathed heavily with one hand on the Colt. It irritated him that this man was tramping over a potential crime scene. There just wasn't enough news to go around. Reuger had heard rumblings that Charles Kroning's children were none too happy with their father's generosity and had been out several times to check on the radio station and paper.

"What are you doing out here, John?"

Mcfee shut one eye against the sun with his mouth small.

"Ya, well the press has a right to conduct their own investigation and the *Ely Standard* is now launching their own continuing series into the mysterious murders of loggers up here in the Boundary Waters," he announced, smoothing his mustache with the notepad in his shirt pocket like a handkerchief.

Gus hissed through his teeth.

"Where in the hell does an old drunk like yerself get off spewing off that kind of water-rotted crap here?"

"Yer getting a bit ornery in yer old age, Vanzant." Mcfee kept his eye shut like some old sea captain. "We old shaders have to stick together here!"

Gus jabbed a finger into his face.

"Since when were yer ever a logger except when yer came beggin' for whiskey!"

"Tsk-tsk..." He shook his head and pulled out his notepad. "Might do an article here on what happens to bitter old shaders who like to masquerade as law enforcement."

Gus grabbed the pad and flung it into the high grass.

"Yer write anything about me, Mcfee, and I'll show you the long end of some double-ought buck!"

Mcfee squinted. "Threatening the press is a serious offense, Vanzant."

"All right, John." Reuger pushed back his hat, resting his hands on his gun belt. "What do you want?"

He nodded over his shoulder.

"Like my reporter's notebook first there."

Reuger picked up the pad and brushed the mud off the flyleaf. He handed it to John, and Mcfee slipped the pad into his pocket. He then turned to the burned truck with the saw already rusting along the edges of the blade. Mcfee gestured to the clearing.

"Ya, well, way I see it here we either have a serial killer on our hands, or I figure we have environmentalists killing loggers and, from my investigation, I'm beginning to lean toward the serial killer here."

Gus scoffed and spat on a jack pine beetle.

"*Yer* investigation!"

"That be about right," he nodded. "I have conducted a thorough investigation here of the crime scene, and I have my own conclusions."

Reuger rubbed his eyes.

"What does the press want, John?"

He hooked his belt like a gunslinger taking careful aim.

"*End of the Road* show is going to do a special feature on this here story."

"From what I heard, you already have."

He gestured toward the burned timber again.

"Sorry about that, Reuger, but I need to have exclusive here on this crime, or I'll have to reveal everything I uncover."

Reuger kept a tight rein on his emotions. He could order John to stay the hell away from the scene of the crime and tell him if he saw him out here again he was going to arrest him. He could tell him nothing and say it was just a suicide. But John Mcfee had an unerring way of getting in the middle of things, with a knack for survival that thrived on chaos. The Kroning children had probably discovered this. John would not go quietly anywhere.

"I gave you an exclusive."

Mcfee stroked his chin.

"I intend to write a book about all of this, and I'll give you an acknowledgment, Reuger."

"Yer couldn't write yer own name," Gus muttered, turning away.

Mcfee looked at Gus reproachfully then turned back to Reuger. A bee hovered, and Mcfee ran from the dive-bombing black dot.

"Them damn bees...like I say...tell me what happens here, and I'll keep a lid on things while yer investigation goes forward."

"All right, John, no more *End of the Road* commentaries."

He crossed his chest solemnly.

"Give yer my word."

"Wouldn't get yer a bad cup of coffee," Gus grumbled.

Mcfee puckered his lips, stoking an index finger down from his brow.

"Yer really ought do something about yer bitterness Vanzant."

"All right, John," Reuger nodded tiredly.

"Yer have my word," he said shaking his hand. "Well," he announced slapping his hands together. "I would like to continue this, gentlemen, but the *End of the Road* show requires my time!"

"Gettin' yer polka records lined up, are yer?"

Mcfee pulled his cap low over his eyes.

"Jealousy is an ugly trait in a man of yer years, Vanzant."

Gus lunged toward him, but Mcfee fell back out of his grasp and rolled on the ground, jumping up like a wrestler. He whipped his pad out.

"Threatening the press is a serious offense!"

"Get yer sorry lot out of here before I kill yer," Gus shouted, watching him back across the glade. He turned to Reuger and nodded. "I know, but he...well he jest burns me with his talkin' that way... ever since that Charles Kroning give him that station, he thinks he's something special....I think he'd kill his own mother to get a story."

Reuger crossed the fireweed with insects swarming up into the harsh sunlight.

"Take a look here, Gus, and tell me what you think," he called back.

Gus stared at the fire-blackened landscape with the burned-out truck and the claw hanging over scorched metal. Reuger looked over the charred logs with bark sheathing off like skin. The truck with the fire-scorched claw and the saw on the trailer had settled into the land. There was already an air of a junkyard about the scene as if the destroyed machinery had been in the woods for many years.

"Bushwhacker probably ruined the crime scene," Gus muttered, looking into the cab of the truck as a butterfly landed on the stick shift then flew out the window.

He stared at the truck and the claw, glancing at the burned logs. Reuger saw pain in his eyes, maybe even sadness. This was a death of a man but also a way of life. The independent loggers were like the small farmers of the Midwest. The family farm was vanishing, and the big corporate farms were taking over.

"Maybe old Foster did catch it with the gas here, Reuger," Gus murmured.

They high-stepped across the timber with logs crunching under their boots. Reuger walked slowly with his head down examining the logs and burned weeds. The scene was more final somehow, he thought. He cussed John Mcfee again. If there were a clue as to what happened, then it would be on the ground somewhere. Mcfee could have mashed something down into the dirt, or, worse, he might have found something and taken it. Reuger glanced up and pointed over to some mashed-down fireweed.

"Found him over here."

They crossed through the brown grass. Blueberry brambles surrounded the area, and Reuger wondered he hadn't seen that the day before. The weeds were flattened and blood-blown from the discharge of the round.

Spattered brain and blood were sprayed like paint under pressure on the weeds. Reuger stared at the ground and wondered whether a man would really put that cannon to his own head. A .45 was a nasty weapon. The shell was squat and all powder. The accuracy was not great, but that wasn't the point of a .45. The gun was designed to stop and kill whatever was coming at you, and it did it in a very ugly way.

They stopped in the high weeds and heard wind volleying the treetops like a distant train. Gus chewed on his beard and gestured to the ground.

"How was Foster layin', Reuger?"

"Curled up on his right side."

Gus looked up one eye closed.

"Shot himself on the left side of the head then?"

"About right."

Gus squatted down and clasped his gnarled and swollen hands together. The wind waved the jack pine and rustled the wild grass around them. Reuger felt the man who had flattened that grass in front of them. The blood-soaked grass was not unlike what was left behind when a deer who was dressed out in the field.

"I'm going to have a look at these logs here, Gus."

"All right," he nodded. "I'll jest be a minute."

Reuger climbed the piled and fire-blackened timbers and fell down through the crunchy wood. The wood was a lot of jack pine with some cedar here and there. Foster had piled the timbers up and was going to call in a truck to pick them up. It was strange the fire had jumped all the way over, but he could see the way it had burned the grass and of course sparks carried by the wind.

"What in Sam Hill you looking for, Reuger?"

"Know it when I see it," he grunted, lifting a log and blackening his hands with creosote.

"Well, let me give you a hand then."

Gus climbed up and they dug through the piled timber. The logs were like giant black matchsticks thrown into a pile. Cork blackened their hands and clothes. Ash puffed out of the heated creosote as they threw logs until they were winded and wet. They gasped and sweated in the suffocating breath of burned wood.

"Logs underneath burned through—nothing left here." Reuger stood up breathing heavy and wiped his wrist over his brow. "Foster had a lot of wood here."

Gus nodded breathing hard.

"Yer thinkin' too much?"

"Maybe."

Gus pulled back his long hair, sweat glistening delicately on his brow.

"Somebody may have had a grudge with old Foster and wanted to make sure he didn't get any of his timber in."

"Possibility," Reuger nodded, climbing down and walking toward the large saw grappling air.

He ran his finger along the hydraulic hoses leading to the truck. He went over the scenario of Foster's operation. It was a portable mill bucking trees into eight-feet lengths on the spot. The logs were fed into the whirring teeth creating a mountain of sawdust. The sawdust became red oatmeal after the rains. Chunks of splintered wood scattered the base, and Reuger sunk into the soft bedding under his feet. He stared at the slasher again, not burned at all. The fire didn't touch the saw.

"Never seen a truck burned like this," Gus called from the door of the cab. "Ah—Reuger? Maybe yer better come over here."

Reuger stood and crossed the charred timbers to where Gus stood like a man who had discovered oil. He took off his hat, shading the sun over the logs and saw a discus the size of a quarter lying on a burned log.

"Have your handkerchief there, Gus?"

"Sure do."

Reuger reached down between the logs scraping the back of his hands and picked up the disc. The button had been seared face to bottom but was still legible: *Earth First.* He held it flat against the white cloth, and the scene changed.

"Ain't that what Tom Jorde calls himself?"

"You betcha," he murmured, turning the button over slowly. "Mind if I keep the handkerchief?"

"I got a plenty, Reuger."

He wrapped the button carefully and put it in his vest pocket. He glanced around the area and heard wind in the trees.

"Looks like that Jorde's mixed up in this thing then, eh, Reuger."

He felt Gus's stare and saw the eager light in his eyes.

"Don't know about that."

Gus eyed him hard and spat.

"What yer...well, then, what in hell that button doing here then?"

"Don't know," he said hunching down, resting his elbow on his thigh.

Gus hissed through his teeth.

"Can I ask yer what yer *do* know about, then?"

He kicked up the brim of his hat, nodding toward the saw.

"I know there's a lot of sawdust over there by that slasher." He turned to Gus, one eye shut against sun. "Want to get your hands dirty?"

"Well sure...if yer has some idea you want me to follow," he grumbled, following him and getting down on his knees in the brown muck. "Jest tell me what it is. I know this police work is complicated, but I sure thought..."

"It was." Reuger looked up and nodded. "The button is something, Gus. It's a good clue."

He shrugged. "I just would've thought is all."

The sawdust was like quicksand around the slasher, and they reached down above their elbows. The smell was like a cedar closet. The wet pine dust was pungent and they mucked their arms up almost to their armpits. Reuger strained his reach and felt something large.

"I feel a good bit of wood down here, Gus."

"He must've dug a pit for this here sawdust," Gus grunted, getting the coated wood shavings in his beard.

Reuger pulled hard on the piece of wood. Remnants of his woodcutting was down there and he found it strange he should dig such a pit. Most men just left the piled sawdust and moved the saw around when it got too big, but Foster had dug a pit.

"Can you lift it, Gus?"

Gus's cheeks reddened over his beard. "Maybe...but she's heavy, Reuger."

"Ready, one, two...*three!*"

They lifted together and pulled a slab of wood out of the muck in the shape of a half-moon and dropped it in the grass. Reuger pushed his hat up and wiped his brow then sat back with arms coated in reddish paste.

"Pine, old Norway pine." Gus nodded. "That wood's from a big tree there."

Reuger brushed the wet mush from the wood and saw the rings. The rings spun from the center of the wood like a spider web. Old wood had a different color and heavier density.

"You logged a long time, Gus. How old do you think this wood is?"

He licked his lips and squinted at the remnant then ran his hands across the rings.

"Haven't seen a tree like that there for the last fifty years."

"How old then?"

Gus rubbed his jaw, scratching like sandpaper.

"Bet that wood there is from a two-hundred-and-fifty-year old tree." Gus's watery blue eyes hardened. "Maybe more."

Reuger whistled and stared at the pine.

"Trees that size were all logged out a hundred years ago."

"Yep," Gus nodded, looking up with a strange gleam in his eyes. "Except the Old Pines up in the Boundary Waters."

Reuger stood and stared down at the remnant. You log and log and hit a few old trees. The treasures. Men stop in the forest and stare at a tree like they would a beautiful woman.

"I don't know, Gus. I don't think Foster's dragging trees that far," he said, shaking his head.

Gus rolled his shoulders and stood, brushing the wet paste from his knees.

"Jest sayin'. I only been up there once, but I've seen wood much the same, Reuger."

The Old Pines. They were a legend when he logged before. Men spoke of them in reverence, and many breaks were spent contemplating the worth of such wood. The trees were the last of the giants. A two-hundred-acre swath of trees the loggers of 1890 had missed. Some of the men said it was because they just made a mistake and didn't go up far enough. Others said that the Old Pines used to be swamp, and the loggers just took the easier trees. But whatever happened, the trees were left and had been federally protected along with the rest of the Boundary Waters when Teddy Roosevelt created the Superior National Forest in 1909.

Reuger reached down and ran his finger along a ridge chattered in the bark.

"What do you make of this, Gus?"

"Only one thing makes those kind of marks." He tapped the wedge of pine. "Choking the tree with a chain, but I don't see why Foster would be dragging logs with chains when he can pull right up with that cherry picker." Gus chewed his lip. "One thing's for sure here, that tree ain't from around here, Reuger."

"Ya, come in Reuger."

He hefted the radio.

"Go ahead."

Reuger... I finished with that .45 automatic, over."

"What'd you find?"

"Well, the shell and the gun match. Foster's prints were all over the gun, and I just about give up on it but then I dusted the barrel and found a couple of prints right before the sighting pin."

"Foster's?"

"Ya. Affirmative, sure is there Reuger, how'd yer know that?"

Gus stared at Reuger and shook his head. Hector was the Barney Fife of the Lake County Sheriff Department. He was bone-thin, short, and never left the station. He handled the paperwork and bookings and a lot of the evidence testing.

"Gun was clean then, Hector?"

"Noooo...so then I dusted under the barrel you know and right below the aiming pin was another print there."

The two men waited in the forest. The drone of a seaplane whined in the distance. Gus hissed through his teeth.

"He goin' to ever tell us what he found there, Reuger?"

He clipped the radio again.

"Foster's, too, Hector?"

"Negative, that was the one there. Definitely not Foster's. Could be your perp's, Reuger."

"Anything else?"

"Not so far but I'll let ya know."

"Thanks, Hector."

"You betcha."

"Barney catch yer crook?"

"Nope. But might have one now," Reuger nodded slowly.

The seaplane came into sight and banked along the trees. Reuger waved as the Blue Phantom scoured the pines and vanished.

"Irene must be giving rides at Pine Lodge."

"Well yer wouldn't catch me in one them little planes." Gus shook his head and spat again. "Especially with *a woman* piloting the dang thing."

"Best bush pilot in the Boundary Waters. Done many a search-and-rescue with her."

Reuger hunched down with the radio and looked at the quiet forest. There was no wind, but it had rained last night. Wind and rain were now his enemy. This was a crime scene. The clues had collected, and he felt now he could turn away from a suicide. Foster was not just a logger falling on hard times. The controversies of the last fifty years seemed to have found a purchase in this remote part of the forest.

He brought the radio up. "Hector!"

"Ya," Static showered in. *"Go ahead, Reuger."*

"Call the crime lab and let me know when they can get some people up here from St. Paul."

"Ya, 10-4."

Reuger hooked the radio and stared at the burned-out slasher and fire-blackened logs. He tapped his gun belt and waited for something. He tore open a pack of jerky and chewed the dried meat slowly. Gus hunched down.

"What yer thinking?"

"Wait a minute."

Gus looked away and stroked his beard.

"Are yer thinking..."

"Wait a minute here."

Reuger balled the wrapper in his vest and nodded. Gus breathed heavily. Reuger stared at the burned truck, the sprawled support legs like some pod.

"Are yer ready yet?"

"Yep," he nodded, standing up and looking at Gus. "Let's go and see Ben."

15

REUGER AND GUS sat with Jim on his lodge porch watching the storm on the north side of the lake. Reuger thought about his visit to Johnson Timber. Ben wasn't there, but Al Hane's wife, Penny, was. Reuger regarded her smoldering vitality that pushed through with dark eyes and full red lips.

"Al says you stopped him from logging this morning."

"Had an injunction, Penny," he shrugged.

"Ya," she said lifting a tired eyebrow. "You know they print those things themselves."

Reuger sat on the desk edge and plopped his hat down. He could smell her perfume and watched the rise of her breasts in a white blouse.

"Your husband always call you during the day and tell you his business?"

Penny Hanes let the magazine fall to the desk and picked up a cigarette.

"Ben's not going to be happy about that. He was counting on those trees, and now they'll drag it through the courts for months."

"Had a legitimate injunction, Penny."

"Ya?" She shot smoke toward the dirty neon panel light. "Never bothered you before."

Reuger lifted his hand. "Times are changing, Penny."

"When you cut trees, I think I remember someone who didn't let anyone get in their way."

"People change."

She fished another cigarette from her purse and sparked a lighter.

"Ya, I guess I should have known that about you."

Reuger noticed her left eye powdered over and knew Al Hanes

swung from the right. He took the small town girl and beat her in a provincial way. Ely was the end of the road. Mining or logging. Take your pick or leave.

Reuger put his hand on her desk and lowered himself. It had started in the Ely Motel with the red light shining in through the half-pulled shade. Penny was younger then, and so was he.

Gus and Jim sat silent as Reuger squinted across the lake. What Penny had told him about Foster Jones was troubling. He was six months behind on his lease, and Ben was about to throw him off the land. She said they had one hell of an argument she could hear clear out in the lumberyard, then Foster stomped away. Foster was a man with not much to lose. Once he lost his lease, he was done as a logger.

* * * *

Diane Carpenter pushed open the door with the screen wangling closed. She flared her cigarette in the storm light. She stared at the man leaning against the porch post with his hat low. She looked at his arms, then his sunburned skin and sandy mustache.

"Stay for dinner, Reuger? Gus too."

Reuger glanced up, eyes brighter in the reflected light.

"Don't have any pressin' engagements."

"I'll tell the girls to put two more on, then."

The screen door slammed, adumbrated by distant thunder. Sun knifed off the lake but over the far trees were shadows, and in the shadows lightning danced. Diane's son, Tim, emerged from the boathouse and walked up the ridge the lodge was built on with his flannel shirt whipping in the storm wind. Jim crossed the porch and called out.

"Seen the boy and his mother from cabin eight?"

"No sir," Tim said, pushing back his flat hair. "Their boat's gone, too."

Another blue bolt touched ground. Thunder rolled up closer, echoing majestically over the lake. Jim had seen the boat, that morning, go to the center of the bay. Voices traveled the flat water, and he heard the boy giving his mother hell. Then the boat took off whining toward the north end of the lake. Jim glanced at his watch.

"How long they been out?"

He turned to Reuger.

"Since this morning."

"Mind if I use your boat?"

"No, because I'll go with you."

They ran into the rain just beginning to darken the sand road. Gus looked up and watched electric spiders crawl the sky. He saw a hazy column falling from mushroom clouds over Center Island.

"Reckon they got fifteen minutes before hell breaks loose," he said to no one in particular.

* * * *

The storm flowed over the lake from Canada in a rolling glob of dark thunderheads stretching out over the trees and throwing down rain and lightning around the aluminum boat. Reuger sat in the front and searched the shoreline. Rain pelted his cheeks and dribbled from the brim of his hat. Flashes of light exploded, and they heard trees crack apart in the distance. The thirty-five horsepower motor strained against the whitecaps and water splashed up over the two men.

"I'll head over towards the Second Sister," Jim shouted with his hair slicked back and his shirt soaked to the skin.

Reuger nodded and wondered whether he might have to call in the seaplane. They would have to wait until the weather calmed before they could fly. But if they wandered off the lake, they could be lost in the interior of the Boundary Waters. The world slipped to the color of a flashbulb, then they heard another tree explode. He cleared his eyes twice before he saw the boat on the Second Sister. The boat was half in the water.

"See it, Jim?"

He pulled off his glasses.

"Oh, ya!"

Reuger saw the oars lying on the pink granite. He had a bad feeling. Wind sheeted the boat, and he saw water splashing white against the motor. Two bodies lay side by side on the rocks. Jim looked at him with his glasses pimpled with rain. Jim ran the boat up on the rocks, and Reuger jumped out, splashing ashore like a drunken man. He reached the woman first, with hair whipping like wet rope. He felt sick to his stomach as he turned over her sodden body.

16

THEY BROUGHT PATRICIA and Kurt back to the lodge. Patricia had blinked at Reuger in the rain then smiled when he turned her over. It was a moment she would remember for a long time. They had become lost then stranded on the island and when the storm began had laid face down on the granite rocks next to the lake.

The long table in the lodge hall was set with plates and covered with food. The fireplace crackled heat, and the pine walls made Patricia think she had walked into a movie of frontier life. The room filled with people. Two dock boys and two girls who helped Diane with the cabins walked in. Patricia thought the blond girl might be Diane's daughter. The owner, Jim, ambled in with an old man, and the deputy sheriff who had helped her move into her cabin.

She watched Reuger hook his hat on a chair and push his gun to the side. She thought about the island where she and her son had been stranded, and how he rescued them.

She had seen an eagle on the island, which was only about a half-mile from shore. So she and the boy hopped into a lodge boat with a small outboard and motored over. She figured it'd be a fun adventure for Kurt and a research trip for her. The engine prop hit bottom and busted in the shallows by the island. They sat stranded when the sky grew ominous. The storm blew up swiftly with the first cracks shaking the ground. They hugged a tree until lightning split another pine nearby. Then they ran to the shore and lay down.

* * * *

Patricia shut the porch door, feeling the night wind caress her cheek and stared at the yellow cabins around the cove. The fish house spilled light on the gravel of the road and a bulb shone in the boathouse like a candle in a barn. She stared at the moon over the pines laying a blue path on the water. Something recoiled before her and she screamed.

"Oh, I'm sorry, I didn't know anyone was out here!"

"Sorry to scare you," Reuger said standing up.

They stood close in the darkness. A boat puttered across the lake. She could feel him watching her. Patricia smiled past him, both of them hearing the video game coming from the lodge.

"My son has found a little bit of civilization."

He turned and nodded.

"I think he's enjoying himself here."

"I do too." She paused. "It was rocky at the start with..."

"Tough age," he said quickly. "Sorry I cut you off."

"No, no, that's fine...to cut me off...because I just cut you off...I think," she murmured.

They looked out together then turned in. She was annoyed that his man made her feel inadequate. Since her divorce, she had depended on no one but herself, but up here she felt unsure. It seemed each way she turned in the wilderness there was something to learn and this man seemed to be there.

"Well," she said brightly. "I think I'll go back to my cabin and take a shower."

"I'll walk you, then," he said.

She held up her hand.

"*No!* I mean no that's not necessary."

The hat moved against the darkness.

"Do you have a lantern or flashlight?"

Patricia smiled quickly.

"No...but I'll be fine."

The dark hat moved in front of her again.

"Never walk without a light in the woods."

She breathed heavily. Suddenly she wanted to poke a hole in this man's stolid exterior. She had seen his eyes when he helped her with the groceries. He was very adept at covering himself but she had seen the flickering glances at her body, and she had surprised herself by returning his stare once. She liked his blue gray eyes that held a gleam of self-mockery in them. She liked the calmness he exuded that allowed her to find no purchase, no glaring error of personality so she could dismiss him easily. The few dates she had gone on ended with a cold handshake. The men broke up like brittle glass against her critical eye.

"A Northwood's edict or another law in the Boundary Waters?"

"Common sense." The hat moved again. "Better to have a light in the woods."

Reuger turned and walked to the bottom of the stairs. The afterglow of the sky cut his figure into some Western she had seen long before.

"It's a good night for a walk here."

Patricia hesitated then came down the stairs. Her tennis shoes squeaked slightly and his boots clicked the oversized gravel where Jim had filled washouts. Patricia thought of her windblown hair and the makeup washed off hours ago and was thankful for the darkness.

"Give me your hand."

"Oh," she said smoothly. "You want to hold my hand already?"

"Nope," he said, taking her hand. "It's just dark."

* * * *

A loon called on the lake as Reuger examined her books. *Amelia Earhart, The Life of Eleanor Roosevelt, It Takes A Village, Virginia Woolf, Reader's Digest, Tuesdays with Morrie, Food Your Miracle Cure, Chicken Soup For the Soul, When Bad Things Happen To Good People, Silent Spring.* Empty suitcases were by the door, a vase of flowers over the sink, her son's tennis shoes in the corner, lotion in a pump dispenser on the table. The old pot hissed and percolated coffee. Patricia emerged in a fresh pair of jeans and a loose red flannel shirt. The sun had burned her cheeks into a healthy red and raccooned her eyes. She passed him in soft tawny colored moccasins and he noticed the curve of her ankles and a perfume lingering like spring.

"Cream, or do real men drink it black?"

"Black."

She brought over the cups and he felt awkward in the small cabin. His hat and his gun and his boots and radio seemed out of place. He felt too big for the space. He was six-foot-one, and he realized then how small she was. He guessed she was less than five-three.

"Sorry about the china cups. Kurt used the mugs for his milk. Baileys? Well, I'm going to have some."

She had a braid in her hair like a young girl. Patricia poured the coffee then filled her cup to the brim with Irish Cream. She turned to the door then looked at the man leaning back against the enamel sink. She saw him look at the door and the silence lay between them. Why didn't he say something? She sipped her coffee. He held the mug and the saucer and smiled. They heard the wind. They heard nothing.

"Let's go look at the stars," she blurted out.

"Sounds good," he nodded.

They rolled up and down on the current unseen beneath the steel drums. Coffee warmed their hands under the glitter bowl of electric circuits, winking, dying, streaking the night like some child's fantasy. They stared into the sky at the glitter arcing the horizon.

"It's so beautiful," she whispered.

Reuger stood on the floating dock and stared up into the sky. Sometimes he took his night vision goggles and looked at the stars. There were millions and it was then he felt he was looking at something akin to God.

"You don't have the pollution or city lights up here," he nodded.

"I just can't believe it," she murmured. "So..." Patricia glanced at him. "Were you raised in the woods by a band of Indians? Or do you just go around saving distressed women and children naturally?"

Reuger set the cup and saucer on the planks.

"Chippewa raised me."

"Really?" Patricia stared across the lake to the moon frosted trees. "Are there Indians out there still?"

"Taking aim right now at the two people on the dock." Reuger pointed across the lake. "Most of the Indians are on the reservations now. A few stragglers still out there."

"So you weren't raised by Indians then?"

"Nope." He pointed across the lake. "But there's a cave on the far side of the lake that has Indian paintings from a thousand years before. You can see a whole nation there if you're quiet and let your mind take you."

"You don't sound like you were raised in the suburbs," she murmured.

"My father was a logger."

Patricia walked the dock with her back to him. She turned around and pawed the planks with her moccasin. Her movements again reminded him of a gymnast.

"Does your father still log?"

"He was killed in a logging accident when I was a boy."

"I'm sorry, I shouldn't..."

"No problem," he shrugged. "We moved down to the Twin Cities, then I came back."

She couldn't see his face under that hat.

"OK...so why did you come back?"

He looked out to the lake.

"I didn't feel free."

"Ah," she nodded, feeling as if she had just found a map. "Thoreau then? The man who leaves civilization to live in the old way."

He turned from the lake with his eyes glimmering.

"Something like that, counselor."

Patricia looked down at her cup.

"Maybe...maybe I just have trouble with taking help from people, and you seem to be around just at the right time."

"It's my job," he shrugged, gesturing to the lake. "You needed help carrying your groceries, and I drove by. You got stranded on the north end of the lake, and it's my job to help folks who get in trouble."

She looked up.

"Even environmental lawyers?"

"Most people don't care what you do up here." '

She nodded and looked at him sideways.

"Is that why you have a dead logger and burned-out logging equipment?"

He stared at her wearily.

"I can read." Patricia gestured out to the trees. "It's no secret that this is some of the last old timber of the Northwoods and the loggers want it and the environmentalist want to keep it. It's going on all over the country. We're expansionists and there's no frontier any more, so that leaves everyone to fight it out over what's left."

"The paper had it wrong," he said shaking his head. "It was a suicide. People want to make it more than it is, mostly people who want to sell papers."

Patricia turned and could see his mustache and liquescent eyes. She turned and stared across the lake. A loon called out.

"That sound is so lonely."

"Mating call."

"Like I said," she murmured.

Reuger glanced at her.

"Your son doesn't see his father?"

"My ex-husband created a new life that doesn't include Kurt." She shook her head. "We met in law school, and we were going to change the world. He went to work for a corporation, and I defended people I knew were guilty." Patricia glanced at Reuger. "I thought I knew him, but maybe it's hard to really get to know anyone. It wasn't even the affair that destroyed our marriage." She paused. "Kurt's been in some trouble...right before we left, the police had brought him home for shoplifting. I thought if we could get away, it might help."

Reuger rested his hands on his gun belt. He thought of the first moment when he saw the boy in the forest. There was that hurt in those eyes even then. A deer caught in the headlights kind of hurt.

"Your son was driving the boat today?"

She nodded slowly.

"He must have hit a dead head then."

He watched her lean down and put the cup on the dock. A boat crossed the lake and they listened to the whine. She was somewhere else, and he wondered if he had been too personal.

"It just seems like we can't get a break anymore," she murmured.

The silence returned, and Reuger felt hamstrung again. He couldn't think of one commonplace thing to say. Nothing. He was so out of practice. His days consisted of talking to men much like himself, and he realized then how isolated he had been. She was staring moodily out at the lake. He cleared his throat.

"I'd be happy to take your boy fishing—"

She turned quickly and held up her hand.

"No. I'm not looking for a handout. I appreciate everything you've done, but I really can take care of my son."

He nodded and looked at her and saw the stiffness had returned. She had loosened up and now they were back at the car with her groceries.

"I wasn't saying..."

"Thank you, Deputy, all the same," she said crisply.

Reuger watched her for a moment then turned to the lake.

"I'm just offering to take your son fishing."

Patricia turned to him, her eyes snapping.

"Deputy, maybe you should..."

"Reuger...most people call me Reuger."

She turned away and her coffee cup fell into the water. Patricia leaned down and stared at the black water.

"Shit."

"It's gone," he nodded slowly. "Probably take a million years for that mug to decompose and ruin the ecosystem for all time."

Patricia turned slowly, her eyes flashing light.

"You really are—"

"I've been told before," he said, pulling the brim of his hat low. "Just tell your son day after tomorrow to be ready to catch walleye. I still think you can take care of your son."

Patricia stood up and regarded him in the darkness. "I'm sure he'll be thrilled."

"Good."

They stood silently together under the starlight. Patricia looked at him.

"Why do they call you Reuger?"

He gestured to his thigh.

"Type of gun I carry is a Colt .44."

She pursed up her mouth.

"So why don't they call you Colt .44?"

"I used to carry a Reuger that was a replica of the old peacemaker."

Her eyes flicked down to his thigh then back up.

"Do you mind being named after a gun?"

Reuger smiled then laughed.

"Uh oh, the mountain man laughed."

"People are named up here a lot of times for what they do. There's a man named Refrigerator Dave and Barber Lewy and Trapper Bill."

"Did you have a name before?"

"Matthew London."

"I hear a lot about tree huggers up here, Matthew London."

He shrugged.

"Just something the people call those who want to stop the logging."

"They are still logging then?"

Reuger turned to the trees.

"Below the Boundary Waters, but this whole area including the Boundary Waters was logged out in the 1890s." He gestured to the dark forest. "Trees you see are all new growth—mostly jack pine. The old growth, the Norway pine, is mostly gone except for the few trees the environmentalists and loggers fight over. These trees don't hold a candle to what used to be here." He pointed across the lake. "There's a section up in the Boundary Waters called Old Pines. Loggers missed these trees for some reason, and there's acres of three-hundred-year-old pines."

"They would be valuable," she murmured, staring at the shadow of the Northern forest.

"Priceless." He turned and smiled wryly. "But I'm sure you know all about endangered resources."

"I know some people don't want to share the land. Natural resources are for everyone now, not just the people who want to rape the land."

"Spoken like an environmental lawyer."

"Or a tree hugger maybe?"

"Most city people are."

"Are you?"

"I don't take sides," he replied, shaking his head. "My job is to keep the peace."

"But you must have an opinion?"

"Paid not to."

She couldn't see his face under the brim of the hat again.

"You're enigmatic, you know that, don't you?"

He turned to her slowly.

"Think so?"

Patricia turned back to the sky and saw horizon light raying down cold and blue, and then flashing across the universe. Haze increased in volume brightness toward Canada until the light jumped like a cathode ray.

"What is that?"

Reuger took off his hat and stared at the sky.

"Northern lights."

Sheets of cobalt blue refracted and flashed until the pines were backlit. Green, blue, and red energy willowing the sky and winking like some errant child with a switch.

"What makes it do that?"

"Some say its solar winds over the poles." He paused. "The Indians say it's the spirits of those who have passed on and call it the Spirit Dance."

Patricia watched the swimming light.

"I like what the Indians say," she whispered.

He tilted his head back and spoke in a husky tenor.

"God himself seems to be always doing his best here, working like a man in the glow of enthusiasm."

"You're religious?"

"John Muir. Naturalist."

She was silent and slipped her arm through his and they watched the lights like a couple watching a parade.

"A tree hugger," she murmured.

"One of the biggest," he nodded.

17

CARTER PUSHED THE chain saw into the tree, spraying yellow wood dust into the air like wet confetti; a small wiry man of hardened muscle with a bristly black beard and peppered hair combed back with skin browned and rough from Northern cold and sun.

The saw puttered beside his leg while he surveyed the cut and the angle then glanced up to the top of the pine. Carter swung the saw back up and braced himself against the weight. He didn't feel the weight of the saw the way he didn't feel cold or heat or personal discomfort. He pulled the trigger then stopped and took the pack of cigarettes from his top pocket, lighting one in the corner of his mouth.

Carter hoisted the saw again with the stringy wood chattering out a fountain of sawdust and oil smoke. He smoked meditatively. The bank would only wait so long. He had fallen two months behind on his equipment and logging hadn't been good. Prices were down and the quality of the wood kept getting worse. The tree huggers kept him from going after the good stuff. One Norway pine three-feet thick could fetch a hundred times more than a pile of two-foot-thick jack pine.

Carter let up on the saw, resetting himself, then pulling the trigger again with the vibration moving through his hands into his shoulders. Five minutes later, he pulled the saw back and let it putter down to the echo in the trees. He squinted up. Fifty feet, he guessed. He took a deep breath and saw mist in the tree line. He was down in a valley and he couldn't tell whether the mist rose up from the swale or hovered in the far trees. A tree moved. He took the cigarette from his mouth. The man moved again and became part of the pines.

Carter turned back to the tree and revved the saw with the stub back in his mouth, concentrating on the cut with the wood dust flying up around him. Marcus had said he saw a man the other week. So there was a man in the woods. If he wanted to come in, then he would give him a saw or he could run the skidder. God knows when Marcus would get up or whether he would show at all. That was the hell of it when you worked for yourself. More times people didn't show up. It wasn't like the days when men went to work early and left at dusk and you missed a day then you might as well not bother showing up because someone took your place.

Heat warmed Carter's back like sun breaking through trees. He pushed the chain saw deeper into the wood as the chain sparked against the spike then snapped free and slashed his neck open neatly before landing in the fireweed. His jugular vein pumped blood on the pine like red paint on bread. Carter fell to his knees with the smoking saw. The blood on his chest felt like bathwater.

The ground rushed up as the skidder's gas tank exploded into a yellow and orange donut of fire before combusting into thick black smoke. Carter kept his hands to his neck and felt the tips of his boots get hot. His watched his skidder burn. Black roiling smoke billowed from tires with the steel bands glowing red. He looked at the tree line and saw a man raising his arm. He saw the cab where his shotgun lay under the seat and the man in the tree line again. The man raising his arm again, fired.

18

REUGER WAS WALKING toward a tall angular man smoking like a general in the morning sun. Jim Carpenter and Ben Johnson stood off by their trucks. The man was all curves and elbows and jaw with a shiny gun belt and holster. His uniform was green with military starch, and the only things missing were the ribbons and medals he kept in a drawer. He approached Sheriff Riechardt with the last swallow of coffee still in his mouth. The sheriff looked at his watch, then stubbed the cigarette and palmed his mouth full of sunflower seeds.

"Spiked his tree," he muttered, walking toward a blanket draped over work boots.

Reuger stared at the smoldering skidder as Riechardt lifted a green-and-white blanket of bears and wolves to a man with his mouth open and eyes glazed. His beard was dark and feathered in around the gash in his throat. The wound opened over a candy red Adam's apple and pink epiglottis. The blood had coated the bristles on the man's chin then flowed down his shirt and filled his top pocket then hardened into a glaze. His suspenders were shellacked to his shirt.

"Shot in the left side of the head," the sheriff nodded, pointing to the red hole above the ear. *Phsit*! A sunflower seed hit the blanket. "Crime lab will be up here first thing in the morning." *Phsit! Phsit!*

Sawdust peppered the man's black bristly hair, and Reuger fought the urge to brush it out. Carter Grisom was just a little younger than Foster Jones. He was an independent logger with chain saws and a skidder that were at least twenty years old. He had been logging as long as Foster. Reuger saw the knurled hands coated with oil and clutching at the air. Seeds rained behind him. *Phsit! Phsit! Phsit!*

"Skidder burned here probably after he hit that spike," Riechardt said curtly.

Reuger kneeled down and ran his hand over the surrounding fireweed. He looked up at the sheriff.

"This where he was found?"

Riechardt palmed more seeds from his pocket and nodded.

"Jim Carpenter found him here," the sheriff nodded again. "Came back here after some hiker reported seeing smoke." He dropped the blanket and puckered seeds in the high weeds. "So there's a link here between the two loggers now." Riechardt spat another seed. "So much for your suicide."

Reuger studied the flattened weeds pulled toward Carter. He had tried to move after he fell to the ground. The wood was mostly jack pine. It was just like Foster. He was a man just staying ahead of the bank. Reuger lifted the blanket again to the hands reaching as if they still wanted to hold the chain saw.

"Next of kin?"

Phsit...a split seed popped to the left. Riechardt stood behind him with his hands on his belt. He smoothed his thin mustache and shook his head, running a finger along a ruler-straight part.

"Don't think he has anyone in town here, Reuger. You know these old shaders usually die alone and broke."

"I'll run them down," he muttered walking to the tree.

The spike was long and silver. It was a tried-and-true way of stopping logging, a fierce weapon for the radical environmentalist. Reuger leaned closer and saw chattered edges where the chainsaw had lost the quick battle with the harder metal before flying loose. The spike had been driven in from above then gummed closed with bits of bark and tree sap. He saw where Carter Grissom was pushing the saw into the wood when the chain snapped free and slashed his neck. Reuger saw the rush of hot blood filling his throat as his jugular pumped blood on the pine, then the ground rushing up as the skidder gas tank exploded. The doomed man dragged himself along until a shot rang out.

Reuger turned to the blackened skidder throwing up dying tendrils into the cooling air like some old buffalo and smelled the burned wood as a warm breeze crossed the valley. He noticed a fire-blackened lantern hooked on a low branch. Gus walked up with eyes glassy and haunted.

"Pretty tore up," he nodded. "Known Carter as long as Foster there."

"I called an ambulance to meet you on the Fernberg here, Reuger." The sheriff chewed quickly then spat two more seeds. "I wasn't sure if you hadn't gone back to the Boundary Waters on a fishing trip to chase Indians."

Reuger turned around and eyed the man in the pressed uniform. He knew the fact he didn't take a seaplane up to the Boundary Waters racked him off. Everything with Riechardt was procedure and by the book.

"It wasn't a fishing trip, Sheriff."

He palmed more seeds and spat three to the side.

Phsit. "Ya, well, I don't give a fuck what it was. You aren't John Wayne here, so let's quit fucking around and get on these here murders. Obviously have a pattern here, and if you want to go looking for someone then the proper procedure is a seaplane with flare gear, not this Lone Ranger and Tonto shit here."

The sheriff took off his glasses and showed fifty-eight years of craggy lines. Seeds propelled into the dying light like photons.

"I don't pay my deputies here to be up there on camping trips when I need them down here. Now, I want you to talk to Jorde, Reuger." He pointed to the blanket. "This is *his* work here."

Reuger walked the ground, looking at the logs, then walked back to the logging road where Ben Johnson and Jim Carpenter stood with the sky in the east becoming bright. "That how you found him, Jim?"

He cleared his throat with his watch catching on his oversized belt buckle. His eyes were back behind his glasses, but Reuger could see he was unnerved.

"Ya, come out to see if the forest here was on fire after the people in cabin three said they saw smoke. Drove on back here and saw smoke above the trees and when I got back here, saw his skidder burning there."

"Burning or smoking?"

"Ya, maybe it was smoking. Radioed the sheriff here." He licked his lips again. "Got out of the truck and saw Carter lying there dead, all chewed up and such, so I went and got one of Diane's blankets and put it over him."

"That all?"

"Yep."

They turned to the man with the construction boots sticking out of the blanket.

"Those bastards will stop at nothing," Ben Johnson growled with his eyes small under his Stetson. "You know it was that Jorde now. Has his fucking fingerprints all over this one. Clear to me what's going on here," he nodded grimly. "The sonofabitch is killing loggers because he can't buy off any more judges."

The sheriff walked over and spat a seed. His eyes narrowed in.

"Environmental issue here, Reuger. I want you to go hang Jorde upside down there until he confesses to these two crimes or reveals who did it!"

Reuger let the sheriff posture for Ben Johnson, then nodded slowly.

"Let me see what the evidence..."

"Cut the crap, there, Reuger. I've got your evidence."

"Sheriff Riechardt, this is Hector, come in."

He stabled the receiver on his shoulder.

"Go ahead."

"I have that registration number for you... or I have that name... ya, the computer was down and..."

"Give it to me, you fool!"

"Ya, registered to a Tom Jorde, T-o-m J-o-r-d-e...Ya, like I say..."

The sheriff let go of the receiver on his shoulder.

"There you go, Reuger."

Reuger felt the irritation between his eyes and stared at the man spitting sunflower seeds. He wondered when he was going to tell him about the gun. Riechardt was playing his game, sounding him out until he could play his card for Ben Johnson. He knew that, but still it pissed him off.

"Where's the gun?"

A seed hit his shoe. Riechardt turned and gestured to his SUV.

"Sorry. Front seat of my truck there. Found it ten feet from the body." A seed spiraled over his shoulder like a dove. He stepped closer. "You have your fucking evidence, now go hang his ass upside down."

The sheriff turned and walked stiffly toward his jeep with Ben Johnson.

"Bruce won't give me a felony warrant without a witness," Reuger said dully.

Riechardt climbed into his jeep and leaned out the window.

"Then get one!"

The sheriff spun away with Ben Johnson's truck following. Exhaust angulated in the damp air. Reuger watched until the last taillight faded into the trees, then he turned back to the man under the blanket.

"I'll be danged!" Gus shook his head slowly. "Didn't think the sheriff coulda got his nose any further up Johnson Timber's ass, but I guess I was wrong, by God! Maybe he gives him them seeds, Reuger. Never seen a man spit so much shit from his mouth."

Reuger turned from the road then walked over the crackling seeds clinging to fireweed and peppering the blanket like bits of snow. He hunched down and stared at the man under the blanket, then at the spike rutting the tree like a silver dagger. Reuger dropped the blanket and stood.

Jim Carpenter looked at him.

"Do you need a hand?"

"Much obliged," he said. "C'mon Gus, let's get Carter out of here."

19

A COLD MOON hung over Center Island. Reuger sat with his hat low and guided the puttering outboard through the rocks with the Winchester on his lap. He watched the fire belch sparks, dancing on the oily smooth water like flames on syrup. The fire yellowed the clap rock and graywacke and driftwood along the shore. He saw someone next to the fire and handed the Colt to Gus.

"Think that's our man, then?"

"Not taking any chances."

He weaved around the boulders in the shallows, gliding toward the fire laid into a leaning teepee. Flames crackled fast like a tumbler of BBs.

"Keep an eye out, Gus. That boy didn't build that fire."

He nodded, holding up the Colt.

"Don't yer worry."

They cleared the boulders and slid onto the gravel. Reuger saw Patricia Helpner's son Kurt standing with his hands behind his back as Gus swung out and splashed ashore. An hour before she had come up to the lodge and said her son was missing. Now the boy walked toward Gus and waved shyly.

"Hi!"

Gus grabbed him by the shoulder.

"You all right, boy?"

He shrugged. "Yeah... I'm fine."

Reuger swished the shallows past the fire with the rifle. He walked the tree line with his finger in the trigger guard then circled back. Kurt's large brown eyes shone excitedly. Reuger stared at the flames devouring the driftwood like paper. He turned to the boy.

"Who built the fire, Kurt?"

He spread his arms wide.

"A real Indian!"

Reuger pushed his hat off his forehead. "Where'd he go?"

Kurt pointed toward the northern end of the lake.

"He paddled off just like you see in the movies. He was real fast too and had a big knife and a gun and..."

The fire popped and a spark arced into the water and sizzled.

"Maybe we should move off toward the boat here," Gus nodded, glancing toward the trees. "Git out of *arrow* range."

They backed up to the boat nudging the sand from a lapping surf. Reuger turned by the bow with the Winchester in his right hand. The day already seemed a distant memory. They had taken Carter to the morgue then scoured the crime scene then covered the area, asking canoeists and hikers whether they had seen anything unusual. Of course no one saw a thing, and they had ended up at the lodge bar exhausted. That was when Patricia burst in with the kind of fear in her eyes that could only mean a missing child.

"Want to tell me what happened here, Kurt?"

The boy shrugged again. "Me and Tim and that Cliff guy and the girl from the other cabin went looking for this Indian and found him! He was real nice guy even after those jerks left me here."

Reuger rolled his tongue against the inside of his mouth. He looked at the trees again and then at the boy. Tim Carpenter had already confessed to leaving the boy on the island. Apparently they panicked and somehow Kurt became lost and Cliff managed to get them off the island but left Kurt behind.

"How'd he find you?"

Kurt glanced to where the lodge was a small, lit house across the lake. "Those guys had taken off with the canoes, and there he was. He said they had left and he would make a fire for me and stay until someone came looking." Kurt peered up. "I think he hoped it would be you."

"And why's that?"

He squinted, one half of his face in the firelight.

"Because he gave me a message for you."

Gus turned from watching the island and looked at the boy then Reuger.

"If that don't beat all."

"Let me get this right." Kurt rubbed his forehead. "He said to meet him at the south side of Second Sister at three a.m. Oh, yeah, and to come by yourself."

Kurt swung his hands self-consciously.

"Anything else?"

"Nope." He shook his head. "He just talked about how badly the Indians got screwed over and how white people stole all their land and logged it out and didn't pay them anything for it. Hey," he looked up shyly, "did you ever hear of a book called Bury a Heart at the Knee?"

"You mean Bury My Heart At Wounded Knee?"

"Yeah, that's it!' Kurt nodded. "He said I should read that book."

Reuger held his watch to the fire and yawned. The wood had burned down, and the droopy silver trees emerged like ghosts behind a dark stage. He turned to the north end of the lake where the Boundary Waters began.

"I'll drop you and the boy off."

"Ya, now Reuger." Gus spat in the water. "I don't think that's such a hot idea here."

Kurt pointed down the beach and pointed.

"He left a canoe in those bushes. He hid it there after the jerks left me here."

"I'll take that," Reuger nodded. "Won't be as noisy as a boat. Take him back to his mother, Gus," he said, holstering the Colt.

"Now, like I say," Gus began, shaking his head. "I don't think that's such a hot idea after he tried to spear us."

Reuger nodded to the boat.

"You'll be the first person I call if I get in trouble."

"You ain't back by six, and I'm bringing in the Mounties," he muttered climbing into the boat with Kurt and starting the motor.

Kurt hopped in and Reuger pushed the boat into the oily darkness.

"Kurt, you and I are going walleye fishing tomorrow evening."

The boy silhouetted the water.

"I thought we were going in the morning?"

"They'll bite at dusk just the same."

20

THE SECOND SISTER emerged just before two a.m. It was a small island resembling islands in the Pacific where the government blew up atomic bombs and life returned years later, strangely mutated. He had been paddling steady for three hours and was tired. He dipped the paddle again, leaving a foamy tail behind like an afterthought.

Reuger glided into tree shadow with rocks scarring the bottom and pulled the canoe further up on the rocky beach. He picked up the Winchester and began walking the tree line. A chorus of night birds and crickets breathed low. He smelled the sour scent of a dead fish and rounded the island to moonlight calcimined on the bottom of a canoe.

"Ya. Over here."

The voice in the trees was heavy and dark. Reuger kept his finger on the trigger of the Winchester and felt the vibration of the trees, the lake, and the earth. A figure stretched from the pines with hair braced to shoulders from a camouflaged cap. Reuger kept the rifle waist level and walked slowly toward the large man staring out at the silver lake. Tommy Tobin brought his hand across the land with the impassive face of a Buddha.

"You know, the Ojibwa once had all of this, but we lost it all when they come up with their barges and took the trees and stripped the land. My ancestors couldn't understand these people who destroy everything around them like fucking locusts." His eyes flickered under the brim of his hat. "They couldn't figure out why people want to take all the trees and leave the land to burn under the sun and starve the animals and leave the old men and women crying because they couldn't fucking leave." He shook his head. "But the Indians they trusted them a lot of times when they shouldn't have, you know. They give them a blanket or a horse or a gun for millions of acres, and the Indians give it to them. They give them these worthless treaties, and you might as well go make a treaty with the wolf because he'll at least look in your eyes before he tears your throat out." He turned. "You ever read Bury My Heart At Wounded Knee?"

Reuger nodded slowly. "A long time ago."

"Ya," he said, tilting his head. "You should read it again, you know. That book tells it like it was. Worst thing was the way the Indians turned on each other, you know." He shook his head. "Did it all the time you know, the Pawnees would attack the Arapahos and the Cheyenne and for what? Some guns or whiskey. You know, if the Indians could just quit selling each other out then they could fucking do something." He glanced over, his eyes glimmering chips of polished coal. "That's what my grandfather always said, anyway."

Reuger gestured to the north.

"You ought to work on your aim with a bow and arrow."

Tommy turned, his hooked nose more pronounced in the ash light.

"Don't use one." He raised his rifle. "Why would I bother with that when I can shoot twice the number of deer with a rifle?"

Reuger kept his eyes steady.

"I saw some arrows coming my way at your cabin."

"Nope." He frowned. "That's my sister. She lives there now, you know. I was up there checking traps, and that old cabin is a fucking wreck. She uses a bow and arrow and chases off people from the cabin." His eyes slipped the corners like dark moons. "She all painted up?"

"Yep. Black face."

"Ya, that's her," Tommy nodded. He breathed heavily. "She's watched too many old movies and thinks she's a Comanche or something."

Reuger turned to the flat lake pooling under the moon.

"It's a good way for her to get killed."

Tommy's mouth flattened, spinning a finger by his temples.

"I've got problems all right, but she's *real* hard-headed, that one. You can't tell her anything. She thinks she's Joan of Arc of the Indians and is always getting ready for her last stand. I told her nobody gives a fuck that she's up there, and if she wants to play Fort Apache then no one is going to try and take it from her, you know."

Reuger turned and sat down on the overturned canoe with the Winchester on his lap. Tommy Tobin was a big man, at least six-five, and he didn't like looking up at him. It was better to talk to a man on the same level.

"So what's been going on out here, Tommy?"

He turned slightly. "What so?"

"You know what I mean here."

"Ya," he shrugged. "That's why I told the boy to give you the message. Figured you wanted to ask me some questions about Foster and all that shit, you know."

Reuger nodded, his brim low and saw the girl again in Pine Lodge. Her description of the man with the lantern in the shed fit Tommy.

"You been in any woodsheds lately?"

He turned all the way around with his mouth open. Reuger couldn't see his face under the camouflaged cap.

"You'll go back this time, Tommy."

"Ya?" He shrugged, rolling the green army coat. "So I'm on parole, big fucking deal. Am I taking too many fish from the lakes or something?"

Reuger tapped the canoe.

"Have a seat here."

He sat on the canoe with his knees like end tables. The bow sank slowly into the sand, and they had to lean toward the stern. They watched a bird glide across the glassy lake.

"So then…what about Foster, Tommy?"

He raised his arms slightly and frowned.

"Ya, heard he was dead, and his slasher burned there."

Reuger leaned forward, seeing the scarred lines on his cheek.

"You didn't do it?"

"Nope."

"Do you know anything about it?"

"Nope."

His lower lip curled out, and he turned.

"I didn't work with him that day. He was an asshole, you know, about me being late and said if I was late then not to bother coming." Tommy rolled his shoulders again. "So that day I was sleeping it off and figured I'd go anyway because when he calmed down he needed help to run the slasher or the cherry picker, and he was getting pretty old there. But when I come down the road there I could smell it, you know." He touched his nose. "His truck was burning, and I left straightaway."

"What time?"

"I don't wear a watch."

"Where'd you go then after you saw the slasher?"

Tommy nodded toward Canada.

"You know, up the Boundary Waters. Figured, you know, it was better to stay away for a while."

Reuger pushed his hat up and wiped his forehead dry.

"Why for?"

He cradled his hands to the sky.

"All the shit that's been going on lately. Tree huggers getting worse, and Ben Johnson taking more trees than ever, and I just figured they need somebody to blame it on, and I couldn't think of anybody better than a Indian with a record, you know."

Reuger leaned back and regarded the man hunched forward. He could have been fishing or playing checkers. He could see no evasiveness in his posture or his eyes.

"Have you been talking to them?"

He turned but didn't look at Reuger.

"Who?"

"Tom Jorde."

Tommy reached down to the sand and picked up a rock.

"No. That asshole, he come out to the reservation a bunch of times looking for anybody to talk to, and so I talked to him a couple of times, and he talks the shit about wanting to help us get back our lands and reparations and all, but I know it's a bunch of shit."

The stone splashed white far out on the lake.

"Good throw."

"Ya, thanks." His mouth clamped together and he blew air out of his mouth like steam. "Ah, they're just like the loggers you know. They want to bring up more of their kind so they can eat their granola and wear their sandals and tell everybody else to get off the lakes and shit. I'd rather have the loggers."

Reuger leaned forward again with his hands on the Winchester.

"What'd he ask you?"

Tommy tilted his head and frowned.

"You know, he knew I was working with Foster, so he wanted to know where he's been logging. Wants me to say he's been logging in the Boundary Waters, but I know that's what he wants, and so I just say Foster he just takes scrub trees down below the line, but I don't think he believed me." He turned and grinned yellow teeth. "He's a real obnoxious motherfucker." His eyes surfaced from the dark. "More than most white people, you know."

Reuger sat back and squeezed his hat brim.

"Ya, you look pretty tired there."

"Long day." Reuger yawned. "So why'd you run?"

"I told you," he shrugged. "I saw the slasher burning and figured they try and blame it on me. That Jorde, he'd do anything to stop the logging, I figure, and I didn't want to be around when they say who burned Foster out." His eyes flickered. "But I didn't know he was shot then."

Reuger rolled his tongue against his teeth.

"How'd you find out?"

Tommy grunted.

"You know you can't keep a secret in the Boundary Waters. I have friends, you know. Besides, that radioman John Mcfee make sure everybody knows."

Another loon splashed down. A lilting call rising to an echoing crescendo. Tommy clasped his hands together like knotted bones.

"Know anything about Carter Grissom then?"

His cap moved. "Nope."

Reuger paused and watched him closely. "Someone spiked his tree and shot him, then burned his skidder. Same as Foster."

Tommy's cap moved again and he scratched the hair up on his forehead.

"Man, that's fucked up. Them tree huggers are really going crazy."

"What makes you say that?"

He pursed his lips and looked to the sky.

"That Jorde, he asked me about Carter too and says he thinks he's been going over the line after the big trees too. He says he has proof and all this shit and that he just needs somebody to be a witness, you know." Tommy shook his head slowly. "But I tell him I don't know anything about it you know, because you get involved with those people and you never log again."

Wind skitched the lake and lapped their boots. Reuger didn't move or speak. A man who lied was uneasy in silence a lot of times. He found people really did want to tell the truth if given a chance. Lying wasn't natural and sat with someone like bad food.

"I knew it would happen sooner or later with the trees running out and all." Tommy stared at the dark eyes under the hat. "People are going crazy now."

Reuger watched him for a long moment.

"Jorde say anything else to you?"

"No." He shook his head. "He just asked if I wanted to make some money."

"Say what you'd have to do?"

Tommy rolled his neck.

"No...but I knew what he was saying, you don't have to say something like that."

"Spiking the tree, you mean?"

"Oh, ya. "

The loon yodel echoed across the lake again. Tommy squinted and shook his head.

"They always do that right when I'm going to sleep you know."

Reuger yawned again and turned toward where he left his canoe. He thought about paddling back and thought he might get back before dawn. He stood up.

"I need you to make a statement, Tommy. What Jorde said to you and where you were the night before and that morning."

Sure," he nodded. "I'll come to the lodge tomorrow afternoon. I want to get some reading in tonight, you know."

Reuger lifted the Winchester to the sky.

"Don't make me come looking for you again here, Tommy."

"Ya." He waved his hand. "I'll be there."

21

THE OLD GROCERY store was planted on the far side of town away from the tourist streams looking for a coffee mug or a buckskin coat. It shut down for lack of business, and now it was a rag-tag headquarters for environmentalists. Printed letters were taped to the window: E-A-R-T-H F-I-R-S-T. A faded green sticker was low in the corner: *We Take Food Stamps.*

Reuger drained his mug before pulling the door to a faint scent of paper bags. He walked to a college girl with hair reaching to a gunmetal desk. The old plank floor groaned loudly.

"Here to volunteer?"

Reuger squinted at her book.

"Silent Spring. Any good?"

She flipped the tree-covered book around. Rings on her lower lip creased her expression like dashes in a sentence and Reuger guessed her hair somewhere between vermilion and green. He could see where the dye stained her scalp. "It really started the whole movement," she declared, then she farted. Her face darkened. "Eating too many beans, I guess," she said under her breath.

"I didn't know that," he said glancing at the other desks with pamphlets and fliers and phone cords snaking into a tangled mess. Most of the desks were empty save for a man eating a doughnut.

"Tom Jorde around?"

"He's back there." She turned around then smiled up. "The center door."

"Mind if I leave this here?"

"Ya, sure, no problem," she said turning back to her book.

He set his mug down and saw a man walking toward him in a Calvary hat with crossed swords. Reuger hooked his arm like a dancer as John Mcfee squeezed his right eye shut, puffing his small mustache.

"Police are now manhandling the press, I see!"

Reuger kept his hand locked on his arm.

"What are you doing here, John?"

He arced the space with his finger.

"That's between the press and their client!"

Reuger stared toward the back of the store and nodded.

"What did you tell him, John?"

He pursed his lips, squinting like a man taking aim.

"The *End of the Road* program has many guest appearances and since this is not part of the ongoing investigation launched by the *Ely Standard* into the murderous rampage of loggers, then I don't mind telling you I was firming up his interview for my show."

Reuger tapped his gun belt, pulling him closer, speaking to him directly.

"Listen to me John, go find some old fisherman and tell all your listeners about the best walleye holes, but you screw this investigation up with Mcfee shenanigans and I'll put you in jail."

His eyes closed to half slits.

"So then, yer threatening the press again, are yer?"

Mcfee reached for his pocket.

"Touch that pad, and I'll break your fingers."

He paused then nodded slowly.

"Don't matter. When you're talking to me you're talking to a tape recorder." He tapped his forehead. "Yer talkin' to the *world* here." He tipped his Cavalry hat forward. "I bid yer a hearty farewell, sir!"

Reuger let him go and watched him tip his hat to the girl then disappear into sunlight. He turned and walked the old planks to a door of faded letters.

"Yeah, it's open, Reuger!"

He pushed the door and inhaled a scent of fried food. Tom Jorde stabbed a computer resembling a large egg in a green T-shirt of white lettering—SAVE THE SPOTTED OWL FROM EXTINCTION. Empty coffee cups and potato chip bags and paper littered the desk and overflowed a trashcan. The room smelled of coffee, paper, and smoke.

"Have a seat. Almost finished," he muttered.

Reuger sat in a chair with one arm missing and looked at a calendar with three gray wolves in snow next to a sign: NO ONE IS TO USE THE COMPUTER WITHOUT PERMISSION. A framed yellow map of the Superior National Forest was behind the desk. The printer hummed, and Jorde leaned back and squeezed his eyes shut. Reuger crossed his boot over his knee and moved the Colt out.

"Long night, Tom?"

"Have to get a petition off this morning." He opened his eyes. "Let's see, you're here to accuse me of killing loggers, right?"

Reuger pursed his lips and moved his shoulders.

"Mcfee would be better off sticking to the fishing reports."

"I would think he must be a damn fine journalist for Charles Kroning to leave him a radio station and a newspaper. I'm going over there this afternoon to tape a show with him and give him the real story about what's been going on around here!"

Reuger leaned back in the chair. "Be careful there, Tom. Mcfee plays both sides against the middle, and then he plays the middle."

"He's not accusing me of murdering loggers," Jorde scoffed. "He's not sticking a gun against my head like the Hitler youth you have running around out there."

Reuger lifted the clear plastic bag he had been holding in his left hand. It dropped on the metal desk with a loud thunk.

"I have another dead logger on my hands. Carter Grisom was cutting a sixty-foot white pine when he sawed into that steel. Then someone shot him next to his burning skidder."

Jorde stared at the chafing marks glinting through the plastic wrap. His red-rimmed eyes drifted up.

"So...what's that got to do with me?"

"Environmental sabotage, don't you think?"

Tom backed up in his rollaway chair and smiled slowly.

"Okay...so you think I'm jamming spikes in trees and then shooting loggers?"

Reuger slapped another baggy on the desk.

"I found that next to Foster Jones's slasher."

Tom picked up the baggy."I haven't had this button for years!"

Reuger rubbed his chin and stared into the washed-out eyes. "Anything you want to tell me here, Tom?"

"I've got nothing to do with these dead loggers," he muttered, throwing the button down. "Why don't you go ask Ben Johnson or his fascist son what he fucking knows? It's more their style than mine."

"Have you been protesting up around there?"

"No!" Jorde jumped out of his chair and stared at the yellow map of the Boundary Waters Canoe Area. "But I probably should be with the shit that's been going on up here while you've been looking the other way." Jorde turned. "But you're a logger and don't give a shit, do you?"

Reuger bit his lip.

"Wouldn't say that."

Jorde leaned close to the desk.

"This land was raped once before at the turn of the century when they came up with steam barges and stripped the trees. The same way they destroyed the Ohio River Valley, the same way they tried to destroy the trees in Washington State Park." His eyes burned with a feverish glow. "When I was up there I realized something. I had been tracking the owls and we had to stay in that forest all night. I woke early one morning and saw those old trees wet with dew, and I knew then they were the last ones and that if someone didn't do something, they would all be gone from the planet, and my children would never see real forests."

Tom Jorde's eyes burned even brighter. Reuger could see a fine sheen of perspiration on his brow. "That's when I decided to speak for the trees, and I joined Earth First. So when I got up here and saw what had been done to this land, I vowed to never let it happen again. I know what Ben Johnson is after..." Jorde nodded slowly. "He wants the Old Pines in the Boundary Waters."

Reuger crossed his boot over his knee.

"What makes you say that?"

Jorde sat down in his chair.

"What's it matter to you?" A slim smile crossed his lips. "I haven't been murdering loggers, but if some poachers got what they finally deserved, then I'm not going to cry any tears for them. They knew what they were doing, and they knew the risk. They're killing the trees, so maybe the trees are getting back at them finally. Ever think of that?"

Reuger stared back at the excited man. He found zealots as bad as the people they fought against. For the first time, Reuger considered Tom Jorde might have killed Foster Jones.

"You ever talk with Tommy Tobin?"

Jorde leaned back.

"I've spoken with Tommy before."

"What for?"

"That's my business," he answered coolly.

"You still carry your pistol, Tom?"

His faced flushed suddenly.

"It was stolen out of my truck right after I saw you."

Reuger scratched his jaw, thumbing his hat farther up.

"You really think so?"

Jorde's faced reddened. "You think my *gun* was used. This is just a fucking setup..."

The door opened at his back, and Jorde glanced up.

"What!"

Reuger didn't turn around.

"I'm sorry...I'm looking for a Tom Jorde."

"You found him," he said slapping the desk.

Reuger stared straight ahead and felt muscles knotting along his upper back with the voice continuing like the haunt of a drowning woman. If he had been standing, he might have stepped back.

"I'm your lawyer. They called and said you might need..."

"Perfect timing!" Tom Jorde shouted, jumping up around the desk. "I was just telling the deputy sheriff here I'm not murdering loggers, but now *you* can deal with what passes for the law in this town."

Reuger stood and turned like a soldier to Patricia in a dark pants suit and clutching a burgundy briefcase. Two diamond studs were in her ears, and all traces of the single mother with a son were gone. She extended her hand and met his eye firmly.

"Patricia Helpner."

22

The creaking stairs smelled of cigars, wood, and the slight old scent of papers and erasers. Reuger strode past the fuzzed glass doors of offices, remembering the light in Jorde's office as he faced Patricia. They had stood under the glare of the neon lights, and then the veil came down.

"Do you have a warrant, Sheriff?"

He shook his head slowly.

"Nope. I don't," he said meeting her eyes.

"Then you had better leave and please don't question my client again without me or some other representation present."

He nodded and stood up.

"All right, Patricia, if that's what you want."

Jorde's mouth dropped, and he looked from Reuger to the woman who just walked in his office.

"What the fuck…you two *know* each other?"

"Sure, we know each other," he said easily. "Tell your son we're going fishing this afternoon."

"We know each other professionally," she nodded coolly.

"That's right," he continued, walking to the door. "I showed her the stars, and we saw the northern lights, professionally of course, then I helped her with her groceries. All very professionally."

Her eyes snapped like a light winking out.

"I think you have made your point, Deputy."

He nodded to the cell phone on her belt.

"Don't know if you can pick up much there with that phone."

"Let me worry about that."

"Just trying to help," he said touching the brim of his hat.

"Oh great! Just fucking great," he heard behind him. "They send me a lawyer *dating* the deputy sheriff!"

* * * *

Reuger came to a door with black-stenciled oversized letters: COUNTY ATTORNEY. A blob moved behind the opaque glass. He opened the door to a small office consisting of a desk and a coat rack in one corner supporting a charcoal fedora. A man studied a plate of eggs crisscrossed with ketchup over a newspaper. His long mustache and slow blinking eyes gave him the air of a walrus. The air smelled of eggs, ketchup, and coffee.

"How she go there, Bruce?"

"Just a minute," he muttered. "Let me finish this article here."

Reuger settled into a chair missing an arm and watched the man mouthing words. Bruce Anderson's shaggy peppered hair and droopy mustache hadn't changed for decades. When he first became the county attorney he only wore three-piece suits. He had been a corporate lawyer down in Minneapolis until he got on the wrong side of a federal judge and was held in contempt. He quit the firm and drove until he found a place where he could hole up and write the great American novel.

After a year of doing nothing more than producing prose he could barely read without flinching, he drifted back into the law. Bruce married a local girl, had children, and roared up to three hundred pounds. Reuger never saw the suit after that, and Bruce's uniform became a pullover sweater and khaki pants.

Reuger glanced at a calendar hanging crookedly behind the desk advertising Durning Hardware, then watched Bruce devour the rest of his eggs.

"Lot of fat in that food, Bruce."

His eyes rolled up gray and almost colorless.

"Since when did you come here to comment on my eating habits?"

Reuger tossed his hat on the oak desk that creaked as Bruce shifted his weight.

"Came to talk to you about some dead loggers."

Bruce flicked the paper with his forefinger.

"Ya, and so I heard."

Reuger leaned over.

SECOND LOGGER FOUND MURDERED IN BOUNDARY WATERS.

"John Mcfee's handiwork there, I'd say."

Bruce looked down and shook his head doubtfully.

"Going to have an environmental war soon here, Reuger."

"Maybe."

"For sure," he nodded, closing the paper.

"Think so?"

"Guaranteed."

Reuger kicked back in the chair as Bruce sugared his coffee. Nothing was on the walls, save the calendar and paint from a tired 1930s era of pale green. A steam radiator hugged one wall and gas outlets poked plaster. Sun blared an open window behind. The only thing missing was a fan rotating slowly overhead. Bruce raised his eyebrows as he swiped sugar from his desk.

"I assumed you would be getting around to solving these two murders some day."

Reuger rubbed mud off his boot.

"Thought the first one was a suicide." He dropped his boot to the floor. "Foster caught his slasher and finished the job with his .45."

Bruce sat back like a pregnant woman and stared at him blankly.

"So what made you change your mind?"

Reuger paused.

"Second murder…physical evidence."

Bruce reached inside his sweater.

"You're thinking they're related?"

"Don't you?"

"Asking you here."

"Maybe."

"Uh huh," he nodded, drawing out a cigarette.

"I'm going to try to make a case here, Bruce."

"Oh ya?" He wiped his chin and leaned back with the cigarette dangling. "What do you have?"

"A gun that probably belongs to Tom Jorde."

"Probably?"

"It's his gun," Reuger nodded, clasping his hands.

"Okay."

"Probably matches the bullet in Carter's head."

"Whose head?"

"Second logger with the spike."

"Oh, ya, sure, OK then." Bruce reached forward and flared the cigarette, then lifted a foil-covered plate. "Smoked salmon?"

Reuger leaned over the desk. The fish was smoked brown and piled around a sauce dish.

"Smoked it last night. Try the sauce there. I made that too."

"Didn't know you smoked your own fish, Bruce."

He nodded sucking on the cigarette.

"Bought it on that Ronco show. Works pretty good here. Bought the rotisserie there, too, for turkeys. You can smoke just about anything."

"Didn't know that," he murmured, taking a piece and dipping it in the sauce. "So...I found an Earth First button next to Foster's slasher."

"Convenient." Bruce popped the cigarette from his mouth. "Think it's a plant?"

"Maybe," he nodded, reaching for a napkin.

Bruce sat back with the piled gray fish and the bottle of tartar sauce and the ketchup eggs and coffee. And the cigarettes. Ashtray.

"What else then?"

"Spike driven into the center of Carter's white pine."

Bruce drilled his ear with his finger.

"Any prints on the spike?"

"Nothing yet." Reuger shook his head. "Have the crime lab going up there this afternoon."

Bruce rolled back on his weight and his neck jowled his sweater. He sucked the cigarette dry and stabbed it in the sand ashtray.

"Need a witness here, Reuger."

"Might have one."

"So then it's getting better. Who?"

"Big Indian who worked with Foster out there just before he was murdered, Tommy Tobin."

Bruce whistled out a blue stream.

"You're going to need more credibility than that there, I'm afraid. We get in court with Tobin and any lawyer will shake him upside down, and we won't like what falls out, I can guarantee you that."

"He says Jorde asked him to burn out Foster and put the spike in the tree."

Bruce came down like an avalanche.

"Ya? Did he really say that?"

"So many words."

"How many?"

"Maybe twenty." Reuger shrugged. "Maybe more."

"Ya."

The two men stared at each other, then Bruce shook his head.

"So there Reuger, you want me to believe now that Tom Jorde's latest tactic here is murdering loggers to stop the logging going on here in the Superior National Forest and Boundary Waters?"

"Short of it."

Bruce reached forward with the cigarettes small in his hand.

"You want me to believe he's going back there and *shooting* these loggers thinkin' he's going to get away with it and using his own gun and leaving his buttons scattered around?"

"Yep."

Bruce put the aluminum foil back on the fish and clasped his hands like a priest.

"Okay then, convince me here."

"I think things may have gotten out of hand. Tom Jorde has driven more than a few trucks into the lake, Bruce. I think he went out there to burn that slasher and Foster come on him and pulled down with his .45, and they struggled then *boom*."

Bruce stared at him.

"Boom?"

"Boom," he nodded.

Bruce swiped his hand across the desk with a stickpin in a red tomato.

"Mary off today?"

"Ya, her mother's sick again." He put the cigarettes down, his eyes flat like two pennies. "Look here Reuger, this is very treacherous water with these environmentalists. They use big time New York lawyers and don't worry about the fees. We could get blown out of the water."

"Using a Chicago lawyer this time."

"Ya, well, whatever." Bruce raked a donut from a wax-coated bag and sprinkled the desk with snow. "I'd like to help you here. I really would because I don't need this kind of shit up here, but you need a witness." A cloud of powdered sugar escaped his mouth. "A credible witness who I can put against these environmentalists." He shook his head. "I have to say I don't hear a case yet."

Reuger nodded slowly. They did this little dance every time. Bruce played the skeptic while he was the salesman. He wasn't sure himself what he was going to say when he walked in the door, and Bruce saw this. They nudged each other into new areas. Bruce had his own ideas about the murders, but he wanted to know what he had to say first. Bruce was waiting for his trump card.

"Tommy saw more than he let on."

He nodded slowly. "What do you think?"

"I think he knows who shot Foster. I think he's scared to say anything."

Bruce leaned forward and stared at the box of donuts. His eyes drifted up.

"Then find out what the Indian knows there." He pursed his lips and breathed tiredly. "Get him to write out a statement, and we'll see if we can sew something together here before Mcfee has us burning the forest down."

Reuger grabbed his hat and stood. Bruce leveled his finger like a gun.

"But I can't go up against environmental lawyers with circumstantial evidence, Reuger. That Jorde will say his gun was stolen, and that will be that then." He held up another powdered donut. "Get Tobin to give you more here, like saying he actually saw the crime committed by Jorde."

Bruce inhaled another donut and Reuger opened the door.

"Maybe the crime lab will find something."

"Ya, let me know here..." He tilted his head up. "Heard you had some trouble the other night at the lodge?"

Reuger fingered the brim of his hat.

"Girl said she was attacked in the shed then recanted her story."

Bruce leaned back.

"Say who did it?"

"Said it was a big Indian."

"Jesus, Reuger."

23

THREE SQUADS WITH peace signs fingered on the hood dust were parked in the weeds. Bright yellow and black police tape wrapped the trees and ringed in the cars. Reuger ducked under the tape and saw Jerry Abrams striding out of the swale. He breathed heavy through his nose and wiped sweat from his brow.

"How she go, Jerry?"

"Ya, not too bad. *Hot*."

Reuger reached him inside the tape. Jerry's owl glasses were dusted and his tie was loosened to his chest. He smoothed a wisp of hair starting behind his ears like a bonnet. In the harsh sunlight he was bald. Reuger grinned at the man with the fussy air of a professor.

"So then, find anything here?"

Jerry squinted into the midday sun.

"Boy, it gets hot up here."

"We have our days," Reuger nodded, breathing the dry scent of pinesap.

"Thought the Twin Cities be hotter you know."

"Have air-conditioning down there."

"Ya, you bet."

Jerry put back on his glasses and stuffed the handkerchief in his pocket.

"Well, she's pretty dry up here, so we took some soil samples and dusted the trees and dug up the dirt here." He turned and hair loped out like a string hanging down his neck. "But I don't think she gave us much, you know." He tucked the hair firmly behind his ear again. "We did find another bullet in the tree with the spike there and a shell."

Jerry walked to the splintered tree.

"And from the looks of her, she matches the caliber of the handgun you found at the scene," he murmured, bending over to the bark. "See here is where we found the bullet." He leaned closer, pushing up his glasses. "And from the penetration, I'd say the shooter was close here."

Reuger hunched down and put his finger on the hole.

"Man, it's hot! Windy, too." Jerry wiped his forehead then bent over with his hands on his knees. "Small-caliber round, so the penetration was minimal." He stabbed his glasses back again. ".22. So the shooter missed here with his first shot and then fired again and hit the victim here." He stood and pushed his hair back in place. "It wasn't point-blank, you know, but darn close."

Reuger stood and squinted at the sun-field of broken stumps littered with sawdust and limbs. Wind volleyed across the field and moved the trees like a distant ocean. Jerry grabbed his hair like a man holding onto his hat.

"Have that cartridge, Jerry?"

He reached into his pocket.

"Here she is."

Reuger held the baggy up.

".22 with a silver percussion cap," he murmured.

Jerry took off his glasses.

"Well, she sure is. Must be a reload then."

Reuger handed him back the baggy.

"Appreciate your time here, Jerry."

"Ya, well." He shook his head. "We went by the other site, but you have too many rains up here to get much, and the sun cooks it all away then."

Jerry stared at the pine with the stain slopping the trunk. A gust blew his hair back and he was bald again. He sighed and shook his head.

"You have someone doing some nasty business, for sure."

24

RATCHETING LIKE A boy pedaling backwards, the line arced out then gulped below. Reuger waited until the bait popped the bottom then hooked a boot over the gunnels. He dropped his hat next to a thermos of leeches and looked at the boy staring at the evening colored lake.

"Beautiful evening,"

"Sure is," Kurt nodded, scratching a mosquito bite on his leg. "I'll bet you fish all the time."

"First time this year."

They held rods off both sides back to back.

"Jerky?"

"Um..." he said, studying the petrified meat. "No thanks."

Reuger split the package and bobbed his line again, and then again. A dog barked somewhere. He looked up and saw smoke hazing the trees.

"Sounds like a terrier there."

Kurt looked up.

"Where is he?"

"Sound travels a long way over the open water." Reuger pointed to the trees hanging smoke. "Probably that campsite over there."

Kurt nodded then reeled his line.

"So there, having a good time on your vacation?"

"Yeah."

Reuger turned and opened a red cooler.

"What'll be? Root beer, orange cream or 7-Up?"

Kurt examined the contents of the cooler.

"Orange cream," he nodded.

"One orange cream coming up," Reuger murmured, cracking open the plastic bottle and handing it to Kurt.

"Hey..." He held the bottle high. "These are pretty cool."

"No cans in the Boundary Waters," Reuger nodded, taking a root beer. "All right, we have Oreos or one of Diane's caramel rolls or some peanut butter cookies."

Kurt shut one eye. "How about an Oreo?"

He handed him the cookies and they ate in silence. They drifted closer to land and Reuger smelled swamp. Birds shot the horizon as early night hovered the water like cold breath. He gestured to a far tree spidering the dusk.

"Eagle over there."

Kurt jerked around.

"Where?"

He jumped the other way and the boat rolled. Reuger saw his rod seesaw over the edge and hooked the reel with his tip.

"There you go," he said handing him the dripping rod. "Your first fish there, and she's a keeper."

"Sorry about that," Kurt muttered, his face crimson.

"Seeing your first eagle is worth a rod overboard," Reuger pointed behind him. "You see him there, right at the top of that tree."

Kurt squinted at the old pine against the sky.

"That's really an eagle? A bald eagle?"

"Right there on the third sister island" Reuger nodded. "You can see the white on his head." He handed Kurt a pair of binoculars. "Take a look with these. Should be able to get a pretty good look."

Kurt held the binoculars to his eyes.

"I don't see anything."

Reuger sited the bird then handed the binoculars back.

"There, go up the tree to the very top there. See him, he's that dark blob."

"I see him!"

His mouth opened slowly and Reuger saw the bandage on his elbow and scrapes and mosquito bites. It was the tattoos of being a boy he remembered from long ago when he was a different man in a different life. They were little soldiers, these boys, he thought, and they went unthinkingly along.

"Man, is he *big*, Reuger!" He held the binoculars down. "You think he sees us?"

"He's watching us," Reuger nodded. "They always go to the highest tree and usually it's one without any branches so they can see for miles."

Kurt lifted the binoculars again.

"*Wow!* He's huge!"

Reuger checked their lines and watched the portable depth finder. They were shallowing for walleye and he thought Kurt might like the play of some rock bass closer to the island. He felt the old role descend on him. He was thinking in a way he hadn't pulled out for fifteen years.

"There he goes, Reuger!"

He turned and saw the eagle plunge down flapping wing bellows then ride the current and arc toward Canada. The eagle flapped twice and glided into darkness. Kurt held the binoculars down and shook his head, his eyes shining.

"That was really cool! I didn't know there were still eagles around."

"Oh, ya," Reuger murmured, checking his line. "They were endangered for a while but they've come back."

Kurt looked down.

"Sorry about dropping the fishing rod."

"Not a problem."

Reuger saw a fire gleaming the tree line. He leaned over to the boy.

"See those campers, Kurt?"

"Yeah."

"They're canoeist headed up into the Boundary Waters there," Reuger gestured across the northern forest. "They'll follow the same portage trails Indians have used for thousands of years."

Kurt frowned, squinting at the man in the big green hat. "What's a portage trail?"

"Paths running between the lakes no wider than a man." Reuger pointed north. "You can go all the way up to Canada by connecting lakes."

"Think we can do that sometime?"

Reuger glanced at him then down at his line.

"I'm sure we can sometime.... Why don't you pull in your line there, Kurt, and we'll motor back to the reef."

He started the motor and turned them into the wind blowing from the island. Reuger saw fishermen in the distance likes monks bent over a poetic pursuit. He cut the motor where water slapped underwater boulders and sprayed the boat. Gulls preened oily feathers on boulders in the lantern light of dusk.

"Throw your line in toward the island, Kurt. You still have a leech?"

"Yeah."

"Now, I'll bet there's a ten-pound walleye in there."

Their lines dolloped the water, then they rolled in the gentle swing of current. Water drained from the outboard like a leaking gutter. Kurt looked at the man with one boot on the edge of the boat.

"Can I ask you a question?"

"Shoot."

"You think I could hold your gun?"

Reuger turned to the boy with big brown eyes.

"I don't know about that."

"I mean I wouldn't fire it or anything." He gestured to the Colt. "I've just never touched a gun before, a *real one,* I mean."

"Just felt a bite there."

Kurt turned back around and jerked on his line.

"I'm ready!"

Reuger let his line back down to the bottom. "What would your mother say?"

"She wouldn't care! I mean we wouldn't have to say anything to her about it."

He felt the Colt against his thigh and the old emotions. He had compartmentalized his thinking long ago and there were areas he did not venture into. His old life did not exist, but it bothered him now to have these errant emotions creeping around like water leaking into a ship.

"All right." He reeled his line. "Set down your rod."

Kurt put the fishing pole down with both hands flat on the bench. Reuger stowed his rod in the front of the boat and turned.

"Now, this will be our secret here...you ever handled a firearm before? All right, then."

Reuger drew the weapon and pulled open the cylinder wheel and ejected six brass shells into his palm. He pulled back the hammer and glanced into the barrel then clicked the cylinder wheel closed.

"These are the bullets," he said lining the brass cartridges on the weathered bench. "Do not touch these."

"I won't." Kurt crossed his chest solemnly. *"I swear."*

Reuger held the lead-colored pistol in his hand.

"This is a Colt .44 caliber pistol, a six shooter. You ever see any Westerns, Kurt?"

"Yeah."

"Well this is the gun that won the West. All right," he hefted the gun into his other hand. "You always keep the firearm facing out of the boat."

"All right."

Reuger opened his small hands then the laid the pistol in.

"It's heavy now, so you better use two hands."

Kurt cradled the pistol like a baby.

"Wow! A gun," he whispered.

Kurt stared down at the piece of metal gleaming slightly from oil on the barrel. The cold metal was rougher in his white hands.

"It's not at all like you think."

"What'd you think?"

"I don't know." He shook his head. "In movies and television it's different. But this is like a machine or something."

Reuger watched the boy and felt strangely old. He put Kurt's hand on the stock and clasped the other around it.

"Curl your finger into the trigger guard there," he said. "There."

Kurt had both hands on the gun, holding it out like a statue.

"Whoa!" He grinned pointing toward the shore, his brow descending. *"Hasta la vista, baby!"*

"All right." Reuger took the gun and cracked the cylinder open. "Gun lesson over."

"Hey, can I put a bullet in?"

Reuger handed a shell to Kurt and held the gun.

"Line it up and push it all the way until it seats."

Kurt pushed the brass round into the cylinder jacket.

"Wow, I loaded a gun!"

Reuger finished putting the bullets in and clicked the cylinder wheel closed.

"Can I put it in your holster?"

"Better let me do that, partner."

"Man, that was *cool!* Wait until I tell the guys..."

"Our secret. Remember?"

"Oh yeah, I forgot," he nodded. "I mean I won't tell them for a couple years."

Reuger handed him his rod and picked up his own.

"Can I ask you something?"

"Sure."

You ever find any dead guys or anything really weird?"

"Comes with the job." Reuger cast with sound suspended before the plop. "Watch the tension on your line there."

Kurt reeled his line in slowly with his fist circling air. Reuger sat and saw planets burning cold in the dusk.

"Can you tell me about some of it? You know, the dead guys."

"Well, let's see here." Reuger pursed his lips, feeling the line. "Had to go up and cut a man down from a tree on Basswood Lake once."

"He hung himself?"

"Oh, ya," he nodded. "Three days before somebody called it in."

"What'd you do?" Kurt shrugged. "I mean what did he look like, you know, when you got there?"

"Didn't look good. It was August and decomposition had set in already, so when I got to him he was falling apart."

"Oh, *yuck*!" Kurt screwed up his mouth and shivered. "Gross! How'd you get him down, you know, from the tree?"

"Body bag." Reuger held his hand out from the rod. "Put it under him and cut him down."

"Did it stink?"

"Sure it did."

"Didn't it make you sick?"

"Nope, but the Forest Service guys puked in the weeds when he broke open."

"Ugh!" Kurt shook his head. "How can—Hey! *I got one, Reuger!"*

Kurt's reel sang out line like some mindless intelligence. Reuger reached over and adjusted his drag and the line slowed.

"I got a fish!"

"Reel him in there steady there."

Kurt jumped up with his fist cranking fast.

"You're tiring him out now, Kurt, keep it up," he said reaching for the net. "Doing a great job now. All right, bring him in. Don't want to let him go deep again."

"He's a *big one,* Reuger," Kurt shouted like a man bringing in a shark with arms bunched close to his chest.

"Careful, you don't want to fall out of the boat there."

Kurt fell down reeling and they saw the white belly darting the green water.

"Looks like a walleye."

"OK, OK," He shouted. *"Get the net ready!"*

"You just keep reeling him in there."

Reuger sunk the net hoping the fish wouldn't shoot the boat and snap the line.

"Keep bringing him in, Kurt. You're doing a good job."

"Get the fricking net ready!"

"Don't worry." Reuger leaned close to the water and threw his hat off. "Keep reeling, but don't lift him up, let me net him in the water."

"Get the net ready!"

"Keep reeling. All right, hold on there.... Hold on."

Reuger slipped the net deep under the swirling white and lifted the walleye. The slick skinned creature flexed in the netting. Kurt breathed hard with the rod over his head.

"ALL RIGHT!"

She's good size," Reuger nodded. "Maybe two pounds."

Kurt stared at the fish slapping the bottom of the boat.

Really, think so? *Two pounds*. Is that huge? I mean for a fish?"

"Be some good eating for you and your mother."

"Oh, we have to eat it?" He looked up, light fading. "I mean, shouldn't I stuff it or something for our den?"

"Well..." Reuger shut one eye and pulled the fish out of the net. The walleye flexed in his hand, mucus painted with twilight. "I tell you, she might be just a little small here for a taxidermist, but you'll have a great dinner. Nothing better than fresh walleye."

"Oh." He stared down at the fish. "Seems kind of a waste to just eat it."

"We can throw it back. Catch and release is practiced widely in the Boundary Waters."

"Oh no!" He held his hand up. "I got to show it to my mom!"

"All right then, let's get the hook out," he nodded, unlatching the green tackle box.

Reuger fingered the hook from the lip while Kurt watched closely.

"Caught him on the first bite here. Ever put a fish on a stringer?"

"No." He shook his head. "My dad never even took me fishing before."

Reuger held the walleye and pulled out a green stringer with the rusted needle eye hooking the end.

"All right, you slip the needle through the gill and out the mouth," he explained threading the fish onto the stringer. "Then you just put him over the side here."

Kurt leaned out and watched the fish splash around and slap the side of the boat. They had drifted out from the land now with the North Star gleaming toward Canada and the lake burning a gentle pink. Kurt turned around.

"That was a good fish, huh, Reuger?"

"No doubt," he murmured, hooking a leech.

"You say that a lot up here."

The big hat stayed bent over the tackle box.

"Think so?"

"You say that a lot, too!"

"Ya, Reuger, come in."

He hefted the radio by his right ear with the shade brim over his eyes, the last twilight gold on his mustache.

"Go ahead."

"Ya, Reuger. Jim Carpenter called from Pine Lodge. You have someone waiting for you there...Tommy Tobin."

"10-4, on my way."

Reuger clipped the radio and turned to the motor.

"You have to go?"

"Yep," he nodded. "Better reel in your line there."

Reuger stowed the rods and tackle box and opened the cooler.

"Another cookie before I stow the cooler?"

"No, thanks."

"After I finish up at the lodge, I'll show you how to clean that fish," he said, reaching back and jerking on the pull-start of the motor. "You can tell your mother I'll be stopping by."

Kurt stared at him flatly.

"Think so?"

25

THE MOON WAS over Canada. The air was a chilly sixty-five. He watched fishermen motoring into the bay. The lodge looked like Christmas, all twinkly and bright against the dark frontier of forest. He held up the binoculars and saw the Indian sitting in the lodge at a table with his hands clasped in front of him. He set the binoculars on the cross seat of the seventeen-foot motorboat. It was still as death. One big mirror of stars and moon. He moved the radio scanning the frequencies. He might as well be on the force. He listened in to every stupid fucking thing Reuger had to say.

He hefted the Remington 30.06 with the high-powered telescopic site. He put the sling under his arm to steady the rifle. His hands were steady as a surgeon. The world through a small hole. There the sonofabitch was. The magnified circle moved around in black space then he saw the Indian much closer.

He was wearing a green army fatigue coat. He had on a cap. He could go with a shot through the forehead but that would be showing off. Better to be sure and make it look a little sloppy. He lowered the site to his chest. He breathed in slowly. You found the pause between breathing and the pump of blood. It was there if you listened. It was when the body was still for a moment. He breathed out again and squeezed his finger around the trigger.

The world jumped as another fishing boat headed into the bay. He cursed as the swells from the boat's wake slapped his boat around. All he could do was wait.

26

WIND RUSTLED THE pines like a lost lover and a half-moon pearled the lodge roof. Reuger walked along the lodge road. The woodshed door was open as he passed a breeze of motor oil and woodchips and gasoline. He continued toward the lodge and saw Jim Carpenter behind a pickup with rifles in the back window.

"Your man is inside at the card table there," he said, glancing toward the lodge.

"How long has Ben been here?"

Jim turned to the lodge.

"Oh, come in about twenty minutes after Tommy showed up outside my office door and scared hell out of me."

"Al Hanes with him?"

"Oh, ya," he closed one eye, "they're tanking up at the bar there."

"They talk with Tommy?"

Jim frowned and shook his head.

"Not since I been here, but I had to get gas and bait for some people."

"Appreciate it, Jim," he said walking the porch steps cliffing light then pulling back the screen door.

Tommy sat with his hat low under a wagon wheel of bulbs like some old Western. He cradled a coffee mug. The room was in darkness except for the round table and the man. Reuger passed the bar and returned Ben Johnson's cold glare. He sat at the kitchen table.

"Had my doubts about you, Tommy."

He shrugged sleepily.

"Had to check my traps."

Tommy kept his fingers on the mug, his thick lips and hooked nose heavier under the overhead light. Cold had penetrated Reuger's flannel shirt and vest and the sleepy warmth of the lodge drowsed him. He left his hat on the table.

"Need anymore coffee?"

"Nope. Keeps me up if I drink too much."

Reuger poured himself a cup and sat back down, sipping the burnt coffee, pulling a yellow pad from the middle of the table.

"Diane's grocery list. A lot of toilet paper to run a lodge."

Tommy's lip curled then retreated. Reuger sipped his coffee. They heard the screen door slam and footsteps go into the bar. He set the mug down and stared at the big man.

"You know Tommy, it doesn't look good here. I have a couple of dead loggers, and I have you." He stood up again. "I'm going to make a fresh pot here. You sure you don't want some?"

"Ya, OK."

Reuger emptied the carousel, filled it from a Hills Bros. can, then poured the water and flipped the switch.

"We'll have fresh coffee in a minute here."

He sat and leaned back, then tapped the edge of the kitchen table.

"So," Reuger leaned forward, "you say Jorde asked you about Foster." He stood again. "Tommy, you want one of these cookies here?"

He craned his neck around to the two cookie jars.

"Ya, what kind?"

Reuger opened the jar by the coffee.

"Mmmm, let's see here, peanut butter and chocolate chip."

"Ya, peanut butter."

He handed him the cookie and they chewed in silence.

"So," Reuger swallowed, "it's going to be your word against Jorde's here." He motioned with the cookie. "Say you went to that slasher earlier that morning and left," he brushed the crumbs from his hands, "but then, I have Foster with a bullet in his head."

Tommy nodded slowly still chewing. Reuger clasped his hands like a priest, shadow smudged under his eyes.

"Something else you want to tell me here?"

Tommy's eyes moved with the whites showing like a slide projector running out of film.

"Nope."

"Coffee's ready." He stood and poured the coffee into two mugs. "How do you like yours there, Tommy?"

He squinted. "Cream and sugar. Only fill it up three quarters there. I like it to be sort of milky, you know."

"Coming right up."

Reuger fixed the two mugs and sat. They drank their coffee and left crumbs on the table from the cookies. Red and green lights floated into the bay outside the window. They heard the distant clatter of an outboard motor.

"Ya, good coffee," Tommy nodded slowly with crumbs on his chin. "I like Hills Bros. over Maxwell House, you know."

Reuger frowned. "Folgers isn't bad."

"Too bitter." Tommy shook his head. "I like a mellow roast."

Reuger sat back with one hand on his mug and yawned. He fingered the initials carved into the table.

"So...what do you have, Tommy? Robbery? Nothing really heavy-duty." He drummed the table with his fingers and looked at the big man. "But this is a murder here. You could go away for a long time with something like this."

Tommy Tobin turned, his eyes flickered then his lips slowly pursed. One hand left the coffee cup with three fingers opening like a pledge.

"Ya, I told you the slasher was burning when I got there, you know. I didn't fucking shoot him."

Reuger drummed the tabletop then bracketed the mug. He picked up his hat, examining the fish blood staining his nails.

"I know that's what you told me, but then you disappeared." He motioned over his shoulder. "Now I have a girl who said she was attacked here at the lodge by a big Indian."

Reuger lowered his voice.

"I'm not going to lay that at your doorstep." He leaned close to the table. "The girl wasn't hurt, so I'm willing to forget it. But if she hadn't backed up on her story, you would have been in a world of shit."

"She's lying," he muttered.

Reuger leaned back. "How do you know?'

"I wasn't in the shed."

Reuger watched his powerful hands close over the coffee cup. His wrists were as thick as branches.

"Who was in that shed?"

Tommy faced him and shook his head slowly.

"Wouldn't know."

Reuger nodded slowly. "Like I said, I now have two murders, and you are my only suspect here." He leaned in and lowered his voice. "You and I go way back, Tommy, but I can't look the other way on this one."

His hands closed around the mug again.

"So, unless you can tell me something different," Reuger stared at him, "I have to look your way."

His lips quivered and nostrils flared, a breath of air escaping like some animal tired from the chase. He stared at the cup with cuts and lacerations on blackened fingers. Tommy's eyes went to the bar door then back. He breathed again and shook his head.

"I knew I shouldn't have fucking gone to work that day—"

It was the front window exploding like glass cymbals that dropped both men to the floor. The bullet split the glass and glanced off the mining helmet against the back wall. Reuger rolled off the chair and pulled Tommy down with him. The big man fell on Reuger's chest, and he felt the air leave his body. He pushed Tommy off and scrambled to his feet and pulled the Colt.

Reuger crabbed through the broken glass with the curtains whipping up in the lake breeze. It was the sound of the bullet zinging off the miners' helmet that stayed with him. That helmet was three feet above Tommy Tobin's head. He stared into the night and heard the whine of a motorboat but saw no lights. He stood slowly and could hear the motor heading for Canada.

"Jesus Christ," Ben Johnson cried out, staring at the glass on the floor.

Reuger looked at him wearily and holstered the Colt. Tommy stood by the table, his olive skin now pale. The long white curtains whipped up like an errant ghost.

"Somebody took a shot there," Al Hanes nodded, his eyes bright under his green hard hat.

Ben shook his head and walked through the glass.

"You got an enemy out there, Reuger."

Reuger turned and followed the trajectory of the bullet and saw the dent in the helmet. He looked at the far wall and saw a white slice in the knotty pine. Ben nodded to Tommy Tobin.

"Or maybe he does."

Reuger saw Tommy's face and motioned back to the table. He was scared and he wanted to use that if he could. Tommy stared at the table with his long black hair silky in the dull light. Reuger leaned forward.

"That was a warning, Tommy."

"Ya, no shit," he grunted.

Reuger pulled the legal pad over. He scavenged the man's face, his position, his posture his breathing. Tommy's eyes went to Ben Johnson standing by the open window.

"I can't protect you, Tommy, if you don't help me," Reuger stated, staring straight ahead. "Next time they won't miss."

He breathed heavily, his eyes dull. Then he shook his head.

"It was that tree hugger...Jorde," he said just above a whisper. "I saw him shoot Foster dead."

Reuger stared at him.

"How could you tell he was dead?"

"There was blood all over the place in the snow."

"It wasn't snowing, Tommy."

"Ya, I know," he shrugged. "But it looked like snow with that fucking blood everywhere."

Reuger leaned back and wiped the fatigue away. He looked at the black and white pictures of loggers on the wall and the miner's helmets. The coffeepot swirled a thread of steam. Tommy didn't cross his arms or look away.

"Why didn't you tell me that the first time?"

"None of my business you know. Those tree huggers can make a lot of trouble for a logger. I figured he try and say I did it. You know, blame it on a fucking Indian the way they always do."

Reuger turned to the bar where Ben and Al Hanes had disappeared.

"You aren't blowing smoke, are you?"

Tommy rolled his shoulders.

"Why do I care? I'm telling you what I saw there."

Reuger clicked a pen open and dropped it on the legal pad.

"Write it out for me there. Every detail you remember about that morning."

Tommy sat and clawed the pen and began to print. He scribbled all over the page.

"She died?"

"Ya," he nodded, throwing the pen down.

Reuger reached into a Hershey syrup can of pens and pencils and scribbled on the page.

"That one works."

Tommy tore out the paper and balled it and threw it toward the trashcan. He picked up the pen and began writing again. Reuger heard the screen door slam then boots on the front step. Ben Johnson's truck started up in the night.

27

REUGER WALKED DOWN the path with the .30.06-caliber round in his pocket. He had dug it out of the soft pine with a knife from the lodge kitchen. He saw Patricia in a chair on the dock and approached the dock cautiously and felt the breeze off the lake again. She raised a glass to her mouth and stretched out her legs. He saw the blue flowery dress when she turned around.

"Did Kurt enjoy cleaning the fish?"

"Natural-born fish cleaner," he nodded walking up next to her.

Patricia fingered her drink and looked down.

"I'm sorry," she said, staring at the drink in her hand. "I just didn't know how to tell you."

He wasn't going to bring it up. He had decided he would show Kurt how to clean the fish then leave. But he had seen her on the dock, and he felt angry, even hurt. Even then he promised himself he would just be polite and say hello and leave. But now it was out there, and he lost the tight rein on his emotions.

"You always bushwhack people?"

Patricia nodded slowly. "I guess I deserve that." She looked up. "But you haven't been exactly forthcoming about what's going on around here."

Reuger crossed his arms.

"Why didn't you tell me who you were working for?"

She slid her fingers back through her hair and shrugged.

"You never asked."

"Weak defense."

"I'm not on the defense." Patricia stood up from the chair and faced him. "You obviously weren't telling the truth before. A *suicide?*"

Reuger shook his head.

"I didn't have all the evidence then."

"So you go from a suicide to the easiest target around?" Patricia frowned. "That doesn't sound like good police work."

Reuger felt slightly ridiculous with his arms crossed like a mad little boy, but this woman just kept coming at him. He tried to laugh lightly, but it sounded hollow and fake.

"What do you know about police work?"

She tipped her chin up.

"I know bad police work when I see it, and I know an agenda when I see it."

Reuger laughed again, this time more successfully.

"You mean like working for a radical environmentalist?"

"Or logging interests."

Now she crossed her arms. Reuger considered leaving; he considered kissing her.

"You watch too much television down there."

"Maybe you don't watch enough," she said lightly. "Ben Johnson is playing chess, and you are one of his pawns."

"I don't take sides," he said flatly. "I can't help what Jorde tells you."

"Oh, come on!" Patricia glared through the darkness. "You view anybody who's not a logger as an intruder!" She lowered her voice. "You believe the wilderness is for men like yourself and everyone else are just tree huggers or swampys."

Reuger rested his hands on his gun belt.

"So they brought you up here to defend Jorde?"

Patricia lifted her hand. "I was working for Earth First in Chicago and they asked whether I would consider moving. I was with the EPA before that—*ouch!*"

He waited while she slapped her legs and arms.

"Why aren't the mosquitoes going after you?"

"Are you wearing perfume?"

She glanced at the inside of her wrists.

"Never wear perfume in the Northwoods."

"Whatever," she muttered walking to the end of the dock.

Reuger watched her sway though the darkness, then walked after her down the dock. The barrels underneath sunk in the lake, and he felt a cold mist on his face. The stars burned over the lake. Patricia stood with her back to him. Reuger pushed back his hat and rubbed his jaw.

"We don't know each other very well," she said facing the lake. "But when they asked if I would consider moving up here, I looked at it as a way to get away. My son needed to get away." She shook her head wearily. "Of course just when I come, all hell breaks loose."

The wind teased her hair along the back of her white neck.

"It's been this way for the last five years," she said dully. Patricia turned and he saw her eyes were wet. "Thank you for taking Kurt fishing." She wiped her eyes quickly. "I know he enjoyed it."

She turned and walked back down the dock. He scuffed his heel on the plank wood then followed her.

"Goddammit," he said under his breath. "Hey!"

Patricia turned, and Reuger swept off his hat and kissed her in the middle of the dock. Her lips were soft as he felt her thighs against him and the pressure of her breasts. He kissed her the way he wanted to when he first saw her on the road. When they came apart, she breathed heavily and put her head against his shoulder.

"That was a surprise," she murmured, feeling a tingling in her legs, resting in his arms.

Reuger felt his throat tighten. All he wanted to do now was make love to this woman. They kissed again, this time slower as they explored each other's bodies. He felt her pressing against him and could feel the hard muscles of her abdomen then her pelvis. He pushed his hardness against her with his hands slipping down her thighs. She pulled back and glanced toward the cabin.

"Where's Kurt?" she asked, kissing his neck.

"He's up at the lodge." Reuger glanced to the cabin then kissed her again. He felt her lean back in his arms and stare up at him against the glittering sky.

"Want to go for a swim?"

He smiled. "I don't have a suit."

"So?" She stood back. "Who said anything about suits?"

Patricia reached back and pulled the dress over her head in one fluid motion. He saw her tan lines creasing ivory skin as her bra snapped away. Her breasts were high and erect. Patricia stepped out of her panties with thigh muscles flexing between the small mound. She walked the dock and jumped into the water and re-emerged further out with her hair smoothed.

"Oh, it's *wonderful*! It's warm. Your turn!"

"I'll just watch you here," he called.

"Oh, come on!" She splashed water onto the dock. "Get your ass in here!"

Reuger glanced back toward the cabin then slipped off his vest and flannel shirt, slipping out of his boots and dropping his jeans. He jumped in feeling the rush of cold water, then the buoyancy lifting him to the surface. She swam past him and he felt her thighs and breasts warm and slippery. She floated backward with nipples clearing water then emerged on the dock in a wash of splattering liquid.

Reuger swam slowly to the dock and hoisted himself up. He could feel his heart. He lowered himself and kissed her wet lips then her neck, licking her hard nipples. She arched on the plank wood as her wet hair slapped the rough dock planks. She held his neck and spread her legs further then started to move. She arched again with the downy curve of her neck under his hand. She slapped the rough planks with her hands and lifted her chin to the sky.

He bit her nipples. She clawed his back.

28

"NEVER SEEN A grown man eat that a way before in my entire life!"

Bruce Anderson rose up with his mouth full of yellow paste. An air-conditioner blew red ribbons from the window behind him and teased a smoldering cigarette in a glass ashtray. The sticky residue of fried food clung to the pale green walls.

He motioned to Gus, gasping for air.

"Only way to get your mouth around these deli sandwiches here!" He waved them in. "Air-conditioning," he said after Reuger swung the door shut.

Bruce wiped his mouth with a napkin and sipped from a Coke bottle then hit his chest and burped. They sat down in the cheap green armchairs, then Gus stood and leaned against the wall. Vinyl paper spread out on the desk and splayed points around the room. Cigarettes were snugged in a sand ashtray like buoys on a sea.

"Little early for lunch, Mr. County Attorney?"

"Ya, but this is breakfast here," he said, potato salad sticking to his mustache.

He pushed the food away like a man about to play cards and pulled a Camel long from his desk drawer. He slapped the drawer shut and leaned back in a cloud of smoke and crossed a tennis shoe across his knee. Reuger nodded to the desk.

"What happened to the Marlboros?"

"Ya," he grunted looking at the cigarette. "Lower tar and nicotine." He inhaled again then leaned forward. "What can I do for you, gentleman?"

Reuger pulled out the lined yellow paper.

"Tommy Tobin's statement saying he saw Jorde shoot Foster Jones."

"That was fast," he muttered, studying the paper. "His grocery list here?"

"Other side."

"Oh." He flipped the paper over and shook his head. "Ya, I can't read this Indian scrawl," he grumbled throwing the paper on the blotter with doodlings of coiled springs. "Tell me what it says there."

Reuger pointed to the desk.

"Says he saw Jorde burn the slasher, and when Foster came on him with a gun, they struggled and Jorde shot him."

Bruce yawned.

"How'd he see him?"

"He was going to work. He worked for Foster."

Bruce leaned back in his swivel chair and clasped his wrist over his head, holding the cigarette hostage.

"You believe him, then?"

"So far."

Bruce exhaled smoke and stubbed out the cigarette. He glanced at the egg salad and brushed away a fly.

"And what about Carter, then?"

"Jorde asked him to spike the tree."

"Ya?" Bruce raised his eyebrows. "Did he do it?"

Reuger shook his head.

"Then we'll have to let that ride for now," he muttered, clasping his hands like a sumo wrestler contemplating his next chess move. He picked up a piece of paper next to a letter opener. "Got a letter here from an attorney named Patricia Helpner."

"Jorde's attorney," Reuger nodded.

"Ya, apparently. Letter says you harassed her client there, and she requests I keep you from speaking to her client anymore, or she's going to slap a suit on the county." He put the paper down. "So you see, Reuger, these people don't fuck around." Bruce leaned back like a man on a life raft. "Then your boss comes to see me here yesterday, too."

"Riechardt?"

"Ya," Bruce nodded, picking up the cigarettes and tapping out three.

"They for later?" Gus asked.

"You betcha. Now, I'm getting to feel real important here. I don't usually get a visit from the sheriff, you know." He gestured to the walls.

"I think it was the first time he's seen my fancy office."

He flamed the lighter above his head. Gus pointed to the cigarette.

"How come yer didn't just smoke the last one down there?"

"It's better for you if you just smoke them halfway down, but Riechardt," he continued, clapping the cigarette into his mouth, "he wanted the same thing you did when you came to see me. Wanted to know if I could make a case against Jorde with his gun." He tapped his ash. "I told him he needed more than just a gun here for me to take on these environmentalists. Didn't like that at all."

Bruce looked like he wanted to spit. He moved forward, leaning on his elbows, smoking like a general.

"What's the sheriff getting into this thing here, Reuger?"

"Couldn't answer that." Reuger put on his hat. "Can you make a case?"

He reeled back, hands behind his head. Bruce shook his head doubtfully.

"Mmmm, this Tobin, Reuger, he has these priors, you know."

"I gave him the priors, Bruce." He nodded across the desk. "So did you."

His lower lip curled over his upper. His eyes changed.

"Girl called me a few days ago. Right after I saw you. Said she wanted to tell me something about what happened in the wood shed at Pine Lodge." Bruce frowned and tapped his cigarettes. "So I'm thinking, what the hell is this now? If I use Tobin, and it turns out he's molesting white girls in woodsheds, then I got my dick in the crack."

"What'd the girl say?"

Bruce rolled his shoulders.

"Didn't give her name and said she would come down to my office last evening but never showed." He looked up. "Thought maybe it was the girl who was in the shed, but she didn't sound like she was from the lower forty-eight."

Bruce tapped the cigarette, caressing the filter with his thumb.

"So then...you really think these environmentalists are killing loggers then?"

Reuger opened his hand. "I follow the evidence, Bruce, you know that."

"Ya..." He inhaled deeply. "But what do you *think?*"

"I think we shake the tree and see what falls out."

"Should know better than to ask you that," Bruce muttered, nailing the cigarette dead. "I'm just saying here we can't have any funny business here with these environmentalists. So, if it says what you say it does here…but Reuger, you get me in court with these high-priced environmental lawyers here, and this thing goes south then I'm not going to look to do business with you after that."

He slid over the egg salad sandwich and the large drink. Reuger motioned to Gus and opened the door.

"Have I steered you wrong before, Bruce?"

"Oh, ya, plenty of times," he muttered, getting his hands around the sandwich. "But this isn't Floyd beating up Emmy Lou, here. We're taking on a national movement." He lowered his head. "So I wouldn't want to be in your shoes if you're wrong, or mine for that matter."

"Warrant?"

Bruce hefted the sandwich the fly landed on.

"I'll get the judge to sign it here this afternoon."

* * * *

At about three o'clock, they pulled up in front of the old Ely Grocery and charged the door. The desks of college kids froze with phones plastered to ears. The voices died like a drowned fire at the site of the two armed men. The office door in back opened and Tom Jorde stepped out with Patricia. Reuger noticed the dark pants suit of shiny material and the heels.

"Ya, Reuger, you at Earth First? Sheriff wants to know if you need any backup there?"

"Can do her, Hector."

Reuger clipped the radio and walked toward Tom Jorde. He stood open-mouthed in a blue nylon coat over a T-shirt with sandals and white socks. The planks groaned under the weight of the two men. There was a jingle of keys and the leather slap of the Colt. Jorde glared at Reuger hotly.

"So the Gestapo is right on time!"

Reuger stopped in front of him and tipped his hat to Patricia.

"Tom, I have a warrant here for your arrest for the murder of Foster Jones."

Patricia stepped forward with hair curled under and makeup deep in her eyes. She snapped the paper out of his hand. She unfolded the white document as Reuger watched her eyes dart back and forth. She finished and handed back the warrant.

"My client will come peacefully," she stated in a cold voice. "Just give us a few moments, and we'll follow you." She paused, directing her eyes. "We'd prefer to not make a spectacle."

Reuger nodded. "Wait for you outside, then."

They retreated to the lot of heated tar and put the shotgun in the jeep and clipped the Winchester. Reuger leaned against the bumper, squinting in the glare from the store windows. Gus hooked his thumbs in his jean pockets, sniffing the oily tar.

"Now, I ain't one for questions Reuger, but ain't that the lady from Pine Lodge you seen?"

Reuger shifted his weight and hooked a boot on the fender.

"Oh, ya."

"Then she's a lawyer for this Jorde and you..."

"That's right."

Gus held up his hand, grappling his white beard, rolling his shoulders.

"What yer do is yer business, but it could make it a bit warm for yer down the road, if yer know what I mean."

"Here he comes," Reuger nodded, unsnapping a pocket on his vest.

They heard clapping from inside the building. Tom Jorde gaited stiffly out with Patricia holding his arm. Workers surrounded them clapping and chanting, "FASCISTS! FASCISTS! FASCISTS!" Patricia walked toward him with eyes like cut glass. Reuger remembered the feel of her wet hair as he clicked the manacles open.

"Tom, put your hands on your head, please."

His face was red as he glared. "How long have you been sucking Ben Johnson's dick, Reuger?"

"Turn around, Tom."

He patted him down while Patricia watched.

"Where are you taking him, Deputy?"

"Down to the station," he said standing up. "You can follow me; it isn't far," he nodded, bringing Jorde's hands down and slipping the handcuffs on.

"I'll meet you at the station, Tom," Patricia murmured, squeezing his arm.

Reuger helped him into the back of the jeep, but his foot caught. He sat him up and pushed his legs around and buckled him in. Tom stared at him with hot red eyes.

"You're such a dirt bag. You're just another *lackey* for Ben Johnson."

He spat and Reuger felt saliva warm and slimy on his cheek.

"You fucking phony," Tom yelled hoarsely, tears welling.

Reuger took off his hat and wiped his face with his sleeve.

"You shouldn't do that, Tom," he said steadily, stifling the urge to slap him across the face.

"Fuck you!"

He was crying now as Reuger climbed into the jeep.

"Better calm down there, boy," Gus said handing Reuger his handkerchief.

"Yeah, well *fuck you,* old man!"

Reuger waved Gus off and started the jeep. He heard a car engine turn over once then a clicking like two plates. He glanced over at the minivan and heard the solenoid click again. Gus shut one eye.

"Dead battery there, Reuger."

"Oh, ya," he muttered swinging out of the jeep and walking through the chanting people.

He kept one hand close to the Colt and leaned down to the driver-side window.

"It won't start," Patricia murmured, staring straight ahead.

"Release your hood."

The hood popped and Reuger lifted it, looking at the battery, seeing the fuzzy green and white corrosion on the cables. The volunteers surrounded him like a posse.

"FASCISTS, FASCISTS, FASCISTS." He rubbed away the corrosion and twisted the clamp on the battery post. He scraped his hand on the latch then glanced around the hood.

"All right, try her now!"

Patricia looked out the window.

"Now?"

"Now!"

Sparks arced the post and shot blue smoke. The solenoid clicked and buzzed.

"She's arcing," he called out. "Hold on."

Reuger twisted the clamp on the post crowded by volunteers clapping and chanting. "*FASCISTS, FASCISTS, FASCISTS*"

"All right," he shouted, one hand on the pistol.

"Now?"

"Now!"

She turned the ignition again and the engine roared to life. He dropped the hood and pushed his hat back with the audience behind him.

"Battery is all right, but your cables are loose." He lowered his voice. "I'll come by your cabin and tighten them up for you."

"How embarrassing," Patricia muttered, then her eyes changed like a veil. "Thank you, Deputy, I will follow you now to the station," she shouted.

He touched his brim and walked back to the jeep. Gus hooked an eyebrow and tilted his head back.

"Her battery there?"

"Cables corroded and loose," he said sitting down and shoving the jeep in gear. "Shorting out when she turns the starter."

"That'll do her for sure."

Tom Jorde glowered, shaking his head.

"The auto-mechanic sheriff, fucking great!"

Reuger drove onto the highway then pulled off to the side. He hooked a boot on the jeep and waited.

"What'd we stop for?" Jorde demanded.

Reuger watched the rearview mirror and saw the minivan. The blinker was on and several cars drove past. Patricia nosed into traffic cautiously.

"Give your lawyer a little time to catch up here."

29

REUGER SAT IN his jeep and watched a motorboat drag skiers across the lake. He took off his hat and ran his hand through his hair, enjoying the light breeze. The smooth blue of the lake rippled in large circles. A cloud passed over, and he felt the discomfort of hours before, when Riechardt closed the door to his office.

"Just checked Jorde's print against Foster Jones's .45." He tilted his head up and crossed his arms. "It didn't match, but we got him anyway," *phsit bing phsit bing,* nailing the trashcan with seeds. "Good work," he said, his eyes hard as nickels.

Reuger stepped out of the jeep and began walking the lodge road. He smelled pine sap then wood smoke from a fire by one of the cabins. The whine of a saw drew him along until he saw wood chips spraying out of the open door of the woodshed. There were no crickets or cicadas or loons or frogs; just the click of gravel under his boots and the sound of his breathing.

He passed Cliff Johnson's jacked-up pickup with a gun rack in the back window and a bumper sticker. *Johnson Timber* brandished the right side of the bumper. The son of a timber baron, Reuger thought to himself as he saw another sticker, *Save a tree, kill a tree hugger* on the left side. He passed the cant hooks and other logging tools from the turn of the century mounted outside the woodshed. The saw started again and he noticed the clean scent of his own aftershave as he went into the shed with the screech like a wave crashing down.

Cliff Johnson was bent over the woodworking table with his shirt stained dark and his jeans coated yellow. Sawdust sprayed out and stuck to the bristles of his short hair. When he looked up, Reuger saw silver had rubbed off his sunglasses in spots. The saw ran down like a slowing train.

"How's she go, Cliff?"

He shrugged and spat.

"Repairing cabin four here."

Reuger leaned against the workbench and the phone rang. The phone was old with paint splattered on the receiver and part of the dial missing. Cliff kicked away some two- by-fours with his boot.

"Pine Lodge."

He squinted with the phone to his ear.

"No, we don't have any Chinese food here. This ain't a restaurant."

"Fucking swampys," he muttered hanging up the phone.

Reuger picked up a miner's hat on the bench then some old oilers for chainsaws. He squeezed out a bead of oil then set the oiler down. The phone rang again then stopped. He stared at a *Drink Coca Cola* sign from thirty years before with people waving from a boat.

"Heard you paid Tom Jorde a visit."

"Ya." Cliff grinned with the Skoal stuck on his front teeth. "Gave that murdering tree hugger something to think about."

"Stick a deer rifle in his face then?"

"Ya, weren't loaded, but he sure pissed his pants." He kicked a board away on the floor. "Should a done worse to the murdering sonofabitch."

Reuger turned and faced him in the dim light of the shed.

"Stay away from the Earth First people, Cliff."

Cliff leaned down to the saw.

"Long as they don't get in my way."

He watched him saw three boards with dust sprouting out the door like bright confetti. The saw whined down, and Cliff threw the wood across the shed.

"So…a little trouble on Center Island the other night?"

"Ya, no doubt." He leaned over the table, a lightning bolt on his bicep. "That stupid swampy from Chicago got lost there, said he could canoe when he didn't know a damn thing."

"You mean Kurt Helpner."

"Ya, right, the kid." Cliff stood up from the board. "I took Tim and the girl from cabin nine there back to the lodge when Tim said that Indian was out there, you know. Figured it was better to get the girl to safety and go back and look for the swampy kid."

"Kurt. His name is Kurt."

Cliff shrugged and grinned.

"Ya, whatever. You seen one swampy, you fucking seen em' all."

Reuger picked up an ax head by the grinding wheel.

"You went back and looked for him then?"

"Sure I did."

He set the ax down and watched Cliff line up the saw.

"He was sitting by a fire outside the island there."

Cliff raised his head and smirked.

"Oh, ya? You don't think I went back for the kid? I wouldn't just leave him there, you know."

Reuger continued along the bench past the three chain saws without chains. He spoke with his back to Cliff.

"You wanted to get rid of him to be with the girl, right?"

Cliff stood up and raised his sunglasses.

"Don't you have some poachers or something to go chase here?"

Reuger picked up a Hills Bros. can of spent brass shell casings. He shook out some of the shells and thought they were mostly .45 caliber and a couple .38 jackets. He looked up in the dusty light.

"Still reloading your own, Cliff?"

"Nope." He spat a line of tobacco juice on the planks. "Store-bought."

The saw whined again as Reuger stared out the back door at the old refrigerators and toilets and stoves and hundreds of pop cans. There were old trucks and an earthmover and a small building on two logs for ice fishing. There was even an old phone booth. He turned back in.

"Been seeing the girl?"

The boards chunked across the shed.

"Some." Cliff grinned picking up a two-by-four. "Sixteen-year-old, big tits, right?"

"Sounds like the one," he nodded, walking into the shed. "Give you some advice, Cliff?"

"You going to tell me to use a rubber?"

Reuger stopped just short of the saw. He tapped his gun belt with his forefinger.

"Going to tell you to let this one go."

"What the fuck for?" He muttered, bringing up another two-by-four.

"She has problems. This isn't some logger's daughter whose father works for Ben."

Cliff stood up, his blue eyes luminous in the deflected light.

"At least I'm not fucking some tree-hugger lawyer." Cliff grinned again and brushed sawdust from his arm. "She must be something for you to go to the other side like that. She give good head or..."

Reuger grabbed him by his shirt and pulled him close.

"Watch your mouth, Cliff."

He turned red and looked down at his shirt.

"I'd appreciate it if you let my shirt go, Reuger."

He pushed him back, and Cliff bent down to the saw, kicking boards out of the way.

"Should have left the little shit out there on Center Island, little tree-hugger kid...give that lawyer something to think about. Come up here and stir up a bunch of shit," he grumbled.

Reuger stood in the doorway of the shed and felt his heart pounding. He had let Cliff get the best of him and cursed himself for letting his emotions play in like that. The little shit knew right where to fire. He would be on guard next time. Cliff bent down to the saw.

"Yeah, maybe, I'll go on over there and get a little tree-hugger ass myself."

Reuger stepped near Cliff then leaned down to the woodworking table. He spoke into Cliff's right ear.

"Go near her or her son and I'll give you the beating you never got."

Cliff leaned back and held his hands up. "Whoa...big talk, Reuger," he said flexing his arms over his head. "But I don't think you could whip me and if you tried, I might just have to kick your fucking ass. You take off that gun sometime and I'll show you.

Reuger unclipped the gun belt and laid it on the workbench. He turned and faced him.

"All right, then."

Cliff spat a brown line of tobacco on the planks.

"I got some wood to cut Reuger, and then I have to talk to my father about the way the deputy sheriff hassles me and keeps me from my work. Maybe he'll tell Riechardt to get rid of your ass, and you can go back to being the lowlife you are."

Reuger picked up the gun belt and stood in the door.

"Just let me know, Cliff, when you're ready."

He spat again.

"Ya, you bet." "

30

THE SEAPLANE SHADOWED an underwater missile on the lake. Irene Peters sat close to the windshield with a black headset, black aviation sunglasses, and blond hair ponying out of a baseball cap. She throttled the plane down, skimming the pines with a flock of geese before dropping like a brick and hydroplaning on the lake. She cut the engine as a bald man in a uniform paddled with the *slip-slop* ricocheting the canyon. Reuger unbuckled his seat belt and opened the door.

"Want me to wait here?"

"Appreciate it, Irene," he said stepping into the canoe.

"Think we have a John Doe, Deputy," the balding man in the Forest Service uniform nodded, swishing away from the plane.

Reuger picked up the other paddle.

"See him, Bill?"

Bill Henderson's angular face darkened, and he smiled the thousand smiles of a man who lives in a wilderness.

"Haven't gone in the water here, but the fellow up there is convinced there's a skeleton down in those shallows up ahead."

They paddled the water cliffed by shadow and saw two people in hiking boots and matching sweatshirts. The man had three day's growth and dark circles under his eyes. The woman's short blond hair was tied up tight in a scarf. She watched the two men paddle the still pond of the lake.

"I hoped to have a diver up here," Reuger called back.

"Water shouldn't be too cold," Bill said, steering toward shore.

The bottom rutted, and Reuger pulled the canoe onto the granite. Bill Henderson splashed ashore and gestured to the blond woman.

"This is Deputy Sheriff Reuger and this is…I'm sorry…"

The man jumped forward.

"Jack Higgins! I saw the body."

"Jack!"

The man breathed heavy and whipsawed to the woman. She crossed her arms and pushed past him.

"This is my wife, Cathy, she was with me when I saw the…"

"How do you do, Deputy?"

Her handshake was firm.

"So you think you saw something in the lake?"

"No!" The man waved his arms wildly. *"I'm* the one that saw it, and I know I saw something!" The man jabbed his finger down. "There's a skeleton in a boat right there. My fishing rod went overboard and I was leaning down to get it when I saw it."

The woman gestured toward the lake.

"We would have reported it earlier, Deputy, but we didn't see a ranger until yesterday and maybe it was just the way the light…"

The man thrust himself forward, almost falling into the lake.

"I saw a body, all right!"

"You *think* you saw a skeleton, Jack. My husband has quite an imagination."

The man's face reddened.

"I saw it!"

Reuger thumbed his hat back and turned to the inky water in shadow.

"Well, only one way to settle it." He sailed his hat onto the rocks. "Let's have a look then."

He unbuckled his gun belt and laid the gun next to the radio and wallet and vest and handcuffs.

"Shouldn't be too cold there, Deputy," Bill Henderson shouted.

"Been in colder," Reuger called back, walking down the slope of the lake and wading though swamp grass and seaweed that tickled his stomach.

"It's right there," the man shouted. "Right in front of you!"

Something clipped his knees. Reuger reached down feeling the gunnels of a boat then hollow chicken wire then oar locks. He felt a branch long and skinny and slipped his hands over a bumpy stem to a hard basketball. His chin dipped in the water as he hooked two holes up to his knuckles. The chills moved up his arms and he wanted to recoil his hands from the creature beneath him.

"What have you, Deputy?"

Bill Henderson was hunched down like a football player. Reuger broke his hands down over shoulder blades then the knotted sticks of fingers. The bones felt like porcelain branches underwater. The flesh was gone. The body had been down there a while. He could tell by the gunnels of the boat it was older, and he felt where the stern was broken away. The soggy clothes pulled at his hands, and several times he felt as if he might be sucked below.

"This is it," he shouted, louder than he wanted to.

Bill Henderson licked his lips and squinted.

You really think so, Deputy?"

Reuger looked up then stood in the water.

"Put that down!"

The man held the Colt by the stock like someone convicted. Reuger watched him open his mouth.

"Put the gun down *slowly*."

His wife ran toward him and fell.

"Jack, you ass!" she shouted from the ground. "Put that gun down!"

Jack dropped the Colt and Reuger watched it hit the granite.

"I'm sorry." The man's mouth opened and closed like a fish. "I just was looking. I had never seen a gun like that before...I'll pick it up."

"Leave it," Reuger commanded.

The woman shook her head. "Jack, you fool!"

"Oh, bite me," he shouted, flipping her the bird.

Reuger waded back and leaned down to the boat. He felt the cloth again, the spidering bones of the rib cage then thick cables lapping the torso. So that was how the man stayed in the boat, he thought. The lakes were all down. The rainfall had been scant, and the boat may have drifted into shallower water. Whoever put him in the boat intended him to stay there for a long time.

"Boat here, maybe seventeen foot," he called out. "I think this fellow is tied in."

Bill Henderson cuffed his mouth.

"He's tied in?"

Reuger nodded, following the cable across the boat.

Some sort of wire cable...I think it might be loose enough without the flesh," he said, down to the inky green water.

"Can you get him free, Deputy?"

"Maybe." He pulled on the cables and felt the waterlogged wood give way. "If I can get these cables off—" he shouted, falling back when the cable tore out of the wood.

"I told you there was a body there," the man shouted. "*Ha!*"

"Jack, you fat fool..."

The man chased his wife, jousting his finger as she backed away.

"You're just mad because for once I was right! Everything you do is the right way, paddle this way, pitch the tent this way, carry the canoe this way!"

The man ran toward his wife.

"Jack, *please*! You're making a scene!"

"Cook this way! Make a fire this way! Well you know what, Cathy!" He held his hands to the sky and bellowed out. "This is *my way*, so *FUCK YOU!*"

"Long trip then," Reuger said to Bill Henderson, reaching under the arms of the skeleton.

Bill stared at the green pooling water and lifted his head.

"Need some help there, Deputy?"

"Ohhhh, I think I got her."

Reuger slipped the boots under the cables and pulled upward. The skull rose like plaster in ink as he pulled the legs free. A red-checked shirt and faded jeans slowly developed as water caressed the cloth in waves. The skull turned over in the current with the mouth gaping teeth and seaweed.

"Yep, that's got her," Reuger called, pulling the skeleton behind like a string of garbage.

The woman turned with her hand to her mouth. The man watched the grinning skull gulping water with a finger trailing like a rudder. Reuger walked toward him.

"Fuck...that's sick!"

Reuger hefted the heavy-clothed bones by the rib cage and climbed to where the rock leveled. He heard something behind him and turned as the skull fell off and hit the slab of graywacke like a football helmet, then rolled down the slope and splashed into the water.

"There she goes, Deputy!" Bill Henderson shook his head, watching the skull sail out onto the dark green plane. "Wants to take another swim, I guess."

Reuger dropped the torso, and one foot detached. He waded back into the lake but the current floated the grinning skull head out into the bay. Water flowed in the mouth and out the ears as the skull gulped happily along. The two people stood transfixed as the skull seemed to be propelled from below. Reuger cursed and turned back to shore.

"Throw me that paddle there, Bill."

Bill Henderson handed him the canoe paddle, and Reuger waded back out until the water was up to his waist. The skull seemed to have a mind of its own. He reached out and clipped the skull head with the paddle. The skull spun around and he swung again. The three people stared at the man swinging the paddle. *Swack*! He smacked the skull again. *Swack*! The eyes turned toward shore. *Swack!* He skiffed the bone head around. *Swack! Swack!* Reuger reached out and grabbed the skull like a bowling ball and slogged back to shore.

Bill Henderson's blue eyes twinkled.

"Sure seemed to have a mind of its own there, Deputy."

"Oh, ya," Reuger muttered, plopping the head on the shoulders and picking up the foot then dragging the skeleton further up the rock slab.

The skull bumped hollowly with seaweed sprouting eye sockets and the mouth like colored pasta. Reuger lay the skeleton down and put the foot by the lower femur. He stood and surveyed the remains. Bill Henderson licked his lips and shook his head. The two men stared at the grinning skull leaking water still from the ear holes.

"Well, Deputy..." He turned. "I wonder how long he's been down there?"

Reuger hunched down with water squishing from his boots. He pulled at the suspenders and felt the cloth of the heavy wool shirt. He ran his eyes down the body and saw it was a big man. Reuger estimated he was over six-foot-four, and he remembered Al Knudsen from the year before. He was a man with flashing dark eyes and a black beard. He had disappeared in the winter while checking his traps.

"Ohhh, I'd say he's been down there a while," he murmured. "This skeleton is clean and the clothes have begun to disintegrate," he said pointing to where the shirt had torn like tissue.

A crayfish spidered out of the collar and ran down the leg. Reuger kicked it away with his boot.

"Oh, shit," the man groaned.

He had crept up behind them, and now they listened to him wretch in the weeds. The woman stood with her back to them. Reuger slipped his hands through all the pockets and smelled the sour scent of dead algae. He noticed the man's clothes again and the waterlogged construction boots.

"By those clothes and suspenders and work boots..."

"A logger," Reuger nodded slowly.

Bill Henderson breathed heavy.

"Jest what I was thinking, Deputy."

The forest ranger clicked his tongue and swore softly at the mouth of fillings winking light.

"So... guess he was up here camping?"

"I don't think so," Reuger murmured turning the skull slowly to the side.

"Think he was from around here, Deputy?"

He palmed the skull then pivoted the head like a melon. Reuger smoothed the cranium with his hand and felt his finger slip a nickel-sized hole just above the neck. He turned the skull around until it faced the rock. Reuger tapped the drilled hole with his forefinger and pulled a round from his gun belt. The .44 shell slipped perfectly through. He looked up at Bill Henderson.

"Oh, ya."

31

HE LOOKED AT his watch. The trees had become black wiry ghosts. Shit. This was a long time to stand in the woods. He looked at the kitchen window again. The square of yellow light bled through the pines. He lifted the rifle and sited up the window again. He had no scope, just an aiming pin.

He dropped the rifle down and pulled a cigar out of his top pocket. The match flared against pale green needles close to his face. He smoked slowly and saw a moon over the cabin. Fucking Reuger was taking his time about coming home. Things were getting crazier, that was for sure.

He smoked with the gun cocked under his arm and waited. He just needed a few more nudges, and then he would understand. *What will be, will be.* You couldn't change things. Important issues were at stake here. Still, things seemed pretty fucked up. He sighed and stared at the window again. So he found Knudsen. *What the fuck.*

He pulled on the big cigar and shook his head in the dark. Things were unraveling fast. They were all getting nervous now, and he had to do the shitwork. He had to stand in the woods with a Winchester and wait for him. They should have put him deeper. *Stupid motherfuckers.* So now he had to risk his neck again. He shook his head again. *What the fuck?*

The woods breathed around him. He stared at the trees. It was all about the trees. It was all about the land at one time, and now it was about the trees. He felt the tobacco numbing his brain and tried to relax. *What will be, will be.*

32

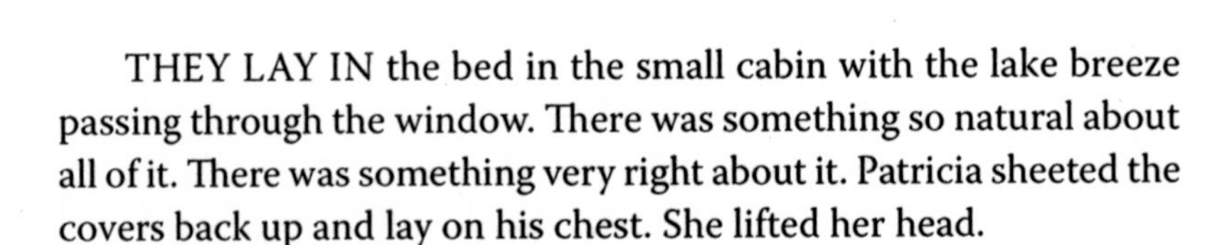

THEY LAY IN the bed in the small cabin with the lake breeze passing through the window. There was something so natural about all of it. There was something very right about it. Patricia sheeted the covers back up and lay on his chest. She lifted her head.

"Tell me what you did before you were a deputy sheriff."

Reuger opened his eyes and could see his hat on the bedpost.

"Are you awake?"

"Yes," he murmured.

"Then tell me what you did before you were a deputy sheriff."

He squeezed his eyes shut and felt her thighs around his leg. The scent of warm bodies puffed from beneath the sheets. The bed was wet, and he moved from the spot.

"Logged trees for Ben Johnson."

Patricia stared at the knotholes in the ceiling and saw a face then a comet in the wood. Curtains rose over the window with light filtering down. A moon perhaps just outside the small cabin window in the forest.

"What was that like?"

"Hmmmm..." He shifted beneath her with his chest rising. "Hard work from morning until night, and then you slept like a dead man."

She kept her ear to his chest, hearing the organ groaning deep within. She bit his skin, watching the play of light on his blond mustache.

"Why didn't you keep doing that?"

"Seven years of hard labor is enough."

He felt her head lift from his chest.

"But you must have liked it to do it that long."

"It was good hard work and you ate well and then at night you slept well."

"And your father was a lumberjack?"

"Yes. A tree broke his back."

"How..."

Patricia sat up with hair falling on her shoulder like a waterfall. They stared at each other in the small cove of light. He watched her in that changing light. She was so alive and here now.

"My father was a cutter and used a chain saw." Reuger sat up slowly against the headboard and smoothed the sheet over his dark stomach. "It was windy and the trees were old. You don't want to cut on a windy day."

"Why's that?"

Reuger raised his hand. "You need to know which way the tree will go, but if it's windy, then a tree can fall a way you don't expect."

Patricia lay back down on his stomach."And your father cut on a windy day." She paused. "So why would he do that?"

"He was working for Johnson Timber," he nodded slowly. "You do what you're told."

Reuger paused.

"Somebody said he was alive for a while with the weight of a sixty-five foot white pine lying on him. When I was a boy, I used to have nightmares where I woke gasping for air."

"I'm sorry," she said, wiping her eyes.

She turned to him with his mustache golden and his hair waving back from his forehead. He grew in her hand and she closed her palm around him. He kissed her neck then slid down to the hard nipples as the cover fell back behind him. Reuger stopped with her legs apart. She was staring at him.

"What?"

"It's nothing. Go on," she whispered hungrily.

He slid his hand down her stomach.

"Tom Jorde's innocent, Reuger."

He stared at her.

"I thought we weren't supposed to talk about it."

"I know, forget it," she said kissing his neck and reaching for him again. "I just wanted you to know that."

Reuger stared at her coolly then rolled off.

"What?"

"Your timing could be better," he muttered, feeling as if someone had just walked in the room.

Patricia swallowed and sat up, fluffing back her hair.

"I'm sorry," she whispered reaching again. "I'm sorry, it was just bothering me. When you told me Ben Johnson caused your father's death..."

"I didn't say that," he said with an edge coming into his voice. "I said he worked for Ben Johnson."

Patricia turned away then looked down at the covers.

"You and I know what's going on. Tom Jorde is being framed."

He looked at her a long moment and felt himself stiffen. He had a set of interior rules that had to be satisfied before he came to a conclusion.

Reuger thought about Irene's stricken face and the smell that filled the enclosed cockpit of the plane. When they landed, he pulled the skeleton out, and he and Gus stuffed him into a body bag and drove to town.

"So yer think it was Knudsen then?"

Reuger turned from the road and saw Gus's pale blue eyes.

"We'll see what Floyd comes up with, that boat was from Wilderness Lodge. "

"Medical examiner," Gus nodded, cleaning his pipe with a pocketknife. "You think maybe Jorde done this one too, shot him and tied him into that boat, then." Gus shook his head, hair flying back in the wind. "But if it ain't Jorde and that's Knudsen, don't it mean..." He turned and stared at the two flat glimmering points under the hat. "Jest a thought," he shrugged. "But sure seems like somebody trying to keep somethin' a secret here."

Reuger looked at the woman beside him.

"I follow the evidence, Patricia, and bring in the man. It's not my job to decide guilt or innocence here. You should know that."

Her eyes hardened. She was sitting up Indian style with the dark mound between her legs.

"I've been a lawyer long enough to know a case that's fucked," she said in a low voice.

He shook his head slowly. "My job is to follow the evidence."

"What are you, a robot?" Patricia's eyes flitted back and forth. "You don't think for yourself?"

"I can't help it if my decisions aren't popular with the tourists."

"What does that mean?"

"It means most people see logging as bad and don't look much beyond." Reuger gestured to her. "You're an environmental lawyer and..."

"I see a town run by one man who has everybody doing his dirty work," Patricia snapped. "You won't even admit he was responsible for your father's death!"

"I shouldn't have told you that," he said.

"Why not?" she shouted, her eyes flashing. "So I wouldn't know you're *afraid* of him!"

He stared at her. Patricia shrugged, looking away, pulling back her hair.

"I think we both know what side you're on now," she said dully.

Reuger pulled back the covers and picked up his pants and boots.

"I shouldn't have brought it up. The lawyer in me..."

"I keep forgetting that's what you are," he murmured, standing up and tucking in his shirt.

She sat back."Oh! So that's what this is?"

"Think what you want," he shrugged.

He felt her eyes following him as he picked up his boots.

"You have a thing about lawyers, then?"

"Whatever, Patricia," he muttered, roping up his gun belt.

"I'm sorry what I do *offends* you."

Reuger clipped the radio and stared at her. She pulled the covers up and covered her body.

"What!"

"Have you seen my other sock?"

She rolled her eyes.

"It's over there behind the door."

Reuger put on his sock then his boot and walked back and fingered his hat like a man in a lawyer's office. He was leaving, and at this moment he didn't think he was coming back. She saw this and looked down quickly.

"You only said what you think, Patricia."

"I'd appreciate it if you leave now."

He snugged his hat and walked out of the room. She heard the cabin door close then his footsteps by the window. Patricia rubbed the bridge of her nose. She heard him pass the window again and the door open. She watched him walk in the room and take off his hat and finger the brim. She handed him the wallet from the side table.

"Thanks," he said and walked out for good.

33

THE BELL CHATTERED the cold thin air and he woke from the dream lost and cold. Reuger lay with the quilt pulled up to his nose. With the third ring he looked at the alarm clock, but it wasn't the clock that rang but the phone next to the bed. He picked up the black receiver.

"Reuger, Sheriff here." Static. "Bad trouble at Pine Lodge last night... at the Ely hospital with the Reynolds girl from Pine Lodge and her family."

White noise filled his ear again.

"Ya...seems...raped last night...woodshed."

He was wide awake and out of the bed.

"On my way."

"Family doesn't want to deal with you...had some trouble before... father... rude to him...covering things here and have already conducted an interview with the girl... apparently told you... of the earlier incident...So there...want you...pick up that Indian...Tobin."

He stood with the phone pressed against his cheek.

"She identified ... mug shot... bet we... match...DNA... complicate other investigation..." Static washed him away again. "Jorde anyway..."

"Sheriff, let me talk to her—"

"Don't want to talk... Reynolds ...moving into town...investigation... an attorney and give a nickel...future of... Lodge... Jim Carpenter...lucky... can keep shirt ... back."

Clicking on the line.

"Go pick up the Indian and bring him... me."

* * * *

Reuger stepped off the boat onto Center Island with the shotgun, and Gus carried the Winchester. They passed through the dead sour scent of fish guts. His boots sunk in the sand as he trudged like a man with a heavy pack before he got to the rocky granite. Sun glazed the stagnant water around the granite slabs where turkey buzzards flocked up on the flat rocks. The lodge was small across the lake.

"Don't see his canoe," Gus muttered with the Winchester clenched tightly, his face pale and old in the harsh light.

"Go look at his camp then," Reuger nodded, ducking into the trees with flotsam in the branches.

They passed scraggly jack pines with foam green mold running the branches like an infection and dead branches curled in like a witch's hand. Gus dropped down to a chipmunk raising fireweed. Reuger kept the shotgun close to his body with his finger snugged. He spied the clearing and bulled ahead with the branches shishing leaves like canastas.

Reuger reached down to the burned sticks and walked the flattened grass.

"Just pulled out here by the looks of that there grass, Reuger."

He hunched down and thumbed up his brim.

"If he raped the girl, then he took off last night."

Gus raised a bushy brow.

"Yer don't sound convinced there."

"Nope," he said pulling up the radio. "Hector!"

"Ya, go ahead, Reuger."

"Get hold of Irene Peters, tell her I'm going to need her plane soon as she can work me in."

"Ya, 10-4."

He turned among the wiry ghosts of dead trees. Reuger stared toward Canada and knew he had gone into hiding. He looked down at the flattened grass and the crusted black logs. Reuger picked up a burned stick. He turned it over slowly then looked up at Gus.

"Let's go see that lawyer's daughter."

34

THE INN HAD been a Victorian mansion built by a lumber baron to bring grace to the Northwoods. The trees ran out, John Stafford died, and the mansion became a boarding home, then a restaurant, then a bed and breakfast. Gus and Reuger sat in the jeep across the street.

"They in there?"

"Oh, ya," Reuger nodded.

"We goin' to jest wait?"

Reuger slumped down and pulled his hat forward.

"I take it that's a yes, then," Gus said leaning back in the seat.

At four o'clock, Reuger woke and saw a man and a woman step into a black Mercedes. They drove slowly past. The lawyer had on a light cream sports jacket and dark glasses. Reuger wondered how long Jim had before he had to close his doors.

"Ya, Reuger."

He swung up the radio.

"Go ahead, Hector."

"I have the medical examiner on the line, I'm going to patch him through...Hello! Hello!"

"Go ahead, Floyd."

"Ya, Reuger, I've been working on the skeletal remains here you brought in, and I found something I think you should know about. You were right, that hole in the back of the skull is a bullet hole, I would think maybe a .44. Now I couldn't find an exit wound so it either lodged somewhere in the brain and then was lost in the lake or it went out his mouth or eye socket there."

"Anything else, Floyd?"

"Oh, ya. I was examining the bones for any other contusions or breaks or any other sign of trauma, you know, and I found along the vertebrae in the neck these strange chippings here and I examined it close, you know, and there is definite signs of trauma here."

"Think so?"

"Looks to me like it was struck here with something very sharp and very fast—almost strafed, you know. Maybe with an ax."

"How about a chain saw?"

"That could well be, but for a chain or something to strike those vertebrae it would have to have nearly cut the man's head off you know, but it could leave these type of marks here on the bone."

"Thanks, Floyd."

"Sure, come on by the house sometime."

He clipped the radio and paused. Floyd Habershaw was a transplant from the Twin Cities. He wore a buckskin coat in the winter and sported a Teddy Roosevelt hat from the Rough Rider days. He was as blustery as TR and had built himself a magnificent log cabin just below the Boundary Waters. Floyd was a loud man and he tended to brag a bit about his wilderness adventures, but he was thorough and a crack medical examiner.

"Gus."

"Yep," he said, sitting up from a dead sleep.

"When you talk to these hardware stores, look for someone who bought a lot of these spikes."

"Fer sure," he yawned, spatting to the hot pavement. "Now, yer sure yer want to do this?"

Reuger climbed out of the jeep and squinted across the parking lot.

"I know you're going to do what you're going to do, but that Mr. Reynolds could cause a lot of trouble and if Riechardt...all right, all right."

"Be back directly," he nodded.

Gus slumped down in the seat and closed his eyes.

"I'll be here."

* * * *

Reuger walked across the lawn passing lounge chairs under a willow that Stafford managed to baby through the winters, an angel gurgling into a birdbath, and a sprinkler that whipped around then chattered back. Flowerpots bright with red impatiens lined the porch steps. He climbed to a door of leaded glass and entered the parlor. A man with wired lenses stood behind the hotel desk. The Inn still carried the moldy scent of a Victorian home.

"What rooms are the Reynoldses staying in?"

The man pushed up his glasses and clicked his tongue then drew a book open and lined it with his finger. He turned to a row of keys.

"I'm sorry, the key is not here."

"I just need the room number."

"Oh, I see, police business. "He drew his hand across his mouth. "Mum's the word."

"I still need the number."

"Ah," he said leaning forward and lowering his voice. "The Reynoldses are in 211 and Dana Reynolds is in room 212."

"Thanks."

Reuger climbed the carpeted stairs to a landing settled by a love seat and a crystal lamp. He walked the hall with the Colt slapping his thigh. The plush carpet was wobbly under his boots as he passed dignified numbers on brass plates. He came to a lacquered door with 212. The brim of his hat touched the wood.

"Dana." He knuckled the door. "It's Deputy Sheriff Reuger."

He heard the sound of a suitcase falling to the floor. Reuger knocked harder and tried the door handle. He smelled something like a napkin burning and saw smoke misting from beneath the door.

"Dana!"

He banged the wood with his fist and jammed his shoulder against the door. A woman in pink curlers thrust her head into the hallway. Reuger drew back and kicked the door. He kicked it again with his booted heel marking the door like a horseshoe.

"Help! Somebody! This man is breaking into a room!"

He stepped back and drew the Colt and fired. Blue smoke roiled the space and he banged four shots until the metal perforated the hasp. He kicked the door open breathing burnt powder and stepping on lathe and plaster. Curtains waved over the four post Victorian bed and mahogany tables.

Reuger saw a trashcan by the bed flaming up toward the ceiling and dumped the burning paper in the tub and saw a cigarette still smoldering. He turned to an old man in the hall doorway.

"Get back!"

"Yes, sir! Something wrong?"

Reuger walked into the room and turned the television off.

Painted toenails peeked out from the far side of the bed. He kneeled down to Dana Reynolds in lacy panties and a bra. He put the gun on the carpet and gently turned her over. Blood smeared her stomach and breasts. She moaned like a child and then he saw the weak trickle pulsing from her wrists. He clamped the wounds and felt warm blood flowing between his fingers.

"Hang in there Dana, you're going to be all right," he murmured, pulling up the radio. "Hector!"

"Ya, Reuger."

"Get me an ambulance to the Stafford Inn. Female with slashed wrists."

"10-4."

He pulled the pillows from the bed and wrapped pillowcases into tourniquets. He bound one arm just above her wrist then the other. She groaned again as he tied each cloth off tightly and saw her hands turn white. Reuger hoisted her like a baby and she moaned against his chest. He could smell a scented shampoo when her hair brushed his lips, then he ran down the hall like she was his child.

35

"SO THEY DIDN'T even thank you?"

Reuger looked up from his biography of *Scott and Amundsen.* "Who?"

"Them *Reynoldses!*" Gus stared through the smoky light. "They just up and come to the hospital and don't say nothin' to you about savin' their daughter from bleeding to death?"

Reuger sipped his beer and snugged his toes in the thick wool socks. He remembered Joel Reynolds whisking by him in the emergency room. He remembered standing there with his blood-soaked shirt, then Riechardt barging into the room. He had returned to his cabin, and it felt very cold and alone.

"Nope, they didn't," he said, setting his beer down.

"Don't beat all." Gus shook his head with pipe in hand. "What's wrong with them people? They so sick with all their nastiness, can't take the time to thank a man for saving their own namesake!"

The fire crackled in the room. The polka music had ended, and a nasal whine filled the room. Reuger glanced up to the radio on the mantle.

"Ain't that..."

"My opinion here that the recent spate of murdered loggers turning up in the Boundary Waters is the doings of a single madman, better known as a serial murderer, who the deputy sheriff and his lackeys are trying to cover up for their own design. It is through the tireless ongoing investigation of this reporter that I have uncovered the discovery of another dead logger just yesterday that was also murdered in the gruesome style as Foster Jones and Carter Grisom. And the End of the Road show has learned that this logger's head was chopped clear off

and was found floating in the lake."

Gus shook his head.

"Where does he get that kind of crap?"

"This reporter has always maintained that a clear and open discourse between law enforcement and the press is the best policy, but this is not the case and instead we have an elaborate cover-up along the lines of the John F. Kennedy assassination. And now the arrest of a leading environmentalist, Tom Jorde, who was just on this show last week, has told this reporter that he is being set up for much bigger forces at work. After much investigation, this reporter must agree. For End of the Road this is John Mcfee..."

Gus snapped off the radio with eyes burning.

"Where in the hell does he get off with that?"

"Free country."

"But he talks out of both sides of his mouth here!"

"Good for his show."

Gus sat down and shook his head.

"That dang Charles Kroning has left us with a curse, and his name is John Mcfee!"

Reuger drank from the beer again, feeling the cold rush. The windows rattled again, and he set down the book then walked to the glass panes. The storm was pricked out in the heavy coal sky. The Boundary Waters had performed one of those abrupt shifts from a pastoral day to a blustery cruel night.

He had gone out to Center Island several times, but Tommy hadn't returned. "One thing's for sure." Reuger turned around and walked back to his chair. "I'd say there is something that girl is trying to get away from."

"Take a razor to her own wrists like that." Gus crossed his legs like a professor in the wing chair. "Mighty young to be throwing all that life away."

Headlights shone in the door. Gus craned around.

"Expecting guests?" He stood up. "It's the sheriff."

Reuger picked up the eagle feather from the table for a marker.

"Know what this is going to be about."

The steps on the porch were loud and officious.

"Ya, door's open there," Gus hollered over.

The sheriff opened the door. He carried a Campbell's soup can in his right hand. He peppered it with a sunflower seed. *Phsit pop!* His jaw turned and he spit into the can again.

"Come warm yer bones, Sheriff," Gus called without turning around.

The sheriff stood in his wool coat with the star emblazoned on the left side. The overhead light flicked on and blinded the men.

"Reuger, I'd like a word with you here," he said moving out from the wall switch.

Gus leaned forward and tapped his pipe on the hearth.

"Well, yer don't have to beat me over the head," he said standing up.

"Talk to you in the morning, Gus."

He nodded to the sheriff by the door.

"And it's been nice talking to yer too, Sheriff!"

The door slammed behind him with his boots fading into the forest. Riechardt tipped the can slightly. *Phsit-pop!* His mouth moved in fast rotation. Reuger gestured to the other chair in front of the fire.

"Have a seat, Sheriff. Mind turning off that light?"

Riechardt switched off the light then walked stiffly and sat down in two-time fashion like a man in an electric chair. He lifted the can up. *Phsit pop*!

"Coffee, Sheriff?"

He shook his head and rested the soup can on the arm and fired from the corner. *Phsit pop*! The patent leather holster next to the old upholstery and the stripe down his pants gave him the air of a retired general. The sheriff lifted the can.

"So, I'll get right to the point here, Reuger. You're not to go near the Reynolds girl again. If you do, I'll take your badge."

"Let the girl bleed to death next time?"

Riechardt leaned to the can again.

"Ya, going in like Custer and shooting up the Stafford Inn didn't help matters," he said, sitting back up. "You scared the guests half to death there, and Mr. Reynolds feels it was your fault his daughter tried to commit suicide by barging in on her. Said you scared her into doing it."

Fire snapped between the two men. A green spark landed on the rug and Reuger reached forward and pressed it cold. The sheriff inventoried the books, fire, and the mantle with the hat next to the brown-holstered pistol.

"What do you think, Sheriff?"

He lifted the can like a staff. *Phsit pop!*

"Doesn't matter what I think here. I had the mayor in my office today. Mr. Reynolds might well sue us anyway, but you're to stay away from this girl!"

"I need to talk to her and find out what's she's sitting on." Reuger said quietly.

The sheriff leaned forward with his legs wide.

"I don't need any heroes up here. I know what happened down there in Minneapolis, Reuger." He paused. "I've always known." He sat back with the can planted. "Seems you were on the wrong side of things there too."

"Funny way to look at stealing, Sheriff."

Riechardt took off his glasses and looked at the lenses.

"Look Reuger, I've heard some strange things out there. Rumor is you know where Tobin is but won't bring him in. I'm not going to listen to that shit, but you better get on the stick and get this Indian into custody."

Reuger leaned back in the chair.

"I don't think he did it."

"Oh, ya, then who did?"

"I don't know that yet.

"Listen, Reuger." Riechardt touched the part in his hair, drawing the tip of his finger along the line. "We have a way things work up here. It may not be to our liking, but it's our reality."

"Why do I feel like I'm being offered a bribe?"

"Watch yourself there."

Reuger set his beer on the table.

"Why protect the girl?"

"Because she's the link between Jorde and the Indian!" *Phsit pop!* His eyes drilled the soft light. "She saw Jorde and the Indian in the woodshed the night before she was raped. Don't you get it yet? This is all part of a conspiracy. *Phsit*...sorry about that."

He leaned down and retrieved the seed from the floor.

"Are you saying Jorde killed Knudsen, Sheriff?"

"Why not?" The sheriff stood and walked to the mantle. "It's Jorde's goal to halt the logging and get everyone out of the Boundary Waters any way he can!"

He turned slowly against the flames.

"This is a war, Reuger. It may be undeclared, but this war over the land is being played out all over the country. You have these radicals who think they know what's best for everyone else, but they don't see what it does to people. They don't see the jobs and communities they destroy so they can drive their SUVs and drink their fucking lattés in the woods."

Riechardt shook his head. "We lose logging, and this town has had it! Johnson Timber employs this town, and I can't let a bunch of radicals destroy our way of life."

The sheriff hit the iron poker on the hearth and it fell and cracked a tile. He picked up the poker, blackening his hands.

"Anyway," he gestured, wiping creosote off, carrying the wadded napkin, "Jorde knew a rape at Pine Lodge to the daughter of an attorney from Chicago would spell the end, and God, ya, it looks like they're right. They've wanted Jim Carpenter out of there for a long time so they can burn that lodge to the ground."

The sheriff looked at the can and shook the seeds. "Look here, Reuger. I'm fifty-five-years old. I can't go looking for another job now." He raised his head and nodded. "So, my job and *your job,* is to bring these radicals to justice and make sure the town's interests are looked after."

Reuger pursed his lips, staring at the man in the changing light.

"How much Ben give you for re-election, Sheriff?"

"Ya," he nodded slowly, "fuck up one more time here, and you'll be packing for the Twin Cities there." He pointed down. "You get that old man or whatever you need here and go arrest that Indian. Then we'll have Jorde there for the loggers, and the Indian for the girl, and people can forget all about this."

Riechardt stood and walked to the door with the can extended.

"You better learn which side you're on here, Reuger."

36

REUGER SHUT HIS eyes and smelled the early dew. His neck hurt from hunching over the infrared scope in the seaplane for three hours. It had been a futile search for Tommy Tobin. He was almost asleep in the chair by the fireplace when the phone rang in the kitchen.

He stood up and walked into the kitchen and picked up the phone.

"Hello."

The line clicked dead. Reuger hung up the phone and set the cup on the sill, steaming in the damp night stream. He leaned closer to the window and saw a flicker deep in the dim forest. An orange muzzle flash flared as glass rained the sink like fine crystal and he dove to the floor with glass tinkling from his head and shoulders. He pulled the Colt and crawled to his feet, then moved low out of the kitchen, knocking over magazines by the chair with brass cartridges rolling on the floor. He ran across the porch and into the trees.

Reuger was swallowed into a gloomy half-light and saw things between the trees that became men then turned back into trees. Silvery light touched the pistol in his hand as he hopped a fallen tree then smelled gunpowder, then saw smashed-down foliage and branches bent and snapped. He approached a cedar, placing his boots like a surgeon, then snapped the branches back.

He found twenty feet of mashed ivy and honeysuckle in a small clearing. Reuger breathed heavily and turned, staring at his shattered kitchen window. He lowered the pistol and knelt to the ground and touched a boot print, then picked up something greasy. He dropped the cigar and reached down again. The casing was a spent .44. The percussion cap gleamed like a dime.

37

ROSS HABER SAWED the tree with sawdust spewing his shoes and pants, and blue smoke funneling out the sides. His pickup was parked under some cedars with a green metal gas can and a pair of tan gloves on the hood. He pulled the saw away and took the cigarette from his mouth, then killed the motor and silence rushed in the same way.

"How she go, Ross?"

"Deputy," he nodded.

Reuger glanced up to the tree.

"Must be about forty-five feet."

"Fifty-five, Deputy."

Reuger sat back on the motorcycle and rested his boot on the foot peg.

"So, you've heard about what's been going on then?"

"Oh, ya." He grinned, a cleft of chin hair moving up. "Them tree huggers come this way they're goin' to get the wrong end of some double-aught buck." He shook his head. "My granddaughter come home the other day, you know what they teach her in school now, Deputy? *Hug a tree!"* He moved the tobacco wad. *"Hug a tree.* She asks me why I hurt the trees and tell me how you can explain to a little girl that this here is just agriculture when they get them that young?"

Ross held the thirty-pound saw and scratched a cheek as rough as sandpaper with oil-blackened fingers. Reuger swung off the motorcycle and looked at the trees again. A man could hide in the foliage easily.

"It's a rough game now, Ross."

"Ya." Ross grinned and nodded. "So yer been rolling in the dust, Deputy?"

"Gets dusty on these old logging roads." He brushed the sand off his jeans and boots and stood up. "You've been logging a long time, Ross, and you know more about what's going on than most men."

He smiled gently.

"Just mind my own, Deputy."

"Let me give you my card, here." He reached into his vest pocket then pulled out his wallet from his back pocket and found a card. "Anything you want to tell me we can keep it between us," he said putting the tan card with the star into his hand.

"Sure, Deputy," he nodded, pocketing the card. "Not much really to tell there. I just log out here and mind to my own business and expect others do same."

Reuger rested his hand on the Colt.

"You think the environmentalists are killing loggers, Ross?"

He shrugged gruffly.

"Wouldn't know, Deputy, but it wouldn't seem to serve no purpose. Just make people hate them more and that just helps the loggers."

"Anyone else you can think of who might gain from something like this?"

Ross smiled, the lines at the corner of his eyes running back to his temples.

"Couldn't think of a one, Deputy..." Ross tilted his head back and gestured to a transistor radio on the hood of his truck. "Except that crazy John Mcfee. He's the only one seeming to get any mileage out of this."

"Keep my card, Ross."

"Got it right here, Deputy," he said, patting his blue jeans with brass rivets on the sew joints.

Reuger walked back to his motorcycle and flipped out the kick-starter. Ross pulled fast on the chain saw, then pulled three times and cursed. He put down the saw and walked toward the pickup with spidery glass on the windshield and pulled a plug wrench from a toolbox. Reuger leaned on the gas tank like the pommel of a saddle.

"Plugs fouled?"

"Oh, ya."

38

THE OWNER OF Wild Outfitters fitted a polar fleece parka on a manikin next to snowshoes and a canoe leaning against the storefront window. Gary Chatoee wore calf-high mukluks tanned the color of a deer with stitches of colored beads on top. A silver and turquoise bolo snugged the collar of his shirt.

"So, Tommy Tobin's gone then," he said, pulling up the furry hood around the manikin's eyes and mouth.

"Looks that way." Reuger nodded, leaning against the wall with his boot on edge of the picture window. "I kept Irene up there for three hours."

Gary picked up a mitten and frowned.

"Straighten out the thumb there."

"Ya, I did, these fucking manikins fight back, you know." He put his own hand in the mitten. "That's infrared right? Ya, he's too smart for that. He'll stay with his canoe and travel the rocks or stay in the caves while you fly above like an eagle looking for a mole."

"Nice analogy."

"Ya." He grinned big yellow teeth. "I can wax literary you know, been reading some Fitzgerald. Pretty good stuff, you ever read the *Diamond as the Big as the Ritz*?"

"Nope."

"Good stuff," he nodded." You should try it."

"Sounds a little heavy for me."

Gary shrugged. "It's not really. You know what Saul Bellow said about men who read boring books?"

"What's that?"

Gary Chatoee picked up the other mitten and shook his head.

"Must be losing my fucking mind. Something about you don't get to heaven or some shit like that."

Reuger stared out the window and watched the tourists streaming past.

"I found several trails that ended at the water's edge." He turned in and looked at Gary. "If they were Tommy, he might be heading for his cabin."

Gary fought with the manikin's hand, pulling the mitten down with both hands.

"Maybe you should forget the mittens, Gary."

"No!" He grimaced. "I can get these fucking things on—*there!*"

They stared at the misshapen hand with the thumb bulging the middle.

"Missed the thumb again."

"Fuck it, " Gary muttered.

"So, Bruce Anderson told me you're testifying against Jorde."

"Ya," he shrugged. "I started thinking about our conversation and all you know, and then I wondered if he tried the same thing with Foster. Guess Riechardt found a bunch of them wires and bulbs at Earth First."

Reuger nodded and hooked a thumb on his gun belt.

"Seems odd that Jorde would keep things like that around."

"Ya…but he must've thought no one would catch him, you know." He moved around the manikin. "Anyway, only way to find Tommy Tobin is to track him, you know," he continued, grabbing a pair of mukluks. "He's a good Indian and can disappear if he wants to."

He picked up the flesh-colored leg.

"That's why I need your help, Gary."

Gary put down the leg picking up the other mukluk that draped over his hand like a dead animal.

"Ya, looking for him in connection with them dead loggers?"

"Nope." Reuger shook his head. "Rape of the sixteen-year-old girl at Pine Lodge."

Gary stopped then moved slower.

"Oh, ya." He slipped the mukluk on. "I read about that in the *Ely Standard* there. Shit, that's fucked up."

"When did you read about it?"

"Just today, you know," he shrugged.

Gary stood back and raised the arm of the manikin. He squinted at the scene.

"Some little girl from the lower forty-eight decided that Tonto raped her, then?"

"That's what she says."

"Ya." Gary turned the other manikin inward. "What do you think?"

Reuger stared out the window and saw a man in a new buckskin coat.

"I don't know… I haven't talked to her yet."

"Her father rich then?"

"An attorney," he said meeting his eyes.

Gary moved the manikin back.

"Ya…so they hang the Indian for it. You and I know that's fucked up, Reuger. These people come up here and get in some shit, and then they leave us with the mess, you know." He shook his head disgustedly. "Always the same. White people get into some shit and they hang it on the Indian."

Reuger walked the old store planks, inventorying the wall of moccasins.

"I don't know what kind of shit Tommy's in." He put the moccasins down. "But I have to find him either way."

Gary moved the teepee back in the window and fluffed up the snow.

"So you want me to go help you clean up the mess." Gary's eyes flashed dark. "Help you catch the Indian who wronged the white woman again?"

"Raped the white girl." Reuger hooked a heel back on the window ledge. "I better bring him in, or Jim Carpenter won't have much of a lodge left when the girl's father gets through with him."

Gary raised his eyebrows.

"Those lawyers will take everything but your shirt, and then they'll come back for that, you know." He fluffed up the shredded paper some more. "You can't change what will be with some people. Tommy Tobin has been headed for trouble since he was born, and he'll die that way, you know."

Reuger looked at the big man in the picture window and the snowy scene. He wondered then whether Gary would have stopped on the road that day or would he have driven by.

"Tommy reload his own?"

"Think he does." He squinted. "He used to anyway, you know."

Gary stepped back from the window and jumped into the store. He reached forward and moved the snow around again and pushed back the teepee.

"You know things are changing for us, Reuger. We're winning in the courts now." He nodded slowly with his arms crossed. "I think we might get Ben Johnson to pay reparations on land he logged out. It won't be much because he'll pay what prices were then, but at least we're getting something here."

Gary raised the other manikin's arms until it was almost straight up. He pulled the green canoe closer and propped the snowshoes. Sun slanted across the two plastic Indians as he moved the aluminum foil fire closer to the teepee.

"People's perceptions are changing too, you know, but all it takes is one bad Indian and people say 'See, you see how they are.' " He gestured to the manikins. "You can't trust an Indian."

They both stared at the scene from long before.

"So then, when you thinking of going up there?"

"Tomorrow."

Gary pointed to the Indians waving cheerily above the fire.

"You know, I would come in and buy something here if I saw these fucking people in the window."

39

THE NEXT MORNING, they slid into the soft mud with the two canoes nudging the motorboat like fawns with their mother. The lodge boat was jammed with packs and extra gas tanks and firearms and ammo in sealed zip-locked bags. Gary Chatoee kneeled with the fringe of his buckskin coat touching earth then nodded to Reuger and started up the trail.

Reuger carried the shotgun, watching Gary's coat blend with the forest as they climbed. Gus breathed heavily, his mustache fluttering with each exhale. Gary held up his arm with buckskin tassels falling in succession. His black eyes mirrored the trapper's cabin as they watched two squirrels leap from the porch with weeds flying up like wind.

Reuger nodded to the cabin.

"What do you think, Gary?"

He shook his head.

"I'll take a look, I don't think anyone is in there, you know."

"Better let me do it," Reuger said, moving forward.

Gary stared at him.

"You come up there with that gun? I've known Tommy all my life, and I know he wouldn't shoot me down, at least I hope he wouldn't," he muttered, standing slowly.

He crept forward and ducked under the hanging roof then pushed the door open. Reuger handed Gus the shotgun and levered a shell into the Winchester. Gary walked into the cabin then returned to the door and fell on a loose plank.

"Fuck!" he shouted. "Ya, what a shithole!"

Reuger and Gus walked slowly toward the porch.

"He's not here," Gary muttered, looking around.

Gus cocked his eyebrow.

"And how in the hell can yer tell that?"

"I'm a tracker," he grunted, turning to the cabin and staring at the painted refrigerator and the table with the gallon of Jack Daniels. "So this is what the Ojibwa have come to." He gestured to the cabin with both hands. "Hundreds of years come down to this shithole in the woods the government allows us to keep?"

Reuger walked the cabin with the dirt floor soft and dusty like flour. The same smell of old clothes and damp mud was there. He examined the hole in the door from the arrows and looked around the cabin. Gary was brushing his new coat, trying to get the mud off.

"Make anything out of any of this Gary? Do you think he's been here?"

"How do I know?" Gary pointed down the trail. "But somebody went that way recently. Might be just ahead of us, you know."

Gus scoffed and spat out the door.

"Don't know how yer can tell that. Last time we was here, we thought this cabin was empty and had them arrows flying at us!"

Gary stared at him dully.

"You have to know what to look for."

"Is that right?" Gus spat again. "What you looking for, a broken twig or somethin' like that?"

"Nope." Gary shook his head. "That's the movies. You look to the ground to track, but you either feel it or you don't. You either have that extra sense or you don't. Most Indians have it." He nodded toward Reuger. "He has it too, from what I've heard."

"And how would yer know if yer had this *sense?*"

"You'd know," Gary said solemnly. "I'll show you," he called, leading off on a trail away from the cabin.

"Do yer believe all that Indian hocus-pocus, Reuger?"

"I wouldn't know, Gus," he said starting down the trail.

They hiked for ten minutes until Gary kneeled and pointed to a yellow plywood teepee with a plastic tarp covering the top and leather crisscrossing the seams. The dark oval opening faced them with a zigzag of red paint. There was a clearing with a fire ring in front of the teepee.

"Must be his sister, Running Bear," Gary whispered.

"Think I met her with a couple of arrows before."

Gus huffed up to the two men and stared at the teepee.

"Tommy in there?" he whispered.

"No." Gary shook his head solemnly. "That lodge is empty."

Reuger grabbed Gary's arm.

"You sure there?"

"I *know* these things here, Reuger," he said gesturing to the clearing. "Something that is handed down, you know, through the generations." He motioned to his forehead. "You either have this sense or you don't and I can tell you that lodge is empty for sure." He stood up. "Here, I'll show you."

"Gary, why don't we go around back just to make sure?"

"You hired me for this, you know," he said, pushing through the underbrush toward the teepee.

They watched Gary stride into the clearing with his buckskin coat and calf-high mukluks and long black hair flying back in the sun.

"Well, he sure looks the part, Reuger," Gus nodded.

Gary continued toward the teepee as a black missile streaked over his head. He dove to the ground.

"Fucking bitch!"

"Got yerself one hell of a tracker there," Gus murmured, shaking his head.

Gary spit dirt from his mouth then called out in Ojibwa, then English.

"*Hey! Running Bear!* It's Gary Chatoee. I'm coming in. We want to talk to you!"

A thin voice rose like a violin note in an empty hall.

"Hey fuck you, Gary Chatoee. You can eat shit!"

"One hell of a tracker," Gus nodded as another arrow streaked out of the forest.

Reuger picked up the Winchester and levered a shell in the chamber. "Cover Gary. I'll get behind her."

Gus called out in a low voice.

"Stay there, Reuger's goin' to get behind her!"

Well, I'm not going anywhere here," Gary muttered, spitting more dirt.

Reuger slipped back through the pines then began to circle around. He watched the feathered branches for movement, tripping on granite knifing the forest. He smashed whorls of bunchberries with juice squirting his pants then veered into sarsaparilla with the greenish white flowers tickling his legs. The forest was still and quiet.

"Hey, fuck you, Gary Chatoee! You and your asshole friends can get off my property!"

Reuger continued pushing through light and shadow, walking slowly toward the voice.

"Hey, fuck you, Gary Chatoee. You just a white man in Indian skin."

He heard the whoosh of another arrow and saw a woman in a corduroy coat with a jean skirt and long dark hair. She pulled up another arrow as he raised the rifle.

"Hold it, Running Bear!"

Her eyes crossed like marbles against a plane of white. She was a statue of an Indian with her arm breaking the curve of the bow. Reuger advanced slowly.

"Put the bow and arrow down slowly." He stepped through the bushes with the rifle tight to his shoulder. "Now!"

"Fucking Gary Chatoee," she muttered, dropping the bow and arrow.

"Any other weapons on you?"

She turned away and Reuger grabbed her arm.

"Come on."

They passed through the forest to Gary Chatoee on the ground by the teepee. He raised himself to his knees and brushed off his coat. Dust sanded his hair white and he couldn't get it out of the rough of the buckskin.

"After everything I did for you and your brother, you shoot *arrows* at me! That's the kind of fucking thanks I get here! You ruined my coat!"

Running Bear stared straight ahead with defiant eyes the color of thick black ink. Large hoop earrings jangled her neck and a string of colored beads looped her hair. Gary Chatoee walked to the teepee and whipped back the cloth opening.

"Gus, keep an eye on her for me," Reuger nodded, kneeling down by Gary.

The teepee smelled of wet blankets in a trunk with plastic bunched in the corners. Light peeped slats in the plywood. A Buddha incense burner crested a box of kitchen matches on folded blankets. Gary reached in and picked up a Sony boom box.

"Hmmm, Diana Ross and the Supremes." He turned. "I gave those to her, you know," he said pointing to the brown calf-high moccasins. "And this is the thanks I get. You tell these people to let this shit go... look at this," Gary said disgustedly. "Is this any way to live?"

Reuger stood.

"Let's go ask her if she's seen Tommy."

They stood around Running Bear with her arms crossed and back ramrod straight. Gary spoke to her in Ojibwa. She turned her nose up and said something that sounded like "Fuck you." Reuger nodded.

"What did she say, Gary?"

"Ya," she said. "Fuck you."

Reuger gestured with the rifle.

"Tell her that if she doesn't answer our questions here I'm going to put her in jail for assaulting a deputy sheriff."

"I didn't assault anybody," she snapped.

"I saw an arrow my way a few days ago from someone with their face painted black."

She glared at him, black eyes snapping like onyx.

"Poachers and trespassers are the only ones I chase off." She frowned and moved her shoulders. "Which one are you?"

Reuger walked in front of her. She jerked her chin away and looked over her shoulder.

"Running Bear, if I have to, I'll call in a seaplane here and have you picked up and taken back to a dark cell in Ely, where you'll sit until I get back."

"Ya, she's too stubborn and dumb to help herself," Gary muttered.

Her eyes narrowed, and she spoke quickly. Gary retorted and gestured to the woods. She jerked her chin up and spoke.

"She says Tommy came and went a day ago," he said glancing at Reuger. "She thinks he was headed for Manomin Lake....He said he was going to meet somebody."

Reuger pulled out his map and traced the lake with his finger. He looked at Gary.

"Trust her?"

"She might be lying, you know, but I told her if she wasn't telling the truth we would come back for her. She said her brother is an asshole who never fixes the cabin, and she wouldn't bother to lie for him."

Reuger squinted down the hill toward the lake.

"Then we have some portaging ahead of us then."

Running Bear spoke over her shoulder.

"Reuger, she wants to know if we can leave her some food?"

"Leave it on the shore," he nodded.

She broke her stance and went into the teepee with the leather flap coming down. Her hands appeared, then the flap was pulled in and lashed. Gus pissed by a red pine then went further into the woods with a roll of toilet paper. They waited around, and Gary walked to the teepee.

"We'll leave the food by the shore," he shouted outside the flap.

Gary waited then clapped his sides and shrugged. When Gus came back, they started down the narrow trail toward the boat.

40

PAIN BRANDED REUGER'S neck with the muddy path flowing under the curved tip of the canoe. He breathed heavily in the aluminum cavern with sweat banding his hat and tickling his nose. The shoulder pads of the canoe hammered his neck as Gus trudged behind carrying the fifty-pound pack with their tent and food. In each hand, he lugged a gun.

They had taken the boat as far as they could on Basswood Lake and left it in Rice Bay on a beach of slate-colored rocks. On Basswood, they passed an old scarred, wooden sluiceway, a remnant of the big log drives where water churned through in a white torrent. Through this narrowing wood trough, thousands of logs had passed on their way down to the mills on the lower lakes. They hiked a narrow portage trail with the canoes, headed for Manomin Lake.

After twenty minutes gluing the dark line, Gary stopped and swung his canoe down. Reuger lowered his canoe with relief rushing through his shoulder muscles as he stretched out the cramps moving through his neck. Gary had shed the buckskin coat and soaked his shirt through the back. Gus was hunched over with the pack, his arms weighed down by the shotgun and the Winchester like some old miner.

"Must be an old logging camp," Gary nodded, pointing through the trees.

Two headlights winked through a patch of wild sarsaparilla. The truck had bowl fenders and a rounded top with cyclopic headlights earring the radiator grill. The windshield was spidered with cracks and the truck body had rusted graveyard orange.

"CCC, I'd wager. Had camps all through here in the thirties,"

Gus nodded. “Somebody want to help me get out of this here mule harness?”

Gary lifted the heavy pack.

“Damn! That thing there will make yer old before yer time,” he said, stretching his back.

Reuger walked to the truck. He could smell the cooked leather of the seats and saw weeds below the floor where the metal had rotted. Gary put his boot on the running board.

“Ya, that Civilian Conservation Corps brought unemployed men to the forest and put them to work during the Depression, and they replanted these trees in straight rows. They were from the cities and were given white shirts and floppy hats.” Gary pulled on the radiator cap and shook his head. “They didn’t know shit.”

Gus shook his head.

“Yep, most had never handled an ax before and when the war came they all left.”

Gary Chatoee bent down and picked up a clear bottle and a flat red Folgers can.

“Syrup and coffee, ya, they were loggers, all right.”

“Yep, I was just a boy, but I remember these men come into the forest and weren’t a damn thing there, and they had to build their own cabins to sleep in.” Gus chuckled. “Cut a lot of trees and planted a lot but they was the skinniest bunch you ever saw.”

Reuger followed a series of rocks laid out in a walkway and looked over the clearing. An amber hunk of metal in a shrub of beaked hazel turned into an iron stove. An old water tank became a circular edifice of rust. He walked to a blackened fire ring and kneeled down next to Gary.

“What do you make of it?”

Gary brushed his hands in the ash then handed Reuger a brass shell.

“He was here, all right. Still warm. I found this in the coals. It’s a .44 you know.” Gary raised his eyebrow. “Magnum load for a Winchester.”

Reuger flipped around the shell and blew ash off a silver percussion cap.

41

THE FIRE BURNED fast, crackling cedar and birch and glimmering blue on the Winchester and shotgun. When they finished the three frozen steaks, they sat around the fire and drank coffee sweetened by condensed milk. The lantern hissed from a branch and the coffee pot spouted; a strip of cold dusk lined the pines.

Gary Chatoee rested on his elbow with his coat spreading out like amber grass.

"So...who's this girl Tommy's supposed to have raped."

Reuger stoked the fire up then leaned back. "Sixteen-year-old looking for answers in the wrong places."

"Like a woodshed," Gary scoffed. "What was she doing in there?"

"I don't know."

"So what's she say now?"

"Haven't talked to her since it happened," Reuger answered.

"Well, he must have done it if she said Tommy was the one!" Gus cocked his eyebrow. "But that damn Riechardt won't let us near the girl now."

"Ya." Gary nodded. "He wants to protect her and make sure they lay it on an Indian."

"Tried to kill herself sure as day, and if Reuger there hadn't gone a knockin' on her door at the Stafford, she would have!" Gus spat off to the side again. "Dug into her wrists with a razor, that one did."

"Ya, she's sitting on something then," Gary said with the flames in his dark eyes.

"Somebody's getting nervous," Reuger murmured. "Had a bullet through my kitchen window a couple of days ago."

Gary sat up.

"They tried to shoot you?"

"They wanted to make a point."

"Things are getting out of hand here," Gus gestured with his pipe. "Yer better be more careful."

Gary frowned and stoked the fire, shooting sparks toward the trees.

"Sounds like Tommy maybe. Probably thinks you betrayed him or some shit by going after him. I don't know much about this police work here, but when I saw Jorde out there at the reservation trying to talk to Tommy and then these loggers end up dead, you know," Gary gestured to the darkness. "I started thinking that maybe they're in it together, and maybe Jorde hired him to do it, you know. Maybe even rape the fucking girl."

Reuger crossed one boot over the other.

"You and the sheriff think alike."

"I don't know," he shrugged. "But maybe they figured you know it would get the lodge in trouble there or maybe Tommy just went crazy and did it anyway." Gary gestured to the darkness. "I've known Tommy a long time, and I always hoped he'd change his ways, you know. I hoped on the reservation he would grow up to be somebody that would help the people." He shook his head. "But he was always just a fuck-up and made a lot of trouble for everyone, and now he's done it again by raping this white girl."

"Innocent until proven guilty," Reuger pointed out. Gary stared at the eyes under the brim.

"Maybe." He turned. "But it's probably better if this thing here is solved and done with you know. Tommy Tobin fucked up one too many times the way I see it, and somebody has to hang for it so the tourists can feel safe again."

"Doesn't sound like justice."

"Ya, since when did this country give a fuck about justice?" Gary's dark eyes burned with the firelight. "Maybe when they exterminated the Indians and corralled the rest into concentration camps so they would starve and die of disease and took their lands, their trees, their nation. Is that justice?" Gary plunged another log into the flames. "The only justice in this country is what you take."

The crackle of the fire returned then a wolf howl echoed in the cavern of the lake.

"Song of the kill," Gus said, turning. "Toward Canada."

"Best those wolves stay there," Gary nodded, pushing a log into the center. They listened to the howl echo through the forest again.

"Ya, Tommy Tobin's had some bad troubles," Gary nodded slowly.

A cedar log popped, sending a spark outside the lava rocks. The coffee pot boiled and steamed from the spout. Gary's mouth turned down.

"He should enjoy his last night in the forest of his fathers."

42

THEY PADDLED OVER boulders beneath the water with the old logs from the drives just below the surface. The water was so clear a person could reach down and grab one of the yellowed rocks. Reuger dipped his paddle, passing through water lilies floating on the water like coasters. The sun glared hotly off the lake as he paddled for the trees and saw a portage trail leading into the forest.

They pulled the canoes into the pebbly beach then into the trees. Gary kneeled to the ground, touching low branches, examining the chopped mud of the path. "Reuger. These tracks are old." Gary walked hunched over. "These are fresh here. The mud is dried, but a heavy man walked over this and broke the crust down."

Reuger stared at the hacked-up mud.

"Where?"

"Right there." Gary pointed. "See the ridge in the mud there?"

"No."

"Well, it's there," he nodded. "Maybe last night someone walked down the path you know. Maybe this morning."

Reuger stood up and stared down the portage trail.

"All right, you take the lead for now, Gary."

They moved quickly down the trail with the tassels of Gary's coat flying back. The trees closed in for a mile into the forest then pulled back for a clearing of swamp and tamarack then a wall of pines.

"Fresh tracks here, Reuger, maybe this morning," Gary nodded, kneeling.

"We better get going..."

"Wait a *goddang minute* for an old man to take a piss will you, darn it!"

Gus pissed on a pine while they waited.

"Don't know how you two can go all day and not take a dern piss!"

"Don't drink as much water as you do," Gary shrugged.

"All right." He zipped up. "Let's go."

They moved back into shadowy darkness and sweated heavily in the close air. The trail opened as they followed the snaking path around trees and through dry creeks and into swamps. They hiked through the forest for another twenty minutes when Gary hunched down suddenly. Reuger crawled up next to him and saw sawdust blanketing the fireweed and second growth like yellow lava.

"Looks like someone cut up some trees here, but I don't see any stumps," he murmured.

"Someone's doing a little poaching," Reuger replied, nodding. "Let's go have a look."

They walked through the sawdust and examined the fallen tree.

"Must've dragged it," Gus nodded, "I don't see any cut trees around here."

Gary stopped and kneeled down.

"Reuger..."

He lifted a pie-shaped remnant.

"By God, that's from a tree the size of a mountain, Reuger," Gus nodded.

The old wood was deep red. The rings were so close together they looked as if someone had drawn them with precision.

Gus shut one eye. "Lot like the piece we found there at Foster's slasher, Reuger."

"Oh, ya," he nodded, fingering the wood.

Gary walked into the sun. Light shone in his black hair and laced the shoulders of his coat. He turned then fell to the ground as a shot cracked from the trees. Reuger dove and held the shotgun by his cheek in the wood shavings. Gus fell back with the Winchester clutched to his chest as bullets puffed sawdust like spouts of water.

"Gary!"

Blood stained his shoulder in a long creep toward his waist.

"Yeah," he muttered toward the ground.

"Can you move?" Reuger called just above a whisper.

"Maybe, but I think I'm shot in the shoulder." He talked into his arm like a man sleeping. "Don't think it's bad, but I have to let them think they killed me because they have you pinned down there."

Reuger searched the trees. Stump wood exploded and two more

spouts jumped from the ground. The shots died back into the silence. He squinted into the forest again then looked at the glassy blood on Gary's shoulder.

"All right...stay there, Gary."

"Ya, well, I don't think I'm going to run a fucking marathon, you know," he mumbled into his arm.

"Gus!"

Gus lay on his back with the Winchester.

"I'm going for the woods and need you to cover me."

"Yer think yer can make it with them firing at us?"

"You just reach up there and empty your shells."

"I'll do it but don't know what I'll hit..."

"Ya, you guys want to stop your discussion group there while I'm fucking bleeding to death here?" Gary muttered into his arm.

"All right," Reuger nodded. "Count of three...one... two...*three!"*

Gus wheeled and fired as Reuger dove into the trees then grappled shells from his vest. He slammed the loads into the slide of the shotgun and started through the forest. Sharp branches whipped his arms and face with the shotgun slippery in his hand.

Reuger clambered up a ridge heaving breath, running through high weeds falling down into a swale then through a wet glade dampening his arms and pants. He clambered up another ridge and was knocked back. The shotgun flew from his hands and he fell back and tasted dirt. He stopped rolling and struggled up to the dark hole of a barrel.

Al Hanes shook his head slowly.

"Always where you're not supposed to fucking be."

Reuger saw the trigger squeeze before the short, whiffing, *bang!* Then something dark flew toward him and he was rolling down the ridge in the iron scent of blood.

43

GUS PICKED UP the Winchester and blew sawdust out of the loading sleeve then cocked the rifle. Two men trudged like convicts in the gray light with one man slightly ahead of the other. Gary Chatoee saw them and said nothing as Gus pressed the rifle to his cheek, then brought it down. He lowered the gun to his waist.

"Called in the seaplane, should be here in an hour or two," Reuger called walking up behind Tommy Tobin.

Gus shook his head slowly.

"Almost shot yer there."

"Glad you didn't," Reuger said, coming to a halt.

Gary Chatoee stared at him.

"What the hell happened to you?"

Reuger looked down at his vest of blood from pocket to waist. Blood matted the hair of his forearms and reached down to one hand like crust.

"Al Hanes bled all over me," he said slowly. "He's dead up there in the forest."

Gus's face drained of color, his mouth ogling for air.

"Yer mean to say, the foreman of Johnson Timber, *Al Hanes*, was pumpin' them bullets?"

That's right," he nodded. "He was waiting for us."

Gary Chatoee glared at Tommy Tobin and touched his own shirt covered in blood. "You put this here, then?"

"Al put that bullet there," Reuger nodded. "He was dressed from head to foot in hunting gear."

"How about that blood on yer vest?" Gus asked, pointing with the Winchester. "How'd yer get that close?"

Reuger gestured to the forest.

"I came up over a ridge, Al knocked me back, and I lost the shotgun. He was going to finish the job when Tommy shot him from behind and we went down the ridge together."

Gus pointed to Tommy Tobin. "He done that?"

Reuger sat on a stump and lapped the shotgun, one boot over his knee. Heat rolled the cut pine and sawdust like the inside of a barn. He remembered pushing up the man with so much blood he wasn't sure whether it was his own. He panicked under the weight until Tommy pulled him off and threw Al Hanes to the side like so much beef.

"You want to tell us what's been going on, Tommy?"

"God, ya, I like to know what in damnation been going on too," Gus grumbled, propping the Winchester against a stump and sitting.

Tommy stood with his hooked nose flattened against his cheeks like a fighter. Hair caved his neck as he squinted against the glare with the rifle crooked in his arm. His army coat was covered in dried mud. No jack pine beetles, no wind, no droning plane, loons, wolves, nothing. Gus spat. Once.

"Ya ain't deaf, are yer?" he nearly shouted.

Tommy shrugged.

Reuger stood up with the Winchester in his right hand.

"Why'd you run, Tommy?"

He stood like a man in a courtroom. Crickets flipped backwards over the stumps and logs and sawdust. His eyes hardened, and Reuger saw nothing at all, then his eyes blinked slowly.

"What are you doing up here?"

Tommy rolled his big shoulders.

"That Al Hanes." He gestured the rifle. "He come to Center Island and say he had some work for me up here. But I didn't trust him, you know, so I come up to see what he's going to do." Tommy looked up, eyes dull like an iron frying pan. "So I stay hidden until I heard him start shooting at you. Then I tracked him. I watched him, and I could hear you coming, and I knew he could too." Tommy paused. "I saw him raise his rifle and wait, and I knew he had you..." Tommy nodded slowly and raised his rifle. "So I drew a bead on him, you know, and when I saw you come out...I shot him."

Reuger felt chills down in his stomach and his bowels felt weak. Al Hanes was going to kill him, but this man had stopped all that. This man had saved his life twice.

"You reload your own, Tommy?"

"Nope," he said shaking his head.

"Let me have your rifle there."

Tommy handed the Winchester with the barrel to the sky. Reuger levered the shells into his hand. He flipped the .44 magnum loads around in his hand; the percussion caps gleaming like diamonds in coal. He felt his soul shrink. The percussion caps matched the shell he found behind his cabin. It matched the one he found in the fire by the old logging camp. "Do you have any more ammo?"

He pulled out his hand and clutched loose cartridges. He palmed them to Reuger. They were .30.30 rounds and .44 magnum loads, all reloads. Reuger jumped the shells in his hand and there was a .22. Reuger held up the smaller cartridge and saw the silver cap.

"I need you to turn around here and put your hands on your head for me."

Gus held both rifles while Tommy turned and touched his head. Reuger pulled his handcuffs off his belt and reached up.

"You're under arrest for the rape of Dana Reynolds," he said in a low voice.

The handcuffs clicked tight. Reuger turned him around and took the Winchester from Gus. Tommy stared down, his eyes like lanterns up on a dark mountain.

"Maybe I should have let you get shot, you know."

Reuger didn't turn from his gaze and felt wooden.

"I can't let this one go, Tommy. You're too far in."

"No," he nodded. "But you let the other one go, don't you?"

Gary opened his eyes with his back against the stump.

"Ya, you fucked up this time, Tommy."

44

THE LAKE WAS corrugated with ripples and small white triangles. Reuger sat in the copilot's seat with Tommy and Gary in the second seat and Gus in the back. He stared down at ovals of glass and bushy trees as they glided toward the gray finger of the dock. Thunderheads passed the plane, and Reuger smelled rain. He turned and looked at Gary and remembered their conversation in the woods.

"So what do you think?"

"Ya, he did it. I think he's lying about everything," he nodded while they were waiting for the plane to land. "It's his destiny you know. It's the path Tommy has followed all his life. You can't change these things. " Gary nodded slowly. "He knows that too."

"I wonder where he got those reloads."

"He bought some ammo from me at the store, but I don't carry any reloads."

Reuger saw the sheriff and two deputies looking up from the pier. He glanced at Tommy crammed into the plane, staring at the uniformed men. They floated through the clouds toward the green surface with his stomach leaving like a Ferris wheel's descent. Water became a solid mass then rippling green, then the plane jerked back and skied the surface. Irene Peters turned off the engine as water slopped over the pontoons. The two deputies grabbed the wings and secured the plane.

"All right, now let's get the wounded man out here," Riechardt commanded while paramedics lowered Gary to a stretcher.

Tommy stepped out from the pilot side door and squinted. Reuger took him by the arm and heard thunder over the lake. The sheriff waited on the dock with his hands on his gun belt. He spat a seed into the still water.

"Ready to receive the prisoner, Reuger."

He raised his hand.

"I can handle it, Sheriff."

The sheriff stepped forward.

"I said I'm ready to receive the prisoner."

Reuger felt Tommy stiffen as the two deputies fingered their revolvers. Thunder rumbled the lake again. The sheriff glanced at the deputies, and they pulled their pistols.

"Now, give me the prisoner, Reuger!"

Riechardt grabbed Tommy and spun him around.

"Hands on the plane and spread your feet!" The sheriff kicked his boots wide and patted down his coat. "What do we have here?"

He pulled out a silver bracelet with two small diamonds in the center.

"This is that girl's bracelet here," he nodded. "You're under arrest for the murder of Al Hanes and the rape of Dana Reynolds. Turn your head around! "

"Reuger..."

Tommy said it under his breath. He said it the way an animal might grunt when trapped. Reuger saw the fear in his eyes.

"Shut up!"

Rain spotted the planks and, lightning touched down on Center Island. Sheets of wind gusted and wavered the wings of the plane.

"You're going away for a long time, boy."

"Reuger..."

"He's not going to help you, boy," Riechardt sneered. "He's done his duty here," the sheriff nodded as the deputies struggled with the handcuffs. "You'd go to the chair if this state had the death penalty."

The rain came down heavily and jumped in the water and darkened the planks on the dock. They all stood silently, and then Tommy turned, and Reuger saw his eyes when the snow hissed down.

He had his forefinger on the trigger of the .38 with the hammer back. The cold steel in his hand. He was about to put it in his mouth.

"Go away."

"Nope."

The shaggy head of snow draping down black silk. Reuger stared at him, a man at the gates of the abyss.

"Why do you give a fuck?"

Tommy shrugged, holding the cold joint like a cross.

"I don't know...but maybe you'll do something for me one day, you know."

Tommy turned suddenly and whipped the free handcuff across the deputies' faces. He lashed the men twice as they fell back to the dock. He turned and ran down the planks of the dock as the deputies recovered and pulled their pistols. Reuger watched the men crouch into the firing position with Tommy running like a figure in a slow motion movie. He stepped forward and swung his Winchester down, cluttering their guns to the dock then into the water.

The sheriff unsnapped his holster and pulled his Smith & Wesson.

"Goddammit, Reuger..."

Reuger clamped the gun down and they struggled like two men dancing cheek to cheek.

"Let go, you son of a bitch!"

He shouldered the sheriff back and tore the gun from his hand. He threw the pistol into the corrugated lake. Riechart's face turned red. "You just made one fuck of a mistake, mister!"

The sheriff grabbed the shotgun from Gus's hand and brought the nineteen-inch barrel up. Reuger stared at the two eyes hard as nickels and felt his heart in his chest. He could see the pulse in the older man's temple.

"Easy now, Sheriff," he said in a low voice. "You're making a mistake now..."

"Shut up!" He shouted. "Disarm this man and cuff him for assaulting a police officer!"

The deputies were still holding their wrists. They hesitated.

"Do it!"

Reuger let the two men take his weapons and motioned Gus back. He knew the deputies as younger men who Riechardt had recently hired. They had identical crew cuts and pink skin. Hector told him they followed the sheriff around like bodyguards.

"Cuff him!" Riechardt commanded.

Reuger felt his arms pulled back and faced the sheriff with water dribbling from his hat brim. He motioned the shotgun.

"Put him in the car! "

The sheriff spun around then and faced Irene Peters. Lightning spidered down from a thunderhead over the lake. Rain swept the lake sideways and the concussion of the thunder rolled over the land.

"I need you to take me up now to recover an escaped prisoner!"

Irene stared at him in her dark aviation sunglasses.

"I'm not going up in this shit here."

"This is police business!" Riechardt shouted with the gun up.

Irene pushed the barrel of the shotgun away.

"And this is my business, you sonofabitch, and I'm not going to auger my plane into a lake in the middle of a storm!"

The deputies pulled Reuger down the pier and shoved him in the back seat of the squad car. Rain hammered the roof and dribbled down his back. He struggled against the handcuffs biting his wrists then turned toward the rainy forest where Tommy had disappeared. He saw a low mist rolling the tree line like snow.

45

REUGER OPENED HIS eyes in the cabin darkness then picked up a .38 from the bedside table. He crossed the cabin and saw Patricia outside the front door in a jeans jacket, white shorts and hiking boots. She shaded her eyes against the porch light.

"I didn't mean to wake you."

"It wasn't loaded," he muttered. "Let me throw on a shirt."

Reuger yawned back into the bedroom and looked at the covers and headed pillow. He put the gun back in the drawer.

"If it's too late, I can leave."

"No, I'll be just a minute," he called back, slipping on a T-shirt, socks, and a pair of mukluks with the strings missing.

She was in one of the armchairs.

"Coffee," he grumbled, putting on his hat from the mantel.

Reuger popped the Hills Bros. can open and loaded the grounds, spilling granules on the counter, then poured water that slopped and mixed. He struck a kitchen match and flared the pot then walked back and sat down. The cloth of the chair was rough against his legs. A scent of creosote and pipe tobacco smote the cold corners of stone and wood.

He yawned again.

"Time is it?"

"Three a.m.," she said quietly.

"Early ..." He rubbed his eyes. "How's the work going?"

Patricia stood and walked to the mantel with the jean jacket pulled around her. He noticed her legs against the shorts and the way her calf muscles flexed. She stared at his empty holster on the nail and turned against the hearth.

"Tom Jorde fired me."

"We're both off the case then." Reuger waved his hand. "It's a long story."

Patricia fingered the holster again, and it fell. She picked up the leather worn dark from the oil of the Colt.

"I'm sorry."

"Don't worry about it—it's an old holster."

"No, I meant about the case."

"Don't worry about that, either."

Patricia put the holster back on the nail and patted it lightly. The buckle swung free like a tendril.

"Where's your gun?"

"Long story again." He crossed his legs and took off his hat. "So what happened with Jorde?"

She stared at the blackened firebox. Wind roared outside like some low creature passing over the cabin. He thought he could hear her breathing.

"If you don't want to talk about it, that's fine."

"No." She turned around. "Tom Jorde felt he wanted a lawyer who…well…"

"Wasn't having sex with the deputy sheriff?" He tilted his head up. "You could have told him we weren't having sex anymore."

She smoothed back her hair and put one foot on the fireplace ledge. Her calf balled up above her sock.

"I won't deny that having a relationship with you complicated matters," she nodded running her finger along the curve of the lantern glass.

"Thought that was over too. Did you tell Jorde that? He could talk about it when he went on John Mcfee's program again and say, ya, I think the deputy sheriff and the lawyer for Earth First were having a relationship, but from what I hear it's over."

She stared at him again. The coffee sputtered and scowled in the kitchen and the room smelled like morning suddenly.

"Let's talk about something else," he suggested, waving his hand. "Kurt back from Outward Bound yet?"

"How…"

"I know the leader of Outward Bound and told him to keep an eye on him and let me know how's he doing."

Patricia leaned back against the stone chimney.

"You don't want to hear this. Not after the way I acted…"

"Nonsense. I'm glad you came by."

She shook her head slowly.

"It's just, it's just I woke up tonight and felt so lonely. I hope Kurt is all right."

Reuger kneeled on the hearth and began throwing newspaper into the fireplace. The balling paper was loud and tufted open on the grill. He scraped a copper bin over and tossed in stick pine with his knees on the cold stone. He chunked a log in and struck a match.

"Outward Bound is a professional organization, Patricia." He pushed the wood further back and lit the paper. They watched the flames curl the paper then leap to the dry stick pine. "I'm sure he's having the time of his life there."

She sat down and held her hands out to the small flames.

"How do you like your coffee?"

"I'll take some milk if you have any."

Reuger went into the kitchen and poured the coffee then added milk to her mug. He walked back and handed Patricia the mug and scraped the chairs up close.

"That should take the chill out here."

"Thank you."

She sipped the coffee then tapped the enamel with her fingernails.

"Johnson Timber?"

"Worked there a long time."

Patricia looked back at the lettering on the mug.

"Uh oh. There's that Earth First lawyer look."

She held the coffee between her knees and looked at him.

"Reuger, Tom Jorde told me you still work for Ben Johnson."

"He's wrong," he said, sipping the coffee.

She leaned forward with firelight in her auburn hair.

"He said you did security work for him."

"I did before." He lowered the mug. "But haven't for a long time."

Patricia paused and looked down at the floor.

"He said you're still on Ben Johnson's payroll and could prove it."

"Do you think so, Patricia?"

"Are you?"

"I get a check every now and then for security work." Reuger breathed heavily and shook his head. "Make no mistake, Patricia. Tom Jorde has his own agenda."

The fire popped and threw shadows around the small cabin. Patricia watched the fire with amber playing on her cheeks.

"Ben Johnson controls the town, doesn't he?"

"Only industry around to employ people. Johnson Timber leaves or gets forced out by environmentalists, then there's only tourism. And that's not enough to keep people working." He held the mug down. "So, in that way, he does control the town."

Patricia stared at the large stones of the fireplace and the scorched smooth marble of the hearth, then the soot-blackened lantern next to a row of books next to the empty holster. She felt herself relax.

"I'd like to apologize." She looked down. "For the way I've acted toward you."

"Not a problem. I think I was probably a little pigheaded myself."

She smiled faintly.

"Not much ruffles you."

"Not much."

She tapped the coffee mug again and stared at him.

"Uh oh, here it comes again," he murmured. "The lawyer just walked in."

"Why are you off the case?"

Reuger walked into the kitchen and picked up the pot of coffee. He walked back in and filled Patricia's cup then his own.

"I mean we can talk about it now..."

"Hold on."

He returned the pot and wiped down the stove then went back and picked up the mug from the floor. He felt her eyes and leaned back in the chair and was suddenly tired. He thought of the moment on the dock when he swung the Winchester down on the deputies. He had destroyed his career in that moment. He wasn't even sure what sort of choice he had made. He had saved Tommy Tobin's life, but as a deputy sheriff he had failed.

Reuger told her of the events up in the Boundary Waters. He told her of the reloads in Tommy Tobin's rifle and how that proved to him he was lying. Then he told her what happened when he returned.

"I let myself be affected by something that happened long ago," he said dully.

The crackling fire filled the silence.

"Tommy made a break, and I didn't want Riechardt's deputies to shoot him in the back," he said flatly. "So I knocked their guns down and kept the sheriff from shooting him." Reuger frowned and shook his head. "But that doesn't change what I did."

Someone tapped the window and Patricia jumped.

"It's a dogwood too close to the house."

"It sounds like someone tapping the glass," she said, pulling her jacket tightly around her. "You arrested him for the rape of that poor girl?"

"Yes."

"A lot of people have left the lodge." Patricia stared at the fire. "I considered leaving."

"I wouldn't blame you."

She brushed back her short thick hair and looked at him. He had lost something. There was a different air about him now, she thought, almost like a bewildered boy.

"But you don't think this Tommy Tobin raped her?"

"It's my job to bring the suspect in regardless of my feelings."

"Or keep them from being shot," she said quietly.

"Tommy knew the risk of his actions."

Patricia pursed her lips, blinking through the smoky light.

"You sound like someone trying to sell something he doesn't believe in."

Reuger stood then pokered a log to the back of the fire box.

"I didn't create the situation here." He held the poker against the flames. "And I can't change it."

"So you just turn the other way like everyone else?"

Reuger turned around.

"Come again?"

"Maybe I don't understand everything going on up here, all right." She gestured to the ceiling. "But I see Ben Johnson doing whatever he wants, and I don't see anyone stopping him!"

"That's not my job," he muttered, turning back to the fire.

Patricia stared at him in his T-shirt without his hat or gun.

"I also see someone hiding from himself," she said in a low voice.

Reuger leaned the poker against the hearth.

"You sure you're not still working for Tom Jorde?"

Patricia snapped up the mug.

"He owns everybody, Reuger!"

"That what Tom Jorde thinks, Patricia?"

"Of course he does!"

"Who's he think killed Foster Jones and Carter Grisom?"

Patricia stared at him. "I don't know..."

"Maybe someone used Tom Jorde's gun to murder Carter and maybe someone left his buttons by Foster and maybe someone happened to leave a spike in Carter's tree." He sparked the fire again with the poker. "But that doesn't change that he's a radical environmentalist who has said he'll do whatever it takes to stop the logging up here. Jorde may have been right about the logging, but it didn't give him the right to murder."

"It's all a set up, and you know it, Reuger," she muttered.

He turned back to the fire and stoked in another log. He didn't know what he thought anymore. All he knew now was that the problems of the world had found him once again, and he wanted to get away. He wanted to leave.

"Tom Jorde should have never let you go," he said, leaning the poker against the chimney.

"Fuck it." Patricia stood up. "You want to play your little games, then go ahead. But I don't have to take your patronizing shit."

"What about yours?" Reuger faced her. "You come up here and think you know what's best for people, then you go back to your home in the city while people up here have to deal with the mess you've created. I've seen more dead wildlife in these lakes from your acid rain than a hundred fishermen or hunters could ever create. I've seen pine trees turned ash white from the shit that floats up from your factories and down on the forest up here. Do you know there's fish up here with PCBs? That didn't come from logging or hunters," he said shaking his head. "That came from people who consume three-quarters of the energy of the planet."

"Why don't you say it," she snapped. "The mess a bunch of tree huggers created."

He sat down and looked up at her.

"You just did."

Patricia marched across the room and slammed the door behind her. A breeze flared the fire brimstone red. Reuger sipped his coffee. It was cold and the fire had burned down. The cabin was closing in on him as he listened to the expiring wood. He stared at the curved white lettering on the mug then stood and walked back into his bedroom. He pulled open the top drawer of his dresser and dug below some socks and underwear. There were ten envelopes rubber banded together. The last one had a postmark of just last month.

46

THE FOREST RIMMED the galvanized link fence. A mill saw whined across the parking lot of Johnson Timber as Reuger parked. John Mcfee walked out from behind a truck in a stovepipe hat.

"So yer been thrown off the force I hear there, Reuger," he called one eye closed against the sun and gesturing to where his badge was.

Reuger breathed heavily. "What are you doing out here, John?"

"I came here to give Ben Johnson a chance here to discount what this reporter has found through tireless investigation."

"What's that?"

"Well now Reuger, yer will have to do your own gumshoe work here but I will take this opportunity to ask yer a few questions on the rape here of this sixteen-year-old girl and yer having let go the perpetrator, Tommy Tobin."

"No comment."

"Yer mean to say yer don't want to tell your side of it here? I know Riechardt fired yer, and you must think he is innocent to have stopped law enforcement from apprehending the perpetrator."

Reuger rested his hands on his gun belt.

"You mean shooting him in the back?"

"That's good," he muttered scribbling the pad. "But I need to know yer motives here..."

"You're loving this aren't you, John?"

"What say?"

Reuger gestured to his pad.

"You have your story now. Your environmental war."

Mcfee grinned wide and cocked his shoulder.

"Can't say I'm not enjoying the ride, but like I say, I need to know your motivation there for letting Tommy Tobin go."

"Don't tell me your sources, then you get no comment."

Mcfee bit his lip and squeezed one eye closed.

"I'll tell you then," he nodded. "It was that Jorde who told me Johnson Timber has a plan to log out the Boundary Waters."

"Too thin, John," Reuger said turning and walking toward the office.

"You mean…yer aren't going to tell me your side of it here? And what I might ask are yer doing at Johnson Timber, Reuger?"

"Make it up, John. That's what you do best anyway," he called back, pushing open the door to a blond girl with flawless skin.

"Ben here?"

"Yes…" She glanced nervously at the door. "May I help you?"

"Nope," he said walking in with his boots loud on the tile floor.

"I think he's on the phone…"

Reuger swung the door open to a slant of sun creasing the brim of a Stetson. Ben Johnson held a cigar below his mouth then leaned forward.

"Call you back," he muttered, dropping the phone next to his Stetson. "You always barge into a man's office unannounced?"

Reuger walked to the wide mahogany desk corned by two brass lamps with gold pens saluting the front. He tossed a rubber-banded wad of dirty envelopes on the desk.

"Only when I'm returning money."

"What the hell is this?"

Reuger swung into a chair and booted his knee.

"Checks you keep sending me in the mail. Taking up to much space in my sock drawer."

Ben fingered the envelopes. Behind him were pictures of men shaking hands with the big money of Northern Minnesota. A double-headed ax was propped in the corner.

"You saving up for something?"

"Thought about a new jeep but the price was too high," Reuger replied, staring at the chair. "Bruce Anderson has a chair just like this with the arm missing. You two should meet sometime."

"That right?" Ben leaned back and nodded to the window. "You with that crackpot Mcfee out there?"

"No. Can't say I am."

"You notice Penny is not here," he said nodding to the open door. "She's making arrangements for her husband's funeral after that fucking Indian murdered him."

"That Indian kept Al from shooting me." Reuger held his hand up. "Unless he was up there deer hunting, and I got in the way."

"I don't know what happened up there. All I know is, I have a dead foreman and you let the sonofabitch *go* who shot him!"

"What was Al doing up there, Ben?"

"How should I know? It was his day off, maybe he was fishing."

"Maybe he was logging."

Ben nodded to the phone.

"That was your sheriff. They just brought Al Hanes back. Doesn't seem like things happened the way you said there, Reuger. He was unarmed and shot in the back and your friend Gary Chatoee says he thinks Tommy Tobin shot him and then murdered Al Hanes."

Reuger felt a shock but kept his face smooth. He stared at the man behind the big desk.

"Right before Al decided to have a little target practice, I saw a mountain of sawdust, Ben. A mountain of sawdust far up in the Boundary Waters and a remnant the size of a man's leg." Reuger stood up and walked to a yellow map of the Superior National Forest going all the way up to Canada." Here's where it gets interesting, Ben. I was looking at this map last night. Here is where Gary Chatoee was shot by Al Hanes, and this is where I found the remains of a very large tree," he said tapping the map just below the Canadian line.

"You going fishing Reuger?" Ben gestured toward the window." Because the fucking lake is that way if you are."

"See the way you can almost draw an arc from one location to the next? Guess what's behind this arc, Ben?" Reuger faced the man in his chair. "…The Old Pines."

Ben yawned and lifted his hand.

"So what."

"I just want to know where all that sawdust came from, Ben."

"How the fuck should I know?" Ben leaned back and nodded. "If I wanted to log up there, I would just go ahead and do it. I have Indian treaties going all the way up to Canada that give me the right to log."

"Those treaties are worthless, Ben."

"Not according to the Indians or the government." Ben Johnson laughed shortly. "You are one queer duck. You let go a rapist and a murderer, then you come here. Are you still screwing Tom Jorde's lawyer too?" He laughed shortly. "She's not bad looking, Reuger. Bet you two talk about all the terrible things being done to the forest after you're done fucking."

Reuger nodded slowly.

"She was right about one thing."

"What's that?"

"No one's ever stopped you."

Ben shook his head.

"You know who was in my office the other day, Reuger? The governor. That sonofabitch doesn't give a shit about a bunch of trees. What he does give a shit about is how much money I give him for his campaign. He was going to send troops up here to protect my loggers. It's all over the Minneapolis papers about how loggers are getting murdered by radical environmentalists."

Ben crossed his arms and nodded.

"Surprised you're still here. Figured when Riechardt gave you your walking papers you'd drift somewhere else, because that's all you are, a drifter, my friend, who never learned what side he was on up here."

"You don't own the land anymore."

"Shit!" He stabbed out the cigar and rolled back his sleeves. "They just wanted the wood to build, and they didn't give a fuck how I got it or where I got it from!" He kicked back from the desk. "And now for some sons of bitches who live in a city a thousand miles from here to come up and tell me what I can and can't do in the forest. The woods belong to the men who work in there and not to a bunch of goddamn swampys who decide on their two-week vacation they want to look at the goddamn trees!"

Reuger listened to the screech of the mill outside the window. Ben jabbed the cigar across the desk.

"And for you to back these sonofabitches after what people done for you up here." He leaned back. "The men in this town need work, and I give them that. I wouldn't want to get between a man trying to put food on the table for his family and his job."

"You don't give a damn about the men in this town."

Ben turned and stared out the window.

"People know what you're doing too. I wouldn't go down too many logging roads at night if I were you."

"Who raped the girl, Ben?"

He turned in from the window.

"That Indian you let get away at Pine Lodge."

"Think so?"

Ben shook his head and smiled faintly.

"Best thing I ever had the sheriff do was get rid of you. You think people in this town give a shit about some spoiled slut from Chicago and some drunken Indian?" He pointed out the window. "What they care about is trees that will bring millions of dollars into this town and give the men work."

"Millions of dollars for you."

He leaned back and nodded.

"I am this town."

Ben picked up the wad of checks and threw it across the desk.

"Now take that and get out, and maybe I'll tell Riechardt you learned your lesson and can play deputy again."

"You keep it." Reuger stood and opened the door. "You'll need it."

47

EARTH FIRST WAS empty and the light from the picture windows wavered on the far wall like sun through an aquarium. Reuger crossed the old planks of the grocery store that still smelled of paper bags and faintly of spoiled beef. He saw light from under a door stenciled MANAGER. He paused then pushed the door open slowly.

Tom Jorde was bent over his computer. Reuger pushed the door open farther, and Jorde looked up.

"What the fuck are you doing here?"

"Thought we might have a little talk...I heard you made bail."

He leaned back and crossed his arms.

"Oh, so *now* you want to talk."

Reuger nodded, pulling up a folding chair and taking off his hat.

Jorde shook his head slowly.

"You can't play deputy anymore, and you want to be my best friend. What's the matter? You aren't bending over for Johnson and the sheriff anymore?"

"Never did."

"Get out of here" he muttered leaning close to the screen again.

Reuger picked up a pencil from the desk.

"What makes you think Johnson Timber is logging up in the Boundary Waters?"

"Why should I tell you?"

"Might be able to help you."

"Yeah." He continued, typing on the keyboard. "Help me do what?"

"Stop him."

Jorde paused then slid back from the screen and turned.

"You stick me in jail for a murder I didn't commit, and now you say you want to help me?"

Reuger nodded.

"About right, but I need to know why you think Ben Johnson's logging up there."

Jorde laughed shortly.

"What's the matter? You let Tommy Tobin go so now you can just kill him up there in the woods, and no one will know the difference." Jorde shook his head. "You cover yourself with this charade of being a deputy, but I know you're a logger on the take and have been for years."

"You know what, Tom?" Reuger faced the smaller man. "You think too much."

He opened the door and crossed the planks of the store.

"Reuger!"

He turned and could barely see Jorde in the shadows.

"What do I get?"

Reuger shrugged. "A chance to see Ben Johnson behind bars."

They faced each other across the dusty space.

"It was a logger…a logger told me about Johnson Timber."

"What'd he say?"

Jorde paused.

"He said they were going for the Old Pines."

Reuger turned and walked back into the store. He saw stubble dark around Tom Jorde's chin.

"Anything else?"

"He said he had evidence. He said he could prove it."

"Did you get it?"

"No, they shot Foster before he could tell me. So now what the fuck are you going to do?"

Reuger paused.

"Think I'll go to Canada."

48

REUGER STEPPED OUT of the cab in Toronto and entered Mother of Mercy Hospital. The sergeant had been skeptical about his coming. He was used to that. Jurisdictional squabbles went on all the time around the Canadian-American line. They were Americans who had been camping and crossed into Canada. They had been attacked in their tent with baseball bats. The husband was dead and the girl was just hanging on. But they were still Americans, and the sergeant said the woman was slightly better.

The sun was blinding, then the lobby was dark. Everything was very clean and cheery. A few people looked up at the man in the large brimmed green hat and cowboy boots. He nodded to a few nurses and asked at the desk for the name the sergeant had given him. They had identified the couple as being from Chicago. He was a photographer for National Geographic, and she was a lawyer. They were to be married this month. It was tragic.

Reuger counted off the room numbers and found the intensive care ward. He walked quietly, trying to stifle the heel of his boot. A man in a red uniform with a hat bigger than his own and a handlebar mustache was at the door. Reuger noticed his ruddy skin and absurdly blue eyes.

Sgt. Haverford," he said with a handshake as crisp as a salute.

"Deputy Sheriff Reuger."

"Right, well, I'm not sure what you hope to accomplish here, Deputy. She is quite weak and still unable to talk." He lowered his voice. "The doctors feel that even if she survives she will be severely handicapped."

Reuger nodded, staring into the dim room. He could hear a respirator and the whir and beep of life support machines.

"I just wanted to show her a picture, Sergeant. My guess is she and her husband ran into some people up there who didn't want to be seen. That's why his film was taken."

The sergeant bit his lower lip and nodded, clasping his hands behind his back.

"Hmm. I see. Very interesting. We have been pursuing the robbery angle, as it were, and I must say we haven't had much luck." He nodded vigorously. "Yes, yes, I like it. Good detective work, Deputy!"

Reuger nodded to the room.

"Do you mind?"

"No, no, by all means. Her parents just went for a bite to eat. I'll take you in."

A twenty-two, maybe twenty-three-year-old girl was fighting for her life. Where the tubes and wires stopped and she began was anyone's guess. He could see she was pretty. A widow's peak stood out on her white forehead. Her head was a turban of bandages.

"As you can see, she is very, very sick, Deputy. Maybe it's best you come back another time. She appears to be sleeping—oops—there she is."

Reuger felt his eyes moisten. She seemed to have come back from the dead. Her eyes were large and brown and almost serene. She blinked several times. The two men felt as if they were in the presence of a newborn.

"Her name is Katie, Deputy," the sergeant whispered in his ear. "Ah, Katie, this gentleman is from the United States...he has come all this way to see you and ask you a question. I told him you couldn't answer, but that's an American for you."

Reuger glanced at the sergeant, who had already clasped his hands behind his back.

"Katie...I want you to show you a picture." Reuger leaned closer. "Can you blink your eyes in response?"

She stared at him and then slowly her eyes descended.

"By Jove," the sergeant expounded behind him.

"All right, if you saw this man in the woods before you and your husband were attacked, then I want you to blink your eyes once for me."

Katie breathed heavy. The respirator seemed to increase. The mask on her face covered everything but her eyes. Reuger leaned closer and held up a three-by-five photograph.

"Here it is, Katie. Take a good look."

Her eyes wandered then settled on the picture. Reuger held his breath. It was a hell of a shot in the dark. Katie stared at the picture and the machines whirred and hissed around them. Her eyes seemed to widen, then slowly the lids descended.

"That was a yes, Katie?"

She blinked again.

"By Jove, Deputy, you are communicating with her!"

Reuger stood up from the bed then reached over and squeezed her thin wrist.

"Thank you, Katie. Get well soon."

49

JIM CARPENTER'S GLASSES were two orbs of light under the porch when Reuger pulled up in the jeep.

"Hot for the walleye today," he nodded.

Reuger squinted at the pines and sky mirrored in the still water. He was still shaken by his trip to see the girl in Canada the day before. He had been awake most of the night and couldn't get her eyes off his mind. She was so close to death. A boat drifted by Center Island, and a cabin puffed smoke. The Boundary Waters had produced a perfect day out of its handbasket of blustery weather. When the dawn came, he found himself driving over toward Pine Lodge

"Patricia Helpner around?"

Jim brought his hand across his body like a conductor.

"Ohhhh, think she's down at her cabin there."

He stepped out of the jeep and started down the logging road. Jim watched him. The conversation around the lodge table that morning had been disturbing. A man who logged for Johnson Timber suggested Reuger was working for the environmentalists and that's why he let Tommy Tobin escape. Jim had brought up the man sharply, but he had to admit the thought had lingered with him all morning.

"Have some coffee on when you get back," Jim called behind him.

Reuger waved and kept on down the dusty road smelling of ozone and pine dust and passed swamp pools trebling frogs. A girl walked toward him with a basket of laundry, and Reuger slowed on the road. Her face was blotchy and red and she kept her eyes on the road. The piled sheets reflected pink light on to her face. She walked by him hurriedly and kept her head bent over, and he watched her go down the road.

He turned and counted three paths then swung down through a trellis of sunshine and greenery. Cliff Johnson stood in the lake and lifted a ten-pound sledge, clanging down on the dock. He was a fitter, younger version of his father, Ben, even when he was that young. Oil shined the crease of his shoulders and the baseball swell of his biceps. Reuger walked out on the dock.

"Out chasing poachers, Reuger?"

"Looks like the lake won out with this dock here," he nodded. "Annabel just come from here?"

"Just delivered the sheets," Cliff grunted, slogging through algae and picking up another six-inch spike.

He shoved the spike into the plank and backed up with the sledge and swung down. The clang rang back from the trees. Reuger stared at the deep green with algae and high weeds waving below. A snake slithered along the shore. The hot wood smelled like railroad ties. He reached down and picked up a spike from the dock.

"Bet these dock spikes go through just about any kind of wood."

Cliff brought the sledge up with muscles bulging like snakes under a tan cloth.

"Catch that raping Indian you let go?"

"Nope. Seen him around?"

"Not safe around here with someone like that running around."

"Worried about getting raped, Cliff?"

The sledge smashed the spike and split the plank wood. He shook his head.

"You let a murdering rapist go there and then crack fucking jokes?"

"See anybody around that night?"

"What night?"

"The night Dana Reynolds was raped in the shed."

Cliff picked up another board and swished through the water with sweat streaming his temples.

"I was wondering if anybody would ever get around to asking me that."

"Then you did see someone?"

"You betcha. I saw that fucking Indian running down the lodge road like all get out you know."

"You tell anybody?"

Cliff snorted.

"Why should I?"

Reuger squinted across the lake and saw a boat by Center Island.

The sky was as blue as a robin's egg.

"Crime committed then you want to let someone know."

"That's a laugh." He swung the sledge. "Let you rent-a-cops know so you can let him go again, then? Ya, I don't think so."

"Better than nothing."

"I told my dad," he nodded. "He knows. He'll get that Indian for sure."

Reuger hunched down and nodded and felt pieces falling into place. It was so clear to him that he felt like a fog had lifted.

"Good to have a father like Ben," he nodded.

"You betcha." Cliff backed up, water swishing white around him. "He stands up to those tree huggers and these fucking Indians who think everyone owes them a living for wood that ain't even theirs."

"I heard your dad was going to settle up on that."

"Shit!" Cliff slammed two spikes into another plank. "Those dumb Indians believe anything you tell them."

"Then Ben's not going to pay up?"

Cliff stopped. "Why am I telling you any of this? You're a tree hugger, from what I hear."

Reuger stared at the hard blue eyes.

"How old are you now, Cliff?"

"Twenty-three."

Reuger looked across the lake.

"You know what the trouble is when people get what they want all their life?"

"Got a feeling you're going to tell me."

He turned and looked at the young roughneck.

"They believe they can take as much as they want."

"You're a real poet, Reuger."

He paused.

"You didn't leave her alone, did you?"

Cliff stopped with water falling from the sledge.

"Ya, who's that?"

"Reynolds girl."

He laughed.

"Sure I did, Reuger."

Reuger smoothed back his hair feeling a breeze like cool water on his brow. He watched a boat pass.

"You think you can hang it on Tommy Tobin, but you fucked up this time, Cliff."

He wet his hair from the lake and grinned. His back curved out like a cobra.

"You going to tell me how you're going to kick my ass again, Reuger?" He laughed shortly and hefted the sledge. "You better get on this Indian." He shut one eye against the sun. "Hell, I guess you're not even a deputy sheriff anymore, so I don't have to listen here to a goddamn thing your tree hugger ass has to say."

"This isn't some girl from Ely you can scare into not talking."

"Hey! Go fuck your *whore* in cabin eight with her bastard kid and leave me the fuck alone!"

Reuger jumped down into the water as Cliff raised the sledge. Reuger grabbed his wrist and slipped his other arm under his bicep and broke his grip.

"You fucker," Cliff cried out, swinging with his right.

Reuger stopped the punch with his forearm and grabbed Cliff's head in a hammerlock. He dunked his head into the water and held him down then let him up for air.

"You should have had your mouth washed out a long time ago, Cliff."

"You motherfucker..."

Reuger cranked his head back down into the lake and held him, feeling his fists beating his back. He brought him up and let him go. Cliff coughed and spit water and grabbed onto the dock. Reuger picked up his hat from the water and hoisted himself up onto the dock. He looked down at Cliff still hacking.

"I'm going to get you this time, Cliff. The girl is still alive."

He looked up.

"When she can talk, and it will be soon, I'm coming to get you, boy. Then I'm going to nail you for murder."

Cliff Johnson spat an oily glob of mucus onto the water and glared up.

"You're dead."

50

TIM CARPENTER PUSHED the wood plane into a board with his back to the door. Burning wood smoked up with the sawdust. Reuger walked into the shed and leaned on the workbench. Tim pressed down with both hands and the plane snagged the wood.

"Shit!"

"Pushing too hard there," Reuger nodded, walking back into the woodshed. Sunlight filtered in through the dusty windows and spotted the floor.

Tim stood up and stared at him.

"Where's your badge and gun?"

"Ohhh....I'm off the force for a bit."

Tim paused, then closed one eye and gestured with the plane.

"So then...why'd you let him go?"

"What's that?"

"You know, Tommy Tobin ....Why'd you let him go?"

Reuger walked back through the shed and leaned against the wood table.

"I didn't want him to get shot in the back."

Tim tapped the plane on the board.

"My dad says you're going out with the lady in cabin eight working for Tom Jorde...he says you must need money."

Reuger felt like someone had just knocked the air out of him.

"What else your father say?"

Tim kept his eyes on the floor. Outside were birds and scrunching sand as people passed down the road.

"He said you're trying to stop the logging and take away people's jobs."

Reuger thought of the strained expression on Jim's face that morning. He had felt the reticence, the suspicion of his glance.

He walked to the door and stared down the lodge road. Sun creased his neck, slashing the brim of his hat.

"Know what I can't figure out here, Tim." He turned in. "How someone could rape Dana Reynolds and hold her down and keep her from screaming."

Tim slid the plane down the fresh white pine.

"How do you think someone could do that, Tim?"

"Wouldn't know," he muttered.

"Seems like someone would hear."

The board fell from the sawhorses and Reuger pinned it with his boot. Tim looked up from the floor.

"It would be just between you and me. Sometimes you have to tell the truth, Tim, even if it hurts people you looked up to..."

"I told you...I don't—"

"What did you see that night, Tim?"

He tried to wrench the board up and fell back then jumped up with his face red.

"Fuck this," he grumbled, bolting out the door, passing his father on the road. Jim Carpenter watched his son go down the road then turned and walked in the shed. He pulled off his glasses and set them on the workbench.

"What kind of bullshit are you pulling here?"

Reuger leaned against the bench with his head down.

"I was just asking him a few questions, Jim."

"Ya... what about?"

"About Cliff and the Reynolds girl."

Jim Carpenter's eyes narrowed.

"You don't think Cliff Johnson—or my son would—" His faced darkened. "You aren't even a deputy sheriff anymore and you have the balls to come in here and accuse my son..." Jim trailed off, wiping a line of sweat from his lip. "I've been willing to not listen to things being said about you here...even when you let that Tobin go and I'm about to lose the lodge when we could have had that lawyer off our back if you..."

Jim's voice tightened and wavered. He moved close, his breath a mixture of coffee and cigarettes.

"You don't have shit here," he said, his voice cracking unevenly. "I've got a family, and this is my fucking life here" He grabbed Reuger's shirt and pushed him against the bench.

"This is my life here, and if they take this...this..." His lip quivered. "You get that Indian back here...you understand?"

Reuger stared at his old friend in the dim light. Jim let him go and picked up his glasses from the workbench. He unlatched the door, and a lake breeze flexed through the shed.

"I want you to get off my property...now."

He stepped out of the door and paused.

"And take that fucking woman in cabin eight with you, too."

51

IT WAS DARK by the time Reuger left. He had waited for Patricia and Kurt to return from town and watched a storm over the lake swim toward land then listened to the rain on the porch roof. He sat feeling the rain on his face and watching the lightning dance over the trees toward Canada. Reuger left a note on their porch, and by the time he reached his jeep the drizzle had started again.

He wiped rain off the seats with water falling from the branches. He started the motor and the engine sputtered then caught. The blurry yellow gauges were oddly comforting as he jammed the shift into gear.

The jeep lights shadowed the trees and flared the wet overhanging foliage. Insects swarmed the headlights and puddles splashed up as he bounced down the road of sinkholes and washouts. He turned off the lodge road onto the more desolate stretch through the forest and accelerated a hill. A truck pulled into the road. Reuger waited for it to move then glanced in his mirror to headlights behind.

He rolled to a stop between the two throbbing diesel engines with insects swarming the beams. He glanced at the empty clip for the Winchester as men melted out of the darkness with plastic face shields and green hard hats. Flits of mosquitoes and water bugs swarmed thicker in the lights. There was a chorus of cicadas and night frogs. His mouth was dry and coppery as he stepped out of the jeep.

"I don't think you men can cut many trees with those ax handles..."

Blue light flashed his eyes and electric pain dropped him to his knees. The second blow slammed his shoulder and he slid into the mud. He pushed himself up with his good arm and ducked. The ax hit another man in the face and he dropped his ax handle.

"Jesus Christ, Parker!"

Reuger picked up the club and crouched in the truck lights with the men staying back. He swung from the shoulder and caught a man across the neck. Three of the hickory bats smashed his back. Another handle split his cheek and he fell to the ground, tasting warm blood. He pushed himself up slowly and turned his head.

"If you had a rope then you could do this right here..."

Stars cascaded his vision like streaming rockets. He rolled slowly through the caressing mud. The hard wood punched his arms and legs. He puked when an ax handle collapsed his stomach. He was far away now. He heard a shout distantly and saw a boy running toward him while men scrambled to their trucks.

52

THE SUN WAS where the moon had been outside the window. Reuger lifted his body, feeling every muscle complain. He was in his underwear and saw his clothes hanging in the shower. He willed himself to stand, then he was sitting. Then he was standing, then he walked into the bathroom. He pulled his clothes from the shower rod and saw a bandage on the right side of his jaw and blue circles under his eyes in the mirror.

Reuger turned slowly and pulled his underwear down enough to urinate. He finished and walked back to the bedroom where Patricia sat with hair tousled and marks from the pillow on her cheek.

"Where do you think you're going?"

"Home," he grunted pulling on his pants slowly.

She stared at him.

"I don't think you're in shape to go anywhere."

He stood unsteadily and shut his eyes against the electricity.

"Have any aspirin?"

"You think you're going to be able to get through the day with aspirin after what happened to you last night?"

He pulled the shirt on then matched up the buttons then didn't bother. His body had been beat so badly that just breathing hurt.

"Let me at least make you some breakfast."

"No thanks."

Patricia shook her head and threw back the quilt then walked into the bathroom. Reuger bent over his socks like a surgeon. His fingers even hurt. He saw her painted toenails.

"Shake me out five, will you?"

He pulled on his boots and Kurt sat up sleepily on the couch.

"So," he yawned. "How she go?"

Reuger saw his hat on the dresser. Kurt's hair stood on end from his pillow.

"Slowly, how about getting my hat for me, cowboy?"

"Sure." He looked around. "Where is it?"

"The dresser," Reuger nodded.

Kurt stood in his underwear and crossed the room with the angular body of a boy. Reuger felt the flood of emotions but checked himself. Things had changed now. He had to remind himself of this. There was nothing to do but leave, and he had to ready himself for that.

"Are you leaving?"

"Ya, afraid so," he muttered, punching out the hat and shaping the brim.

Kurt squinted at him. "You look better than last night."

"Thanks," Reuger nodded, pushing himself up from the bed. "Patricia, can I get some water for these aspirin—thanks," he said taking the glass and swallowing. "Thanks again."

She held the glass and shook her head.

"Those men who beat you up all work for Ben Johnson."

"You can't prosecute a mob," he said shortly.

"Oh, great." She clapped her sides. "You're just...let me at least make you some coffee."

"No thanks."

He was moving now.

"Reuger, you should go to the hospital, the amount of blood..."

He lifted her to the side and winked.

"Thanks for washing my clothes."

"You should rest today at least." She whipped her hair back. "I just hate to think what would have happened if we hadn't driven down that road—those men would..."

"Let him go, Mom!"

She stared at her son then at the man. Kurt gestured to the door.

"He's got some things he has to do."

Reuger stared at the boy and clipped the radio. Somehow he knew. The boy knew, though his mother didn't. He stood next to his mother with his thin arms crossed. Reuger stared at the boy who had come between him and death, remembering the way he ran from Patricia's car between the trucks.

Reuger held out his hand.

"I want to thank you, Kurt."

He grasped his hand shyly.

"You'd do the same for me."

Reuger stared at the boy then walked to the door.

"Hey!"

Kurt raised his hand from his waist like a gunslinger.

"Be careful out there now."

* * * *

It was bright by the time he parked the jeep and walked into his cabin. He climbed the porch steps slowly. Reuger felt better with the aspirin and the movement and walked into the bathroom and turned on the shower. He sat with his head between his hands and rubbed his neck. Steam rolled the bathroom in a vaporous cloud.

He urinated again and stripped and stepped into the swirling steam inside the shower curtain. The scalding water pelted his body. He leaned against the shower wall with his head under the stream and let the water caress his body. Then he rubbed himself down with soap and washed his hair, shaving in the shower and brushing his teeth just as the water became cool.

He turned off the shower and looked in the mirror. Bruises colored his body like dye and charcoal shadowed his eyes. He pulled the bandage to a deep vertical cut down his chin. He rubbed himself dry and combed his hair back and rubbed on deodorant and touched the gash on his cheek.

Reuger walked into the kitchen with the towel pinned and drank some orange juice, then pressed the answering machine.

"Ya Reuger, Bruce Anderson here. I have these Earth First lawyers all over me pressing for disclosure. I guess the woman is gone and they brought up these real assholes from New York, you know, and I can't say anything because I don't have a witness here, and Riechardt says not to worry about Tobin because he has a gun with Jorde's print on it and some girl says she heard Jorde and Tobin talking in some shed. I can already feel these lawyers here roasting me like a pig on a spit, you know, and then when I ask about you he says yer suspended indefinitely here...so you have to call me here Reuger. Beep."

"Reuger, this here's Gus. Heard you was beat up pretty bad last night by them thugs from Johnson Timber, well, that man down in Winton, at the hardware store, he got back to me and found a ticket for them spikes showing he sold a bunch of dock spikes to Pine Lodge

that match the description and type of metal that was in Carter's tree. I'll try yer later and hope them ax-wielding sons of bitches didn't beat yer up too bad."

The machine clicked off. He turned slowly to the boarded up window then stared at the glass of orange juice in his hand. He was leaving that house again in early morning. He was leaving those people behind and closing the door. He remembered suddenly he had drank orange juice and left the glass on the counter. That was the last sign of him. The last act of that life was leaving a dirty glass.

Reuger stared at the glass in his hand, then carefully set it down on the counter and walked upstairs. He went to his bedroom and into the closet and pulled down a battered brown suitcase. He pulled open drawers and lifted out socks and underwear, then shirts and pants. He went to his closet and took out wool and canvas shirts, a down vest, a jeans jacket, then picked up a vinyl Adidas gym bag from the floor. He zipped open the bag, throwing in toiletries and a dopp kit then a leather case.

"Hello?"

He stepped to the window and saw Patricia's car. Reuger slipped on a robe with his gun belt around his waist. She was in the doorway in a jeans jacket and khaki slacks.

"Hopalong Cassidy in a robe?"

He smiled faintly. "I couldn't find the sash."

She stared at him strangely.

"Are you going somewhere?"

He crossed his arms and felt pain shoot his neck.

"It was in the way you said goodbye. "Patricia tilted her head. "I had the strangest feeling I would never see you again."

He didn't avert her eyes.

"You are," she whispered. "Aren't you?"

He nodded slowly. "Yes."

"But…but where will you go?"

Reuger balled his fists in the robe and hunched his shoulders.

"Canada for now," he said in a low voice.

Patricia fell back against the door and stared at the man with his hair combed and mustache dark from the water.

"You can't just keep running from your problems, Reuger," she said dully.

He kept his hands in his robe pockets. Patricia stared at him, then reached forward and tugged the empty holster.

"Who are you anyway really? Reuger, who is Reuger? Are you some sort of fantasy you made up a long time ago? Some boyhood fantasy?"

She walked around him."You're like some action hero, but now you don't have your gun or your badge." She pulled on the holster again. "So, who are you... really?"

"I have to pack, Patricia."

"You look like a salesman. Is that what you did?" She stopped and nodded quickly. "Oh, right you were *a logger,* but you only did that for a while. What were you before that? Did you sell vacuum cleaners or aluminum siding?" She leaned close. "What kind of a con man were you?"

Patricia stood to the side of him and shook her head.

"You had to be a con man of some sort to create this persona. You were what, twenty-five when you came up here?"

"I don't have to listen to this shit," he muttered.

"Hey!" Patricia grabbed his arm. "Don't you think every person in the world thinks about leaving? I've wanted to run away for years, but I have people who depend on me..."

"That's you, Patricia."

"It's you, too!" She stared at him and stepped back. "But you've pulled this stunt before, haven't you?"

She shifted her weight, a breeze curling her hair around her ears.

"What about Tommy Tobin?" She pointed to the door. "You didn't let him get shot because you know he's innocent. The same way you know Tom Jorde is being framed—"

"You're describing someone else," he said, shaking his head.

"The fact that you're leaving shows it's true!"

He stepped away, irritation throbbing his temples.

"What would you have me do?"

"I don't know," she cried out, shaking her head. "But now's not the time to run away!"

Reuger gestured out the door and shook his head.

"All right. I'll say it. I'm scared. That what you want to hear? If they want to steal the trees, then why the fuck should I care?"

"We're all scared, Reuger," she continued. "But what is happening is wrong and you can do something about it!"

Reuger breathed deeply and held up his hands.

"Look, just... just leave and let me go. I have to pack," he muttered, staring down at the floor.

Patricia stepped back as if someone pushed her.

"So, you weren't going to say a word... you were just going to leave?"

He stared at the floor. She shook her head. "You're pathetic."

Then he heard her walk to the door and stop.

"What about Kurt?"

Reuger glanced at her.

"You weren't...you weren't going to say anything to him?"

Reuger moved his arms out slightly from his robe.

"He doesn't depend on me that way," he said in a low voice.

Patricia stormed across the cabin and stood in front of him.

"What are you talking about, Reuger? You're his goddamn hero!"

He held up his hands like a man stopping traffic. "You can't put that at my doorstep—"

"Oh, really? What can anybody leave at your doorstep, Reuger?"

"You can't even give of yourself to a boy who can't find anything to believe in until he meets this *mountain man* who rescues people and talks to him the way his father never did and takes him fishing and shows him how to cut wood." She wiped her eyes, smearing mascara. "He didn't think people like you existed anymore, Reuger! Don't you see? You gave him back something he had lost...he believes in you!"

"I can't help you," he said in a low voice.

Patricia was crying. She shook her head.

"You bastard," she whispered.

Reuger heard her footsteps then the door closing. He slowly walked up the stairs into the bedroom. He stared out the window and watched her car go down the road. He picked up the leather case from his dresser and smelled the old leather of his father's closet. He used to hide in the closet and wait for his father to come home from work. He was never so happy in that darkness with the shoes and work belts. He sat down on the bed with the leather case of the man who had left him then lifted a false bottom and took out a faded picture.

Reuger held the picture of a small boy.

53

HE TIED THE bow off with the back of the canoe sliding around like wood on ice. The lantern yellowed the planks. Reuger walked the dock then climbed the porch noiselessly and pushed open the cabin door. He passed into the bedroom past the boy sleeping and kneeled down then touched her cheek. Patricia's eyes rolled open as his hand went to her mouth.

"Get dressed and meet me on your dock," he whispered.

She stared at him then he left the cabin. When he reached the canoe she was already letting herself out the door. Patricia walked toward him.

"Do you always sneak into women's bedrooms?"

"Didn't want to wake Kurt. Get in, I want to show you something," he said holding the canoe steady under the slash of amber.

Patricia stood in a jeans jacket and gray sweat pants and tennis shoes. The air was cool and damp and still. "I thought you would be in Canada by now."

He looked up.

"I'd like you to come with me."

She waved back her hair and stepped primly into the canoe.

"You'll find a paddle up there," he said untying the bowline.

Patricia picked up the paddle and swished the water into foam.

"A J stroke is what you—"

"I know how to canoe." She dipped the paddle. "I took canoeing in college one summer."

He watched her create white explosions on the dark plane, her hair over her shoulder like a cape. He switched sides and ruddered the canoe north.

"Do you mind telling me where we are going?"

"Wilderness slot. Tributary on the north end."

Patricia turned farther, eyes glimmering.

"There's a cave there I want to show you," he explained.

"It couldn't wait until morning?"

"Do you want to go back?"

"What time is it?"

Reuger glanced at his watch.

"Four a.m."

She breathed heavily then began paddling again. Loons called across the lake cavern and answered in the same note. Thirty minutes later, they paddled into a corridor hidden behind an island. He turned up the lantern, and guided them with light rolling pale and colorless over swamp grass.

"Are there snakes out here?"

"Steady as she goes there," he murmured, paddling carefully.

She kept her arm outstretched while reeds swished by.

"You didn't answer my question about the snakes."

"Aren't any."

"Why don't I believe you?"

Reuger searched the high grass and saw an ogling mouth and turned into high reeds breaking down like skinny soldiers. He paddled slowly toward the cave, close enough to see quartz rimming the mouth. They glided into a pond of ink water and slipped toward the opening. The cave reminded Patricia of a carnival where she rode into a lurid world of devils and witches.

"We aren't going in there, are we?"

"Oh, ya," he answered watching the canoe roll the water. "Have to duck your head to get through the mouth there, but she opens up nicely then."

"As the man, don't you think you should be up front?"

"Put your head down and turn the lantern down at your feet."

"What if something's inside there?" she asked, ducking down as they entered the echoing cavern.

"You'll find out first."

The walls appeared like a movie theater out of darkness. Light skimmed the silky water and ricocheted off imbedded phantoms. The cave rose up then spread out twenty feet to either side. The air was damp and smelled like an old well.

"What is this?"

"Cave paintings."

Reuger held the lantern high like a priest.

"Indians came here thousands of years ago." Patricia saw etchings in the surface of the stone. The red stick figures sparkled and wavered in the light. Water dripped from the walls, plunking in the echo of time. She felt as if she was looking at the soul of a people. Their lives flashed before her eyes on the curved wall of granite and greenstone.

"This is a moose," Reuger nodded slowly. "I think this is a canoe, looks like a man smoking a pipe here, see the head?"

"Yes! I see it!" Patricia shook her head and whispered. "It's amazing!"

He swung the lantern over, and the light left the wall then collected on a single spot. Reuger looked like some geological explorer from an earlier time. The propane light glanced off his cheek, silhouetting his hat against the far wall. The canoe seemed to float on glass.

"Here is a man doing some sort of dance," he nodded. "This looks like a man shooting a bow and I think this is a fish or maybe an otter. See the tip of the canoe here and the man with the paddle?"

"Yes..." Patricia squinted closer at the mineral-colored figures. The canoe had large curves at the end. The figures reminded her of hieroglyphics she had seen in some magazine. Patricia leaned closer. "What's behind it?"

Reuger held the lantern closer with his shadow large on the cave walls.

"Looks like another canoe, must be his squaw and child."

"A family," Patricia said softly.

Reuger stared at the primitive family then put the lantern in the canoe and sat. He reached into his vest pocket and handed Patricia the picture from his father's leather case. She stared at the photograph and smiled slowly. She looked up.

"Your wife was very pretty, and your son is adorable."

He kneeled in the canoe and they stared the way parents look at a baby. With the ancient people overhead, Reuger began to explain his own journey.

* * * *

"He had enormous hands, Patricia. I saw him heft a thirty-pound chain saw with one hand like it was paper—"

"Your father," she nodded.

Reuger gestured into the darkness while they floated under the earth. The propane light spread pale gold on the water as he told her of a man who had left him years before. She saw the wounded boy as he talked. She saw the love lost when a parent is gone.

Patricia sat in the canoe with the picture in her hand.

"All I wanted to be was a lumberjack like my father. When he took me to the site and let me watch, it was amazing. I remember the snow on the trees and my father breathing steam like some machine and those chain saws whining through the air and then the tremendous crack when those trees fell."

Reuger looked at his own hands and shook his head. He wondered why he should think of his father now, but he was trying to understand himself. He was trying to understand what he did.

"But then he died," Patricia said softly.

His face darkened like some sunny day snatched for a slide of a dark thunder. He took off his hat and held it by the brim.

"I was there when they told my mother." He turned the hat slowly. "The men came in and told her and never even looked at me. They left sawdust through the house, and the trail went back into my brother's room. I don't know why that was, except my mother was there when they told her and there she stayed."

Patricia reached across the canoe and took his hand.

"That night, a logger came to the door and spoke with my mother. He told her the owner's son had told my father to cut even though the winds were high. He had told him to cut or he would never log again." Reuger stared at her. "My father cut that tree perfect and it fell clear, but he told him to keep cutting. It was near dark when the tree from another logger broke my father's back."

Patricia watched the rage reach into their space of yellow light.

"Was it..."

"Ben Johnson," he nodded grimly.

Patricia looked away and wiped her eyes.

"Does anybody know this?"

Reuger stared at her with hard gray eyes.

"Gus," he nodded slowly. "He told my mother."

They continued to drift around in the cavern of vanquished people. He told her of his life in the lower forty-eight. He told her of his mother cleaning houses and the many different apartments they lived in. He explained the feeling of suffocation that gripped him at night as a boy and the dreams he had of a wide-open land away from the cities and the noise and the chaos.

"I felt like the Indians," he said, pausing. "I never felt like I belonged to that society."

"So why did you become a policeman?" She asked softly.

Reuger paused and shook his head.

"I don't really know. My best friend and I took the police test. It seemed the only place where order existed, and I had no sense of it anymore."

She lowered her head and pulled back her short hair.

"Then you married?"

"That's right."

Reuger squinted at the picture and smiled again. Patricia felt like crying when she saw him smile like that.

"What was your son's name?"

"Matthew," he murmured, staring at the three-year-old boy who was now a man.

Intellectually, he knew he had grown up, but he had stopped his memory fifteen years ago. His son was three. He would always be three.

"Funny how it never leaves you," he nodded. "You know what I remember most about my son? Having him lay on my chest and sleep." Reuger looked at her. "Is there anything better in this world than having your child sleep on your chest?" He wiped his eyes. "I've wondered what he's like now many times, when I let myself wonder."

Patricia tapped the picture.

"He looks like you, Reuger."

"Think so?"

She smiled faintly.

"Oh, ya."

He continued holding the picture with his head toward the canoe. She asked him the question under the men holding spears, under the buffalo and bears and moose and canoes and women holding babies. She asked him the question under the people who had walked the land before and still haunted the soul of the nation.

"So why did you leave them?"

He held the picture as a man might hold a crucifix. He explained it to that little boy the way he had done a thousand times before.

"We stumbled onto an apartment of dealers. It was just my partner and me....He was my best friend." Reuger pursed his lips. "We found the heroin, and then we found the money. He put the heroin on the front seat of the squad and the suitcase of money in the trunk."

Patricia tapped out the moment on her cheek. The tip of her index finger lifted like the beat of a judge's gavel upon her temple.

"What did you do?"

He looked up from the canoe and rubbed his jaw, a deep cut on his wrist. Lacerations of his life plain in the cracked palm and chiseled fingers, the crow's feet cornering the eyes, the windburn leathered skin pulled tight over the jaw. His life was plain to her now; the raw wind of isolation burning into his soul as he roamed over the nation he had left. He was not unlike those men who had ascended the Rockies while civilization surrounded them who preferred a frozen death to muddled complacency.

"He put the suitcase in his garage under his lawnmower." His voice seemed to her still be swirling around the cavern even as he went on. "We both had young families. He was my best friend, and suddenly the lines were blurred." Reuger paused. "There was probably fifty-thousand dollars in that suitcase."

Patricia tried to hide her eyes, but he saw the question on her lips. The canoe turned slowly in the black syrupy water. Her finger pulsed against her temple like the bang of a gavel.

"Did you use it?"

"I came home one day early," he said softly. "It was earlier than I was supposed to, and there they were." He looked at her and saw her grimace. "All the clichés fall away when you see it. It is this physical act between two people, and you happen to see it. Like coming onto a car accident, and what you see changes you forever."

She sat back like someone had just pushed her.

"Your best friend and..."

"My wife," he nodded.

Patricia shook her head slowly.

"Oh, Reuger."

He nodded, remembering the bodies in white sheets, the murmurs, the groans, the door creaking, and then the frightened stares. Then he was running away. That was when his running began. That moment. He wanted to get away from all of it.

"So you turned him in then?"

He raised his head, eyes gray as slate. He remembered going to the station and walking in. His heart was in a riot, and he wanted revenge. He had said nothing to anyone about the money, but it was his word against his friend's. He told them and said he would testify.

"I turned him in to internal affairs."

Patricia nodded slowly, sitting in the canoe with her hands clasped.

"Then you left?"

He nodded slowly and remembered finishing with his testimony and knowing where he would go. His best friend was going to jail, and he was lauded as a hero by the department but hated by his fellow officers. His wife and child had left him the week before. He lumped it all into one package in his mind. He would leave all of it and go back to the Northland. He would go back to when he was happy.

"Then I left," he nodded slowly.

* * * *

Sun flooded the cave now and danced on the minerals in the walls like embedded glass. Reuger stood examining the figures of men gesturing to the heavens. Patricia watched the sunlight outside the cave, hurting her eyes, then looked at him leaning close to the slick rock formations.

"They used something from the mineral ochre and mixed it with glue from sturgeon skeleton and bear fat," he said, his voice echoing off the walls. "The glue and oil disappears but the iron hematite binds with the stone...that's how it lasted so long."

She looked up at him and felt the long night. He nodded slowly.

"Pretty smart...these old cultures knew a thing or two—"

"What happened to your mother, Reuger?"

He stared down.

"What?"

"I said what happened to your mother?"

Reuger lowered himself down and turned the lantern off in the canoe. The hiss faded and they could hear birds outside the cave. Dry light creased his cheeks and cornered his eyes.

"My mother died of a broken heart. They called it cancer, but I think she died with my father. She left this earth the week before I left."

Patricia shut her eyes for a long moment.

"So you lost your mother while all this was happening."

He looked out the cave and she saw the gray hairs at his temple.

"My mother remarried. George London was his name. He insisted she change her name and mine. I always hated him for that," he said distantly. "He was a traveling salesman... they divorced after five years."

"What was your father's name?"

"Jim Hurley." Reuger stared out of the cave. "I remember in the hospital, the last week before my mother died, they told her to eat. The cancer was in her stomach and unless she could eat, then there was nothing they could do. So we all sat in the hospital room and encouraged her to eat...and she did," he nodded slowly. "But then, everyone left and I was alone with her. She was so thin by then and there was light coming in the window the way it is coming in this cave...dry light, pale...harsh."

He squinted at the opening.

"And then she vomited up all the food, except it was bright green. It was like a fountain of bright green vomit. I'd never seen anything like that before. It was all bile."

Patricia watched his gray eyes mist then fill like iron cauldrons.

"There were no nurses around, and she had this little vomit tray she held below her. And I remember I didn't know what to do for her. I just called for the nurse and my mother held that tray with vomit all over everything and I saw her finger move, just sort of rub the side of the tray." He paused. "But I knew then she understood that she was going to die."

Patricia leaned forward and put her head down on his arm.

He raised his eyebrows slowly.

They sat in the bowels of the earth as light glimmered the water like a train coming to the end of a tunnel. Reuger turned the lantern down and looked at the woman who had her hands clasped to her chin.

"Anyway, my wife was leaving me, and I didn't have the heart for the fight."

He said this as if they had been having a conversation.

"For the child?"

Reuger nodded with the skeleton of light creasing his brow, dark in the tired sockets. Patricia kept her hands to her chin with her eyes moving up.

"I couldn't stay, and I didn't want to. I wanted nothing to do with any part of that life. When I was done testifying against my partner, I drove out one morning and got on a train and never looked back. I used to think you could just go somewhere and start over. I believed you could leave your past behind."

Patricia looked at him tragically.

"Did you really think you could escape?"

Reuger shrugged.

"I thought up here a man could start over. It was where I was happiest. I think this is probably the last untouched wilderness of this country." He looked at her. "I think that's why those people went west a hundred years before. You think you can start over and become someone else." He smiled slowly.

"For a while it worked, and I did become someone else." He paused. "But when I saw you...I knew I couldn't do it anymore. It only worked if I stayed out of life, but when I saw you and your son, it all came back."

Patricia nodded, biting her lower lip.

"When you left, did you know what you were going to do?"

His eyes darkened. "I had an idea."

"Become a lumberjack like your father?"

He looked up at her with light in the creases beneath his eyes.

"After I left, I knew it was no good. I kept seeing my son's face and the guilt was crushing. I saw my partner as they hauled him off to jail. When I reached Ely, it was snowing very hard, and the town was empty. I picked up some supplies, and by the time I had reached the forest, I knew what I was going to do. It was snowing very hard, and I just knew." He paused. "It's like a darkness overtakes you, and you can't get out. I knew death had to be better than what I was feeling."

Patricia stared at him, afraid now.

"You mean...you..."

"Kill myself," he said, looking through her.

"What happened?'

"A big Indian came along and found me sitting in the snow with a gun."

"Was he—"

"Tommy Tobin."

Patricia was quiet.

"What did he do?'

Reuger looked at her and nodded slowly.

"He saved my life."

54

REUGER HELD THE canoe steady while Patricia stepped out. Sleep circled her eyes; and her face was pale. She read his eyes and ran her fingers back through her hair like a young girl trying to imitate her mother. A boat motor whined far outside the bay and the scent of bacon frying was in the air.

Patricia stared at him and thought of their earlier conversation.

"So if you think he's behind it all.... Are you going after him?"

He stared at her with stubble on the tip of his chin.

"I need to go back up there and catch Ben taking out those trees... and I need the girl to say it was Cliff who raped her."

Patricia felt how flat her hair was and wondered whether her eyes were as red rimmed and hollow as his.

"But they won't let you near her?"

Reuger shook his head slowly. Patricia watched mist roll up from the lake in the early light. She had the loss of time people experience when they stay up all night.

"You asked me in the cave about something." Reuger looked up. "You asked me if I used any of that money."

She stared at his clear gray eyes and held onto herself. Reuger shook his head slowly.

"I didn't use any of it, but I didn't say anything about it either. I just let it happen, and now I realize that was as bad as if I had spent all of it."

He looked across the sunny bay.

"It's the same as the night I saw Annabel Günter.... I knew what happened, I just didn't do anything about it."

"What happened, Reuger?."

"Local girl. Father worked for Ben Johnson. I found her walking the Lodge Road in the middle of the night after being with Cliff... .Shirt torn up, bruised, scared, one shoe gone. I knew what had happened. I told her to press charges but she knew it would mean her father's job and she kept quiet..."

He paused and breathed tiredly.

"And I did too I guess."

* * * *

Patricia watched the water lap the barrels under the dock.

"Don't be too hard on yourself. It's still not too late."

"Her father still works for Ben. She won't say a word."

"But if you could get her to say it was him. ...At least you can talk to her, Reuger."

He nodded slowly. "I just don't understand why these girls are so reluctant to say it's him when..."

"You're kidding?" Patricia shook her head. "They feel guilty! He may be the worst thing to ever happen to a woman, but if he smiled at them and made them feel good and somehow talked them into a compromising position, then it all gets very fuzzy. They feel they are to blame somehow and brought it on." Patricia slashed the air with her hand. "This girl Dana Reynolds has to face the rest of the male community that will ask her why she went into that shed with this creep? So, they gave her someone else to pin it on. Someone acceptable. It happens to be an Indian with a record this time. ...Many times, it's a black man."

Patricia moved her tennis shoe on the plank.

"So why did you stop logging and become a deputy sheriff?"

He held onto the dock and looked at his hand.

"After seven years of cutting trees, I discovered I wasn't my father." He squinted across the lake. "It wasn't enough. I suppose I still wanted to right some wrong."

"The wrong done to your father maybe..."

"Mom!"

Patricia turned back to the cabin.

"I'll be right there, Kurt," she called to the boy in his underwear on the porch. "Put something on...you'll catch a terrible cold."

"Hey, Reuger!"

He waved to the skinny boy with the big smile. She turned around, and their eyes met. Reuger looked at the boy again and then his mother. He smiled slowly.

"Light of your life... huh, Patricia?"

"You betcha."

55

A YOUNG WOMAN came to the screen with eyes suspicious and blue. Reuger took off his hat and looked through the screen door.

"What do you want?"

"I'd like to talk to you, Annabel," he said, nodding slightly.

Her eyes narrowed in. "Ya, what about?"

Reuger paused.

"I think you know."

"Oh," she nodded. You want to talk about it *now,* then?"

She stayed behind the screen, eyes burning blue. Reuger saw she had come a long way since that night. She wasn't the girl he saw working in the lodge anymore. She was a beautiful woman with shining blond hair and an ample figure.

"I'd like to talk about it now. Your father around?"

"He's at work."

Reuger stepped back from the door.

"Why don't you come on out."

She paused then let the screen slam behind her and squinted out from the porch. Reuger saw a rose tattooed on her left ankle and remembered again the small figure in the headlights struggling down the logging road. She sat in the swing of rusted chains and sagging boards and flicked her silky hair behind her shoulder. Reuger leaned against the porch railing and felt the heat at his back.

"Your father's gone then?"

"I told you he's at work."

Reuger held his hat between his knees.

"Is that an engagement ring, Annabel?"

"Ya," she nodded, fingering the small diamond. "Carl Hibbing and me were engaged last week."

"Congratulations."

She touched the diamond again and flexed her fingers. She was wearing a halter-top with tight brown shorts. A light talcum smoothed her thighs.

"We're going to move down to Minneapolis. Then I can get away from this fucking town here."

Annabel fingered the ring again and touched her eyes. She looked up at Reuger with the flawless skin of a newborn.

"You been in an accident or something?"

"Might say that," he nodded.

She dropped her hand.

"Now, tell me what you want here."

Reuger squinted out to the drooping trees.

"I need your help with something, Annabel." He turned in. "You know about the girl raped at Pine Lodge."

She jumped up and pulled the screen door open. Reuger slammed it shut. She shook her head.

"I don't want to talk about it!"

"I know you called Bruce Anderson," he said in a measured tone. "I know you want to stop him and so do I. Things have changed now."

She swung on him.

"Ya, you were only too happy to have me not say anything about the little prick before. What now? Yer conscience get you? Well it's too late now, and I'm out of here, so you can just forget it. Now let me go."

She opened the door, then slammed it. Reuger knocked on the door again and waited. The door opened suddenly.

"You want me to say something here!" Her eyes were red and tearing. "You want me to tell you how he pinned me down in the back of his truck and ripped my bra in two and then tore my shorts down and pushed my face into the hay and shit in the back of his truck there..." She wiped her eyes again and pinned his arms. "And how he held me like this and *fucked me* then!"

Annabel squeezed his arms so hard he flinched, then turned away with her back heaving and shaking her head.

"Is that what you want...you...you who didn't want to hear what fucking happened," she sobbed.

Reuger still felt her hands and stood like a man submerged. He then picked up his hat from the porch and walked to the edge. Annabel wiped her cheeks with the back of her hand. He hesitated then spoke.

"I need this girl to tell me what happened."

She pulled her hair back and sniffed, wiping her eyes again. He saw the pink watch on her wrist and nails bitten down. She turned with sun creasing her eyes like small jets.

"So? She's not from here then—why doesn't she just say it's him!"

He looked at her and she turned away.

"Fuck..." Annabel shook her head. "Another month and I would have been gone from this town."

She shook her head slowly.

"Fuck!"

* * * *

A cottonwood dropped gossamers on the jeep until it looked like snow from the porch. The muffler popped and contracted in that old CJ7. They sat like a couple with platinum slinging off the smooth fall to her shoulders. He looked like a cowboy.

"Won't have much time," Reuger said getting out of the jeep.

They crossed the street smelling of kerosene onto the porch with hydrangeas in copper pots. A scent of lemon oil was rubbed on the chairs and rich brown chests in the foyer. A woman with curly white hair and granny glasses stood behind the turn of the century post-office desk. Reuger opened his wallet.

"What can I do for you, Deputy?"

"I need the key to Dana Reynolds room."

"Well let's see here, they moved her to room 215. Oh, here you go," said handing him the key with the green plastic ring. "But the Reynoldses just left you know, although I'm not sure I saw their daughter." She leaned close. "Terrible thing that happened to her. Those damn Indians..."

"I'll check the room," he nodded.

They climbed the stairs then walked the narrow hallway of lacquered doors. Reuger counted off the doors then knocked lightly.

"Dana, it's Deputy Sheriff Reuger from Pine Lodge."

He could hear the television.

"Go away! I don't want to talk to anybody."

He keyed the door to the smell of cheese popcorn and dirty clothes. Dana Reynolds was on the bed in pink sweats. Her suntan had faded to a sallow hue and bandages wrapped her wrists like a boxer. Food wrappers littered the floor. Newspapers and tabloids and teen magazines were strewn on the bed.

She jumped forward.

"Hey! You can't just come in here, I'm going to call the police!"

"I am the police," he nodded, motioning Annabel to a chair. "I'm the one who found you when you slashed your wrists." He leaned back against a mahogany desk. "I want to talk to you about what happened in that woodshed."

She scowled and switched channels. "Ask the guy in the uniform with the mustache. He spits those seeds everywhere. He's been here about twenty times."

"Riechardt?"

"Whatever his name is," she muttered.

The pale flickering washed over her. Game-show laughter, rock videos, weight-loss gurus. "Why don't you tell me why you cut your wrists?"

"I felt like it," she muttered.

"Felt like killing yourself then?"

She stared at the television. Reuger pulled up another chair and straddled it, holding his hat over the back.

"You have something pushing against you, and you don't know which way to go," he began in a low voice.

"You better get out of here right now!"

Dana flicked channels faster. Reuger walked to the door and motioned with his hand for Annabel to come in.

"Dana, this is Annabel—"

"Yeah, so. "

"She has a story to tell you—"

"I don't want to hear her fucking story," she mumbled.

Reuger put a micro recorder on the bedside table and turned it on. Annabel took off her dark glasses and set them down with a trembling hand. Dana's eyes flicked over then back to the television.

"Dana, about a year ago I went to a party..."

She stared stonily at the blue screen. Annabel leaned forward with her blond hair draping her knee.

"A senior party out in a field here..."

Dana continued flipping through channels, staring straight ahead into the TV. Annabel wiped the tears away silently. Reuger glanced at the turning tape recorder. Annabel Günter looked out the window with the light bleaching her cheek. She tilted her head and looked at the girl in the bed with the bandages on her wrist.

"My date was Cliff Johnson."

The blue screen was gone, and they were three people in the middle of the day in a hotel room. Dana straightened her legs, and Annabel sat clutching the seat like someone ready for a ride.

"We laid down in the back of his truck and he pinned my arms and started tearing at my clothes..."

Dana closed her eyes then and saw the glaze of night in the woodshed. She smelled pencil shavings. The moon was in the saw chains over the workbench and flat and wet in the windowpanes. She stared at the woodworking table and the axes and cut boards and drifts of sawdust.

"...I couldn't stop him..." Annabel wiped tears from the corners of her eyes. "He tore my panties in two and pushed my legs apart with his knee and kept his hand on my mouth." Annabel wiped her eyes, smearing mascara like soot on an orphan.

Dana stared at the table in the center of the room. It was the table in the woodshed with sawdust scattered over the surface. She took another step, walking slowly toward the table of sawdust. He had been so nice to her again at the campfire. She had been walking by the shed after the fire. She heard something behind her and turned but saw only the pale road.

Annabel stared at her and told her how Cliff Johnson turned her over in the back of his truck. She told her how she struggled, and then how she felt it was her fault. She said she felt she had brought it on, and that no one would believe her. She said Ben Johnson employed her father and most of the town, and no one would convict the son of Ben Johnson.

She paused and shook her head. "He raped me in the back of his truck, and if he did something to you—you should say something..."

Dana stared at her, then she was standing in the door of the shed. She heard footsteps. A hand clamped her mouth, and she was moving into the shed like she was flying through darkness and the door slammed behind her. She slammed down on the woodworking table in the sawdust and smelled alcohol on labored breath and the sticky scent of perspiration. Muscles strained against her thighs and rough calluses bruised her face. The hand pressed her mouth while another ripped her shirt up then plunged down between her legs. Her thighs spread as her sandals clopped the floor.

Air washed her body like cool water. She smelled oil used for chain saws; much like bicycle oil and the bark of trees and the needles of Christmas trees. Gasoline was in her mouth. The rag was suffocating her. She couldn't scream and felt sawdust sticking to her body then the pushing between her legs. He was splitting her apart. His face was wet above her and his eyes glittery. Someone was holding her arms, and she felt something cool inside her leg then blood trickling down her thigh. He grunted loudly and drove into her thighs again and again. It felt like he was cutting her in half. She cried with the rag in her mouth. He was off her, and she fell off the table onto the rough plank floor.

Annabel and Reuger watched the motionless woman. She was sitting in the bed. Annabel stood up wearily.

"There, I did it. Can I go now?"

Reuger nodded slowly, staring at the girl on the bed. Annabel crossed the room. She reached the door and pulled it open.

"You're a whore!"

Dana said it like someone waking up from a long sleep. Her expression remained unchanged, but Annabel stopped like someone had jerked her back. She turned slowly to the bed.

"What did you say?"

"I said you're a fucking slut," Dana nodded, stabbing the television back to life.

Annabel walked across the room. She faced Dana, standing between her and the television.

"I'm not a slut!"

Dana shrugged lightly, a small smile creeping over her face.

"You knew what he was going to do."

Annabel turned and stormed to the door then stopped. Reuger watched and didn't move. Annabel turned around to the girl in front of the television. Dana flipped the channels. Annabel shook her head slowly, walking across the room.

"You think you're too good for someone to rape."

She tore the remote from Dana's hands.

"Give that to me!"

Annabel held it over her.

"Let me tell you something, bitch he raped me in that truck there like he fucking raped you in that shed!"

Dana reached up and slapped her with her open hand. Annabel shook her head. "Go ahead and slap me again, bitch. You're hoping it will go away," she nodded. "If that would do it, you could slap me twenty times, but it's not fucking going away!"

Dana raised her hand again, but Annabel slapped her first. She fell back to the bed holding her cheek with the silence in the room. Reuger saw the first dark spots on the sheets. She wiped her eyes quickly but the tears came faster. Dana put the palms of her hands against her eyes. Annabel sat down on the bed next to her. "

"Ya. Go ahead and cry." She pulled out a cigarette from her purse. "God knows I cried my eyes out."

56

THE SHERIFF STOOD with his hands behind his back, flecks of aluminum glinting in his hair. The soup can was on the desk with seeds in a brass tray. An American flag drooped next to a silver edged frame of the Marine Corps motto. His desk mirrored a woman and a girl with hairstyles from 1985. On the center of the still pond was the micro recorder.

"Think you're pretty smart, don't you?... Think you can walk in here and fuck me over here."

He turned like an old photograph with light on half his face. Reuger watched the man chewing slowly. *Phsit-pop*. He nailed the metal trashcan.

"I fought off a whole unit of Viet Cong. I can handle twenty of someone like you. You think you're some kind of cowboy running around out there trying to right the wrongs of the world. You better think about what the fuck you're doing here."

Reuger nodded. "Ben still has you by the short hairs."

"He has you too, Reuger, you just don't know it!"

"How about I play that recording for her parents?"

The sheriff squinted toward the door.

"Who called them down here?"

"They want to hear about the break in the case."

Riechardt glanced at the black recorder.

"He said, she said, Reuger. Doesn't change a damn thing here." He sat down quickly and picked up the soup can. *Phsit ping!* The Indian did it—Tobin, he did it! You better quit fucking around here when you're *not* even on the force..."

Reuger slammed his hand on the desk and leaned forward. Riechardt's face was a study in craggy lines and acne scars and missed whiskers.

"You bullied that girl into lying, and now you've got a lawyer outside your door. Get in my way again, and I'll have Bruce Anderson empanel a grand jury for obstruction of justice. You'll be bent over in your favorite Marine Corps pose for the next thirty years."

The sheriff held the soup can like a gun.

"No one will testify against Johnson's son."

Reuger stared at the man holding onto his desk for support. "It could have been your daughter in that shed. It could have been your daughter crying for help in the darkness with that psychopath on top of her." Reuger nodded to the picture on the desk. "Your flesh and blood in there in the sawdust, getting torn open with a rag in her mouth. Your little girl getting fucked..."

The sheriff jumped up and turned to the window. Reuger stared at the starched green uniform and waited.

"I need my job," Riechardt said in a low voice. "He employs the town. We lose Johnson Timber, and we're finished."

"The price is too high, Sheriff."

He turned and sat down at his desk. "So what do you want?"

"My badge."

The sheriff looked at him then turned and opened a drawer and threw the silver badge on the desk.

"Your guns are in evidence, I'll call Hector." He paused. "As of now—well, you just get them and tell him to call me if he has any questions. As of now, you're back on the force."

Reuger cupped the badge and sat down in the chair. He realized then this was the payoff as far as the sheriff was concerned.

"Now get out of here," he muttered, beginning to write on a document.

Reuger put the star on and felt the pull on his vest. He looked at the man behind the desk. A single lick of hair sprouted from his part and jumped slightly.

"Now tell me to go arrest Cliff Johnson."

The sheriff looked up slowly, his eyes flat as nickels.

"You're crazy."

"Tell me to arrest Cliff Johnson the way you told me to arrest Tommy Tobin. And I'll give you time to explain all this to the parents out there."

"You aren't going to..." The sheriff reached across the desk and

Reuger scooped the recorder.

"This isn't going away this time."

He stood up. "You're a goddamn fool, Reuger."

"Maybe, but you have to make a stand at some point."

The sheriff looked old. The phone rang and ricocheted around the room. The two men stared at each other. The phone rang three more times then stopped. Reuger opened the door and looked back.

"You'll land on your feet, Sheriff."

"Get the fuck out of here."

57

REUGER WALKED THE white hospital corridor with the gun slapping his thigh. Several people looked at the man in the big green hat with the Colt on his leg and the tan vest and cowboy boots. A man with a black crew cut and olive skin glanced up from emptying trash. Reuger turned into a room where a big man read *Sports Illustrated* with wrist tubes.

"How she go there, Gary?"

Gary Chatoee tented his stomach with the magazine.

"Not bad, you know."

Reuger pulled a chair close to the bed and sat down.

"How they treating you?"

"Oh, not bad," he frowned. "But I don't like the Jell-O, you know." He rolled his shoulders. "The doctor, he says he thinks I can get out of here in a couple days."

"That's good then," Reuger nodded.

Gary motioned to his badge.

"So you're back on the force, hey?"

"Couldn't keep me off."

Gary squinted out the window. "That Riechardt, he came to see me to ask what happened in the Old Pines, you know." He shook his head. "Kept wanting me to say you and Tommy Tobin shot Al Hanes in cold blood there, but I told him he shot at us first. I think he wanted me to say Tommy shot me, too, you know."

Reuger palmed his hat. "I wanted to ask you a few questions about some old treaties."

"Ya, sure," Gary said, sitting up, grimacing.

"Anything you know about what kind of treaty might have been given to Johnson Timber at one time?"

"You mean how did they steal the wood?"

He clasped his hands over the sheet.

"All goes back to the 1881 Allotment Act. It was a way the government had of taking good land from the Indians. Eight-million acres passed out of Indian hands and usually for a horse and a gun, and the whites could log it and didn't pay shit to the Indians then. Logging companies were supposed to pay reparations, you know, and Ben Johnson's grandfather was one of them."

Reuger hooked his boot at the knee.

"Government still honors these treaties?"

Gary shrugged.

"Ya, sure, they have to. Same with the treaty of 1854 for hunting and fishing rights. That's why I can shoot three bears, and you can only shoot one."

"Then the treaty would give Ben the right to log out those lands if he paid up?"

Gary frowned and rolled his shoulders, draping the tubes along side his arm.

"Ya, I suppose so, but he could never do it now because of them tree huggers."

"What if he had an old treaty that said he had been granted the right to log the Old Pines?"

Gary held his hand out flat.

"I guess he could interpret it that way, you know." He shook his head. "But it don't mean shit and, like I say, them tree huggers there wouldn't let him do it, they'd put it back in the courts."

Reuger paused.

"Unless he already logged it."

* * * *

He turned off the ignition to a backfire and watched road dust swirl up behind Ben Johnson's truck. Reuger stepped out with the Winchester, and Gus with the shotgun. They walked toward the men with dark beards and green hard hats lounging on the lodge porch. Jim Carpenter leaned against a support post, and Ben Johnson sat in an Adirondack chair with a boot over his knee.

Ben motioned from the chair.

"Enjoy that badge there, Reuger. I'll have it taken away from you tomorrow."

He stopped with the Winchester in his right hand. The lake wind blew hard, flapping up some trash in the road.

"Where's Cliff, Ben?"

"Who knows," he shrugged and threw a peanut in his mouth. "Can't keep track of him these days."

"He and Tim," Jim pointed north with his mug, "gone camping in the Boundary Waters."

Ben Johnson balled the bag of peanuts into the road. Reuger watched it roll like a tumbleweed between spits of road sand.

"There you go. Gone camping," Ben announced.

Gus stood with wind picking his beard and scraping leaves down the road. He looked at Reuger, plainly asking, "what now?" The two men on the porch stared out.

"You going to go arrest him, Reuger? You and Hopalong Cassidy there?" Ben shook his head and laughed. "You get some whore from Chicago to say what you want, and you think people around here are going to put my boy in jail?" He leaned back and hissed through his teeth. "Shit, you are one stupid bastard."

"They'll convict," Reuger nodded slowly. "When they hear he raped a sixteen-year-old girl in a woodshed."

Ben scoffed and spat.

"You'll never get that far; tomorrow you'll be washing dishes at the Ely diner." He pointed down, drawing forward in the chair like an anxious king.

"You're finished up here, my friend."

Reuger turned.

"Can I have a word with you, Jim?"

Jim walked off the porch and sloshed his coffee in the road. They stopped by the dock in the smell of fish under a sky bridling rain. Reuger smoothed his hand over his jaw and looked at his old friend. Jim cleared his throat.

"I'd like to say something about the other day...I went off half-cocked..."

"Don't worry about it," Reuger said, waving him off. "I want to tell you what's going on here." He breathed deeply. "Dana Reynolds finally said what really happened in that shed... Cliff raped that girl in your woodshed, and I think he's making a run for Canada with Tim."

Jim stared at him with his mouth slightly open.

"She had gone into the woodshed with him after the campfire the first time and was too scared or too confused to say it was him by the time I talked to her at the lodge. Tommy must have come on them and thrown Cliff off her. The second time he just raped her straight out."

Jim stared out to the lake again with his face drained of color.

"It wasn't the first time for Cliff. I found Annabel Günter a year ago walking down the Old Timber road in the middle of the night." Reuger paused. "She didn't want to say anything, and I let it go."

"Shit," Jim whispered.

Reuger saw Ben Johnson over his shoulder and lowered his voice.

"I think Cliff might be involved with these dead loggers too. I pulled a dock spike from the one he was repairing on cabin eight, and it's a dead match with the spike that Carter Grissom sawed into." Reuger paused again and put his hand on Jim's shoulder. "Tim might be mixed up in this thing as well. I just don't know how yet."

Jim turned red.

"I found some wig he had taken from Diane. The wig matches strands I pulled out of the woodshed. My feeling is Cliff corralled him into doing something."

Jim didn't move then nodded imperceptibly.

"You think he would hurt Tim?"

Reuger tugged the brim of his hat down.

"I don't know.... How long ago did they leave?"

"Must have been three hours ago." Jim squinted north to a spider of light touching down. "I dropped them off at the Boot portage with a canoe."

"How much gear?"

"Had an outfitter pack..."

"Don't listen to him, Jim!"

Ben Johnson swung his arm with his voice swallowed by wind. From the dock his face was red under the Stetson. The wind died, and his voice reached them like a radio turned up.

"Just a drifter, and I gave the sonofabitch his first job, and you see how he repays you, Jim! He's one of these goddamn tree huggers!"

Jim breathed tiredly with the small cliff of hair tapping his forehead."Ben's making a play for the Old Pines," Reuger nodded. "He has some old Indian treaty and thinks it'll give him the right to pull the trees out. I think Foster and Carter were burned out and shot to keep them quiet about cutting up the wood with their slashers."

Jim was pale, rubbing his cheek with his left hand. He pulled the top off his plastic mug and winged the cup dry. He looked at the man on porch, then took off his glasses and pushed the hair off his forehead with a trembling hand.

"Sounds like he's gone fucking crazy here," he muttered.

Jim looked down then crossed the road like a soldier and stopped below the porch. His tennis shoes were flat and an extra roll caved his belt on all sides. Rain hazed down on Center Island with the boathouse door slamming shut across the bay. Reuger walked up behind him and felt the first drops.

"Don't listen to a goddamn word…"

"Get out, Ben."

Ben stared down like a man in a practical joke.

"What?"

"Get off my property," Jim repeated, his voice cracking.

Ben Johnson stood on the stairs with cowboy boots over the edge.

"Shit, *your* property! My daddy owned this place before you were even a twinkle in your mama's eye, boy, and I could take it back any goddamn time I want!" He snorted again. "From what I hear, once that lawyer is done with you, you'll be lucky to have a fucking canoe left…"

Diane Carpenter burst through the screen door and winged up the Mossberg shotgun. She shucked a shell with her left hand and lowered her eye to the aiming pin. The barrel glimmered space five inches from Ben Johnson's head. Reuger saw her finger curled tight in the trigger guard.

"Get off our property, ya bastard," she ordered in a low voice.

Ben's eyes cornered with the two loggers flat against the wall. He tried to smile then shook his head slowly.

"Still just a goddamn hillbilly, aren't you, Diane? Just a miner's daughter who'll be back waiting tables again."

"Ya, and that's somewhere you'll never eat," she murmured with her cheek to the mahogany stock. "So just take these two assholes with you and get off our fucking property here."

Ben turned slowly to Jim Carpenter.

"Just signed the death warrant for your resort."

"I'll take that chance here," he nodded.

Ben muttered something, missing a step, then falling off the porch.

He stomped toward the truck with the two men swaggering behind. The doors slammed and the engine turned over. The truck backed up slowly then swung away leaving dust. Diane lowered the shotgun and pulled a cigarette from her pocket.

"Ya, that asshole no-good son of a bitch, I should have shot when I had the chance," she muttered.

"Why waste good buckshot?" Gus asked, spitting in the dust.

Jim stared at his wife.

"Would you really have shot Ben?"

Diane lit her cigarette.

"That sonofabitch Cliff is with Tim now, and I could have shot him for that."

"Tim was upset this morning." Jim glanced at Reuger. "He was here when we were served the papers for the suit."

"Ya, well, can you blame him?" Diane tore the cigarette away. "Expect Riechardt to come and padlock the place any day now!"

She wiped mascara from her eyes and turned to the rain-swept lake. Reuger walked onto the porch and watched the storm darken the sky. They stood side by side facing the dark rolling thunderheads toward Canada.

"Wonder where they're going, you know," she murmured.

Thunder concussed down and shook the windows.

Reuger tapped the rifle against his leg.

"Canada."

58

THEY UNLOADED THE canoe from the lodge boat under an iron sky. They carried no gear besides the Winchester and shotgun and worked quickly in the still woods. Already, several fat gelatinous drops pattered the leaves with a scent of brass and black dirt. The portage trail tunneled behind them with roots snaking out of the ground. Rain sprinkled the water like scattered pennies.

Kurt had come running down the dock just before they shoved off. His face was white and his eyes small and lost. His mother was gone. She had been out on the dock, and he had fallen asleep in the cabin. When he woke she was gone but her book and her chair were in the water along with a pair of Ray-Ban sunglasses. Reuger had run down to the cabin and looked around. They had quickly covered the lodge, and they had no doubt. Patricia Helpner was missing.

"Think I should go with you."

Jim Carpenter stood by the bow of the lodge boat, watching Gus and Reuger unload.

"I can't let you, Jim." Reuger shook his head. "Your thinking won't be clear. These boys have a good three hours start, but they'll camp somewhere tonight, and we'll catch up. "

"I'll have the scanner on, then," he nodded.

Reuger handed the Winchester to Gus and slipped under the canoe, hoisting it onto his shoulders. He hiked down the portage trail with the cavern over his head, and Gus followed with a gun in each hand. The woods were dark already and the trail slick. They walked the edges of the muddy path.

Jim Carpenter turned his boat around as the storm hit.

59

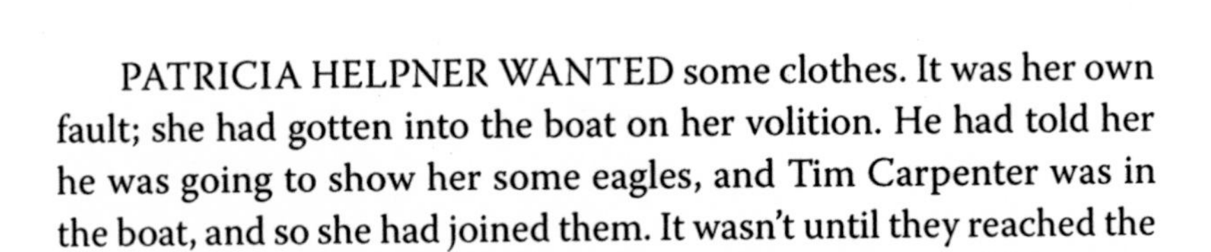

PATRICIA HELPNER WANTED some clothes. It was her own fault; she had gotten into the boat on her volition. He had told her he was going to show her some eagles, and Tim Carpenter was in the boat, and so she had joined them. It wasn't until they reached the far north end of the lake she realized something was terribly wrong.

"Is this where the eagles are?" she asked Cliff as he pulled the boat ashore with the canoe trailing behind.

He had smiled at her then and she felt sick to her stomach. He pulled up a large rifle as his eyes undressed her. Patricia involuntarily drew her hands to her breasts.

"No, it's not, you tree hugger bitch." Cliff pulled back the bolt. "You're going on a little a tour of our endangered resources."

Patricia stared at him, then Tim Carpenter transferring the gear from the boat.

"Tim…do you know what you are doing?"

"Shut the fuck up, bitch." Cliff walked close up to her. "You're the reason he's losing the lodge and you're the reason men are losing jobs. When we get to where we're going, we figure we'll hold a little press conference. With you along, people will listen to our story."

She saw this was bullshit, but she also saw how Cliff had sold it to the younger boy. Tim Carpenter walked into the woods, dragging the canoe. Patricia looked around the darkening woods and realized her situation fully. She saw the pulse in his temples, the gleam in his eyes.

"You don't want to do this, Cliff. Take me back, and we'll forget all about this."

He laughed shortly and smiled. "No, you aren't going back."

He lowered the rifle and Patricia thought she might faint.

"Reuger's been fucking the hell out of you, and I understand why now."

She stepped back and hit a tree, then he was on her. He pushed the barrel against her chest then reached forward, and she felt his left hand on her vulva. Cliff fumbled with her suit, and then he was inside her. His fingers tearing and groping. Patricia winced as he leaned close.

"How's that feel, bitch?"

She spit on him and he stopped.

"Get your hand out of my cunt."

"You fuckin' bitch—"

"Cliff!"

Tim Carpenter was back, and Cliff turned.

"Just putting a little fear in her, buddy."

Patricia didn't know what Cliff had told Tim to get him to go along, but she could see it wasn't holding him. Cliff turned back to her and nodded slowly.

"To be continued," he whispered. "I think we better tie her up, Tim. She could be trouble."

He looked down.

"Just don't hurt her," he muttered.

Cliff walked over to the boat and slit the bowline. He walked back to Patricia with the yellow nylon and grabbed her hands.

"I wouldn't hurt her, Tim," he said, wrapping her hands tightly. "We'll just keep her around and give her a scare."

60

THEY REACHED BOOT Lake with the storm hurling lightning and thunder from the treetops. Reuger swung the canoe from his shoulders to the dark mountains ranging freely across the sky with thunderheads swishing the water white. Graywacke and granite and greenstone glowed unnaturally bright on the far shore. Rain battered the canoe.

"Reuger!"

Gus pointed to a man paddling in an army coat with black hair roping his shoulders. He had appeared with the storm and the lightning and concussion. Reuger watched the man cross the lake toward him like a creeping dusk and remembered his conversation with Bruce Anderson.

"So, you have the girl's statement then?"

"A recording."

Bruce made a sound like steam escaping through his teeth.

"Oh, ya, it's still he said, she said, Reuger, but maybe we can get a DNA match. But I'll bet Riechardt managed to botch that up too, you know, so you still need a witness here with Cliff Johnson. Ben Johnson won't make it easy here."

"I'm taking off for the Boundary Waters."

The radio buzzed in his ear.

"Can you get the son to sing on the father on this logging business here?"

"Do my best."

"Ya, well, it doesn't matter. No jury will think Cliff Johnson acted on his own here—maybe with the rape we can strike a deal. Obviously the son of a bitch is using his own son for his shit detail here." He paused. "I'll swear out felony warrants, and you can go pick him up for conspiracy to log in federal lands. Might as well jump from the pot into the fire here."

Bruce breathed heavily in the radio again.

"So what about Foster Jones here...Al Hanes kill him, too?"

"Maybe."

"Ya, who else you thinking it might be?"

* * * *

Tommy Tobin dragged his canoe ashore and walked under the pines. His army coat was drab olive turned to the color wet tent canvas. His hair slicked his neck like tar.

"So yer made it away after Reuger saved yer ass, there," Gus shouted with his beard wet and clingy like a poodle.

Tommy turned to the lake and raised his rifle.

"Ya, that Cliff Johnson, he come through maybe three hours ago. I think they were headed for Ensign Lake. They were moving fast and carried deer rifles, you know."

Reuger unsnapped the restraining strap on his Colt and faced the big man. "We're even, Tommy."

"Ya," he shrugged. "If that's the way you want to look at it."

"I need the truth about Foster Jones."

A crack in the sky opened and thunder echoed the lake and shook the trees, stones, earth. They stood under the pines with rain dripping like a shower curtain. Tommy breathed tiredly.

"I could have told you before, you know, but you wouldn't fucking believe me."

Reuger watched him against the rain and lightning with one hand to the Colt.

"Try me."

"Ya," he nodded heavily. "And if I had said anything then, then I would be at the bottom of the lake with Knudsen."

Gus shook his head.

"What in the hell are yer talkin' about?"

He frowned at the world, rain oily on brown cheeks, gun to the angry sky.

"You don't hear sounds like that in the woods at night, you know." He shook his head. "A girl making sounds like that. I was walking down the road past the shed when I heard it, you know, and the moon was real bright and you could see a long way. And when I opened the door to the woodshed, I could see him on her there." He halved the air with his fist. "But I didn't know it was him until he cussed me for throwing him."

Gus spat angrily.

"What in hell yer talking about..."

"So I lit the lantern, you know, after he run off, and she didn't have no clothes, and I woke her up that way and she screamed."

Tommy pointed his gun out toward the rainy gray plane.

"So I go up toward the Boundary Waters, figured I'd just leave, you know. Figured they'd say I raped her and all, but then I met a fucking bear on the portage trail, and so I went and stayed in the woods that night and went to see Foster early." He paused, his mouth flat. "That's when I see smoke over the trees and run back there and the slasher's burning, and he's there again. I thought maybe I was dreaming because it was the second time I seen him do something no one would believe, you know, and I was just going to clear out."

"Who?" Gus sputtered. "Who in hell yer talking about!"

Tommy turned from the lake with his eyes black.

"Cliff Johnson," Reuger nodded.

"Cliff!" Gus stared at him. "He done that, too?"

The rain pattered mud along the shore and simmered the lake. Tommy reached out and let rain fill his open hand.

"I knew what I saw could get me killed, and I figured that Cliff Johnson say I did it anyway, you know, so I stayed away in the woods." He drank from his palm like a Comanche. "But then I hear the tree hugger's looking for me, you know, and I meet him in the woodshed. He wants me to tell him about logging in the Boundary Waters, and I figure I say anything he get me killed there, too." He tilted his head. "I come to see you, and that Ben Johnson and Al Hanes they come and sit down at the table and tell me to say I saw the tree hugger kill Foster."

"Why in the hell?" Gus sputtered. "Why didn't yer just *say* it was Cliff Johnson all along and save us a lot of damn trouble?...Yer changed yer damn story three times!"

"Ya?" He looked at him with eyes half-closed. "What would you say? I knew I'd be in the lake like Knudsen if I said anything. Ben Johnson kill me if I say his son shoot Foster and raped the girl." Tommy turned north. "But I know where he's goin' now; that Cliff Johnson is going up there to finish the job on them trees, I think. You didn't see it when you were up there." He gestured with the rifle. "But that

Ben Johnson, he has a cutter up there. He's going to take all the trees, because he knows the tree huggers can't stop him now."

Reuger pushed back his hat.

"How fast can one of those hot saws go through trees, Gus?"

"Good skidder behind her?" He shrugged. "Maybe ten minutes a tree. But Reuger, how could he get one of them big cutters up there?"

"Piece by piece, I imagine."

"Ya," he nodded. "I'm telling the truth here."

"*Oh, hell!*" Gus spat. "It's yer third try, and how do we know yer didn't just shoot Foster yourself there?"

"Because his story matches Dana Reynolds's."

"Ya, you see there," Tommy nodded. "Told you I was telling the truth here."

"Oh, hell," Gus grumbled. "Yer finally just got lucky."

Reuger rubbed his jaw and hunched down.

"Headed for Canada, then they'll take Ensign up to Trident, then Frog Lake to Birch and across the border." He pulled out a resin-coated map. "But if they're breaking off for the Old Pines, might go across to Basswood too."

He folded the map into his pocket.

"I'll need somebody who can track."

"Ya, that's what I was thinking too," Tommy nodded.

"Let's go, then."

61

THEY PADDLED BOOT Lake bailing the canoes with wind chopping water and making small whitecaps. Rain stung their cheeks and ran in their eyes and soaked their clothes and ruined matches and soaked tobacco. The wind was cold from the north and whistled the lake plane and blew Tommy's hat off. He circled to pick it up with his long black hair whipping wild.

"Do yer think that lightning wants a big hunk of metal in the middle of the lake," Gus shouted with his wet beard making his face thin. Reuger shook his head.

"Not today."

"Well, I was jest wonderin."

Tommy reached the far shore first and kneeled in the mud while they dragged the canoes in through jagged volcanic rocks. Gus fell down and climbed out of the water,, pulling out his soggy roll of pipe tobacco.

"God dang it!"

"Maybe two hours ago they come through," Tommy said standing up.

Reuger stared into the dripping red and white pines and brushed through the tamarack to the portage trail. The path was sharp bends and a steep climb to the next lake. He walked back to the two men and picked up his canoe.

"I'll lead off until we reach Ensign."

They slogged through the rainy forest for twenty minutes. Reuger lowered the canoe into the shallows swirling over slate deposits much like gray stepping-stones. Quartz glittered like gold thrown casually across the clear pane of glass. He took off his hat and scooped water onto his face and the back of his neck. Gus trudged up with his mustache puffing and his eyes red and baggy. Tommy swung his canoe down easily.

"I told him he shouldn't make it look so easy," Gus muttered wiping sweat from his brow, smoothing back straw-white hair. "I hate to say it, but I'm gittin' too old fer this shit."

Reuger stared across the lake while Tommy squatted down and pointed to the print of a tennis shoe.

"I'd say this was made in the last hour, maybe two here."

"They head north or crossed to that portage," Reuger murmured.

Tommy swished into the shot scattered water and pointed to two blots of red as an oar snapped off the glacier walls.

"Might be them, you know."

Reuger swung up the radio.

"Hector!"

The radio bridled static then cleared.

"Ya, go ahead Reuger."

"Get me Jim Carpenter at Pine Lodge."

"Ya... 10-4."

He watched the two smudges of red passing slow and steady toward the far end of Ensign Lake.

"Yep, that might be them," Gus nodded.

"Ya, Reuger, I have Jim Carpenter for you."

"Thanks Hector... Jim?"

Static.

"Ah, yes sir?"

"Jim, might be looking at your son and Cliff on the far western end of Ensign Lake here, could you tell me what they were wearing?"

Ya, they were both wearing red hunting vests... Over."

"10-4... that's them. I'll keep you informed."

Reuger clipped the radio and pulled out his map.

"What do you think, Gus, Splash Lake?"

"Well now, that makes sense to me." He rubbed his whiskers and touched the map. "More than if they were headed fer that portage there."

"Ya, going toward the Old Pines then," Tommy nodded slowly.

"Let's see if we can close the gap then."

They waded back to their canoes and slid them into the green sparkling water. Tommy paddled into the lead with his hair flying free over his shoulders.

"See if you can get to where you can keep an eye on them," Reuger called out.

Tommy leaned further down in the sleek canoe and moved away. Gus turned around with one eye shut.

"Where'd he get that there ultra light canoe?"

Reuger shook his head.

"Not going to ask."

62

PATRICIA WAS SHIVERING uncontrollably now. She had a flannel shirt over her swimsuit but the cold was through her and even with the gag she felt her teeth chattering. Her hands were in front of her and Cliff pulled her along behind him. They had made a fire and pitched camp, now she was behind this psychopath in the woods. He had told Tim he was going to get more wood and grabbed the .30.06 and her.

"I'll keep her with me," he announced.

"You can probably untie her, Cliff," Tim said, looking up tentatively. "We don't want to hurt her."

He shrugged, winking. "Sure, after I get the wood, we'll untie. Hell, maybe we'll just let her go. We've made our point here, I think," he said, nodding to Tim. "The tree huggers know what's it like to be scared now."

Tim nodded.

"Yeah…we'll let her go."

Then Cliff jerked her into the woods. Patricia felt every nerve in her body. She knew what was coming and settled it again with herself. She would fight back and maybe die, but she wouldn't let this son of a bitch rape her. Patricia found herself flying suddenly then she was against him.

"Well, Ms. Tree Hugger," he said, pulling his belt loose and yanking down his zipper. "Alone at last."

Patricia pulled against the nylon mooring rope cutting into her wrists. Her eyes teared over.

"Now, don't get all chocked up," Cliff grinned, stripping his shirt off.

Then she felt his arms go under her shirt and rip it open.

"There we go," he whispered, kissing her neck.

Patricia felt her suit break over her biceps then his lips on her neck.

"Let's see what kind of tits a tree hugger has," he muttered huskily.

Patricia felt the top of her suit fall and then the air was on her breasts. His lips traveled down.

"Well, well, well," he murmured, and then she felt his lips on her nipples.

She winced and brought up her knee. It caught him in the thigh and Cliff stepped back. His eyes flickered.

"Fucking bitch!"

Patricia felt the back of his hand break across her face. The pain was inside her jaw, and then the hand came back the other way. She saw stars.

"You aren't going to stop me now, you cunt," he shouted, jerking his pants down.

Cliff pulled her tight as she felt his penis against her stomach then against the outside of her suit. He breathed on her hotly, his breath a mix of tobacco and beer.

"I'm going to fuck the shit out of you right here and now."

Patricia counted to three then brought her knee up as high as she could and this time she felt his pelvis bone. Cliff fell back in a heap and she turned and ran. She broke through some pine trees and then hit a tree head on and fell back stunned. Cliff was on her. He drew back his hand as she heard a shout. Patricia waited for the pain, but he pulled her up. Cliff then dragged her roughly through the trees and stopped.

"Well," he muttered, raising the rifle. "Looks like your boyfriend just arrived."

63

THEY REACHED THE edge of Found Lake with darkness between the trees and the cooler air like compost. Reuger smelled the dew in the pines and stagnant water around the tamarack and the cool scent of cedar hanging low. The dusk was lighter on the water with the forest rimmed in darkness.

"Campfire?"

"Oh, ya," Tommy nodded pulling in the canoe.

Gus held out the pump twelve-gauge, and Reuger checked the slide.

"Where are they?"

"Maybe a half-mile in." Tommy looked over his shoulder. "I tracked them, you know, and waited until they made camp and started cooking. They're on the lower edge of the forest. Old Pines are farther up across one more lake, but these trees are pretty big too. I figured they were pretty hungry and wouldn't move again, you know."

Reuger stared into the close woods and heard the low throb of insect life. The lake pooled the sky behind like some giant mirror.

"Cliff's a good shot," he nodded. "So we want to get the drop on them here. Let's try and keep the fireworks out of this. Tommy leads us to where they are, and I'll take it from there. Let's go."

They hiked the dark forest until there was only lighter sky. They moved through the trees as three shadows until Reuger saw a fire bleeding through pine needles. Tommy crawled up and leaned down by a fallen tree. Reuger crouched and heard the fast crackling of burning branches. Tim Carpenter sat in a hunting vest with his father's deer rifle leaning against a birch log. The outfitter pack was against a tree.

"I don't see Cliff anywhere. We'll get Tim and wait for Cliff to come back," Reuger whispered to the two men watching the fire. "Let's go."

They pushed through tangled growth with guns forward and emerged from the forest like three hunters. Tim was staring at the fire when they fanned out around him. He jumped up and shouted.

"HEY!"

Reuger crouched and covered his mouth. The fire shined on his badge and cylinder wheel of the Colt.

"Nice fire, there, Tim. Need a nice fire on a cold damp night, don't get up," he commanded, keeping his hand on his mouth. "Just sit here with me and let's not make a sound, and you tell me where Cliff went."

He slowly took his hand away.

"Went to get some more wood," he gasped.

"How long's he been gone?"

"Maybe fifteen minutes."

Reuger watched Tommy and Gus walk the perimeter then circle back. They hunched down with their hands toward the flames. Reuger spoke with his eyes on the trees.

"Why'd you run?"

He looked down with the flame light glistening in the trees. The men waited. Tim sniffed then wiped his eyes. He sniffed again.

"Did you help him, Tim?"

He nodded, wiping his eyes with the back of his wrist.

"Ya," he sobbed with eyes red and hot. "He told me to wait in the shed…I didn't think he was going to rape her, you know, I just thought he was going to make out or something…but then…" He broke into sobs with his back heaving up and down. Reuger put his hand on his shoulder.

"Easy there, Tim, easy."

The boy cried harder and shook his head.

"Did you help him, Tim?"

He buried his head in his arms. The fire snapped and popped. The sobs sounded like a wounded animal in the forest. He looked up suddenly, his face wet.

"What could I do?" He cried out. "He started to rape her, and I ran out the back door." He sniffed and looked at Reuger with mucus running from his nose. "Do I have to go to jail? Cliff said I would go to jail if I said anything."

Reuger pulled a handkerchief from his back pocket and handed it to the boy.

"Here, clean yourself up there."

He looked at Tommy and Gus.

"Let's all move out of here into the woods and wait for Cliff to come back. He's close and probably watching us right now." Reuger nodded to Tommy. "Why don't you get that deer rifle there, Tommy, then let's all move out of the camp."

The forest was dead save for the snap and pop of wood. He looked at Tim brushing his eyes on the shoulders of his shirt.

"Does Cliff have his gun?"

"Yeah..." Tim nodded.

Tommy lifted up the deer rifle and turned toward the trees. Reuger watched his body stiffen.

"What is it?"

"Something there," he murmured, staring into the trees.

Reuger motioned to Gus as Tommy slowly brought up his rifle.

"He's there," he nodded. "He's watching us..."

"Count of three here, Gus, we're going for those trees with Tim," Reuger said in a low voice.

"Got yer," he nodded breathily, grabbing his other arm.

Tommy pivoted slowly with the Winchester to his shoulder.

"He's drawing a bead..."

"One, two..."

"Reuger—he's..."

"Three!"

They ran as the clap-roar slapped their ears. Pulmonary blood burst from Gus's chest, spraying leaves and fireweed and splattering a tree like thrown paint. Reuger shoved Tim toward the trees and fell next to the blooded hole in Gus's back. He turned him gently and pulled off his vest then pressed the welling mash in his sternum. Blood frothed his lips, seeping out in a growing pool from his chest.

"Hang in there, partner, not over yet," Reuger nodded, working fast.

"All them trees never got me," he groaned beyond a whisper, beyond a groan.

"Hector!"

Static sizzled and screamed. Reuger dropped the radio, pushing hard against the hole pumping blood. Lurid fire shadows played on the waxy pallor rising from Gus's neck. Sparks flew upward and smoke drifted over. Gus coughed then gurgled blood out of his mouth.

"C'mon Gus," Reuger shouted, pushing against his bare white chest with arterial blood welling up darkly.

"Reuger...Reuger..."

"I'm here, partner."

"Take my hand..."

He grabbed the old hand and felt the heat leaving. Smoke blew over them, and Gus disappeared into white mist. Tommy kneeled and rested on the stock of the rifle.

"Gus...fight! Don't leave...fight! "

He kept one hand on the blood flow, watching the gleam in his eyes grow faint. Tommy reached and held Gus's other hand, and the three men waited by the fire.

"Reuger..." Gus whispered with bloody bubbles on his lips. "Your father..."

"We'll get you back, Gus, just hold on, we'll get you back..."

"...Your father." He groaned again, his eyes fading like candles. "Yer a lot like him..."

He squeezed his eyes tightly as his lips fluttered. Reuger cradled him in the dark wilderness. He saw the light fade in the eyes and heard the final gasp of the lungs, then the mouth opening slowly like some hardening cement.

"Gus! Breathe!"

The beard and hair now blew stiffly. Reuger lay him to the ground as Tommy brought the hand to his chest. The two men kneeled and Tommy began a throaty chant of the original people.

64

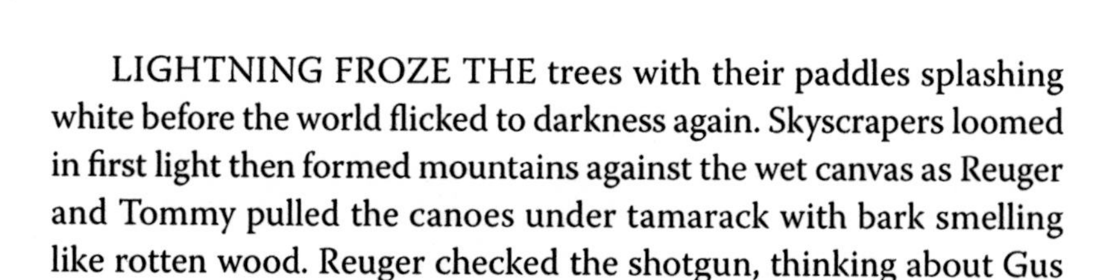

LIGHTNING FROZE THE trees with their paddles splashing white before the world flicked to darkness again. Skyscrapers loomed in first light then formed mountains against the wet canvas as Reuger and Tommy pulled the canoes under tamarack with bark smelling like rotten wood. Reuger checked the shotgun, thinking about Gus wrapped in the rain tarpaulin off the portage.

Tommy stared down the portage trail with his cap pulled low and rivulets streaking his wide brown cheeks. Water dribbled from the barrels like a garden hose as Tim shivered in the green poncho. Lightning blinked then shook the land with the rumbling farther north.

"I need you to watch the canoes for me here, think you can do that, Tim?"

He moved to the overturned canoes. Reuger picked up Jim Carpenter's .30-06 and the sawed-off shotgun and motioned down the path of brown horizon light.

"Take me to that cutter, Tommy."

"Ya, so let's go then."

They splashed down the trail that weaved back and forth and circled around trunks five feet across with water rivuleting antique bark. Moss was green and slick on the bark. Large black birds flapped low through the forest. Rain shook the leaves. They were back in the canopy of trees not much brighter than a canvas tent. Tommy's army coat clung like a wet bed sheet as he stopped. They heard a whine through the forest.

"Cutter," he nodded with rain streaming from his hat in three streams of gelatinous light. "Not far, I say less than a quarter-mile, you know."

Reuger pulled back the bolt on the deer rifle.

"Makes sense he'd run for reinforcement. I'll take it from here."

He slung the rifle and picked up the shotgun with the steel slippery and cold then moved down the washed-out trail. The path turned and Reuger fell into the soft mud and heard Tommy splash down. He wiped his eyes, staring at two men with rifles and hard hats. A yellow John Deere cutter funneled blue smoke as the arm pivoted around. It looked like a steam shovel fitted with a titanium-cutting wheel on the arm. A skidder clambered with moon tires over the terrain, grappling logs with tongs. Men cut the trees, spraying fountains of sawdust in the rain gloom. A long slim delimber whirred branches clean in seconds.

Tommy crawled up.

"Ya, those guys don't look too friendly there," he murmured.

"They have families at home."

"Maybe, but they probably fucking hate their wives, you know."

A screech shot overhead and they watched a white fountain of sawdust shoot out from the cutter. The tree fell back like a lover's death. Reuger looked around carefully.

"See anybody else with a gun?"

Tommy moved his head and spit mud from his mouth.

"Nope, look's like they're the only ones." He shook his head. "Man, they have a lot of shit up here."

"Well, loggers aren't soldiers—let's get the drop and see how she goes." Reuger turned. "But if they shoot… let's take it home…ready?"

"Ya, sure."

"Let's go then."

They charged out of the forest and Reuger lifted the shotgun.

"Deputy Sheriff—*drop it!*"

The man threw the gun and raised his hands. Tommy raised his Winchester.

"Ya, deputy!"

Reuger glanced at the second man and heard a shot. The man fell back with a bullet between his eyes. A second shot threw Tommy back into the mud. A rush of wind whined by Reuger's ear, then the stock of the shotgun splintered in his hand. He dove behind a tree with bark chipping around him and pulled up the Colt. He held the pistol high, then wheeled and fired. He ducked behind the tree and flipped open the smoking cylinder wheel and reloaded.

Reuger heard the tractor clank of the treads. He hugged the earth as sawdust seared the back of his neck like warm batter. Hydraulics hissed in his ears with hot wind blowing on his back. He felt the ground move as the tree cracked away like a shadow leaving sun. Reuger looked up covered in sawdust behind a stump not two feet high. He raised his head and saw the gleaming razored discus spinning at the end of the hydraulic arm.

Cliff Johnson opened the door of the cutter and walked on the muddy treads in sunglasses and a wet T-shirt. He held the .30.06 out from him. Patricia stood with a blue flannel shirt and her hair wet. She was gagged and her hands bound in front of her.

"Come on out, Reuger, or how about I blow a hole through your girlfriend here."

Cliff grinned with a thumb of Skoal in his lower gum like a swollen cyst. He swung up the deer rifle and cocked back the bolt. Men stood around in the rain in hard hats with beards and dark eyes and jeans and suspenders and heavy work boots. Dual exhausts caps tapped a slow rhythm.

Reuger stared at Patricia and felt a rage that blinded him. He thought about picking off Cliff, but he moved around behind Patricia and put the gun to the back of her neck.

Reuger threw his pistol in front of the stump and raised his hands.

"I'm coming out."

Cliff pulled the gun tight to his shoulder and Reuger felt a searing in his stomach and saw the men huddled in yellow slickers, the engine of the cutter breathing, the hum of the titanium wheel. The barrel exploded.

"What the fuck are you doing?"

He looked up from the mud and saw a big man facing Cliff.

"You can't shoot the sheriff in cold blood there!"

Cliff spat tobacco juice on the steel tread.

"Just showing what a chicken shit he is."

Reuger climbed up from the mud, facing the wet and tired men. A big man with a bushy beard stood over him with a rifle. It was Carl Günter. He had knocked the barrel of Cliff's rifle high. Reuger wiped mud from his eyes and looked at him.

"Cliff Johnson is wanted for the rape of a girl down at Pine Lodge," he said hoarsely. "He shot Gus in cold blood last night."

Cliff laughed and smoothed back his short spiked hair.

"That fucking old man probably tripped over his own fucking rifle. He'll say anything to save his skin now." He pointed with the barrel. "He's in it with Jorde and been killing loggers! Hell, that one there shot Al Hanes in cold blood, and *he* raped the girl—and Reuger there let him go!"

Tommy sat in a puddle with long hair clawing his cheeks. A man held a rifle to his neck.

"Ya, that's true, Carl, I heard about that," a ginger-bearded man nodded. "Came up here and shot Al. Maybe we should do same for them here."

"Sure they did." Cliff's face reddened, the pack of tobacco mutating his face. "They're trying to take jobs away from you men and killing loggers—hell, they just shot Jack there!"

"That bullet came from Cliff Johnson's rifle," Reuger said steadily.

"Fuck you, tree hugger."

"Cliff Johnson burned out Foster Jones, then shot him," Reuger continued steadily, not taking his eye from any man's gaze. "He wanted to make it look like Tom Jorde did it."

"Ya, that's a big one." Cliff spat down on the tread, motioning the rifle to the sky. "Why don't you ask your fucking friend Gary Chatoee about that one."

"Might have to do it, Carl," a man called out. "They've been killing loggers…I say we do the same for them."

The rain filled in the silence. Reuger looked at the big man holding the rifle. He paused, feeling the weight in his vest pocket.

"Annabel enjoy that graduation party last year?"

Carl Günter turned slowly and stared at him like he had been slapped. The rain beat down harder and splattered in the mud around them. His dark eyes narrowed.

"What the fuck would you know about that?"

Reuger lifted his chin to the cutter.

"Why don't you ask Cliff there."

"Ya, he's talking shit." Cliff waved down, rain plastering his T-shirt to his torso. "Don't listen to him, Carl."

Reuger nodded to Cliff.

"That one there believes he can do anything. Not hard to believe he'd shoot a man in cold blood or rape a girl in a woodshed…"

Cliff spat on the tread.

"You're lying."

Reuger kept his eyes on the big man staring at him suspiciously.

"A year ago I found Annabel just before the landing. She was wandering down the road in the middle of the night with her shirt torn up and her shorts spilt through the crotch."

Cliff swung the rifle around.

"He's talking shit..."

"She was afraid to tell me what happened, Carl...afraid to go accuse the son of Ben Johnson of rape."

A spidery vein dipped from the swollen sky and deafened the men. Cliff grinned and shook his head.

"Ya, sure, Reuger. This is all more of your tree hugger bullshit here." He turned back to the dark eyes and hair plastered to wet skulls.

"You men have known me here and my dad all your lives. We give you your jobs, and we'll keep you logging." He turned around, jabbing his finger. "This son of a bitch here wants to take that away from you! I told you I would keep you working, and I've been doing it..."

"Keep you men working by logging in federal lands." Reuger stared at the men with the trees lying behind them. "See here the new model—Cliff is going to outdo his father by breaking the law—Ben always bought the law, so why not..."

Reuger heard the bolt of the rifle and saw the stock by Cliff's cheek. No man made a move to stop him and the long dark barrel loomed down from the rain. He touched his vest and looked at Carl Günter.

"I'm going to reach into my pocket...something I want you to hear...

"Get out of the way, Carl!" Cliff shouted.

"I can prove he raped your daughter," Reuger said steadily.

Carl Günter stood close, his hard hat pouring water from the brim, trickling through heavy beard. The ground shook with light.

"Ya, you have one minute here."

Reuger pulled the wet micro recorder from his pocket and pressed the button. He didn't hear anything and hit the fast-forward. He pressed the play button again.

"He's made up some kind of bullshit, Carl..."

Annabel's voice crossed the dead air like a flower in a coal mine.

"He was tearing at my clothes...I couldn't stop him. He tore my panties in two and pushed my legs apart with his knee and kept his hand on my mouth so tightly...I fought him..." Annabel sniffed. "I couldn't stop him. It was supposed to be a graduation party, it was supposed to be fun." She was crying now. "... But that Cliff Johnson... he raped me there in the sawdust in the back of his truck..."

Carl stared as Reuger clicked the tape back and played it again.

The mechanical voice tortured the air. Carl Günter's eyes blinked and his lashes were wet and a rash rolled up from his neck. He was a big Scandinavian. A man who had labored all of his life in the forest and took for granted what was finite. Now, he looked as if someone had just told him the world was composed of air.

"She didn't want to say anything, Carl. She didn't want you to lose your job."

Carl suddenly reached forward and grabbed his bicep, crushing down with a gasping whine from his mouth. Reuger winced, holding the big man off, then he was gone into the rain. He slogged through the mud then stopped and stared up. Cliff spread out his arms.

"You aren't going to listen to this bullshit! Carl, it's all shit he and those tree huggers cooked up!"

Carl Günter stood below with rain falling on his cheeks. Cliff stepped back on the lead colored treads and fell down. He scrambled to his feet and pointed.

"He's fucking crazy!" Cliff swung his arms against the sky and stared down. "Now my father has treated you well—this son of a bitch has you all going now!"

A bolt of lightning exploded in the forest.

"You know me and my dad!" Cliff hit his chest. "We employ you, not the goddamn tree huggers here!" Another roar of electricity flew overhead, and the rain came down harder on the men and the machines. Cliff screamed against the storm. "He's a traitor...he's in it with Jorde who's been murdering loggers..."

Another sonic crash of light broke against the sky. The men surrounded the cutter and looked up at Cliff. The exhaust pipes steamed in the rain. Cliff saw wet beards and eyes and water dribbling off the brims of hard hats.

"You men..." His voice went up an octave. "You men do as I say here!"

The sullen wet men encircled him closer.

"Cliff burned out Foster Jones then shot him," Reuger continued in a low voice, walking closer. "They wanted to keep Foster quiet about what's been going on up here. Then they framed Tom Jorde for the murder. All part of Ben's plan here. He wanted to get these trees out a long time," Reuger nodded gesturing to the forest. "He knew if Tom Jorde was fighting a murder charge then he could log it out."

The men stared at Cliff with the dead man behind in the mud. The cut trees now looked like some unholy accident. The world blinked as a tree split like a rifle shot. Cliff swung the rifle around dangerously, spitting the Skoal from his swollen lip.

"You men know me!" He was almost shrieking. "That old man Foster was dead when I got there...*we wouldn't kill loggers!*"

"Then he shot Gus Vanzant in the back." Reuger shook his head, opening his hand to the trees. "Logging is dying in the Northwoods here. Logged out a hundred years ago and this is all that's left except for the small trees and the jack pine. Ben could set his price on these trees here." He stared at the men. "But it's over now, and Ben knows that—he's known it for years. This was the last act of a desperate man..."

The explosion blinded them, then the crack took away sound. The bolt had struck so close it knocked men off their feet. Reuger saw Cliff pull the rifle tight to his shoulder and the barrel flash and heard the bullet go over his head. Then Cliff was gone. He had flown off the tread into the mud with the rifle clapping beside him. Cliff stared up as Carl Günter marched toward him splashing water and mud.

"Ya little shit, ya raped my goddamn daughter!"

"Don't believe him," he screamed, backing up on all fours. "I didn't touch her! *I swear I didn't!*"

Carl Günter hoisted Cliff up by his neck as another tree burst into flames.

"I didn't do it, Carl!"

"You little fucking shit!"

The muscles on Carl's forearms bulged as he squeezed down on his neck. Cliff struggled against his iron grip and kicked air. Jet engines roared overhead as thunderheads collided and destroyed trees. Carl Günter squeezed his neck closed.

"Ya...little...fucking...shit!"

Reuger brought his elbow down on Carl's forearm and Cliff fell and retched on the ground. He groaned and turned over slowly, rolling in the rain and mud then scooped the rifle Carl had dropped.

"You stupid bastard," he yelled hoarsely.

Carl Günter lunged at him, and the Winchester flamed the damp air with the bang ringing in Reuger's ears. Carl fell in a muddy slide, and Cliff threw the rifle and sprinted into the titanium razor wheel spinning at five hundred miles an hour. A viscous splotch of blood and intestines and body organs splattered the yellow machine. Cliff separated like a man at odds with himself, and his trunk fell next to the cedar.

65

REUGER PARKED IN front of the reservation store the day after he returned. Dust winded down the street and the tin roofs of the buildings scraped and flexed noisily. Farther down the road, he saw two men walking with sledges toward the lake. He swung out and walked up on the store porch and tried the screen door, then trailed around back to a wrecked station wagon and piles of tires.

The back door was older but locked. Reuger pushed up a window and reached around and turned the lock and let himself in. The store was a wreck of boxes and mops and stacked soda pop bottles. He walked steadily toward the front and looked out the window. He turned and walked through the storeroom past the toilet and turned to another door. There was a cot and a dresser and the room smelled of dirty socks. A detective-style lamp was lit over a desk and a device resembling a red bicycle pump.

He crossed to the desk and picked up .22 and .44 caliber brass casings scattered on the top. A tub of gunpowder was on the floor next to three stacked white boxes. He reached down and thumbed open the lid. The percussion caps gleamed like mined silver.

* * * *

Gary Chatoee lay in the hospital room and nodded to a nurse putting down a vase of flowers by a dirty window not open to the late summer day. The arrangement was a mixture of wildflowers. The nurse left and Gary turned and grinned.

"I have a secret admirer here."

Reuger scraped up a chair and laid a brass cartridge on the bedside tray then a silver bracelet next to the cartridge. He doffed his hat and looked at his old friend.

"Want to tell me about it, Gary?"

His face lightened to a sallow hue and he stared down at the sheet with peaks of gray in his hair. Gary looked out the window past the flowers. Reuger spoke quietly.

"I searched Tommy before he got on that plane. He had nothing in his pockets, but you sat next to him."

Gary stared down at his big hands and moved his thumbs. Reuger saw his eyes go to the cartridge.

"Found three of those reloads there. One from Tom Jorde's pistol and one behind my cabin, and one in that fire up by the old logging camp." Reuger dropped a boot to the tile floor and moved so the Colt wouldn't jab his side. "I pulled those shells from Tommy's Winchester. He told me he bought his ammo from you at the store, but he didn't know they were reloads. So I went to your store and saw the reloader and the .22 and .44 jackets next to the box of silver percussion caps." He tilted his hat back and shook his head doubtfully. "Smart to use reloads, Gary. But you know, nowadays..." Reuger shook his head again. "Most people don't reload their own ammo anymore, and you don't own a .22."

The windowpane was growing longer, and the flowers had shadows on the buds. Gary kneaded his hands.

"What'd Ben promise you?"

Gary opened his mouth then closed it.

"Ben promised you he'd pay up if you helped him frame Jorde and Tommy?"

Gary looked down. Reuger pulled his hand back through his hair and stared at the sweat stains on the brim of his hat. Gary spoke in a low voice.

"You know what jack pine is?"

He tilted his head up. "Jack pine is shit. And what did they leave us after we had the land for hundreds of years? We end up with a bunch of scraggly ass jack pine. That's what we been cutting on tribal property for the last hundred years, fucking jack pine after they come and take all the good timber." He paused. "So finally the white man needed something again from the Indian, and I was there to get it."

Gary lifted his head.

"You think I'm not going to throw some drunk to the whites for a chance to better our people?" Perspiration beaded his brow, lips, slicking his sides under the half garment. "He always dragging us down and them tree huggers who want to try and get our timber too. You don't think I'm not going to take a deal like that?"

Gary's eyes burned against the sheets.

"We could have built schools and stores and homes with that money! All they want to leave us is the crap, you know, what they always leave the Indians."

Gary looked at his hands again. "What'd Ben want you to do?"

He shrugged, then breathed heavy and stared out the window.

"He wanted someone to burn out Foster and Carter and make it look like the tree hugger did it."

"Thinking you'd get Tommy to do it then?"

Gary bit his lip, staring at some distant point.

"I knew he'd fuck it up. Before I could even get him to do it that Cliff Johnson goes and kills Foster."

Reuger rubbed his jaw. "Ah, fuck, Gary."

"Ya," he nodded slowly.

"Cliff gave you the bracelet then?"

Reuger stared at his friend.

"Ah, shit."

He stood and walked to the window. From the hospital room, he saw the black line of the Northern forest against the encroaching town. He spread his hands out on the sill.

"After I found those percussion caps, I saw some men working down by the lake, Gary." Reuger kept his hands on the sill with light in his hair. "So I went down there and saw they were building a dock. I kept hoping I wouldn't find any of those spikes. Thought maybe they might use screws, but they were using dock spikes."

He watched a man walk down the deserted street below.

"Ya, what would you do? They slaughtered my people like the buffalo, and you think I'm going to cry for some old logger stealing trees from the Boundary Waters when I can finally get something back from these fucking locusts."

Gary's voice echoed off the hard-walled room. Reuger turned and leaned back, crossing one boot over the other. He squeezed the bridge between his eyes and felt some sort of wonder at the chicanery of Ben Johnson. He had covered every angle, and with one stroke he would solve his Indian problem, knock off the environmentalists, and take the treasure of the land.

"Why'd you shoot him, Gary?"

He frowned like a man lamenting over a technical problem.

"You probably should get a good lawyer."

Gary shook his head. "They just talk a lot of shit, you know."

"I have to do my job, Gary."

"Ya, I trust you," he nodded slowly and looked up. "That Carter, he was still alive when I walked up." He rolled his shoulders. "I figured that spike just wound him and you go after the tree hugger then." Gary's eyes welled up in the window light. "But he was laying there you know, choking on his own blood, and there was nothing I could do for him, and I had that gun I stole out of the tree hugger's truck." The big tears rolled down the scarred brown cheeks. "So I had to stop him from suffering, you know... I can still see his eyes when I pointed that gun at him..."

Gary wiped his eyes and breathed deeply.

"My hand shook so much, I missed the first time."

He wiped his cheeks again as a young nurse breezed in with shoes gumming the tiles. She pulled the shade up farther and touched the flowers and then circled around to the bed.

"Hello, Mr. Chatoee, time to take your temperature here," she sang, slipping a thermometer in his mouth with a cord running to a monitor.

Reuger leaned against the frame of the window.

"It's normal," she announced and touched the bed tray and picked up the bracelet and held it to her wrist. "What a pretty bracelet!"

Gary nodded slightly and the door whooshed closed.

Reuger walked over and picked up his hat from the chair.

"Ben would have never paid you for that timber."

"Ya, maybe..." He shrugged. "But I had to try though, you know."

He stopped by his bed.

"You should work on your aim," he said, nodding.

Gary shrugged.

"I hit that window where I wanted it."

"You sure?"

"Oh, ya." He tilted his head up. "You going to arrest me?"

"I know where you are for now. I'll need you to testify against Ben Johnson."

He gestured toward the open window.

"Ya, sure. Maybe I can get a better deal then, huh?"

"Maybe."

Gary turned in from the window.

"How do you know I won't run for Canada?"

"If you do, I have a hell of a tracker."

Gary Chatoee nodded slowly.

"Ya, Tommy...he's a good tracker, that one."

* * * *

Reuger parked beyond the fence at noon around Johnson Timber. He stepped out with the Winchester and walked with his badge catching light against the vest. He saw a squad car outside the fence and felt the warrant in his pocket he picked up from Bruce Anderson.

He leaned up to the dusty car and stared at the two deputies.

"What are you boys doing here?"

Hank Jennings nodded to the mill.

"Sheriff thought we ought to sit outside of Johnson Timber and make sure Mr. Johnson doesn't get any ideas about taking a trip to Canada."

Reuger squinted at the two men in deputy uniforms.

"I'm going to go serve Mr. Johnson a warrant."

Hank nodded slowly.

"Need some assistance?"

"Better do this one myself."

"I'll give you fifteen minutes, Reuger, then we're coming in."

"Fifteen minutes then."

He walked through the gate standing open and across the lot empty except for Ben's double tandem truck. Reuger walked to the office building and glanced in the window then tracked along the shrubbery line past the reception area. He crossed into the lumberyard with the wood gassing out from stacked boards. He glanced into the mill barns and walked past the piled sawdust and parked skidders and cutters gleaming sun. Reuger turned in the barn quiet and headed for the office. He pushed open the door with leveler shades and the jingling bell. The smell of cigars and cheap leather washed his raw senses as he saw Penny's empty desk. A light was on inside the half-open door. He levered up a shell, pushing the door slowly open with his right hand.

Cigar smoke resined the brass clock and gold pens on the desk and pictures of senators and businessmen. Cliff smiled in his football uniform on the credenza behind his desk. The loggers in the black and white picture leaned back against the treasure of a country. Reuger walked back through the office and heard a faucet drip in the bathroom. The bell jangled again then he was back in the hot dry sun and wispy sand.

He entered the old mill barn with stacked wood and logs on the conveyor belt. Ben Johnson walked out of that light. Reuger stood in the garage-sized doorway. Ben was looking at something in his hand. When he looked up he saw a man with a rifle and a hat silhouetted against the packed sand of the yard. He stopped and put something in the pocket of his jacket and tilted up the dark Stetson.

"What in the hell are you doing on my property?"

Reuger reached into his vest and held up the folded warrant.

"Come to arrest you."

"What the hell for?"

"Conspiracy to commit murder and logging in federal lands."

He snorted and shook his head.

"You aren't going to arrest anybody."

Reuger slipped the warrant into his vest and raised the rifle.

"You going to shoot me?"

"If I have to," Reuger nodded.

Ben shook his head slowly.

"Your sheriff couldn't do it, and you think you have right to arrest me after you destroy my business and murder my son?"

"You murdered your son, Ben."

His eyes filled, his face turning crimson under his white hair. "I'll have you run out of this town on a rail you son of a bitch! I have a call into governor, and then I'll do to you what you did to my son, you fucking bastard."

Reuger held the rifle waist high, standing in the barn light with the boards stacked around them. "You had Cliff go out there and burn out Foster, then he shot him with his own gun."

Ben stepped forward, jabbing his finger through the air.

"That slasher was burning when he got there, and that old man was dead! Why the fuck would I protect him now?"

"Cliff raped that girl and you covered for him, Ben. The way you're covering for him now. You used your son for you own dirty work and never gave him any limits."

Ben stepped toward him.

"What in the fuck do you know about being a father?"

The two men stood across from each other, then Ben wiped his eyes and pulled his hat low.

"I'm walking through that goddamn door."

He began walking toward the lumberyard. Reuger raised the rifle to his shoulder and aimed at his midsection. He felt his heart, his breathing, and his leg muscles. He felt the muscles in his arm tense as Ben walked by.

"I knew you couldn't do it, you yellow piece of shit," he muttered.

Reuger held the rifle low and reached out. Ben punched with his right fist and the blow hard-balled the side of his head and knocked his hat off. Reuger staggered a few steps then set the rifle down and reached Ben in the lumberyard. He grabbed his fleshy arm and pulled the large man to the ground.

"Get your goddamn hands off of me," he roared, his Stetson flailing dust and face flushed red.

Reuger cocked back and punched him. Ben scraped his neck with fingernails and tried to strangle him. Reuger hammered his nose, and he grunted with his thin white hair wild. Ben tried to slap him, then swung with his fists. Reuger dragged him along the ground by his arm, sand coating his face like granular paint. Ben swore and coughed and spit blood. Reuger levered his arm behind him, then booted his neck and twisted his arm until he had Ben Johnson like a steer.

"You're under arrest," he gasped, pulling out the handcuffs with his free hand. "For conspiracy to commit murder and logging in federal lands."

"You dirty bastard," he croaked.

Reuger clapped one handcuff on his wrist.

"Jim Hurley broke his back in '66 when you were running the crews..." He twisted the other arm back and ratcheted the handcuffs closed. "Winds were high that day and you made the men cut anyway, and a tree fell the wrong way and broke his back." Reuger tightened the handcuffs until they pinched, keeping his boot on his neck. "You killed him same as you had a gun."

He pulled Ben up and heard him pass gas. Reuger stared at the old man with hair on his brow and dust on his cheeks and pants. The expensive blue-twilled cotton shirt with Johnson Timber on the right pocket was torn open. Reuger pushed him back, and he fell into the dust and groaned.

"That was my father, you son of a bitch," he said, watching the deputies come through the gate like the Indians at Little Big Horn.

66

THE CABIN WAS much the same. Fire flickered on the hearth, and the two men sat in chairs by the warmth and light. The pistol shone dully from the nail from the holster from the mantel. The kerosene lantern was fire blackened, and the hat didn't move below it. Tommy Tobin smoked in Gus's old chair, and they heard wind outside the door.

"So what's going to happen to Gary Chatoee then?"

"What say?"

Tommy pulled the cigar from his mouth.

"You going to arrest him there in the hospital?"

Reuger turned the page of his book.

"I gave everything to Bruce Anderson. He gives me the warrant, I'll go arrest him there."

He tilted his camouflaged hat up.

"Ya, but I thought he confessed there."

"He gets a lawyer, and what he said in that hospital bed won't amount to much," Reuger murmured.

Tommy put the cigar back in his mouth and blew smoke toward the ceiling.

"You see? The Indians are their own worst enemy. Here he was trying to throw me to the wolves, you know, and for what? *Fucking money*." He held the cigar down. "It makes you sick to see your people doing the same dumb thing over and over."

"Gary just got mixed up," Reuger said, picking up his beer.

"Ya, one way to put it...so, what's the book?"

"One you lent me."

"Oh, ya, good book," he nodded putting the cigar back in his mouth. "Gary Chatoee should have read that book you know." He tilted his head back. "That boy and his mother leave Pine Lodge?"

"Tomorrow morning."

He nodded, rolling the fat dark tobacco between his fingers.

"That's too bad. She was a nice woman, you know." His dark eyes lifted slowly. "You should see her again. Boy seemed nice too."

Reuger put the book down in his lap and thought of Kurt's bedroom hours before. He had watched him take out the green-brimmed hat from the bag.

"Wow! Awesome! Thanks, Reuger!"

He plunked the hat on in the pine walled room.

"What do you say there, partner?"

"Let me fix the brim for you there, sum buck," he said shaping the brim and putting the hat farther back on his head.

Kurt stared at him with bright eyes.

"How does it look?"

Reuger squeezed one eye closed.

"Like a North Woodsman."

"Cool!"

"Ya, there's a dead wolf on the Fernberg."

He turned down the squelch on the radio. "A dead wolf, huh?"

"They're around," Reuger nodded, resting his elbows on his knees. "Ever heard them howl?"

Kurt shook his head, and the hat fell forward.

"Well, you never forget it," he said fixing the hat for him again. "The sound goes right down to the bone. It's the ancient song of the kill. Next time you come up, we'll see some wolves."

"Yeah, next time,' he mumbled, trailing off.

Kurt rubbed a scab on his knee and Reuger saw the scuffed tennis shoes, the mosquito bites. He wondered who would tend to the cuts and bruises of boyhood. A working mother could only do so much.

"You aren't going to see my mother anymore, are you?"

Reuger clasped his hands and composed his face.

"Well, your mother and I had a long conversation about that, and we both agreed it was better if she went back to her life, and I stayed here," he said smoothly. "But I'm sure I will see her again when you come back up here."

Kurt took off the hat and laid it in his lap.

"But you didn't ask her to stay up here?"

"She has to get back to her life, Kurt, like you have to get back to yours."

He put his arm behind his head.

"I don't want to go back," he replied in a small voice.

"Well, maybe not now," Reuger nodded. "But once you go back, I'm sure that will change."

"I like it here," he said looking around the room of knotty pine. "I know my mom would like to see you again. She gets lonely at home."

Reuger leaned down and met the boy's eyes.

"Your mother is a very special lady, Kurt, who will meet someone just right for her."

"She should just stay up here," he muttered, rubbing a scab on his knee. "Then she could see you."

"Your mother has a job, Kurt."

"No, she doesn't." He looked up with the large hat back on. "They fired her."

The boy and the man stared at each other.

"I heard her on the phone," he shrugged.

Reuger breathed heavily. "Well, if I know your mother, she'll land on her feet."

"No." Kurt crossed his arms. "She'll just go back to working all the time like before and never meet anybody and die a lonely old maid."

Reuger stood slowly and rested his hands on his gun belt. He paused then pistoled his fingers.

"Now you be careful down there in the lower forty-eight."

Kurt stared up with the big cowboy hat and managed a smile. He put out his hand and they shook, and Reuger pulled him in and smelled his hair and his skin. Kurt sat back down and waved.

"Goodbye, Reuger."

The fire popped loudly and Reuger looked back down at his book. Tommy puffed again like some caricature of a man enjoying a cigar in front of the fire. He shook his head slowly.

"Ya, you should ask that lady and her boy to stay, you know."

Reuger stared at the page, "Think so?"

"I do," he nodded slowly. "If you don't, you're still just as fucking lost as when I picked you up in the snow." Tommy looked over his cigar and gestured. "Maybe it's time for you to go back, you know, Reuger."

He lay the book down and stared at the impassive man.

"Like yourself?"

"No." He shook his head. "But you're not like me." Tommy puffed on the cigar and looked through the smoke. "I'm better alone, and you're better with someone, you know. That boy and his mother saved your ass out there on the old lodge road. Maybe it's time you saved someone's ass you know, maybe it's time you went back."

"Back to the lower forty-eight?"

"Nope." Tommy tapped his chest. "Back in your heart."

Reuger set the book down and picked up the torn ten-dollar bill for a marker. He paused and turned the ripped currency in his hand.

"Ya," Tommy nodded. "That's not much good without the other half, you know."

Reuger put the ripped bill into the pages and looked up.

"Ben Johnson said something in his lumber yard that's been bothering me."

"Ya, what's that?"

Reuger looked up.

"He said that slasher was burning when Cliff got there....What'd you see when you got there?"

Tommy rolled his shoulders.

"Just Cliff standing there, you know."

Reuger stared at the fire.

"What time did you see him then?"

"What's that?"

"What time did you see Cliff at Foster's slasher?"

Tommy curled his lip out and rolled his shoulders.

"Must have been around ten o'clock, you know...but I don't wear a watch."

"What was he doing?"

Tommy squinted through the smoky light.

"Like I say...just standing there." He stood and turned on the radio. "You thinking something else about Foster?"

"Slasher still burning or smoldering?"

"Ya," he squinted into the fire, "must have been smoldering now that I think about it."

The polka music ended, and they both looked up to the voice on the radio.

"And Sheriff, it was these thieves at Johnson Timber all along trying to frame you along with the unseen forces of greed and avarice that has nearly destroyed this country."

"That's right, John. I knew what was going on in the Boundary Waters but needed hard proof. It was a conspiracy, and these things take a lot of investigating to prove—"

"Now pardon me for interrupting you there, Sheriff, but this reporter knew from the start it was a conspiracy here and it was from my tireless investigation that the End of the Road program uncovered these shenanigans of the timber barons, and it was only through my dogged pursuit of the truth that my suspicions were borne.

Tommy snapped off the radio and sat down.

"Nothing fucking changes, you know."

"Nope," Reuger said slowly. "Nothing does."

He leaned back then looked at the radio. His eyes drifted over to the two-way radio on the table next to his book. "Nothing does," he muttered, scooping the receiver.

"Hector!"

"Ya, go ahead, Reuger."

"I need you to run a print for me."

67

JOHN MCFEE SAT at a gunmetal-colored desk and pecked at a typewriter. The storefront was glass and the light played over him like an aquarium of rippling yellow waves. The keys of the typewriter clacked in the staccato of a train starting and stopping. Mcfee slammed the return carriage back and looked up at the man in front of him.

"Never could get used to those computers," he said motioning Reuger to a chair. "Them girls have to scan all my type in."

He laughed and continued pecking. Reuger glanced at his watch and put his hat on the edge of the desk.

"Jest puttin' the finishing touches here on the biggest story the *Standard* has ever had," he muttered.

Reuger looked around the bare office with the computers over empty desks. He watched John Mcfee with one eye closed, pecking at the typewriter.

"Is it big enough, John, to allow you to keep your radio station?"

Mcfee's finger stopped and his right eye opened slowly. He hunched down behind the typewriter like a man behind a bulwark.

"What yer mean by that?"

"I think you know."

"Don't get yer meanin."

Reuger eyed the small man.

"I did some checking, John. Seems Kroning's family wasn't too happy with his donation to you and the town."

Mcfee balled his tongue.

"Still don't get yer meanin."

Reuger looked at the coffee pot against the wall.

"They were putting a lot of pressure on you, John. Ratings had been going straight down for the paper and the station since Kroning made his gift. They said you were destroying their investment and wanted to bring in other people."

Mcfee leaned back from the desk and crossed his arms.

"Yer tryin' some trick here, Reuger?"

He pulled the pad from his top pocket.

"That won't help you, John." He leaned close to the desk. "You know what never made sense to me?" Reuger paused. "How'd you already have that story written that morning at Foster's slasher. I didn't know what happened..." Reuger nodded. "But you did."

John wiped his mouth.

"I told you. I was following up on a developing story there..."

Mcfee blushed suddenly and stood up from the desk. The swivel chair fell straight back to the floor with a crash.

"Intimidating the press is a serious business here and..."

"I have your print on the gun, John."

Mcfee stopped with his hand in the air like a frozen manikin.

"I thought it was Cliff's. But the timing didn't match up. Tommy Tobin saw Cliff out there around ten or so, but Foster was shot three hours before and his slasher had burned down by then. By the time Cliff got there, Foster was already dead."

Mcfee was red. He pulled on his scraggly mustache then glanced to the front door. Perspiration glistened on his forehead. Reuger picked up his hat and touched the Colt.

"You have a record, John. Public intoxication. I had Hector run the print on the gun. It wasn't Jorde's and it wasn't Cliff Johnson's and it wasn't Tommy Tobin's. It was yours, John."

Mcfee's arms came down to his sides. Reuger saw the flannel shirt and the mukluks and the white socks. He had the air of a man who had just retired from a long job.

"Sit down, John."

Mcfee pulled up the swivel chair and sat down heavily.

"Want to tell me about it?"

He put his forehead down on the typewriter. Traffic drifted by the storefront. He breathed heavily like a man tired from a long race.

"You ever been touched by lightning, Reuger?"

"Nope, can't say I have."

Mcfee lifted his head and tapped the return carriage with his forehead. His eyes leaked tears as he spoke down into the keys.

"When that Charles Kroning come along, he touched me with lightning. Didn't have a life until he listened to my *End of the Road* program." He raised his head slowly, his eyes glassy and red. "Then I was somebody. I was somebody, and I went to his funeral and stood by Dan Rather himself. *Dan Rather!* I was on three fucking networks, interviewed by twenty papers..." He shook his head. "Do you know what that feels like to stand next to those kind of people? Yer feel like a millionaire...like someone jest took you out of yer life and put yer up on a cloud."

Tears rolled down his cheeks. Mcfee sniffed.

"I was one of the pallbearers, Reuger...me, John Mcfee, carrying Charles Kroning's body to his final resting place."

He wept heavily and sniffed.

"It feels jest like heaven. Because you are like them and all this shitty life out here is below you." He wiped his eyes. "But then you come back and the damn wave just leaves. For a while, you're somebody, but then you sort of fade away. And them damn Kroning children wanted the station back, and they start sayin' I'm a nuisance and there's no reason I should be employed by the station and paper he give me." He stared at Reuger. "Me! I'm a nuisance!...Charles Kroning loved what I was doing here and if he was here..."

He trailed off and put his head back down.

Reuger watched him and thought how a whim of one man becomes life for another. He wondered how much Charles Kroning really thought about what he was doing.

"Quicksilver fame never lasts, John," he said in a low voice.

Mcfee rubbed his eyes again and smoothed back his scraggly hair.

"I jest didn't think it would all go away so fast," he muttered.

"So, you needed a story."

Mcfee sat up and stared as if woken from a long sleep.

"That's right. I *knew* there was a story. I knew an environmental war was brewing and I jest had to sniff it out, and by God I was right! That Jorde had told me they were taking trees from the Boundary Waters, and he thought Foster was one of 'em. So I went out there to talk to Foster several times, and he wouldn't say what he knew, but he thought someone might try and burn him out....Said it might be the environmentalists and it might be Johnson Timber. So I waited and waited for it to happen..." He looked up. "But it never did."

"So you set the fire?"

Mcfee looked up, his eyes clear and blue.

"Yer have to give a story a nudge now and then, Reuger. I knew this was a tinder keg, and so I just touched the fuse.... Was goin' to happen sooner or later, and I figured it was the kind of thing that radical Jorde woulda done anyway. Charles Kroning said a man has to be willing to do whatever it takes to bring a story out! He said he had crossed the line many a time to bring out a story he thought were important."

Reuger looked at the small man and felt some pity for him.

Mcfee jumped up, his eyes wild.

"I got stations and reporters from all over the country calling me and wanting the scoop! Had the *National Enquirer* just on the phone...*People* magazine was talking about coming down to do a story on the man who investigated the story....You have to get things goin' sometimes is all!"

Reuger clasped his hands together.

"Foster came along then."

Mcfee stared at him.

"He sleeps in that cab there!" He cried out. "I figured no one was around, but he come out of the truck like a wild bear...there should be a law against a man of his years carrying a firearm." John shook his head gravely. "He come at me with his gun, and I just tried to keep him from shooting me. I knocked it up, and it went off."

Mcfee drew himself up then stared glassy-eyed.

"It was an accident, Reuger. I never meant to shoot the old logger, but he jest kept waving that gun around, and I went to grab for it, and it blew off by his ear." John wiped his eyes and shook his head miserably. "I'm sorry for the old man, Reuger, I really am, but justice was served in a bigger sense. Look what was uncovered because of it! The ruthless timber barons' exploitation of the last old growth in the country! Besides old Foster probably would have..."

Mcfee trailed off again.

"Shot himself anyway," Reuger said softly, standing up.

Mcfee stepped back.

"Yer can't muzzle the press!"

"I need you to come with me, John."

Mcfee stared at him then slowly sat down at the typewriter dazed. He opened his mouth several times then collapsed back into the chair and covered his eyes. He didn't move.

"You know what Charles Kroning said to me?" He took his hands away and looked up with pained eyes. "He said I was the last *original*

American...said I was the descendent of the *pioneering* spirit that settled this country! That was why he bought me the radio station and newspaper." Mcfee stared at the floor and rolled his head. "He said he didn't want to see that die out, and that I would have to continue doing my good work in his legacy!"

"That's a heavy mantle, John."

"By God it is, but I carried it, didn't I?" Mcfee's eyes brimmed with tears. "I carried it, didn't I? The mines are played out, and the trees are gone, and I took what was mine by God...I took the only thing left...I took the *story*."

Reuger shook his head slowly.

"A man is dead for your story."

He held up his hand weakly.

"Accident...Reuger... don't yer see that?"

"C'mon, John, let's go."

Mcfee gestured to the typewriter.

"But...but, I have to finish my *story* here!"

"You just did," he said taking him by the arm.

68

THE FIRST REAL snow fell in late October and powdered the land and wisped the air and then settled down and accumulated a good two inches. Reuger drove through the forest, ducking behind the windshield even though the cloth top was on. Air leaked in the sides, and he stayed close to the heater. He swung off the road and bumped across a field to a red pickup and turned off the motor to the slight hiss of ice crystals. His boots left wet tracks and he kept his hands in his coat.

"How she go?"

Ross Haber pulled the cigarette from his mouth in a torrent of blue smoke. The saw puttered by his leg with the bright red lumber jacket like a flag.

"Morning, Sheriff."

"Staying warm here?"

"Oh, it's not too bad, you know."

Reuger squinted out with ice crystals on the brim of his hat.

"First snow."

"Ya, you bet."

"How's the logging?"

Ross smiled and snuffed the motor.

"Oh, I'll make a dollar, but if I was doing it for the money, then I wouldn't be doing it, Sheriff."

"Tough way to make a living for sure."

"Oh, ya, only reason to be a logger these days is because you like being in the forest." Ross waved the sky. "I'll be out here until they take me out stiff as a board, you know."

Reuger gestured to a tree with orange tape.

"Something special?"

"Those trees are the ones they say I can't cut. White pines." He curled up his mouth and smoked. "Probably some of the last of the old growth around here, but they say I got to leave 'em."

"Jorde?"

He shook his head. "Some new fella. That Tom Jorde is gone, from what I hear. The new fellah is a lot less radical. He says Tom Jorde made for a lot of bad publicity, and we all have to work together now. They have their say, and them people down there may think a tree is something more than it is..." He turned with an old smile. "But it's all just agriculture to me."

"More complicated these days," Reuger nodded.

"Oh, ya." Ross brushed snow from the saw. "My grandkids won't see logging in the Northwoods anymore. They'll have to listen to granddad tell his stories here." He clipped the cigarette between oiled fingers. "But like I say, they can push me down to a little corner of the woods, and I'll still be out here among these trees."

"Won't keep you from your work, then." Reuger waved, walking toward the jeep. "Stay warm, Ross."

"Oh, ya, you bet, Sheriff...oh, yer have another one of them cards? I meant to call yer the other day. Having a little problem with the wolves back here and was wondering if I could shoot a couple of them."

Reuger opened his wallet and pulled out a card.

"Yer dropped something there, Sheriff," he said picking up the torn currency.

Thanks, Ross."

"Must be a half of ten there."

"Oh, ya."

"You carry that around a lot, do yer?"

"I guess I do."

Ross's eyes sparkled.

"I'm not one to say anything, Deputy, but I might ask why you carry around half of a ten-dollar bill."

Reuger paused and held the crinkled and ripped currency. The cold nipped his face, and he saw how the paper was lacerated and crumpled.

"Reminds me of someone."

Ross Haber put another cigarette to his lips.

"Someone special, Sheriff?"

"Oh, ya."

Ross picked up the chain saw and popped it with one pull.

"Well," he said turning toward another tree, smoking like a steam engine, "might not be my place to say it, but it's not much good without the other half there, Sheriff."

Reuger looked up at the man holding the whining saw. He thought about the quiet of his cabin and the phone bill that was over four hundred dollars a month. He thought about the boy he had left so many years ago and the boy he was yet to find. He thought about time and the coming winter and the lonely nights. He thought about her and looked at the old woodsman.

"You might be right there, Ross."

69

REUGER HELD AN urn next to Irene Peters as they flew over Basswood Lake over a troop of Boy Scouts heading toward International Falls. He stared down at the curved pools of pink light and the great shelf of the northern continent. He imagined the glaciers coming down and carving the lakes then the trees of the last century filling the land.

Irene pointed to trees rising up above the jack pine like a shelf. Sun skimmed the top of the world and gold lay over the old pines like anointing oil.

"I'll bank over them," she shouted.

Reuger felt the plane dip, and they began a slow bank. Patricia squeezed his shoulder from the back seat as he opened the door and wind filled the cockpit. He opened the urn and Gus's ashes spread like fire down through heavens last light as he watched a man return to earth once again. Reuger pulled the door closed and saw an eagle cross the sky.

The eagle soared over the trees with no effort. Reuger marveled at the grace of that creature. He turned and shouted over the wind and the engine.

"Do you see the eagle, Patricia?"

She leaned forward from the back seat.

Yes!" She smiled with her hair pulled back with an Indian braid. "He looks so majestic!"

Reuger turned to the back seat again.

"You see him, Kurt?"

The boy came forward and moved his head one way and then the next, his large brown eyes searching the sky.

"Where? *Oh yeah!*"
"Looks great, doesn't he?"
Kurt stared at his father and smiled slowly with two large teeth.
"He looks free, dad," he shouted.

ACKNOWLEDGMENTS

Many, many thanks to Joe Coccaro for recognizing *Jack Pine* for being something special. And to Leticia for her great representation. To John Koehler, once again, for pushing ahead with a big logging book that needed to be published. And of course to my wife and her parents, Vern and Shirley Ciske, for showing me the Boundary Waters and the Northwoods for the first time. And to Don and Connie Stocks, for their years of hospitality in the Northwoods. And the deputy sheriff who put up with a novelist asking questions. Many thanks. And to all the people of the Northland with whom I spent many years.

This book is for you.

CPSIA information can be obtained at www.ICGtesting.com
Printed in the USA
BVOW01s0429230315

392706BV00012B/8/P